THE ENDURING FLAME

SOVEREIGNS OF THE DEAD: BOOK THREE

VISTA MCDOWALL

For Brandon. I figure you need some reading material while stuck in that metal tube somewhere in the ocean.

A Brief Summary

The Lantern-Lit City:

Cara leaves her home when her mistress, **Renna**, is kidnapped by a Hooded Man using dark magic. Along the road, her master, **Merick**, is killed, and she learns that she is *sulpari*, a creature bred from a human woman and an undead *fampir*. She enjoys the company of **Alex**, a scholar who knows a lot about the undead. They are attacked again by the Hooded Man, though this time he has turned Merick into a mindless, undead wight.

Sandu is a bounty hunter disguised as a peddler. After his last job, which ended in the supposed death of his friend **Jagger**, he is sent to bring Cara to Riverfen. However, he realizes that he doesn't like his line of work, and ends up befriending Cara instead.

They are hunted by Jagger, who had survived the attack on his home. In his quest for revenge, Jagger murders innocent people. He eventually finds Sandu, but can't bring himself to finish the job. Jagger goes into the swamp where he is drowned by Mist-folk. His story does not end here, as he is resurrected by the mysterious blind man, **Darian**.

In Riverfen, **Gwen** is a young sorceress exiled from her homeland. She marries **Druam Strilu**, the earl, and tries to be a part of his court. When the queen spreads rumors about her, Gwen turns to **Mavian** to teach her more about her magic.

The queen, **Seanna**, is spiteful and petty. She is terrible to everyone around her, except for **Maeria**, a woman she develops feelings for. However, when it's revealed that Maeria is really Renna (and also in love with Mavian), Seanna becomes nasty to her, too. There are two assassination attempts on Seanna, and she leaves Riverfen in disgrace.

After arriving in Riverfen, Cara learns that Alex is really *fampir*, as is Druam. She also learns that Mavian is the Hooded Man, and that Renna went with him willingly. Unfortunately, Renna is killed by Druam, and so Cara is inclined not to trust him.

At the Masque, Gwen follows the call of three Witches and vanishes. Mavian attacks, leaving many dead. Cara survives, Sandu is mortally wounded, and Riverfen is left in shambles.

The Fading Glow:

Cara hates Druam for killing Renna, but doesn't have the power to confront him yet. She decides to go to D'Clet in search of Mavian. Having miraculously survived after being tempted by Death, Sandu goes with her. On the road, they meet Darian along with the resurrected Jagger. A sorcerer, Laris, also comes with them, though his only intent is to exploit Cara in order to regain his lost youth and powers – he was the man who helped her parents conceive, and so is convinced that she owes him.

Due to Laris's interference, Cara's old injury returns. She resorts to drinking the blood of animals to heal herself, and finds that she likes it. She also kills *fampir* and is confronted by Darian. Rather than taking his advice, she continues to kill and drink, eventually discovering the power of her black fire and using it to kill Laris.

Sandu finds his ex-wife, Tambrey, on her deathbed. Her children have gone away with their stepfather to avoid the plague. When Sandu catches the plague, he nearly dies, and Darian saves him. He is depressed and struggling with 'waking nightmares,' and becomes suicidal when he learns that his children are not on Earda. With Jagger's help, he finishes his journey and frees his father.

Gwen is transported to the Whispering Woods, where she learns of the Songs, the real source of magic in Earda. She learns the Songs of Nature, Humanity, and Death, and also cares for Sandu's children, Eaton and Elvy, who have been brought there for safety. When she returns to Earda, Gwen goes to Demarren to depose Olfrick. She is successful, but now has a torn country to heal.

Mavian tries to resurrect Renna, but accidentally revives one of the first *fampir*, **Talnor**. With Talnor and **Rask**, Mavian besieges Stonetree. They are victorious, and Druam is captured. Feeling remorse for this, Mavian frees Druam and learns that his new prowler companion, Ekkar, is actually **Verdon Strilu**, Druam's long-lost brother and Cara's father. Mavian, along with Merick and Ekkar, deserts the army and heads back to D'Clet with the remains of the Mott scholars.

Seanna is captured by a corsair, **Cairn Steel-Eyes**. While in her clutches, Seanna has an unpleasant interaction with the elf prince **Aremo Teru**. With quick thinking – and realizing that Cairn is really **Sura Gellder**, Cara's mother – Seanna is able to maneuver her freedom. Her victory doesn't last, as Henrik is assassinated and their kingdom invaded by Aremo's armies. She gives birth just before being forced to flee Con Salur, leaving it in the hands of Aremo and the Lofalin elves.

Talnor recruits Cara, and as a test forces Cara to kill Alex. Cara complies, murdering Alex in front of Sandu. Sandu, Darian, Jagger, and Sandu's father Cadel all flee into the snow. Darian tells Sandu to go to Demarren in search of a sorceress, and so Sandu and Cadel set off across the sea.

GLOSSARY

Places:

    Con Salur - a cliff city home to King Henrik

    D'Clet - a mountain city overseen by Earl Hjalder

    Dedaria - an elven kingdom of D'Ehsen, ruled by *Kair* Aremo

    D'Ehsen - the large island and surrounding isles on which multiple kingdoms are found

    Demarren - a kingdom of D'Ehsen, ruled by Liegelord Wullum

    Dotschar - the largest kingdom of D'Ehsen, ruled by King Henrik

    Eadrion Empire - a large empire to the west which rules a small portion of D'Ehsen

    Mott - a town which is home to the only university in Dotschar

    Novum - a temple of worship for Dotschar's main religion. Typically has nine sides for the nine gods.

    Rengu - an elven kingdom of D'Ehsen, ruled by *Ameer* Voclain

    Riverfen - a coastal city overseen by Earl Seastone

    Skålland - a kingdom of D'Ehsen ruled by a chieftain

Units of Time:

    Candle - roughly equivalent to an hour

    Quinn - five days

    Deshe - ten days

Creatures:

Fampir - an undead which used to be a human or elf, and can disguise itself as a mortal

Mist-folk - swamp-dwelling creatures which lure their prey into the marshes

Prowler - an undead which used to be a human or elf, but is now feral and predatory

Sulpari - a woman with a *fampir* father and mortal mother

Wight - an undead raised by a necromancer. Mindless and obedient to their master.

Positions:

Ameer - the Rengu (elven) word for prince; their equivalent of a king

Clothman - a low-level cleric of the Dotsch religion; usually practices in small novums

Curate - a mid-level cleric of the Dotsch religion; trained in healing and employed in manors, palaces, or large novums

Exalt - the highest position in the Dotsch religion, either chosen by his predecessor or voted in by his fellow predicants

Kair - the Dedarian (elven) word for prince; their equivalent of a king

Liegelord - the sovereign ruler of Demarren

Predicant - the second-highest position in the Dotsch religion; there are three predicants for each of the four earls.

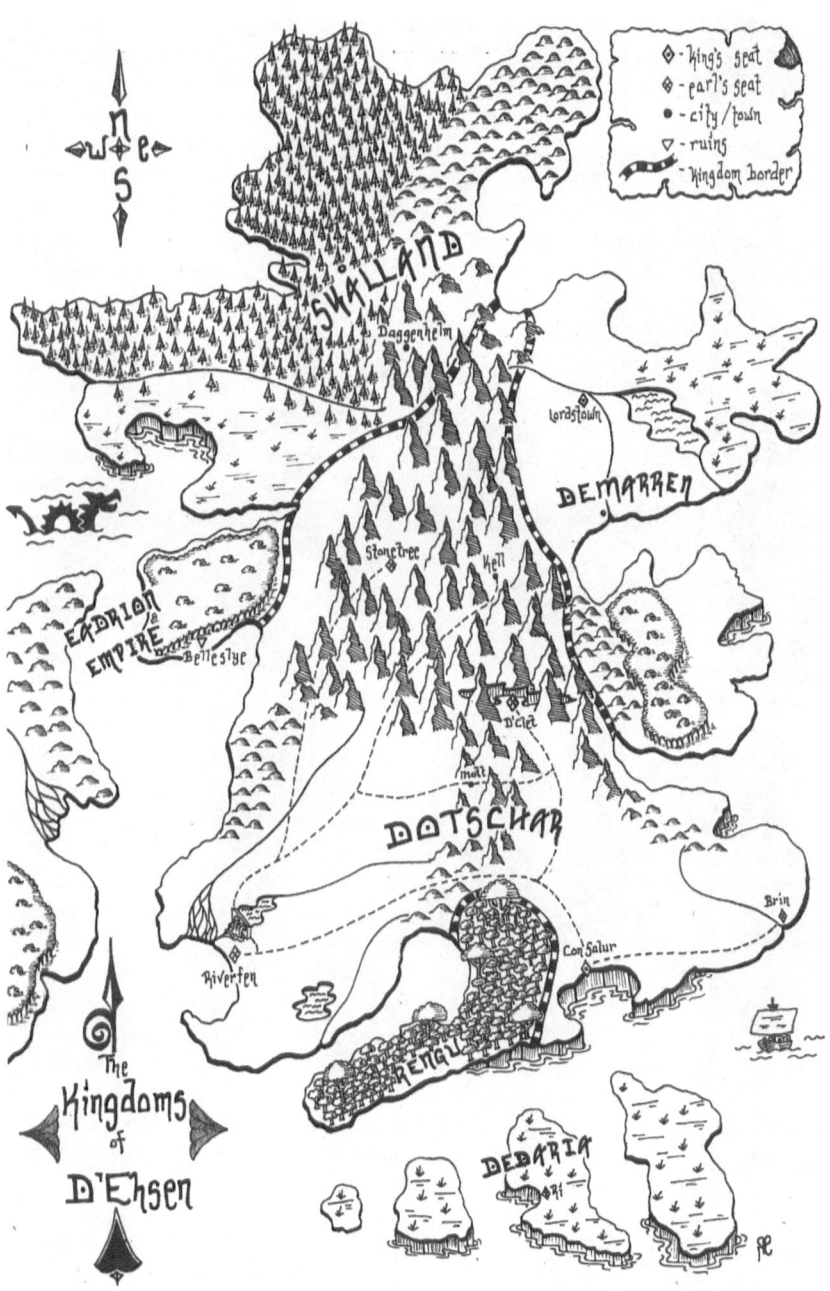

PART ONE

CHAPTER ONE
Seanna

Snow fell continuously. It would have been peaceful, had Seanna been able to watch it from the warmth and safety of the keep in Con Salur. She held baby Landin close, her hands bundled in whatever cloth she had found to cover them. Her breath steamed in the winter air, and shivers passed over her. After days of walking, her feet ached and her still-healing body burned with pain. A hidden root caught her shoe, and she stumbled in the snow. Portia was by her in a moment, her strong hands helping Seanna to right herself.

"Thank you," Seanna said through chattering teeth.

Ahead of them, Dyle Belrose and Gavriel Ropaz pushed doggedly through the snow, leading the way to some unknown destination. The wizard and predicant walked side-by-side, their forms identical in the blizzard. Behind Seanna came a small group of straggling people: rustics, nobles, and servants from Con Salur, all that were left of the mighty city. Barely a hundred had managed to escape the siege. Seanna gritted her teeth. *It won't matter if we all die in the cold.*

Belrose and Ropaz stopped, their heads bent together. Belrose turned to Seanna. "Your Grace, we think we're near the borders of Lord Felder's estate. The town of Larthearth is a few miles past it."

"Lord Felder is obligated to help us," Seanna said, her shivering making it hard for her to think. "We'll go there first."

Belrose nodded. He and Ropaz continued to plunge

through the swirling white, and Seanna followed, hoping for a hot meal and a blazing fire. She blinked away the snowflakes on her eyelashes.

Some of her people struggled as much as her. Though it was hard to pick them out in the storm, she thought that the nobles stumbled and straggled the most, while the rustics stared forward determinedly. *We nobles have been spoiled our whole lives. We've never had to brave a storm, yet these rustics have known such hardship every winter.* Seanna bit her lip and adjusted her grip on Landin. The baby's face was pale, his lips turning blue. If they didn't find shelter soon...her heart clutched at the thought.

Wrought iron gates loomed out of the white. No one manned them. Ropaz pushed them open, and the refugees slowly moved up the long drive to the manor house. Seanna imagined meat and wine and her feet drying by the fire.

A few lights shone from the manor's windows. Seanna surged forward, ready for the warmth. The rest of the refugees huddled in the yard as she, Belrose, and Ropaz made their way to the doors. Belrose pounded as hard as he could on the fine timbers.

After a few moments, a servant carefully opened the door. He peered out at the bedraggled group.

"Rustics are not welcome here," the servant said frostily.

Ropaz stepped forward. "I am the High Predicant Gavriel Ropaz, and I escort Her Grace Queen Seanna Bergfalk and His Grace King Landin the Third, heir to the throne of Dotschar."

The servant paled. He stepped aside, and the three entered. Though the stone halls were chilly, Seanna was grateful for the reprieve from the wind and snow. She and the others followed the servant through a set of rooms to a cozy dining hall where a great fire roared. Seanna edged toward the fire as the servant bowed and went to find his master.

Just as Seanna began to thaw, Lord Felder entered. His gaze darted between his guests, and he licked his lips nervously.

"Your...Your Grace," he muttered, giving a perfunctory bow. He didn't even address Ropaz. "I-I'm afraid...I mean, I didn't—"

"Our people are freezing outside," Seanna said. "We need

food and shelter, and whatever furs and cloaks you can spare for the road ahead."

Lord Felder licked his lips again. "Ah. Well, I-I-I'm afraid I can't help you."

Seanna drew herself up, though she was still shorter than every man in the room. She shifted so that Felder could see the infant's face. "This is your king, Lord Felder. Would you really–"

"Shh!" Felder put a finger over his lips. He turned frightened eyes to the doorway. "They could hear you!"

Seanna stared at Felder. "You don't mean...?"

"Yes!" Felder spoke in a low, furtive voice. "The elves are here! Why do you think I'm still alive? I surrendered the moment they came through. They left a few of their own to keep an eye on me."

He tried to shoo Seanna and the others back to the door, but she didn't budge. "Lord Felder–"

Seanna's objection spluttered to silence as three elves ducked into the room, looking cold despite the many furs slung over their shoulders. The air in the room dropped to an icy tension.

"Felder, who are these people?" asked the first elf in a lilting accent. His eyes lingered on Seanna.

"R-r-rustics begging for some food and shelter," Felder stuttered. "I was just sending them away."

"And where do these rustics come from?"

Felder sputtered, but Ropaz stepped in. The polished edges of his words dropped into a slur, rounding into any rustic's speech. "From Haverly, sir. West o' the capital. We've been walkin' for quinns and deshes, an' with the snows–"

"Enough." The elf waved him into silence. "Give them some food and send them on their way." He swept from the room, the other elves following him. Lord Felder let out a deep breath.

"I'll give what we can spare," he said. "You may have better luck in Larthearth. The elves don't care to guard the rustics."

He looked at little Landin. "And I'll provide something warmer for the child."

He scurried from the room before Seanna could ask for

more. When he disappeared, she slumped into a chair in front of the fire. Her vision blurred, and she angrily wiped away her tears. Ropaz put a hand on her shoulder.

"We're still close to the city," he said. "I doubt any nobles in this region could help us. Be grateful for what he can give."

"I know," Seanna said. "At least we weren't recognized."

"We'll have to be more careful," Belrose said. "The elves will send word to all their soldiers once they realize our escape. It'll take days to search the whole city, but they'll come into the countryside eventually."

Seanna nodded. "Distribute the food to the children and elderly. We'll see if the village can give us shelter for the night."

"Of course," Ropaz said. "And you need to eat, too. You must keep your strength if the child has a chance."

"I know." Seanna turned to Belrose. "You sent word to the prince in Rengu Forest, yes?"

Belrose nodded. "I used my fastest messaging spell. I've received no word in return."

They went quiet as servants bustled in with packages of food: bread, cheeses, and dried meats and fruits. One of them brought a fur to Seanna, which she wrapped around Landin. She nibbled on some cheese and meat as they went back out into the cold. Her belly ached with hunger, and the skies were beginning to darken, but they had to make it to the village before they could rest again.

The weary band pushed back out into the storm.

✳

Seanna and her refugees traveled from village to village, finding little food to fill their bellies. Most villages allowed them to stay in their public houses, but with the onset of winter, they didn't have much food to spare. Whispers followed them, and Seanna showed Landin whenever she could.

"This is your king," she said to the awed villagers. "Keep us secret, and we will win back our land from the elves."

As the distance grew between them and Con Salur, Seanna's

fears shifted from discovery to worrying about survival. Some of the weaker refugees had succumbed to hunger and illness. Noble and rustic alike fell as they walked, and though the others helped carry them to the next village, most didn't survive the night. Though she pitied the ones who fell, her own concern stayed close to her chest, for Landin had developed a cough.

Where are the Rengu elves? Seanna prayed that the Rengus had not allied with the Lofalins. *They will find us. They have to.* With its enormous trees and wild woods, the forest of Rengu was their safest haven. It wasn't far from Con Salur, and if they pressed onward, they could reach it within a deshe or two. *Ten to twenty days, and we could all be safe.*

As they rested in an abandoned hut in a small hamlet, Seanna tried to warm her child. She rubbed his cheeks and nestled him in furs, and fed him the little milk she could muster. She sighed in frustration.

"We must press on to Rengu," Seanna said to Ropaz and Belrose. "Wandering like this will kill many of our people." She couldn't bring herself to voice her worry over Landin.

"Even if we reach the trees, we cannot find the elven cities without a guide," Ropaz said.

"A shelter in the forest is better than none at all," Seanna replied.

"A forest filled with creatures large enough to eat a man," Belrose said. "Have patience, Seanna. I've sent another message to them, but they also must avoid the Lofalin scouts. Help will come."

Unless we've already been betrayed. Seanna said aloud, "Speak with the headswoman of the village. Ask if we may stay another night or two. Perhaps we'll hear from Rengu within that time."

Ropaz and Belrose went out to speak with the villagers. A few minutes later, Portia bustled in with a basket and a pile of sticks. The girl built up the fire and set some food beside it to warm. She held out her hands for the baby and took him into her arms.

"You must be exhausted," Portia said.

Seanna stretched her hands out over the fire. Its little

warmth barely eased the chill in her bones. "I can't take much more, Portia. The walking and hunger and begging for bread and shelter. Landin's cough. I..." Her throat closed around her words.

"He'll make it through," Portia said. "He's strong."

"But is he strong enough?" Seanna took the baby back and held him close to her breast. So many of her family had died in the last months, their absence a constant weight on her heart. *Papa and Mumma and Henrik and Halmer.* "I can't lose him, too."

Landin was hot in her arms, his tiny cheeks flushed. Seanna held him closely, a silent prayer in her heart. He was so small and weak. Winter had killed many a child, no matter their parentage, and without a permanent shelter or supplies, she almost wondered if it would have been better to stay in Con Salur and face the Lofalins. At least their deaths would have come more quickly.

The fire crackled and smoked as Portia separated their meager food. A few mouthfuls of bread each, a dried apple to split, and cheese with moldy spots on it. Hunger pulled at Seanna's stomach, and she ate whatever Portia put in front of her. When she finished, she tried to get Landin to latch, but he cried and struggled. His body burned with heat.

"He's feverish," Seanna said. "Get your brother."

Portia nodded and rushed out. Minute after slow minute crept past. The sky outside the hut grew darker, the wind more chill, before Portia returned with Ropaz quick on her heels. He held out his arms for Landin.

Seanna carefully put the baby in Ropaz's arms. He held Landin gently, running a finger over his forehead and cheeks.

"When did he last eat?"

"This morning," Seanna said. "He didn't latch when I tried earlier."

"He's blazing hot." Ropaz said to his sister, "Portia, please find the coriander in my satchel. One pinch into a flask, and mix it with water." With deft hands, Ropaz put the baby on the ground and began undoing his furs.

"Stop!" Seanna cried. "He'll freeze to death!"

Ropaz shook his head. "He won't be fully exposed. But his body needs a chance to cool, and these furs will trap all the heat inside. He needs plenty of water and milk, if you can get him to feed."

With gentle fingers, Ropaz unwrapped the furs and put a thinner blanket over the child. He took the flask handed to him and wet a corner of cloth with it. He held the wet cloth to the baby's lips, coaxing him to drink. After a couple of tries, Landin finally opened his mouth and suckled at the cloth.

Seanna watched nervously, her hands clutching at her sides. Portia sat beside her, a comforting arm around her shoulder.

In the hush of the hut, Ropaz whispered a spell. His words made Seanna think of warmth and full bellies, of the comfort of a parent's arms. Tears sprang suddenly to her eyes, and she leaned against Portia's shoulder.

As Ropaz murmured, he nursed Landin with the cloth using one hand and traced the child's cheeks and forehead with the other. His fingers went to the baby's chest, resting there. Landin coughed once, then settled. Seanna thought she saw a trickle of light move from Ropaz's hand into the child, but she blinked and it was gone.

With a satisfied look, Ropaz bundled Landin up once more and gave him over to Seanna. She took him, glad to feel his weight in her arms again. Landin eyes were bright, his cheeks their normal color. She felt him all over, but the fever had broken. He quickly latched when she moved to feed him.

"Thank you," Seanna murmured. "I don't know what I would have done without you."

Ropaz spoke what Seanna's soul already feared, "If we don't find a safe haven soon, the odds of his survival will grow slim."

Seanna noted Ropaz's pale face and shaking hands. She knew that magic had a cost, but somehow never thought what that might mean. She said, "You won't be able to practice your magic if you're too weak."

He nodded. "I fear I overextended myself already. I promise you, I will do everything in my power to help him. But I'm only one man, and next time such a spell could leech whatever life is in me."

Seanna would gladly give her life to save Landin, but she didn't know if she could ask the same of Ropaz.

Portia squeezed Seanna's shoulder and said, "We'll keep the child safe. I can help you carry him, and perhaps we'll find a nursemaid."

"No," Seanna said immediately. "He's mine, I don't want another woman feeding him. I'm a good mother. I can care for my own child."

She hadn't expected to react with such ferocity. Her fears over survival and the war had eclipsed the concerns over becoming a mother, yet in that moment of quiet, she realized how deeply those worries were ingrained in her. Much of her pregnancy had been spent arguing with her husband or engaging in petty feuds to fuel her own ends. Though she no longer fretted over her popularity, she hadn't allowed herself to dwell much on what having this child would be like. All her life, she'd expected to have nannies and wet-nurses and governesses and all sorts of retainers on hand to help her raise the child. Now, it was just her.

The truth of it frightened her.

The words of Cairn Steel-Eyes, the corsair queen, came back to her: *Your child needs a mother more than it needs a queen.* But what if Seanna failed? *I've already dragged him from his home into the wilderness. I've risked his life on a false hope.* She knew that staying in Con Salur would have been just as sure a death, but after the fright of his fever, she didn't know anymore if she'd made the right decision.

Portia rubbed a comforting circle on Seanna's shoulder and broke through her dizzying spiral by saying, "Of course you're a good mother. None of us ever doubted that. But even the best mothers need help caring for their child sometimes. Let us help you. You didn't expect to run the kingdom by yourself; why would you expect to be alone in this?"

An immense gratefulness welled up in Seanna. She leaned more heavily against Portia, savoring her touch. She said, "I've always driven away those who wanted to help me. I suppose I thought there would be no one left by now."

"We're here," Ropaz said. He kneeled in front of Seanna. "Do you remember how I judged you when we first met?"

She smiled a little. "If I recall, you called me impulsive and proud."

"Those were weaknesses of Seanna the Queen. They are not weaknesses of Seanna the mother. Now, let me see if I can find a merchant in this town who sells herbal remedies. Even without magic, I can try to keep Landin's humors steady."

She nodded her assent, but before he even stood, the hut's ramshackle door swung open. Seanna clutched Landin close. *What now?*

Belrose entered the hut with a huge grin. Beside him came a slender elf, hair tangled from the wind, nose was red from the cold.

"Seanna," Belrose said, "this is our Rengu envoy. Help has come at last."

Seanna could have kissed them both in her relief. She staggered to her feet, her legs weak. She took the elf's hand and held it tightly. For a moment, no words came to her. When she finally spoke, she only said, "Come in out of the cold. We have little, but we can share it with one who brings us hope."

CHAPTER TWO
Sandu

Cara,

I can't sleep at night for imagining the last time we saw each other. I remember it so clearly.

In my dreams, you come with me. You strike down that demon woman. You help Alex to his feet.

In my nightmares, you kill him again. Over and over. I can't look away. I see darkness in you. It consumes you, and there's nothing I can do to stop it.

But the nightmares are real. You killed him. He begged you. He said he was mortal again. I don't know how it's possible, but I believe him. He wouldn't lie to me. He especially wouldn't lie to you. I stay up at night wondering how he did it, but we'll never know now, will we?

Even when I'm awake, the nightmares don't end. The queen and knight and prowlers are all there together, surrounding me with their lips and their teeth and their claws, and I can't escape them.

Only now, you're with them, too. You don't let me leave. You slaughter me, just as you did Alex.

Sandu left the letter unsigned. It stared up at him from the table, incomplete, yet he had no more words to give to it. Behind him, Da snored softly. Though his mind still reeled, Sandu climbed into his own bunk. He tossed and turned, unsettled by the ship's constant rolling, his sleep plagued by unending dreams and nightmares. In some dreams, his left arm was there again, but the space was always empty whenever he rolled to that side.

Sandu woke with darkness still stretching over the ocean, and put quill to parchment once more.

Cara,

I don't want to remember you as a monster. I want to remember you as that country girl from Kell who wanted only to save her friend. Do you remember who you were then?

You wore your hair in a long braid down your back. Your dresses were plain and open at the sides so your legs could move. Each day you spent candles in the yard with Merick, practicing with your sword. I'd never seen a woman fight before. I've still never seen one quite like you.

When we found the prowlers in the journeyman's tower, you were afraid. I didn't know then the extent of your fear. You saw yourself in them for the first time, didn't you? You realized that there was a monster in you.

It wasn't until Merick died that you really spoke to me. You kept yourself apart at first, not trusting me. Of course, I was trying to sell you. I guess trust shouldn't have been given at all.

But if you hadn't trusted me, I wouldn't have betrayed the Guild. It was your trust that swayed me. You became my friend, and I couldn't sell you. Even if it would have freed Da. There were so many times that I wanted to tell you the truth and the words danced around my lips. But I could never quite string them together.

I've always been a coward. You made me strong. At your side, I thought I might become braver. It was a lie I told myself. I relied on you, and I became weak.

I almost didn't return to you. But still I followed you to Riverfen. I found sorrow there. A queen and her knight, touching me and torturing me.

There was a girl there, too. A noble girl who held my hands when the waking nightmares had caught me. I think she used magic. It made me feel better for a moment. Long enough to find you and feel that everything was right again.

Sandu put down the quill. Each time he wrote a letter, the words spun out of his control. His thoughts leaped this way and that. He couldn't concentrate with the lantern swinging to and fro and the waves slapping against the wood just below his and Da's porthole.

Why even bother? Not as if she'll ever read these letters. Yet Sandu still needed to put his thoughts to paper. Maybe writing them down would tear them from his head, and he could find peace again.

Night still clung to the sky. Sandu put the second letter away and tried to sleep.

Rest came only in bursts. Everything in Sandu held to a mild hope that he would fall into such a deep slumber that he might never wake again. But he only slept fitfully, his bunk too narrow and hard and his head too jumbled. His eyes crusted with tears of frustration.

Pale light eventually entered his cabin, watery under the dark horizon. Sandu sat up, his head aching, his body sore from trying to account for the motion of the ship. This time, he would write to someone else.

Jagger,
I never thought I'd say this, but I miss you.

Sandu remembered the silent giant's expression, both knowing and judging. The words faltered, and he scratched them out.

Eaton and Elvy,

Tears marked the page under their names. What could Sandu say to them? They were far away from Earda. Darian had said that they weren't dead. But what was the difference between living and dead if Sandu couldn't reach them?

He had held their mother as she died. He might never hold them again. Even if he could, he only had the one arm. Would the children be too heavy for him to lift now?

The words only flowed when Sandu wrote to Cara. He didn't know why. She didn't care for him anymore.

Yet Sandu kept writing. Some part of him hoped that his pain would leech from his body and onto the paper, and he wouldn't have to suffer from it anymore.

Cara,

I've been on this ship for a day now. I don't think I'll ever grow used to its movement and sounds. I've never traveled over the sea before. My feet have always sought land.

I don't like it. I don't ever feel grounded, like I can stay in one place. Of course, I never am in one place. I'm on the ship, and the ship is always moving. It's carrying me to Demarren. Far away from you.

If I hadn't been caught up in my own grief, would I have been able to stop you?

Somehow, I don't think so. Your hatred for the undead is greater than your love for me. That's the way of things. Hatred overpowers love, and soon enough, there won't be any love left between us.

Sandu stood abruptly. The paper hadn't taken his suffering, for he felt it more intensely with each stroke of his quill. He clutched the half-finished letters in his shaking hand. Despair throttled him; he couldn't write another word, and neither could he stay in that tiny cabin while his da snored in the other bunk. He stumbled to the deck where mist coated his cheeks and sailors went about their work. None of them paid attention to him.

The rail that separated him and the roiling sea was low and thin, only coming up to his hips. He looked over it into the blue-black waters and wondered how it might feel to sink into their depths. His breath would be replaced with saltwater.

It mightn't be so bad. After all, his breath had been replaced with fear many times in the last few months. The fear choked him and brought images of terrors that haunted him waking and sleeping.

Water would bring only darkness to his head.

The letters fell from his hand before he even realized he'd let them go. The parchment drifted and swirled, ever downward, until they touched the surface of the water. The ship plowed on, heedless of those words that soon soaked and disappeared.

Sandu put one foot onto the railing. This time, Jagger wasn't there to stop him.

One jump, and I'll drown with my words.

Then Sandu thought of Da, trembling and seasick, and stepped back from the railing. He shook himself. Being on the ship unnerved him, its perpetual sensation of movement dizzying. Without his left arm, he was constantly unbalanced. His head couldn't settle, the waking nightmares ever at the edges of his vision, ghosts that reminded him of all his failures.

As he stood on the swaying deck, Sandu took a deep breath. The salt air was fresh and cold with winter's touch. It helped to clear his head a little, so he took another. For a long time, he stayed still, focusing only on his lungs and air and the distant horizon, grey washed with the pink of the rising sun.

Across the sea is a sorceress, Sandu reminded himself. *She will help me find my children and regain myself. I just have to survive the journey there.*

Slowly, the specters in his head receded, and Sandu blinked. He had forgotten how sweet the air could be.

The ship awakened around him, sailors bustling to change shifts and lower the sails. They ignored him, and he didn't beg for their attention. When the morning bell rang, Sandu dutifully went down to the galley for breakfast.

Sandu gathered up a tray of bland food and watery rum. He had to put one end against his torso, the balancing act nearly sending him rolling. It was a long trip back to the cabin, up steps and down, all while keeping the tray as level as he could. He only spilled a little of the rum and broth.

Sandu set the tray on his own bunk and shook his father's shoulder. "Da, it's time for breakfast."

Cadel moaned and rolled over. His face was drawn and pale, a spittle of drool leaking from his lips. He mumbled, "Not hungry."

"Come on, Da. You need to eat something." Sandu held out a crust of bread. Cadel took it with a thin hand. Sandu smiled. "There we go. There's broth, too, when you're ready."

"Any water?"

Sandu shook his head. "Just rum, I'm afraid. We won't get our ration of water until supper."

Cadel finished his bread, though he only managed a swallow of rum and two spoonfuls of broth. When he was done, he leaned his head against the wall and peered at Sandu. He said, "You look terrible."

"You're one to talk." Sandu didn't meet his father's eye. He didn't quite know how to talk to Da anymore. Too many years had passed with too much guilt.

"You've changed, son," Cadel said. "Something's eating at your head. Tell me about it."

"The children are gone, Da," Sandu said immediately. It had taken so much strength for him to tell Jagger and Cara about his waking nightmares, he didn't know if he had any left to tell his father. The ghosts closed in around him again, wavering at the edge of sight, waiting for his weakest moment before they pounced.

"But we'll find them." Cadel's confidence did not assure Sandu.

"We've a long trip to make, Da," Sandu stood to return the tray. "You should rest."

After his trip to the galley, Sandu couldn't bear to go back to the cabin. He knew that he and Cadel would have to have a long conversation at some point, but he didn't know where to start. An apology would sound hollow, and a full confession like the ravings of a madman.

So instead, Sandu sat at the ship's prow, watching as the vessel cut through the water. It neatly sliced the waves, sending sprays into his face. The longer he breathed of that clean air, the longer the ghosts would stay away.

Across the sea is a sorceress. Sandu repeated the hope to himself, over and over, a beacon in his fragile mind. *I just have to survive the journey there.*

CHAPTER THREE
Mavian

Wind whistled through the caves, howling with deadly frost. Its cry sent shivers down Mavian's spine, sounding too like the laments of those he had harmed. Mavian and the scholars were bundled in furs and blankets and huddled shoulder-to-shoulder around the fire.

Mavian thought it was nearing dark, though he couldn't be sure without the passage of the sun to confirm the time. His body weighed him down with exhaustion, fatigued after the day's travels. They had only arrived at the cave system below D'Clet that afternoon. Mavian had selected this specific cavern for its size as well as its distance from the network that connected it to the castle. Even if Chadron had guards posted in the prowlers' old cave, they wouldn't be able to hear Mavian's ragtag group of scholars.

Their journey over the mountains had gone as well as could be hoped, and even then some of the scholars had lost fingertips to the frost. An older man had started coughing on the second day and hadn't stopped since.

But we survived. Mavian pulled his blankets closer around himself. He envied Merick's lack of sensation. The wight didn't react at all to changes in temperature, equally as still in the heat as in cold. Neither did Ekkar mind the winter's chill. The prowler curled up as near to Mavian as he could get, but more from a need for attention than anything else. Though they still gave fearful looks to Ekkar, the scholars had more or less accepted the prowler's nearness as they all huddled together.

"So what now?" asked one of the scholars, Ronan. He was in his forties, his beard and tonsure flecked with grey, his robes patched and mended many times over. Over the past few days, he had become the scholars' de facto leader.

"I'm not quite sure," Mavian admitted. "We need weapons and allies if we want to defeat Chadron. He'll have guards, and we may have to fight our way up through the castle."

"We are scholars and monks," Ronan said. "Men of peace and study. Even if we had weapons, we have no training in using them."

Something in his expression made Mavian pause. There was a hardness there, a grudge that Mavian couldn't quite place. Before he could ask, Ronan continued, "Don't you have dark magic? If I recall, you had the powers of the Underworld when you attacked our caravan."

Oh. Mavian shut his eyes, the shame of that night slithering into his belly. "You were there."

"I held one of my fellows in my arms as he died, cut down by your men," Ronan said. He pointed to Merick. "I watched that *thing* break a woman's leg." He lifted his sleeve, showing scars on his arm. "I tried to rescue my life's work, and your dark tentacles swept me back. So tell me, Far-Eyes, why we followed you from our home when you had no plan?"

The other scholars glanced from Ronan to Mavian, silent save for their chattering teeth. Merick stood against the cavern walls, expressionless and still. Ekkar mumbled in his sleep and twitched. Mavian shifted, not sure what he could say. Ronan was right, of course. He didn't have a plan. He had killed their colleagues. But how could he make them see that he'd changed?

His answer took too long, for Ronan snorted and turned away. "Typical. The last time I followed a Strilu, my friends were slaughtered. And that one knew what he was doing."

The comparison to Alex stung. *No one believes I'm worthy of the Strilu name.* Mavian couldn't fault them. Sometimes he didn't believe he deserved the name given to his family two generations back, a name granted through love and fealty to

Druam Strilu. *A love and fealty I betrayed.*

Ekkar snuffled and pushed up against Mavian's back. Unconsciously, Mavian reached back to pet the prowler. A thought struck him. *Maybe I should tell them the truth.* Would they accept it? *I have to try.*

"Ronan, you worked with Verdon Strilu when he was at the university, didn't you?" Mavian asked.

The scholar nodded, suspicion in his eyes. "I helped him research the *fampir* and *sulpari*. Other than him and Alex, I was the foremost expert on those subjects."

"Did you know he was *fampir*?" Mavian said it as politely as he could, and hoped the scholar wouldn't read any condescension in his tone.

Some of the other scholars shook their heads, and one said, "I didn't realize it until now, but it makes sense."

Ronan waited for them to quiet down, then said, "I suspected. Never asked, though. Didn't think it polite. Both Verdon and Alex had a strange way about them, but they were earnest and hardworking, and I didn't think it my place to judge."

Mavian nodded. *I wish I'd done the same.* He said, "You mentioned the *sulpari*. Did Verdon speak often of it?"

"Yes. He wondered if it were possible to create one. He had a, er, lady friend that was interested, too. One time he brought a young mage to Mott to interpret the scrolls. Never saw the mage after that, though."

"And then Verdon vanished."

Ronan nodded. "Left all his notes and his work unfinished. Except for everything on the *sulpari*. That disappeared with him. Alex had to redo all the research himself when Verdon's companion returned some years later asking about it. Eventually, she didn't come back, too."

"What was her name?"

"Sura Gellder."

At that, Ekkar burbled and raised his head. He settled back quickly, but his half-lidded gaze remained on Ronan. The scholar avoided the prowler's eye.

"Sura." It was the second time Mavian had heard her name. *The woman who stole Verdon's heart and convinced him to conceive a child. And the mage has to be Laris Stanthorpe.*

"Why bring up the past?" Ronan asked. "Verdon's dead and gone, he can't help us now."

"Actually..." Mavian didn't know where to start. *How to explain the impossible?* He said, "Verdon's here with us."

Ronan snorted. Mavian tugged at Ekkar's hand, encouraging the prowler to sit up. Ekkar blinked and sat slowly on his haunches. Mavian said, "This is Verdon Strilu."

Some of the scholars laughed, and Ronan snorted, "That's a prowler."

"I know." Mavian explained it as best he could, starting with Verdon's desire for a child and ending with the revelation that his cousin had become the first prowler during the *sulpari's* conception. Mavian's passion exploded in his words. He spoke louder and louder, his hands gesticulating wildly. Ekkar burbled in response, bouncing on his heels, infected by Mavian's energy. He finished, "I didn't even recognize him, but Druam did. He asked me to find a cure for Verdon and the rest of the prowlers. That's why I'm here: all my research is in D'Clet, and with the first prowler, we may be able to complete the work. We could end the scourge."

The scholars watched Mavian tiredly, unaffected by his speech. Ronan stroked his beard, but then he shook his head.

"Even if you're right – and I don't fully believe you – we still have to take D'Clet from Chadron. We're stuck here in these miserable caves without any weapons, and we have barely a few spells to cast between us." Ronan pointed at Ekkar. "If that truly is Verdon, he would be sickened to know what he became."

"That's why we have to cure him," Mavian said. "Look, I know I don't have a plan yet. But give me time. I'll think of something."

"Hmph."

"For what it's worth, I'm sorry," Mavian said. He wouldn't win over the scholars unless he admitted his past mistakes. "I'm sorry that I attacked the caravan and killed your fellows and stole your research. I was a fool, and I'm paying every day for that mistake. But I'm trying to do better now. I want to help you, but you have to trust me a little."

He knew that words would not be enough when Ronan's unforgiving frown did not lighten. With a sigh, Mavian kneeled in front of the scholar and held out his hands. "Sir Chadron despises me and would kill me if given the chance. If you don't want to work with me, tie me up and bring me to him. I'm sure he'd give you a reward for my capture. You could even watch the execution, if you like."

Ronan didn't move, and Mavian implored, "But if you choose to let me work for your forgiveness, I promise I will do everything in my power to make the university as great as it once was."

All the scholars waited for Ronan's answer. Mavian's knees ached against the hard ground, and his heart pounded. *He's going to truss me up and send me to Chadron.* Mavian's hands trembled, but he kept them held upright. It was no less than he deserved.

After an uncomfortably long moment, Ronan finally pushed Mavian's hands away. "I'm not going to send you to the slaughter, boy. But we're not warriors, and many of us are too old to gallivant through caves on a faint hope."

"You can help in other ways," Mavian pleaded, rocking back on his heels.

Ronan shook his head. "Harnel needs a healer, and we all need a good rest and warm beds. I know an inn or two in the city that would be glad to host us for a time. If you ever do take D'Clet, you can find us and work toward forgiveness."

"But–"

Mavian's objection died on his lips as Ronan said, "We leave in the morning. I wish you the best of luck."

"Don't you want to see Chadron dead for his crimes?" Mavian said. He resisted the urge to tug at Ronan's sleeve like a petulant child.

Ronan's shoulders heaved in a sigh. "Of course I do. But my fellows are hungry, tired, and cold. We followed you on a hope, and you have nothing to give us. At least here in D'Clet we have a chance to sell our services to make a living, but we have no delusions that the university will ever regain its former glory. Even if you manage to kill Chadron, you can't turn the ashes back into knowledge."

"Give me a chance to convince you," Mavian said. "I'll go into my old workshop, I'll–"

"We leave in the morning," Ronan said over him. "If you have anything to prove, you'd better do it by then."

Ronan walked away, and Mavian didn't follow. Though surrounded by scholars, he felt completely alone. Everything Ronan said had been right. Mavian hadn't made a plan before he pulled the scholars from the wreckage of Mott. He didn't know how to deal with Chadron or cure Verdon.

Without thinking, Mavian began the long trudge up to the caverns beneath the castle. He held a glowing red orb in his hand, the magical light casting faint shadows on the wall. Behind him, Merick followed at a sedate pace, while Ekkar pounced and sniffed and ran in spurts, his burbles growing excited as he detected familiar scents.

My impulses have caught up with me. Mavian's mind clung onto the mistakes of his past, darkening whatever glimmer of hope he'd once held. *It was an impulse that allied me with Rask. It was an impulse that made me reveal my plans to Gwen, which led to Renna's death. Have I ever really thought anything through?* Sure, he had laid careful plans to steal the scrolls from Alex's caravan and invade Druam's Masque, but had he ever really thought through the consequences of such things? He couldn't even blame Rask for whispering in his ear or giving him the tools for his wretched work. *I agreed with him. I told myself it was to cast down the old nobility and bring up a class that would actually help the rustics, but it was all for my own greed and ambitions. I'm no better than Rask.*

His steps led him to the cavern which had once housed his small army of prowlers. It was black, no lights flickering and no soldiers pacing the shelf above. Silent and empty, only faint traces remaining of the creatures that he had brought there. Ekkar whined and sniffed and scratched at the floor, as if hoping to bring out his fellows.

"Sorry, friend," Mavian murmured, laying a comforting hand on the prowler's head. "They're all gone."

With a careful tread, Mavian picked his way through the cavern to the stairs on the other side, listening for any cry of alarm. None came. He climbed the steps to the heavy door at the top and pushed. It swung open with a groan. The room beyond was as empty as the cavern.

Mavian kept going through the tunnels, the endless warren wearing on him. The black all around penetrated his thoughts, turning them ever gloomier. *What am I doing here? What hope do I have of curing Verdon or taking D'Clet? Always the fool.* He cursed himself over and over.

At last, he reached his workshop. It was empty and unguarded. The vials and bottles and parchments and books lay exactly where he'd left them, undisturbed save for the fine layer of dust that had accumulated over them.

Mavian stared at them for a long time, knowing that none of them held the secret to curing the prowlers. He'd obsessed over their words and spells in his quest to resurrect Renna. Even if any did mention the *fampir*, none had a method for reuniting a *fampir's* soul with its body. Why should they? Prowlers had only existed for twenty-odd years. Scholars of the past would have no reason to believe something like this could even happen.

But there were sulpari in the past, Mavian thought. *Cara wasn't the first created. So why no prowlers then?*

He glanced at Merick, who had taken up his old position by the wall, and Ekkar, who sniffed at a row of vials. Mavian nodded to himself. He sorted through the pile of books and set aside a few for reading.

It's a start, I suppose.

CHAPTER FOUR

Cara

Cara followed Talnor into the black void, leaving the bloodied tower room behind her. Darkness flooded her vision, an oppressive force that pressed down on her. Somewhere in the shadows, voices of the dead cried out in pain and fear. Something brushed against her, slimy and wet, and she yelped.

A cold hand closed around hers and pulled her forward. As Cara took another step, the world popped back into color and light. She reeled, her body still convinced it was in that dreadful place. Her ears rang as the dread portal closed behind her, and she put her head in her hands as she slowly oriented herself. That cold hand moved to her shoulder.

"Thank you," Cara managed.

"The Underworld is not easy to travel through," Talnor said. The *fampir* helped Cara to a chair.

After a minute, the dizziness receded. Guilt took its place. The guilt felt like sand, gritty and shifting, building layer upon layer inside her, clinging to her organs no matter how she tried to shake it away. Echoes of her crimes beat in her skull: *You killed Alex. You betrayed Sandu. You sided with a* fampir *for the promise of vengeance.*

Talnor put her arms around Cara. *She isn't your friend,* Cara reminded herself. It was hard to remember, for Talnor had Renna's face and smooth skin, the long hair that fell around her cheeks and the sweet scent of lavender. *Talnor isn't Renna. She stole my friend's body and will use it against me whenever she can.*

Regardless of this truth, Cara found herself relaxing in Talnor's arms. *The enemy of my enemy is my ally,* she told herself. *I cannot do this all alone. Use her as she uses me, and never forget what she truly is.*

"Something on your mind?" Talnor asked.

"I killed Alex," Cara said. She couldn't dislodge the memory of his severed head staring up from the floor. "He was *fampir,* yes, but he trusted me."

"He lied to you," Talnor said. "And he would never betray Druam."

"I know." But as Cara forced herself to think about anything other than Alex, Sandu intruded into her head instead, brown eyes wide with hurt and fear. Cara pushed her knuckles over her eyelids, but he obstinately remained. His shout of alarm rang in her ears and made the sandy guilt grow.

"Sandu will never forgive me," Cara said, seeking comfort in Talnor's level gaze. The ring of red around the other's blue eyes only deepened her pain.

"Come," Talnor said. "Don't wallow in your own head. With winter upon us, we have time to unlock the powers in your blood. The black fire is only the beginning."

Cara took her hand and stood. She straightened her shoulders. *Forget Alex and Sandu. They're not your concern anymore.* The sand clung to her heart, and she ignored it.

"Then we should start," Cara said.

"First, Earl Rask will want to meet you," Talnor said. "He will be most interested to hear of your abilities."

＊

In the Great Hall, Rask perched like a giant bird on Earl Stonetree's old seat. He spat at servants and yelled at soldiers, and chewed his meat with an old dog's avarice. His too-clever eyes followed Cara, and she felt naked beneath their condescension.

Talnor swept ahead of Cara, the shimmer of her gown attracting the soldiers' lustful eyes. She ignored them. At her approach, Rask gave a small nod

"I remember her." Rask gestured at Cara. "*Sulpari*, yes? The girl that Lord Strilu dragged from the wilderness. The savior of Riverfen, rescuing the queen from prowlers and defending the king at the Masque." His voice dripped with derision.

Not like you were there to witness it. You were safely away while your men tried to kill the rest of the nobles. Cara gave the smallest bow that could still be considered courteous. She returned his glare with disdain. Rumors had abounded about the earl for many years, questioning his slow rise to power and his long life. Some had even whispered that he hired necromancers to keep himself from dying. *I know of at least one necromancer he employed,* Cara thought sourly. This man had allied himself with Mavian, and she would not trust him no matter Talnor's assurances.

Rask's eyes swept over her again, and she knew what he saw: a pawn in his noble games, a piece to be moved about as he pleased. He didn't care whether she lived or died, only that she served his purpose.

"What can she do that you cannot?" Rask asked Talnor.

The *fampir* smiled. "She has the blood of both mortals and the undead. Once I have found the secrets of her power, she will be instrumental in taking Riverfen. I once witnessed a *sulpari* raze a city with her fire."

Cara bit her tongue to keep from interrupting. *Once Talnor finds the secret? To* my *power?*

"See that she obeys. I won't have another like Mavian. I won't be betrayed," Rask said.

"Why did you support Mavian?" Cara blurted. Mavian was still her sworn enemy, and she hadn't forgotten that it was Rask who had given him the money and tools to steal Renna away.

"He was useful," Rask replied.

Talnor threw Cara a harsh look, but Cara pressed on, "So you approved of his dark magic?"

"It got me Stonetree, didn't it?" Rask's watery glare moved over her. "Don't let your morals keep you from your goals. While others quibble over 'right' and 'wrong,' I take what I want."

"And what do you want?"

Rask gave her a spine-chilling smile. "You are rustic indeed if you believe I would ever divulge myself to you."

Talnor cut between them, and Cara stepped back. Talnor said, "I will keep her in line, Rask. Have no doubt of that."

"Good." Rask leaned back in his stolen throne. "Tomorrow we will begin the trials. I want the *sulpari* to serve as my executioner."

Cara turned away from him and left the Great Hall. Something about him made her tremble, some secret that lurked beneath his age-spotted hands. *He is a dangerous man, for his allies as much as his enemies.* She greatly disliked how he spoke over her, as if she weren't even there, and how easily Talnor agreed to keep her at heel.

I am not their dog. If they fail to see that, well...Rask himself said to take what I want.

✳

The stone walls pressed in on her. Everywhere Cara went was granite and snow. The oppressive grey corridors led into horrid white courtyards dirtied from the feet of soldiers and horses. Everything felt grim and stark.

The soldiers lined up in the courtyard were equally morose. The elves shivered in their armor despite the blankets and furs wrapped around their arms and legs. The human soldiers, used to the cold, fared better. But they still exuded a sense of dread in their tense lips and tightly gripped weapons.

An icy wind blew across the steps of Stonetree's keep. Cara huddled within her furs and stared straight ahead. Rask and his generals gathered on the other side of the steps, grand in orange and grey. Talnor stood with them, unaffected by the chill.

A line of prisoners stretched through the courtyard, their hands and feet chained, their skin haggard and grey. One by one, they were unchained and brought before Cara, then forced to kneel. For most, there was no proclamation nor time given for last words. A few called out brave words, but many met their ends in silence.

The machination of the executions became routine for Cara. She waited for the prisoner to kneel, swung the heavy axe over her head, then brought it down over their necks. Sometimes the heads went down the steps, sometimes they bounced toward Rask's feet. Blood poured across her boots, its sweet scent calling to her. Cara's features kept warping between human and *fampir* as she struggled to keep herself under control.

With every swing, Cara told herself that this was not degrading, that she was indeed proving herself to Rask and earning her place as a leader of this army. With every swing, she knew it was a lie.

Cara wiped the sweat from her brow as the next prisoner was brought up. Unlike the rest, mostly men who had served as commanders in Stonetree's defense, this was a woman. She held her handsome head high as she walked up the steps, every movement purposeful and sedate. Her brown hair was streaked with grey, her eyes lined with wrinkles, but these markers of age only served to increase the nobility she exuded.

The woman examined Cara. "You served in Kell, did you not?" Her gaze flicked to Talnor. "Under Renna Nellestere."

"I did," Cara said. Her mouth was suddenly dry. When she was younger, she had longed to meet Earl Stonetree and his wife, to see for herself their wisdom and grace.

She had not imagined that moment coming like this.

Lady Stonetree frowned at Cara. "Where were you while invaders besieged my husband's keep? Was it not your duty to serve him? Defend him?"

The words slapped Cara, and she gripped the worn axe handle to ground herself. She said, "Any oaths I took were severed upon my lady's death. Earl Stonetree allied himself with undead; I could not serve him in good conscience."

The lady shook her head and raised her chin in defiance.

Rask stepped forward. He growled, "Daughter, this is your final opportunity to denounce your husband's choices. It would pain me greatly to see you die today."

"Then be pained by it." Lady Stonetree turned away from

her father. With a sigh, Rask indicated to Cara.

As she kneeled on the grey granite, the knees of her dress soaking with blood, Lady Stonetree stared up at the clouds. As much as Cara distrusted Rask, she wished that the lady had said what she needed to in order to save her life. Cara hefted the axe but did not lift it over her head.

She glanced at Rask one final time. There was no mercy in him.

Lady Stonetree said, "History will remember me as the woman sentenced to death by her treacherous father and beheaded by her forsworn vassal. Perhaps they will even write a ballad for me."

With that, the lady bowed her head. Cara's gut churned. In a righteous world, she would have stood by Earl Stonetree and his family against all invaders. She would have kneeled beside the lady and accepted her own fate for defending her home, not been the one to swing the axe.

As Cara lifted the heavy weapon over her head, the memory of Alex's death pushed itself into her mind. She could see it clearly: raising her sword as he kneeled on the rug, the hope and dread in his eyes. Eyes untouched by a *fampir's* red ring. She let the axe fall with a cry.

The brave lady's head toppled down the steps. Cara watched the handsome face empty of life. *I have allied myself to these people.* The beast rose at the sight of blood. The liquid shone, beautiful and red, and she longed to take just a taste. Her features warped a moment, and the soldiers cringed away from her.

As the head bounced, it changed from the lady's to Alex's and back again, both smeared with betrayal. Cara shut her eyes and took a deep breath. The sand around her heart grew and grew, rubbing with a painful grit.

I must do as Rask says: do not quibble over 'right' or 'wrong.' There are only actions that will lead me to the Ossuary.

Cara opened her eyes, but did not inspect the body at her feet. She glared at the sky until the soldiers had removed the corpse and led a new prisoner up the steps. Then she continued her grisly work, focusing only on the steady lift, drop, and shudder as the axe met its mark.

As she worked, Cara met Rask's eye. His smile had grown wolfish, hungry. She wondered what piece on the game board she had become.

She grinned back at him, letting the beast into her features. *If he is a wolf, I am a bear. And a bear only tolerates the wolf.*

CHAPTER FIVE
Gwen

The chasm in the throne room yawned wide, its depths spanning the layers of polished granite and dirt to the heavy grey rock that lay beneath the city of Lordstown. A stray piece of floor broke off and tumbled down, striking against the sides until it hit the bottom. Gwen watched it apathetically. She sat on the edge of the ragged stone, her feet dangling into space. Behind her, the nightcat Lintem sat alert, his tail curled over his paws as his gold-green eyes surveyed the room.

On the throne sat a man bound with magic. His gaze alternated between flicking around in desperation and glaring at her. His guards stood at the edges of the destroyed space, not daring to step closer. Fear clung to them, rank in their Songs.

All of them, witch and prisoner and soldiers, waited.

Gwen had sent one of the guards to summon the Liegelord's Council. This arrest must be done properly. The bound man, Olfrick Kron, had deposed Gwen's brother and taken the country of Demarren for himself. His regicide had come in the form of the Trials, a hunt for mages that had ended with more innocents than Gifted swinging from the ropes. Olfrick's hands were smeared with the blood of nobles and rustics alike.

Once the Council comes, they will arrest Olfrick. Demarren can finally heal. Gwen threw a pebble into the chasm, listening to it click and clack its way down into the darkness.

The scorpion stinger at the end of Lintem's tail twitched. He let out a low growl.

A Demar man stood at the archway to the room, his mouth agape as he stared at the destruction. Vines curled over the pillars and flowers bloomed from between the flagstones, their beauty contrasting the dark pit in the center of the room.

Gwen climbed to her feet, sure of her step despite the crumbling floor. She vaguely recognized the man, but couldn't quite place his name on her tongue. "Who are you?"

The man licked his lips and did not step farther into the room. "Councillor Habib Mutaro." He returned her question, "Who are you?"

Gwen didn't answer him. She waited as four more people gathered behind Habib, all of them white-skinned Skals like Olfrick. Her lip curled at the blonde man in the rear, a man she knew quite well. The smell of mint clung to his tunic, and his long mustache had grown since she had last seen him.

"You have done well for yourself, Ambassador Daghorn," Gwen greeted him. "Did Olfrick make you a councillor after you successfully incited war between Demarren and Dotschar?"

The mustachioed man started. The rest of the councillors murmured and shifted uneasily, assessing both the damage and the strange woman who had caused it.

After a moment, one of the Skals said, "You brought that crowd of rustics to our doorstep."

Beyond the councillors, at the far end of the hall, Gwen could see that very crowd, still waiting for her to emerge. She smiled. "I did."

"You used magic against Demarren's soldiers and dared to imprison Liegelord Olfrick."

"I did." Gwen's eyes narrowed. "And unless you wish to meet a similar fate, I suggest you listen to me."

The councillors grumbled and looked to the guards, but none of the men interceded to aid them. Habib took a tentative step forward. "I recognize you. You're Princess Gwendolyn Zaman."

The other councillors protested:

"No!"

"That's impossible, Daghorn told us she vanished."

"That creature could not be our princess."

When she lived in Demarren, Gwen had dressed in silks and worn a veil across her cheeks. Those days were long gone. Animal skins and leather swathed her body now, her hair grown long and pulled into locks, and her skin mottled in grey and green and brown. Only her violet eyes remained the same.

"He is right. I was once the princess of this country," Gwen said. She gestured at Olfrick. "I came to avenge the coup against my brother, Liegelord Wullum Zaman. I demand justice for this traitor and all who stood with him during the Trials."

The councillors were silent. Some notes from their individual Songs floated through the air in chords of disbelief and anger. They would not be easily convinced.

"Let us speak together," Habib said. In his Song, Gwen detected a sharp mind and decisive instinct. He continued, "You must understand, this is a difficult position for us. We will confer and decide what must be done with both of you."

"I will not release Olfrick while you discuss," Gwen said.

"Of course. But, if you wouldn't mind, could you disperse the crowd at the gate? We don't want a riot to break out."

Gwen contemplated a moment, then nodded. The councillors withdrew, and she quickly checked the spells holding Olfrick. His mouth moved angrily, but no sound came out. Satisfied, Gwen strode up the long hallway to the castle doors and the waiting crowd.

The people cheered as she emerged into the sunlight. Some cried, "Liegelord Gwendolyn!"

That made her pause. Did they believe she would become their ruler? *That's not why I came.* Gwen held up her hands, and the people below quietened. Most were Demar like her, but a few were Skals, loyal to Wullum over Olfrick.

"My people, this is a momentous day. I have captured Olfrick Kron, and he will stand trial for his crimes against our country!" As the crowd roared, Gwen desperately hoped this was true. *Perhaps if the councillors disagree with me, I'll incite these people into a riot. Either way, Olfrick will face justice.*

"But a proper trial takes time," Gwen continued. "Go to your homes and celebrate a new dawn for Demarren. Trust that I will remain and devote myself to a peaceful resolution."

After a few more cheers, the crowd began to disperse. A few stubbornly remained behind, and Gwen sent a melody from the Song of Home to encourage them to leave. Eventually they, too, departed, and the soldiers shut the massive gate.

Gwen returned to the throne room. The guards in there had taken advantage of her absence and fled, leaving Olfrick alone in his crumbled throne with Lintem standing watch over him.

Olfrick's eyes flashed, and Gwen dove into his Song. She found the expected hatred there: hatred for her and Wullum, hatred for the advantages Demars had known in the country for so long. To her surprise, she found love, too. Olfrick had a wife and children, and cared for them as deeply as she cared for her own treasured family. He had known his share of suffering and compassion, pettiness and deep-rooted dreams.

I am glad I did not kill him, Gwen hummed to Lintem.

I can rip his throat out for you, Lintem purred back. *Would that spare you the guilt?*

Hush, she smiled. With a few quick notes, she released the magic over Olfrick's mouth, allowing him to speak. He spat, then swallowed.

"What do you wish to accomplish, witch?" Olfrick hissed. "My councillors are loyal. They will never allow this atrocity to go unpunished."

Gwen cocked her head. Despite his arrogant words, fear laced through his Song. His councillors were ambitious, and he knew it. Would they condemn him for the chance of greater power? *Daghorn surely would, and the others may follow suit. Habib...* Gwen frowned. She knew Habib Mutaro from somewhere.

The truth jolted into her. Habib had been the secretary for Councillor Ebarren when Wullum still ruled. Gwen had spent a lot of time with Ebarren, for he had been the first man to ever teach her about magic. She remembered Habib trailing after the councillor, always quiet, studious, and eager.

Eager for any chance at power? She would have to learn more about Habib before she put any trust in him. For all she knew, he had been the one to betray Ebarren during the Trials, sending her beloved mentor to the gallows.

Olfrick's words interrupted her thoughts. "Magic has been taboo in Demarren for too long. Even if they condemn me, they won't hesitate to execute you. You came here on a false promise."

That might very well be, but Gwen wouldn't give him the satisfaction, so she changed the subject. "Why did you incite the Trials? Was it all to kill my brother and take his position?"

Olfrick gave a feral grin. "An opportunity presented itself. I took it. Did you know that the very first executed person was indeed Gifted? The crowd adored it. When I realized that the mob could be directed from afar, I knew my chance had come. Killing the Liegelord in a coup would have spelled my doom. Killing him under suspicion of magic gave me the power to rewrite the narrative. Of course, your escape only served to prove his guilt."

As Wullum knew it would. Gwen closed her eyes a brief moment, remembering the last time her brother ever held her. He had told her that the Trials would come for him whether she remained or not, and so sent her away. *I didn't know the Songs then. I could not have saved us.*

Gwen stroked Lintem's head. "You did not have to kill Wullum's wives and son."

"You really think I could have kept power with them alive? You are a naïve little girl."

She didn't rise to his bait. "As long as there is power, there will be men seeking to control it." She frowned. She had spared Olfrick with the intention of giving him a trial and avoiding war in the streets over his fate. But what if it was inevitable?

Even with the Songs, she alone could not heal a divided country.

Gwen uttered the Song to gag Olfrick's lips once more, then turned away from him. The councillors were at the other side of the room, their expressions grim. In their Songs, she heard a mix of emotions and fleeting thoughts, but couldn't pick out any one over the other. Rather than trying, she tuned out their Songs and waited for them to speak.

Habib came forward, his fists clenching and unclenching at his sides. He took a deep breath before he spoke, "P-Princess Zaman–"

"Just Gwen," she interrupted.

"Gwen," he started again, "we agree that Olfrick has betrayed his country and caused the deaths of innocents. He will stand trial once the Greater Council has been called. However, we also agree that the use of magic has been forbidden in Demarren for many generations. Though you are of royal blood, you must also stand trial for using spells against our people."

Lintem growled, his scorpion stinger twitching. Gwen placed a hand on his head to calm him. She had known that this was a possibility. *Don't worry,* she hummed to the nightcat. *Even if I am found guilty, I have no intention of dying here.*

Daghorn's voice squeaked out from behind Habib, "And that horrid creature must be put down."

Gwen gripped Lintem's fur as his roar echoed over the chamber. The councillors cringed away. Gwen kneeled next to her companion and put her forehead against his. *Go to the forests,* she hummed. *Listen for my call and return when I need you. This is a political matter; you will only frighten them.*

Lintem's tail swished, his frustration evident in his Song. *I don't want to leave you.*

I know.

Lintem gave her a quick lick, then bounded off. He sprang between the councillors, sending them scurrying out of his way, before disappearing down the hall. As his black tail flicked and vanished from view, Gwen's heart sank into the chasm. They hadn't been apart since he was a cub. *Be safe,* she sent out through the Songs.

From somewhere in the distance, his melody returned to her, *I'll eat them if they hurt you.*

Once the councillors regained themselves, Habib said, "You and Olfrick will both be held under house arrest. We have rooms set aside for you. If you'll please come with us? Oh, and release him?"

Gwen complied, Singing the few notes that undid the bounds over Olfrick. He stood, rubbing at his arms, and glared at her. She strode to the councillors, and he followed behind.

As Gwen came next to him, Daghorn said, "You cannot use magic while under arrest."

Gwen couldn't help but laugh. "How do you plan to stop me? Remember, I am your prisoner by choice. I only remain to see justice done."

Daghorn's lips twisted, but he said no more. Though Gwen's words had been fierce – and she would not hesitate to use the Songs if she must – her guts twisted inside her. She had come to help her country mend its rifts, but magic couldn't help her with that.

It's the people who must change, and no amount of spells can force them into it. Gwen held her head high as her steps turned leaden. *I hope that all this will do more good than harm.*

CHAPTER SIX
Seanna

"Welcome, Your Grace." The elven prince, *Ameer* Voclain Etrila, bowed low. Everything he did held an incomparable grace, from the sweep of his arm to his light footsteps on the delicate walkway. His green robes swirled around his legs as he offered Seanna his arm.

Seanna quickly passed her son to Portia, then accepted the elven prince's proffered hand. They settled into a leisurely pace, and Seanna gazed out over the forest of Rengu, astounded at its beauty and simplicity.

They stood on the outer trunk of an enormous silver-barked tree that rose high above its neighbors. Its girth could hold five Silver Keeps laid one next to the other, its height nearly as tall as the cliffs of Con Salur. Above their heads, gigantic blue leaves rustled in the wind, undaunted by winter's touch. Across the bare crowns of the forest below were more of those mighty trees, though none matched the height or width of this one.

Walkways and terraces circled the outer trunk. Inside the tree was a vast hollow space. The elves had built their homes from mushrooms that grew on the inner trunk, connecting their natural buildings with rope walkways or wooden stairs. Pulleys drawn by magic moved platforms up and down the tall city. The entire thing glowed with the light of bioluminescent fungi that spread from top to bottom in an immense network of life.

"What do you think of Rengu Forest?" Voclain asked.

"It's beautiful," Seanna said. "I wish I had come in peaceful times to enjoy its splendor. Are all the Rengu homes built like these?"

"Some," he said with a smile. "There are few minwood trees left in Rengu, and not all of my people can dwell in them. There are plenty of villages on the forest floor, and farms that grow our food and livestock."

Seanna studied the *ameer*. Like Aremo and the Lofalin elves, Voclain's skin was a dusky brown. But the Rengu elves, she noticed, had a greenish tint to theirs, and their hair varied in shades of brown rather than black. Voclain was an elderly prince, his hair and long beard white with age, his cheeks wrinkled from many days of laughter.

The *ameer* guided her up a set of vine stairs to a private balcony. They sat and took tea together, watching the birds that flew above the forest crown. Seanna relaxed a little: her people were dry and safe, resting at the base of the tree. Aremo's armies could not easily penetrate the twisting forest, nor did they know where to find her.

"I am sorry for Henrik's death," Voclain said. "I am old and have seen many kings in my lifetime. It pains me that so many die young."

Many elves lived a little longer than humans, often to a hundred or so. A rare few could live beyond that. Seanna cocked her head at the prince and asked, "Do you remember the last war?"

"Oh yes. I was still a youth, but my father assisted the rightful king in reclaiming his throne. Many of my friends died on the battlefield." His mournful gaze pierced her. "I will not allow my people to suffer again."

Seanna deflated a little. She reached for a pastry to give herself time to think of a persuasive argument, but the old elf's wrinkled hand shot out. He turned up her palm, his dry fingers running lightly over her skin.

"Your grief lines are long," he commented.

Seanna pulled back, her palm tingling where he'd touched her. "I've lost so many in this war."

"And you will lose yet more. Is that a price worth paying?"

He stared out over the wintering forest, his gaze faraway. "Tell me, why do you fight back against the Lofalins? You and your people can remain here in safety and security for the rest of your lives. Start anew."

Sudden tears pricked at Seanna's eyes. She pushed back the lump in her throat and said as steadily as she could, "I don't have a choice. So many have already fought and died. It would dishonor them to give up now."

"That's an excuse, not a reason. Great leaders surrender when they know they've lost. So why won't you?"

Voclain's voice was gentle and smooth as velvet. Something lurked under it, a tension that Seanna couldn't quite understand. She tried to see beneath the veneer of elderly wisdom. What lay in his heart? Cruelty, perhaps? Manipulation and ambition?

His brown-flecked eyes bore into her, and she was struck by a similarity between him and Druam Strilu. Both had lived far past a man's normal life, and both carried the burdens of it.

Seanna swallowed, her mouth dry. What could she say to an elf whose experiences far outmatched her own? At last, she asked, "What would you do in my place?"

He answered without hesitation, "I would surrender."

"They'll kill Landin." *I cannot surrender. I will not.*

"Then flee." Voclain gave a small wave. "It matters not to me. Stay, flee, fight. You cannot bring back those who have perished, and you cannot defeat Aremo. He has won."

"You're wrong." Seanna crossed her arms in a meager attempt at stubbornness. "I refuse to believe that I've struggled this long for nothing. There has to be a way."

His bushy brows drew together. "This isn't a ballad or child's story. Good does not always triumph. You have no army, no city, no allies. You have lost."

Seanna thought of tiny Landin, his round cheeks thinner than they should be, his nose bright red from the cold. She thought of the people who had marched from Con Salur on a faint hope, all of them counting on her for guidance even when their companions dropped from exhaustion.

She could not abandon them now.

"You're right," she said. "We won't win through force or numbers. But Aremo is one man, and the Lofalins are only here because of him. If we can defeat him, we can take back our kingdom."

The elf's look was pitying, gazing on her as a grandparent would a wayward child. "I admire your determination, but–"

Seanna interrupted him, "We destabilize him. Find his weaknesses, discover what might make the Lofalins turn against him. Play a game of politics while he believes to be fighting a war." She stood, warming to her idea, and paced around the balcony. "He doesn't know I'm here. We can use that to our advantage. Invite Aremo's allies here and ply them with drink and merriment. Smile, and all the while hold the knife behind our backs. Then, when the moment is right, we strike. Not with swords, but with words."

Voclain's sad eyes stared back at her, drooping in his ancient wrinkles. He shook his head. "I will not risk my people on a faint hope."

Before she could protest further, the old elf stood and bowed. "You and your people are welcome to our food and shelter. But if you bring war to my doorstep, I will send you out to the wolves."

He swept away, and Seanna's triumphant moment ebbed into melancholy. She slumped into one of the spindly chairs, and not even the aromas from the table could tempt her missing appetite. Her fingers entwined in her lap. *I've failed. I promised my people retribution, and all I've given them is frostbite.*

She could flee. Run away, as Voclain said, as Cairn Steel-Eyes had suggested so many deshes ago. Take Landin and go to her grandfather's land in the Eadrion Empire, begging her distant relatives for refuge. No doubt she would live well there, not as richly as a queen, but with a roof over her head and good food in her belly.

For a moment, the idea enticed her. She could raise Landin and tell him stories of the long-gone king's court and the lights of Riverfen.

A court of ghosts, and a city of lights that will soon be

extinguished.

But what of the rest of her people? They had no jewels or crown to pawn, no extended relations to seek. If they were lucky, the elves would treat them no worse than the lords that came before. If they were not...Seanna shuddered at the atrocities that she knew Aremo could enact.

But how do I convince Voclain to help me? The old elf had stayed in his woods for nearly a century, never bothering with the outside world. He had spent his lifetime protecting Rengu from it.

If Seanna were in his shoes, would she endanger her people for a stranger's crown?

✳

As darkness drew over the forest, the luminescent mushrooms began to glow, their cool light soft and steady. Seanna stood at an archway to the balcony, bouncing slightly as Landin slept, his tiny fist curled on her shoulder. Behind her, Portia hummed and folded down the bedcovers. With so many refugees and a dearth of empty rooms in the Minwood tree, many of them were asked to share. For a group that had traveled together and slept huddled up in whatever shelter they could find, the humble rooms were a luxury.

Moving slowly so as not to upset the baby, Seanna went to the crib beside the bed. She carefully placed Landin down inside it, then caressed his cheeks with her finger. He gave a tiny cough before settling. Her heart swelled, and she didn't move for a moment, simply staring down at the innocent child that she had brought into the world.

"You have lost. Flee." Voclain's words echoed in her mind, as they had been since her conversation with him earlier that evening. It had been easy, sitting alone and filled with righteous fury, to imagine herself slithering past Aremo's defenses and bringing him to ruin. Now, looking down on little Landin, she didn't know if she could stomach defeat.

"You will lose yet more. Is that a price worth paying?"

In the secret places of her soul, Seanna knew that Landin's life would never be worth less than the kingdom. Not to her. She would sacrifice herself if she must, she would wring herself dry, but she would not let harm befall him.

"What are you thinking about?" Portia's soft voice drifted through Seanna's reverie, water that melted the ice in her heart.

Seanna joined her handmaid on the terrace. Even in winter, night birds sang and insects chirped from the safety of the mighty tree. A cool breeze brushed Seanna's hair from her face, and she closed her eyes as she sat down.

"I'm thinking about what to do next," Seanna answered honestly. "Voclain will shelter us, but no more than that. We ran from Con Salur thinking of nothing but food and warmth, and now that we have both, we are lost."

"We fight back," Portia said at once. "We take our kingdom from the elves."

"With what army? What allies? Voclain was our greatest hope, and he will not aid us. The earls are dead or incapable of sending help. We are alone."

Portia reached out and clutched Seanna's hand. Seanna stiffened a moment, then allowed herself to relax. She squeezed Portia's fingers, taking solace in the calluses that lined the girl's palms. *Strong and steady. Not like me.*

"We're not alone," Portia said. "We have each other, Belrose, and my brother. Your people followed you all the way here; they'd follow you to the ends of Earda if you asked it of them."

Seanna smiled, warmth spreading up her arms from their entwined hands. "I wish I could share your optimism."

"The Rangers are here in Rengu. They can help us."

"They are loyal to Voclain, and they're trained to fight against wolves and bandits. They're no army." But as she spoke, an idea came into Seanna's head. *I may not convince Voclain, but I can convince the other elves.* "Yet an army didn't help us the first time. Maybe what we need now are people like the Rangers."

Portia's eyes lit up, and she began to speak in a tumble of words about who they could reach out to and what they could do. Seanna vaguely listened, distracted by the way the moon shone on the Portia's arms and the fall of her hair as it escaped her braided crown.

Once more, temptation flooded her being. How easy it would be to give up, to take Landin and Portia and go across the sea. Maybe Voclain was right. Maybe this was a war that Seanna could never win, and she should flee while she had the chance. She could laugh and flirt with no worries of war hanging over her.

Seanna cut through Portia's string of words, "Where would you go, if you could?"

A wrinkle dimpled between Portia's eyes. "What do you mean?"

"I mean if you could leave the war behind you. Where would you go?"

"Why are you asking?" Portia shifted, her pale eyes wide. "You're not thinking of leaving, are you?"

Guilt washed through Seanna at the girl's stricken expression. She said hurriedly, "Of course not. It's just nice to dream about, isn't it?"

"I suppose..." Portia trailed off. She yawned and stretched, her hands pulling away from Seanna's. Their absence made her feel cold. "Well, I think it's time to sleep. Don't you?"

They crawled into the bed, and though at first Seanna kept herself near the edge – she both wanted to sleep nearer to Portia and feared the emotions such an act may bring – she woke up with the girl pressed against her, her soft breath warm on Seanna's cheek. Seanna didn't move, not wanting to wake her, as the morning sun touched the terrace. At last, Seanna extricated herself and stood, letting the cold floor beneath her feet and the water in the washbasin jolt the feelings out of her.

Portia was kind, sweet, and cared for Landin as much as Seanna did. She could ramble for a candle about nothing, and Seanna would still want to listen to her. But Seanna knew that she couldn't pursue such a love. For one, she had betrayed the trust of every woman she had ever been with. For another...

I can either be a queen, or I can be a lover and mother. I cannot be both. She glanced over her shoulder at Portia's and Landin's sleeping forms. *Not if I want to win this war.*

It was a truth Seanna had long ignored, but could not deny any longer. Whatever love she held for them must be locked away in a corner of her heart. It could not affect her decisions. It could not stand in her way.

I am sorry. Seanna kissed Landin's forehead, then brushed a hand over Portia's cheek. *I can't be the person you want me to be.*

CHAPTER SEVEN
Sandu

Another splinter pierced Sandu's foot. He pulled it out with a curse and threw it aside. His feet had yet to develop the calluses needed to easily run around the ship, and he doubted they ever would. If his shoes hadn't been thoroughly soaked by a rogue wave, he would have happily kept them on.

The ship was a flurry of activity, with sailors running every which way to either trim or let out the sails, wash the decks, and a hundred other myriad chores. Some scurried up and down the mast while others labored below.

Though his seasickness had abated, Sandu still found himself unbalanced by the ship's constant movement. More often than he liked, he reached out to catch himself, only to fall, the stump of his left arm useless.

Sandu tried to help on the ship. He swept and mopped and carried meals to the sailors on watch. Whenever the men found a task for him, he worked to finish it. But all the while, he felt the aching absence of his arm. The rigging filled him with fear, and the one time he'd climbed it, he'd clung so closely he felt as if the ropes might absorb him. Each step up had been difficult, his heart hammering and his palms sweating.

Coming down was even worse. Sandu slipped and only just caught himself before he fell to the deck. After that, he would watch the working sailors, wishing that he were whole again.

Each night, the sailors gathered to drink together in comfortable camaraderie. Some told stories, their red cheeks blown out in exaggerated features. Others played their small instruments and sang ditties that made the rest clap and stomp their feet. In the warmth of the lanterns, with Da by his side, Sandu felt safe.

As soon as the drinking died down and the chill sea wind swept the sailors into their bunks, the despair returned. Sandu lay awake night after night wondering what he was good for. He'd betrayed his friends and watched his wife die. He'd freed his father, but it was his actions that had put Da in prison in the first place. He'd watched Cara kill Alex, unable to stop her. With only one arm, he couldn't properly work the ship, or till a field, or a hundred other jobs that had once been open to him.

With only one arm, Sandu felt less of a man.

Each day that he wandered uselessly about the ship, small under the sailors' pitying eyes, the ocean's dark call grew louder.

Days passed into quinns. Sandu lost count of time's passing, the candles blending within the endless ocean and boundless skies. His heart retreated deep inside himself, too fragile to be exposed to the chapping winds and harsh sun. The waves sang to him, a siren's call to which he said everyday, "Maybe tomorrow."

*Across the sea is a sorceress...*Sandu clutched to Darian's promise, a mantra that kept the flickering flame of his hope from dying out completely.

One morning, as Sandu carried the breakfast tray, an errant wave caused the ship to keel suddenly. He dropped the wooden platter, and food spilled over the floor. Sandu cursed and stooped down to pick up the mess. As he moved, something in him broke. *What's the point?* He fell to his knees, his breeches soaking with broth, and stared at a cup as it rolled across the floor.

"Son?" Cadel rolled over and eased himself up. He looked from Sandu to the mess. "Aren't you going to clean it up?"

"Yeh," Sandu said without moving.

A heartbeat passed. The deck groaned above while the cup rolled, rolled, rolled, bumping against the wooden floors in an endless cycle. Sandu watched it. His limbs wanted to drag him to the floor, even the phantom weight of his left arm somehow too heavy. He could just lay down. Maybe he'd drown in the broth. Maybe a giant creature would come up from the sea and swallow the ship whole.

"Son, it's just a spilled tray," Cadel said. "Let's just clean it up and move on, yeh?"

Sandu didn't respond. His gaze followed the cup, his mind rolling over and over with repetitive thoughts.

Callused hands grabbed at his shoulders. Sandu met his father's worried eyes.

"Barty?" Cadel asked. He brushed his thumb over Sandu's scruffy cheek. "Barty, what's wrong?"

Across the sea is a sorceress. Sandu tried to speak the words, but they wouldn't come. The ghosts closed in on him, ripping at his soul. He tried to tear himself from his father's grasp, but Cadel held tight.

Sandu's mouth moved but nothing came out. The mantra that had become a prayer was slipping away. Why was he going across the sea? Why was he trying when no one cared about a one-armed coward?

"Barty, look at me," Cadel ordered.

Sandu obeyed, staring into those familiar eyes. More wrinkles had grown around the lids, but the warm brown irises were the same as he remembered.

"Think about the meadery. Remember it?" At Sandu's nod, Cadel continued, "You used to help me lift the barrels. They were wide and heavy, but you were strong. At the end of a long day's work, I'd tap one of the cider kegs you so loved, and we'd share a drink in the meadow. The cider tasted of crisp apples, and the grass was warm under us."

As Cadel spoke, Sandu returned to that hazy memory. This was before he met Tambrey, before his life went to ruin. He was still a gangly youth with only a few hairs on his chin, and he recalled laughing and chasing a squirrel that had dared to come too close to their sanctuary.

"Tell me about the rowan tree," Cadel said. "Do you remember?"

Sandu's lips moved, and a whisper came out, "I climbed the rowan."

"That's right. It was after your first full cup of cider, and your head was full of foolishness."

"I fell," Sandu said.

"And you broke your arm." Cadel nodded, his thumbs rubbing a callus in Sandu's cheeks. "I carried you all the way to the healer, and it took deshes before you could use it again."

Sandu nodded slowly.

"And in that time, you still helped me in the meadery. You rolled the barrels you couldn't lift, you wrote in the ledger for me. You weren't useless." Cadel leaned his forehead against Sandu's. "You're not useless now, if that's what you're worried about. You're a smart lad, you can read and write. There's plenty for you to do in this world."

"But I'm not whole," Sandu said. The words shattered inside him, and he spit them out as if they were glass. "I'm broken."

"The world is full of broken men. There are some who give up and pity themselves. But others find a new course. I raised you to be the second kind. We survived your ma's death together, and I'll be damned if I don't help you survive this, too." Cadel's voice was rough and raw, and it cut through the fog of ghosts.

"How do I do it?" Sandu asked.

"One day at a time," Cadel said. "First we'll pick up this mess. Then we'll see what the rest of the day brings. Don't think too far ahead, don't worry about what may or may not happen. Don't dwell on the past, either. It's done and gone."

Sandu nodded, taking a deep breath. He held Da's hand against his face for a little longer, savoring the touch he'd missed for so long.

"Across the sea is a sorceress," Sandu said. "She's going to help us."

"That's right, son. But she can't help you if you never move from this spot. Come on, up you go."

Together, they cleaned the mess Sandu had made, and though they had to eat the spoiled food – they wouldn't receive more rations until suppertime – it was the first thing that Sandu had truly tasted during the whole trip.

✳

They arrived at port on a cold afternoon where waves crashed into the docks and people ran from the biting winds. Sandu and Cadel struggled down the heaving gangplank, then into the nearest public house. Though the purse Sandu had taken from Alex's room was growing lighter and lighter, Sandu purchased a hot meal for each of them. They savored eating without the lull of the waves churning their stomachs.

The man at the counter directed them to a modest but clean bunkhouse a little farther into town. They ducked their heads against the gale and hurried through the empty streets. By the time they reached the lodging, their cloaks were heavy and wet. Like the other men who huddled in the bunkhouse, they hung their cloaks up as close to the fire as they could, then settled into their blankets. Sandu had purchased a bed for each of them, but they lay together for awhile until their shivering stopped.

As Sandu lay with his arm on his father's back, Cadel said, "So what's next? Where do we find this woman?"

"I don't know," Sandu admitted. "I suppose the capital."

"Can we afford to hire a wagon?"

Sandu checked the purse's weight. "Only if we get lucky and find her within a couple of days."

"So we're walking."

"Yeh."

They were quiet a moment, then Cadel asked, "I know you've had a rough time of it, with Tambrey and the children and all. But there's more eating away at you. Tell me. Please."

The words bubbled up Sandu's throat, then died on his tongue. His father had gone through so much; poor Da didn't need Sandu's burdens along with his own. Sandu only shook his head, and Cadel sighed.

"Fine, son. I won't force you. But your arm is chapped after being in the wind and surf for so long. You should see a healer tomorrow, get a poultice or something for it."

Though Cadel didn't say it, Sandu heard the implication: *And maybe get something for your head, too.*

Cadel eventually fell asleep, and Sandu moved into his own bunk. Without the creaking of the ship or the steady beat of the waves, he found it difficult to close his eyes. He didn't quite know when he had finally drifted off, only that he was woken the next morning by a sun ray searing through the window directly onto his eyelids.

Cadel was still asleep, and Sandu left a note for him. He would do as his father had suggested; he'd seek out a healer, and maybe they could help him ward off his ghosts.

As soon as Sandu walked into the street, he was swept along with the crowd. The babble of voices around Sandu were incomprehensible, and he floundered against the tide of bodies until he made it to the edge of the street. Nearby, a Demar man shook his head and smiled. "Never been to the city before?"

Not a city like this. Sandu had only traveled beyond the borders of Dotschar once, a little ways into Skålland where the lands were all wilderness. The press of people and sounds, experienced many times before in Riverfen, were familiar to him, but somehow this crowd fooled his mind into thinking he was trapped in a maze of bodies.

Now that he stood on the edge, Sandu could see that the people all flowed together in the same direction. He took a steadying breath and said, "Where are they all going?"

The man frowned. "There are rumors of Olfrick Kron's arrest in Lordstown. A runner just came from the capital, and they want to hear the truth."

"Oh." Sandu didn't much care for Demarren's politics. Even this small delay could mean the worst for his father. "I'm seeking a healer. Do you know of any?"

The man nodded. "Down the street in the square, look for a green door. Just follow the crowd, you'll find it."

Sandu gave his gratitude and plunged back into the mass. He moved quickly and steadily, no longer fighting against the rush of people. Soon enough, the crowd poured into a large square. At its center, a disheveled man stood on a wooden platform, his face still coated by road dust.

"What did you see?" shouted someone in the crowd.

"Is it true?" called another.

The traveler held up his hands, and the crowd quieted. Sandu edged forward, curious despite himself.

"It's all true," the traveler proclaimed. The crowd gasped and murmured, then hushed again as he said, "Our princess has returned, but as a witch. She used magic against the guards of Lordstown, and proclaimed Olfrick Kron guilty of treachery and regicide."

The people around Sandu wore vastly different expressions: some triumphant, while others had brows furrowed with anger or despair. Some in the crowd backed away, as if they feared being caught up in something dangerous. Others pressed forward, eager and expectant. Tension thrummed through the mass, a wind that could blow either way.

I should leave. But Sandu didn't budge. This princess...surely the traveler meant Gwendolyn Strilu? If so, then Sandu and Da must go to Lordstown.

"What about the princess?" a voice cried out. "Surely she'll be hung for witchcraft!"

A few cheered in agreement while others booed loudly. Though the sky was clear, the air felt humid, a storm brewing within the crowd.

"I don't know," the traveler admitted. "She hasn't been seen since Kron's arrest. Some think she's being held for trial as well. Others that she fled."

Sandu's ears rushed with the pounding of his heart. *What if I'm too late?*

Sandu breathed deeply, calming his fluttering lungs. First he had to get to Lordstown. Then he could worry about the sorceress.

The crowd swelled around him, a churning beast. Voices cried out:

"Let them both stand trial!"

"They should put Olfrick back on the throne."

"She's our princess, she's the rightful heir!"

The storm could break any moment. Sandu darted between the people, heading for the green door not too far off. He reached it just before a fight broke out between two Demars on the edge of the square. Shouts and cries rose up, and the crowd ruptured. Some ran for the streets, others proceeded to lob their fists at each other. Guards swarmed into the fray, trying to break up the fights, but there were simply too many people.

Blood rushed in Sandu's head, his vision swimming as his ghosts swarmed over him. His hand shook on the doorknob. *Across the sea is a sorceress,* he tried to think.

But he was across the sea, and the sorceress might be executed before he ever reached her.

The door opened, and Sandu stumbled into the plump woman who peered out at the square. They both staggered into the entrance before catching themselves.

The woman took a quick glance at Sandu, then pulled him inside and shut the door. The cries of pain and anger became muted, the bright green paint shutting out the ghosts. Sandu put his hand on his knee, breathing deeply, forcing himself to calm.

"I'll put the tea on," the woman said before bustling into a back room. Sandu didn't watch her go. He simply breathed, feeling his palm on his leg and his feet pressing into the freshly swept floor. Slowly, he returned to normal, and he straightened. The woman observed him from the doorway.

She was past her prime, with more grey in her hair than black, and wrinkles in the corners of her eyes and lips. She was dressed comfortably, without decoration. Sandu assumed she was Demar, for her skin was dark, though her brown eyes had flecks of gold in them. She reminded him of his mother, with her long hair swept up out of her face and tied back with a kerchief.

After a couple of tries to work past his stubborn tongue, Sandu managed to say, "Are you the healer?"

The woman nodded. "My name is Tav. You've come a long way."

"Yes."

The kettle whistled, and Tav gestured for Sandu to follow

her into the kitchen. She sat him at a rickety table and poured a cup of strong-smelling tea. He blew on it before taking a sip. The hot water scorched his lips, and Sandu put the cup back down. Tav settled across from him, drinking long gulps from her own steaming cup with no apparent discomfort. Her gaze was fixed on him.

"Your humors are making your head ill," Tav said.

Sandu's cheeks burned, and he stared into his cup. "It's that noticeable?"

"My country is full of hurting people. I've learned the signs well," Tav sighed. "Many are like you. Their past haunts them, and there's no potion I can brew or poultice I can make to heal them. I can give comfort, if you'd like."

Despair blackened Sandu's heart. "There's nothing you can do?"

She gave a helpless shrug. "Only you can heal yourself. Perhaps if you came in every few days and spoke with me, I could help you find that path."

"I don't have that time," Sandu said, shaking his head. "I have to get to Lordstown."

"Why?"

Sandu's hand clenched around his cup. Somehow, he thought this woman would sniff out any lie, but he didn't know how he could explain the truth. Finally, he settled on, "My children are missing. I believe there's someone there who can help me."

"You've come a long way on such a hope," Tav observed. "Surely there was someone in all of Dotschar who could have helped you."

"It's complicated." Sandu sipped again at his tea, which had blessedly cooled to merely warm.

Tav leaned forward, and her hand darted out to grab his wrist. He startled, but then forced himself to calm as her bright eyes searched his. After a moment, she said, "Finding your children will not heal your mind. You know that, right?"

Sandu didn't say anything. If he could just hold his children again, hear their piping voices and smell the sweet soap on their skin, he knew he would be better. *I have to be.* How else could he be a worthy father for them?

He pulled his hand away, and the woman mercifully let go. Sandu stood, leaving a coin on the table. "Thanks for the tea. I should head back to my Da now."

Tav didn't say anything as he left, though he felt the glint of her eyes on his back. He hunched his shoulders and pushed open the green door. Thankfully, the square had calmed down, and Sandu made his way back to the bunkhouse. He'd rouse Da and start their journey that morning.

We don't have much time. We have to reach the sorceress before the trial.

CHAPTER EIGHT
Cara

"I should be out there with them," Cara insisted. She glared out the window at the expanse of snow and rock, searching for the return of the hunting party. "I was born to hunt *fampir*."

Talnor didn't move from her comfortable position by the fire. "You were born for far greater than capturing rustic *fampir* and hauling them all over the countryside."

"But the soldiers—"

"Have been well-informed of the nature of *fampir* and how to defeat them. If a few die, well...we're at war. It's a bit too late to worry about the lives of common men." Talnor popped a pastry between her red lips and chewed slowly. A small bit of cream dotted the corner of her mouth.

"I should not be cooped up in here like some prisoner." Cara tore her gaze away from Talnor and started pacing, her steps marking a familiar path over the rugs. *I need to be out there.* It had been her idea to use the information in Alex's journal to capture *fampir* for their potent blood. It had not been her idea to stay behind while others sought out the creatures.

She studied Talnor for the hundredth time. This woman had Renna's features, every little mole in its correct place, each fleck of her eye exactly as Cara remembered. But the soul inside was no longer her friend's. A stranger occupied that familiar body, one who did not have her old companion's grace and dainty composure. Where Renna was smooth and gentle, Talnor was rough and abrupt. While Renna ate only tiny bites, Talnor consumed food like a hungry animal.

Who is this person, really?

Cara sat across from Talnor with an intent look. The *fampir* gave her a cursory glance. "What?"

"I want to know about you," Cara said. "I want to know why you hate Druam so much."

"It's fairly simple, isn't it? He trapped me for centuries." With a lazy finger, Talnor swept the cream from her lips and licked it.

"There has to be more to the story."

"You want more? Fine. I'll show you more." Talnor reached down and held the finger over her other wrist. She drove her sharp nail into her skin, producing a large ruby droplet. "Open your mouth."

Cara's skin crawled, but she complied. Talnor flicked the blood from her finger onto Cara's tongue. As usual, the coppery taste roused Cara's beast, and she held it down with effort. She closed her mouth and swallowed. "What now?"

"I'm going to show you my sorry tale." Talnor leaned forward and wrapped a hand around each of Cara's wrists. "Look into my eyes."

The droplet of blood burned as it went down Cara's throat, and she could feel its heat in her stomach. The *fampir's* grip was tight, and Cara's wrists already ached from the touch. Still, she followed Talnor's instruction, and gazed into those achingly familiar blue eyes, now ringed with red.

The blue filled Cara's vision. She opened her mouth, but her tongue didn't respond. Her head reeled, and she tried to close her eyes to ward off the dizziness, but couldn't force her lids shut. Talnor's icy blue gaze swallowed her in a flash of cold light.

✳

Cara blinked. She was no longer in Stonetree, no longer in a building of any sort. She stood in a wide field drenched in blood and corpses, pennants hanging from broken spears and dead horses still tied to their chariots.

Though she tried to move her limbs, they didn't respond. Talnor's voice flitted in her head: This is my memory. You're seeing from my eyes. You control nothing here.

Cara relaxed a little. Somewhere distant, she could feel her own body, still sitting in the cozy room in the keep. She was safe. This was a memory.

With nothing else to do, Cara settled into Talnor's mind and watched events unfold.

✳

Talnor surveyed the battlefield, her mouth twisting in a grim smile. *Fampir* spread out, feasting upon the dead before the carrion crows had a chance to descend. Some of the fallen might even rise that night as newly blooded undead, strengthening their ever-growing army.

"Is Landin among the dead?" a deep voice asked from behind her.

Talnor's smile widened at the sight of her mate. A handsome elf in life, Galiyar was even more glorious as an undead, his long hair flowing from beneath a shining helm and his eyes glowing red above his full lips. She sauntered to him and raised up on her toes to kiss him. His tongue darted out, tasting the blood on her lips, and she shuddered with delight.

When they parted, she said, "He's not been found yet."

A frown tainted his brow. "Then we must keep hunting. I will have the king's head gracing the table at our victory feast."

"Soon, my love," Talnor promised. "Soon the world will be ours."

He left, and she strode through the field of the dead, heedless of the grime that coated her boots and the soft cries of the dying. Talnor's sharp eyes swept over the scene, and she paused. A red banner draped into the mud, its emblem faded and spattered with blood. She smiled.

The king lay dying underneath his banner. His cheeks were pockmarked with scars, his beard grey and thinning. Blood dribbled down his chin, and he gave a great, racking cough. His hands gripped a spear jutting from his stomach.

"King Landin the First," Talnor purred. She crouched down next to him. "Where is your son?"

The king spat and glared at her. His eyes watered as Talnor twisted the spear, her grin growing wider.

"Where is the handsome prince?" Talnor cooed. "Surely he wouldn't flee? Surely he's braver than that?"

"He...went...to Valder," the king gurgled. His head slumped, and his eyes stared fixedly at the ground. Talnor hissed and dug the spear deeper, but he gave no response. She wrenched his head from his body. Gripping it by the hair, she stood and held it aloft with a cry. The *fampir* flocked to her, screeching and whooping.

Yet Talnor narrowed her eyes at the horizon, for her enemies were still out there.

*

"Was that the Dead's War?" Cara asked.

"The Dead's War was not how you imagined it," Talnor replied.

"Then tell me."

"It was a race of experimentation more than anything. King Landin I coveted the River Valley and tried to take it from the tribes who lived there. Those tribes banded together and crowned their own king, a man called Erlix. Landin's first forays were unsuccessful; the mountains proved too great a challenge. So he retreated and began his experiments. His sorcerers created the fampir, *including myself and my mate.*

"With the fampir's *greater strength and fortitude, the army made it over the mountains. But Erlix's men had also been busy. They had made the wights, mindless undead cretins, after a spy reported on Landin's experiments. Unlike us, the wights were fully obedient.*

"Wights and fampir *fell on both sides. Victory seemed assured, until he came.*

"Valder Riesk."

The name dropped onto Cara with the weight of centuries. She had heard it before from Darian. The man had somehow destroyed legions of fampir *with a single spell, and had been allied with a* sulpari *like her.*

"What did he do?" Cara asked.

"He had more gems, like what Mavian used," Talnor said. "Ones in all colors which heightened his power. We were forced to flee, for the wights grew stronger under his magic. I remember seeing him on a hilltop, so far away. So small. So young. Barely a man, yet wielding the forces of the Underworld with such confidence. He drove Landin's forces out of the River Valley, and an uneasy truce began which lasted for almost eighteen years."

Did Cara detect a trace of admiration in Talnor's voice? Jealousy, even?

Talnor continued, "My mate, Galiyar, and I knew that we must either persuade Valder to our side or seize his gems by force. Our plan started then: we began to sire more of our kind. Over the years, our army grew and grew. Landin I grew afraid and tried to destroy us. You saw the result of that.

"Yet Landin II, now grown, sought help from Valder in order to contain us. We had to make sure we arrived first."

✳

Talnor tripped over a stone, her free arm flying up to catch herself. The strong hand that held her firmly by the other arm kept her from falling, then wrenched her forward. Though she longed to tear the blindfold from her eyes, Talnor did not resist. She could hear the heartbeats of the men around her, too many for her to fight before they overwhelmed her. They had been wise to insist that she, and she alone, descended to the Ossuary.

They walked and walked and walked, down endless steps and through cold rooms, until at last they stopped. The hand holding her fell away, and the heartbeats receded. Talnor tore off her blindfold, then stopped short.

Wights surrounded her. Each had once been a hulking soldier, with heavy weapons and heavier armor. Their unnatural eyes glinted in the light of the blue orbs that congregated near the stone ceiling. None of them breathed, none of them had blood pumping through their veins. They were silent and eerily still, watching her.

They were in a small chamber with only one archway leading out. Other than the wights and orbs, it was completely empty. Talnor craned her head, trying to peer through into the next room. She could see nothing of the rest of the Ossuary.

Two shapes emerged from the gloom: one young and willowy, a beautiful maiden with flowing hair and bright eyes. The other Talnor recognized instantly: Valder Riesk. He was older now, his hair greying and his robes hanging loosely on his thin frame.

But Talnor was less interested in him. She regarded the woman curiously. The girl had a human heartbeat, but a strange, musty smell. Almost as if...

"It's true," Talnor breathed. "You bred human and *fampir* together."

Valder paused. He stood protectively in front of the girl. "What do you want?"

Talnor gave a small shrug. "I want an alliance."

"Tch." He gave a small, annoyed sound. "You and your mate have been a plague to our people. You massacred Landin's army and destroyed his capital. Why should I bind myself to such evil?"

"Think about it," Talnor said, stepping gracefully toward him. He took a step back. She said, "You could become king. Overthrow both Erlix and Landin II. With us at your side, you would be unstoppable." She breathed deeply, savoring the Underworld magic that sang throughout this strange underground chamber. "We could start a new era."

The girl shook her head vigorously. "You'd only kill us after you got what you wanted."

"Peace, Alesse," Valder murmured. He gave Talnor a calculating look. "You have been our enemies for many, many years, and yet only now have you come seeking friendship. We have tried sending emissaries all this time, and were always spurned. If I recall, you sent their heads in response."

Talnor smiled broadly and spread her hands in an inoffensive gesture. "Grave mistakes, I assure you. We want the same thing, Valder. We want the Underworld and Earda to unite, and to be free from the authority of backwards kings."

"No," he said. "That's what you want. I want peace."

"Peace can only be gained through force."

"Perhaps." Valder turned slightly toward Alesse, his robes shifting to show the glint of a white gem hanging from his neck. Without thinking, she lunged for it. In an instant, wights piled on her, pinning her to the floor.

Valder stood over her, shaking his head. "And your true self is revealed. Goodbye, Talnor. If you or your kind ever return to this place..."

He left the threat hanging as he departed. Talnor wriggled and protested, but even her considerable strength was no match for the number of wights which held her down. She shouted out, "You belong with us, Alesse!"

The girl paused, and Talnor pushed her opening, "You are half *fampir*, child. You belong with your kind. We could show you such incredible things."

"Don't listen to her," Valder said. "Don't be like the others."

"I know," Alesse said, a hint of grief in her voice. "But I do wish things were different."

Talnor grew still, her thoughts racing as she contemplated Valder's words. Others? Were there others like Alesse?

A new plan formed in Talnor's clever mind.

※

"Show me what you can do," Talnor said. She stood in a town square flooded with bright sunshine, the sun hot on her head, sweat beading on her skin and her limbs growing weaker with each passing moment.

A *sulpari*, her beast distorting her features, stood with her feet in a pond. Two dead humans lay next to her. Her glossy red hair shone in the sunlight, matching the red of her eyes. Madness gleamed within them, and she bared her fangs at

Talnor.

"I need more," she insisted.

Without hesitation, Talnor held out her arm. The *sulpari* sank her teeth into Talnor's flesh. The *fampir* allowed her to take a long drink, then tore her arm away. Undead blood dripped onto the grass and stained the *sulpari*'s mouth.

The *sulpari* grinned and plunged her hands into the water. Her eyes lit with a red fire. Talnor sensed the flow of power that the woman used, surging against her chest and running down her arms.

Thunder crashed in the distance. Dark storm clouds quickly overtook the clear blue sky. Villagers rushed out into the square, their fear palpable.

The *sulpari*'s smile never wavered, her fangs white against her lips.

Then blood rained from the sky. It dripped onto the streets and rooftops. People screamed as red flowed down their cheeks. The *sulpari* laughed and laughed, terrible and beautiful, and Talnor looked on with a swelling of satisfaction.

✳

"I found all the sulpari *who had turned from Valder," Talnor said. "I groomed them into weapons."*

"What did Valder do?" Cara asked.

"He hunted them down and killed them. That was when Galiyar and I decided to make our final move. We would take the Ossuary from him."

✳

"You cannot leave me here!" Talnor insisted. She glared at Galiyar with all the hate she could muster. "I have worked for years to bring him down, and you would have me stay behind?"

Galiyar held up a soothing hand, but she pushed it away. He said, "I know, my dear one. I know. But the Ossuary augments his power, and if he should defeat us—"

"He won't."

"If he should, then one of us must remain alive in order to exact revenge. You are letting your anger cloud your mind. I know the loss of the *sulparis* was difficult for you, but you must think clearly now. We don't know what schemes and traps Valder has laid in his Ossuary."

"We have a force of thousands of *fampir*," Talnor said. Her palms itched, wanting to slap him. "Even if we fall, he will be overwhelmed with the numbers. And he's used many of his wights in hunting down the *sulparis*. There cannot be many of them remaining."

"That may be so, but for my sake: please stay," Galiyar said, his voice low and pleading. He ran a finger on Talnor's arm, and she accepted the touch. "I have sired two fine Valadi soldiers. Help them to gain their footing, then join me once our victory is assured."

He leaned his forehead against hers. Talnor closed her eyes, breathing in the scent that had remained unchanged for so many years. She had gone into this journey with him; she did not savor the notion of ending it while separated.

"Please," Galiyar murmured. "It will comfort me greatly to know you live on to accomplish our dreams."

She held his hands and breathed with him. After a moment, she said, "Very well."

✳

"He died in the Ossuary," Cara commented. "Valder destroyed him and the other fampir.*"*

There was no response from Talnor. A deep pain resonated in the strange dream-world they both occupied, and the next memory coalesced.

✳

"Protect me!" Talnor screeched at the *fampir* who huddled by the cavern entrance. They leapt at the two soldiers who waited patiently for them. The *fampir* with her were new, unblooded. They stood no chance against the brothers.

As the still-twitching limbs of the *fampir* dropped to the floor, Mordekai Strilu strode forward, flanked by his brother, Jokim. Their red eyes held no pity. Talnor backed away until she hit the cold stone wall.

She trembled before them, a show put on to make them more confident. They were mere whelps. As the brothers closed the gap, she leapt forward, her talons straining for their pale skin.

Mordekai whipped out a net, and she could not dodge in time. The threads wrapped around her, and she shrieked: each fiber was soaked in garlic that burned against her flesh. She struggled to escape, but each movement only trapped her further. Mordekai's hands turned red as he pulled on the net, but he gave no signs of distress. He looked on her without pity.

Together, the brothers carried her from the cavern and down, down, down into the depths she had not ventured into since the sorcerers had transformed her into a monster.

"Where are you taking me?" Talnor gritted out despite the pain. Her skin bubbled and boiled as the net pressed against it.

The brothers didn't answer. They kept moving, implacable and merciless.

They came into a vast chamber. At its center lay a black sarcophagus, its sides and lid carved with runes. Talnor's eyes widened, and she doubled her efforts to escape. She could do nothing against the *fampir* who held her captive.

"Goodbye, Talnor," Mordekai said. His eyes held no warmth, no malice. Nothing. They were as blank as the cold granite.

They dumped her into the sarcophagus and closed it. Talnor screamed and scratched at the lid. At last, she managed to tear the net from her and shove it into a corner. But no matter how she fought, she could not budge the heavy lid.

She was trapped. For once in her life, true fear crept into her heart.

✳

The connection between Talnor and Cara ended. Cara reeled from the last desperate gasps in that black space within the tomb.

"Do you understand now?" Talnor asked. "Do you see why Mordekai – Druam – must be made to pay for my centuries of imprisonment?"

"I do," Cara said, though her thoughts were not focused on those painful memories. It only had room for the Ossuary, that secretive place where Valder had controlled so many wights and destroyed so many *fampir*. Now that she had seen a glimpse of it, she wanted more. *Talnor is too narrow-minded. She cares only for revenge on Druam. But I want to end the* fampir *scourge forever, something even Valder couldn't accomplish.*

Now that she understood Talnor better, she knew the creature's weaknesses. Witnessing her memories had only helped to separate Cara's ideas of Renna from this monster.

"You once helped the *sulpari* discover their gifts. Is there more than the black fire and blood rain?" Cara asked.

"Oh yes. Would you like me to show you?"

Cara nodded. It's what she came for, wasn't it? A power not even Druam could withstand. Talnor played at kinship, but Cara knew that the *fampir* had no qualms about sacrificing her if necessary. *So I'll meet you move for move. You use me, I'll use you.* Cara smiled at Talnor.

CHAPTER NINE

Gwen

The breeze on Gwen's open balcony made her bare arms shiver. She had been taken to her old room, but was surprised to find that little had changed in it. Her dresses and veils still filled the wardrobe, her childhood toys stored in a walnut chest at the foot of the bed. She didn't know if the Skals had avoided that room simply because they had no use for it, or because of the constant reminders that a witch had once occupied its bed.

Gwen couldn't sleep. Her bare feet stood on the cool stone, the city stretching below. Its lights twinkled, yellow and ordinary. She missed the splendor of Riverfen with the thousands of colorful lanterns that lined its streets every night.

Do they still glow in war?

In the streets below, Demars and Skals completed the errands of the day or caroused in the public houses, their voices raised in drunken jollity. Yet underneath the banality, Gwen heard discordant notes twisting about. *The people do not trust each other. They do not trust their leaders.*

How could she hope to unite them when half feared her magic and the other half resented her Demar skin?

I can no longer be their sweet princess, nor their savior.

A soft knock came at her door, and Gwen called her unknown guest to enter. Habib deferentially approached her, his sandals slapping against the tiled floor. As before, Gwen opened herself up to his Song, listening for notes of betrayal or scorn. All seemed well on the surface, and she relaxed a little.

"Do you come with questions or with counsel?" Gwen asked. She leaned back on the railing, half-listening to the music that floated through the air. Ordinary music played on instruments, not Songs. She had forgotten what it was like to listen to such melodies, and found that they were a mere droplet to the ocean of sound in the Woods.

Habib's dark head shone in the starlight, its shorn half covered in tattoos. He indicated an unlit torch. "May I light them?"

"If you must." Gwen had spent many nights in the Woods with only the light of the moon and stars to guide her, and her eyes had grown used to the dark as well as the light.

While Habib lit the torches on the walls, he said, "I am sorry for interrupting your peaceful night, but..."

Gwen stared out into the city. She kept an ear on Habib's Song, listening to it alongside his words.

Habib hesitated, then continued, "I have been asked to serve as your advocate for your trial. Councillor Daghorn will stand for Olfrick."

Of course. Gwen didn't speak. The thrum of Songs in the city came quiet but steady. *Daghorn will use whatever tools he has against me. What of my so-called advocate? Will he provide his full support?* She cast an assessing eye on Habib and waited for him. His Song was filled with suspicion and fear, oily and black in the night.

"The charges against Olfrick are for treason, regicide, and inciting mobs. The charges against you are for assaults against city guards and using forbidden magic." Habib paused, but when Gwen gave no answer, he continued, "Unfortunately, some of the Greater Council are in their winter estates, and refuse to leave until the spring. Both trials will have to wait until all of them have convened here."

"So we have time to prepare," Gwen said. "What is my best defense?"

"That you used magic in order to bring down a tyrant," Habib answered.

She tilted her head, contemplating this argument, then said,

"Olfrick could make the same defense: he incited the Trials in order to bring my brother to justice."

"Your brother was the rightful ruler," Habib pointed out.

Gwen remembered the shadow of her brother wandering through Purgatory, his cries lost in the grey smog. She shook her head, "Rightful, but perhaps not righteous. We must not rely upon the Greater Council's fond memories of Wullum's reign."

Habib gave a little shrug. "This is a new situation. All trials involving mages have always been to argue that magic was used, not that its use was justified. The law is clear; by all rights, you should have been hanged the moment you were caught. There were enough witnesses, including members of the Council, to justify such an action."

"Hmm." Gwen ran her fingers over the stone, feeling each minute hollow. The Song inside it rumbled, low and continuous, unchanged for centuries. "They are all fools. Whether they like it or not, the threads of the Songs are in everything. Even you."

Habib swallowed, then said, "I have been raised my entire life to see magic as a dark force only used by the wicked. Many killed in the Inquisition were innocent, I cannot argue that, but others who died were secret mages who used their powers for their own selfish ends. You are the first mage I have ever spoken to, and you invaded our city and deposed our ruler within a day. What could have happened had you been an enemy of Demarren?"

He was right. She could have razed the city, could have dominated Olfrick and forced him to do as she pleased. But the thought had never occurred to her.

"I am no enemy to my homeland." Gwen pulled at his Song, parsing through the notes and melodies until she found a familiar thread. "Neither was Ebarren."

Habib didn't look at her. "Ebarren was guilty of practicing magic. His name means nothing to me."

"But you still respected him."

For a long moment, Habib said nothing. At last, he said softly, "He was like a father to me. He taught me everything I know about politics. I wept for him when he was executed, but I also felt so, so betrayed. How could someone I admired do such a terrible thing?"

"Do you know what kind of magic he practiced?" Gwen probed.

He shook his head. "Does it matter?"

"He has known those arts for many, many years. If he wanted to rule or enact evil upon Demarren, he would have done so. You spent time with him; you know that he only wanted to help my brother make this country better." Gwen reflected on all that Ebarren had taught her. Without him, she would never have had the courage to explore her own magic. "I was close to him, too. We share that connection."

In his Song, Gwen heard dissonant notes. This man truly believed that magic was a corrupting force, irreconcilable with his notion of a safe kingdom. He may want, as she did, to preserve peace and forge a new path forward, but he would never agree with her methods. He wanted to help her, but he also feared her.

"You have no reason to be afraid of me," Gwen said. As she spoke, she heard in his Song what truly frightened him. "I will not bring harm to your family."

Habib took a step back. "You can read minds."

"No, but I can understand your Song. The melodies are complex and intricate, but the Song of Love is well known to me. You have a wife and a young son, with another child on the way." Gwen spoke without thinking, reading all the melodies that were strongest in his Song. "Your mother is ailing, and you must support her, too. You are proud of your position, but know it is tenuous. As one of the few remaining Demars in the Council, you must tread carefully. You are caught in a pit of vipers."

Gwen didn't need his Song to understand his wide eyes and stricken expression. He put out a hand to the railing, the other wiping at his robes. He took one step back, then another, until his shoulders touched the wall behind him.

"Stop it," Habib said. "Stop poking through my soul, or whatever it is you're doing."

"Why?" Gwen took a step, and he tensed.

"Because it's not right. You have no right to what's in my mind and heart."

"Don't I? You would hide secrets from me, but now I know where I truly stand with you." His soul was bared to her, and Gwen did not release her grip on it. She heard the melody which had grown cacophonous within him: "You want to see me hang."

"Please," Habib whispered. He fell to his knees in front of her and clasped his hands. "I have been told to advocate for you, and I will do so despite my own misgivings. But please, don't use your witchcraft on me."

"You have political power and use it daily to have your own way. Would you not act as I do, in my place?" Gwen demanded.

"I don't know," he said. A tear dripped down his cheek.

"Magic is a resource, a tool. I can wield it, and so could Ebarren. Yet you think we should die for using what power is available to us."

"That's not true." The lie made a jagged note in his Song.

"I don't need you," Gwen said, stalking to the other side of the balcony. "I will not have a liar advocate for me."

Silence built between them as she listened to his Song. She made an annoyed noise. "You honestly believe in the justice of Demarren's trials? That innocent blood can be spilt as long as a few mages are caught?"

"Stop it!" Habib shouted. He climbed to his feet. "Stop invading me!"

"Then stop me," Gwen said. "Go ahead. Try."

Habib roared and lunged at her. With a quick note, Gwen halted him in his tracks. He stood frozen, one foot off the ground, his arms reaching for her neck. His eyes darted about as he struggled against the bonds of her magic.

"You fear me because you understand nothing about me," Gwen said. She advanced on him. "Yes, magic is to be feared. It is more powerful than you can imagine. So why would you want to make an enemy of me?"

She hummed another few notes, and he was able to pry his lips open and hiss, "Because I do what is right, not what is easy."

"Tell the Council that either I will have an advocate who is truly on my side, or I will be my own advocate," Gwen said. "Tell them, too, that I will witness Olfrick's trial and see that justice is done."

"And if he is declared innocent?"

She smiled grimly. "I will make my objections known."

With another hummed melody, Gwen released him. Habib crashed to the stone floor, wincing as his knees struck the hard ground. He glared up at her. "This is why Demarren has always despised your kind."

"Get out." Gwen looked back over the city as his sandals slapped against the tiles. She didn't move as the door slammed closed. Beyond the lights was the dark mass of the forest where Lintem had gone to hide.

They are fools if they believe they can keep me under house arrest. With the Song of Air keeping her steady, Gwen descended outside the castle walls and into the streets, her feet taking her toward her companion.

✳

A small forest grew on the outskirts of Lordstown, stretching across the river to the foothills. It was quiet and secluded, used for royal hunts but otherwise forbidden for the rustics to enter. Most of the trees had bared their branches for winter, though the occasional pine stood tall among its companions, its verdant green beautiful in the pre-dawn grey.

Gwen curled in the branches of a tall rowan, her feet kicking in the air. Lintem lay above her, his paws dangling down in front of her face. His constant low rumbling soothed her. She leaned her head against the tree bark, thinking over what she had done to Habib.

"I wish we were back in the Woods," Gwen said. The forest around her held none of the Woods' mystery. Its trees didn't whisper to her, its shrubs didn't camouflage stone-hide animals or jeweled birds. Its grass was plain and green, its boulders ordinary. Her heart ached for the Woods' Songs to enshroud her once more, providing her with lifetimes of solitary joy. She murmured, "Just you and me again, hunting and exploring. Remember your first snow? You didn't know what to think of it. You were so small then, I could still carry you. You pounced through the powder and chased the snowflakes, and when you were done, your coat was so white you looked like a ghost."

Lintem huffed and leaned down, his warm breath blowing across her forehead. His rough tongue lapped against her skin. Gwen shut her eyes. "We took care of each other when we had no one else. We grew together."

His rumbling purr encompassed her, and Gwen relaxed in its shelter. He hummed to her, *We still take care of each other.*

"I know." Gwen sighed deeply. The clouds swept by overhead, their whorls painted with the oncoming dawn. She would have to return soon, out of the peace of the forest and into the chaos of society.

Lintem heard the consternation in her Song and rumbled, *I can eat that man if you like.*

Gwen smiled. "We cannot solve everything with violence." Nor with magic. Her smile slipped, and she rubbed her head. "I thought it would be easier. That I could simply come back, depose Olfrick, and restore Demarren. How foolish of me."

We could just leave, Lintem purred. *Go home to the Woods.*

"I wish it were that simple. We cannot return to the Woods; remember what the Witches said? And Dotschar is torn by war. I don't even know if Druam is still alive."

Then we go somewhere else.

"We can't." Gwen hummed snatches of a childhood lullaby, then said, "I started this whole mess. I should be the one to clean it up, but I can't unite them with words or magic."

Lintem cocked his head at her, and Gwen answered his silent question, "I may have to become something far more terrible. Something for them to rally against."

He licked her hair, and Gwen reached up to scratch his chin. From the safety of the tree, she looked upon the city. The city of her childhood, though now she was a stranger to it.

CHAPTER TEN
Mavian

Vials lay scattered about the table, the glass still coated with droplets of various potions. Every book from the shelves lay open, stubbornly refusing to yield the information Mavian needed. Merick stood against the wall, silent and brooding, while Ekkar prodded a tube across the stone floor, the glass making bell-like sounds as it went.

"None of it will work," Mavian muttered. His eyes were gritty with exhaustion, his hands shaking. He hadn't returned to the cavern below since the scholars left. He imagined the empty chamber with only his own belongings and a smoldering fire to greet him.

No, he couldn't face that yet.

Frustration building inside him, Mavian riffled again through the various manuscripts and records. None of them mentioned any creature similar to a prowler, but still he pored through them until his eyes burned.

Just as he was about to throw aside an ancient journal, a scrawled note in the margin caught his eye. Mavian frowned as he translated it: *The music forges a trail to the lost souls.* His brow wrinkled as he contemplated it. He checked the journal, which had belonged to a mage serving under Valder Riesk during the Dead's War. But this note wasn't written in the same hand as the rest of them.

Mavian held the book loosely at his side as he paced and puzzled over the short message. *The music? Could it be like*

Gwen's magic, workings made more powerful with humming? He put aside that notion for the moment and focused on the second part. *The mages of the Dead's War made* sulparis *like Cara. Did they notice that the* fampir *fathers lost their souls, and so disposed of them before they could spread? But then why try to find the souls?*

His mind overflowed, sending his heart into a frenzy. His fingers trembling with excitement now more than fatigue, Mavian pulled out all the sources he had from the Dead's War. He flipped through them, searching for any description of musical spells.

Mention after mention sprouted forth from the pages, passages that Mavian had previously ignored or dismissed as dramatic embellishment. Now, though, he noticed that nearly all the scholars from the Dead's War spoke of music and songs that fueled their magic. One even said that they had been tasked with infusing gems with the music to aid the lesser mages.

None discussed the use of such magic after Valder's death.

But what is this music? Mavian ran a finger over his lips in thought. All of the scholars seemed to take this magic for granted, for they didn't explain its properties or effects, nor did they instruct how to access it. After Valder's death, they discussed using different sorts of magic, the kinds Mavian was more familiar with, but not a word on what happened to the song-magic.

Yet again, Mavian thought back to the way Gwen used her magic. She had been able to manipulate spells using humming or soft singing. Somehow, she had been able to touch upon this magic. *And other sorcerers, even unwittingly, must have been able to as well.* But how could Mavian do it? And could this strange magic be the key to the prowlers' cure?

Before he could think more on it, voices interrupted his thoughts. Mavian stiffened. The sounds were coming from the corridor that led to the castle.

Chadron? But what would that cur want with Mavian's little workshop?

Mavian looked wildly around him. Ekkar had noticed his unease and stilled, his red eyes focusing on the direction of the voices. Merick put a hand on his sword, but otherwise did not move.

The clanking of armor and weapons decided it for him. Mavian didn't have the energy or the ability to fight. He beckoned the others to follow him into the winding tunnel that would take them back below the mountain. With a quick word, Mavian dismissed the magical glowing orbs, plunging them all into darkness.

Crouching around the corner, Mavian held his finger to his lips. He couldn't see Merick or Ekkar in the pitch black, and hoped they would obey.

From his workshop came the sounds of many shuffling feet. Chadron's familiar voice floated over the noise, "Destroy the potions and alembics. Burn the books."

"Let us sort through and save some of the books, Sir," came another familiar voice: Ronan.

Mavian shivered as anger and fear bubbled up under his skin. Had the scholar betrayed him?

"Why?" Chadron asked.

Ronan replied in a calm, measured tone, "Because there is a wealth of knowledge here that your mistress may be interested in saving."

Chadron made a scornful sound, but said, "Fine. Bring up any you find; I'll lock them away in my study."

"Very good, Sir Chadron," Ronan replied.

Mavian heard a good deal of crashing and cringed at the thought of all his alchemical supplies being thrown against the floor. But no soldiers came pouring down the tunnel, no order came from Chadron to search for him. He breathed a small sigh of relief and indicated for Merick and Ekkar to begin their walk back to the cavern. When they had put some distance between them and his workshop, Mavian lit a glowing orb.

What is Ronan playing at?

✳

Down in the cave, Mavian sat morosely by the fire. He had

managed to get it going once more, but its small flickering flame did little to dispel the cold that had settled on his heart.

His workshop was gone. Even if Ronan had saved any manuscripts, they would be locked away where he couldn't reach them. His tools, his supplies, his ingredients and recipes, all destroyed. All he had were the few books he had brought to Stonetree, still stashed in the satchel that lay at his side.

As he had predicted, the scholars had taken nearly everything with them. They had been kind enough to leave a small supply of food and water as well as some blankets and firewood. But they had gone, and apparently gone straight to Chadron. Mavian couldn't blame them; he would rather be warm in the castle than shivering in this damn cave.

Mavian's eyelids drooped, and he no longer fought to keep them open. Ekkar had made a nest for himself from the blankets, and Merick stood guard against the wall.

But before sleep claimed him, some *thing* tugged at Mavian. He jolted upright, suddenly alert. There was no one there, nothing had touched him, yet he had felt a sharp tug. He knew he had.

The grabbing force came again, its invisible tendrils pulling at him. Mavian scrambled up, his mouth gone dry. *What new magic is this?* The force was stronger than anything he had felt before, dragging at his very essence.

Ekkar whimpered and tossed about, then twisted to his feet. Even Merick took a step forward. Both of them stared at the cavern entrance.

"What's wrong?" Mavian hissed. He reached for the small dagger at his hip, knowing it would do nothing against Chadron and his dogs.

Merick moved forward first, his dark eyes glazed over. As he walked past Ekkar, the prowler locked step with him, his mouth hanging open. Mavian resisted the tugging that grew more and more persistent.

"Stop it!" Mavian cried. He ran forward and pulled at Merick's arm, but the wight ignored him. Both of them kept moving to the archway, heedless of Mavian's distress.

Then Mavian heard it. A low *click, click, click* that echoed through the caves. As it grew louder, Merick and Ekkar stopped on either side of the archway like some undead soldiers awaiting the entrance of their leader.

Mavian gritted his teeth, his chest aching with the weight of resisting the magic's pull. Whatever it was, it was powerful. It had completely incapacitated his allies, turning them into obedient creatures. *But obedient to whom?*

More than ever, Mavian wished he had the white gem. Without it, he was helpless.

I can face this bravely, or I can face it as a coward. Mavian squared his shoulders and stood before the archway, waiting for whatever came through it.

Interminable minutes later, two silhouettes approached from the tunnels, one immensely tall, the other using a cane. For a breathless moment, Mavian thought it was Chadron and Rask, come to kill him at last. Then he shook himself, realizing that these were not his former allies.

Mavian drew himself up and said, "Stop there! Who are you? What are you doing here?"

A friendly voice answered him, "I could ask the same of you. A necromancer, a wight, and a prowler walk into a cave; sounds like the start to a jest, doesn't it?"

A chill crept down Mavian's spine. *How does he know...?*

"Who are you?" Mavian asked again. "I demand you come into the light and show yourself!"

The clicking started again as the two figures drew closer. At last, they came into the firelight.

The tall one was blonde and gaunt, his skin roped with scars, knives strapped all over his lithe frame. *That one could be a fair match for Merick,* Mavian thought. He turned his attention to the other. The shorter man rested his cane in his elbow, and though his eyes were blank and white, something about him made goosepimples break out over Mavian's skin.

Mavian said again, "Who are you? Who sent you?"

The blind man ignored him. He knelt down and reached a hand out to Ekkar, his expression pitying. He said, "Come now, little one. I have searched for you for a long time. Poor soul, wandering so long."

Mavian clenched his fist as Ekkar crept toward the blind man. The prowler sniffed the stranger, and it was as if a spell had been broken. Ekkar burbled and slapped the floor, and chirped in the dead's tongue, "*Frrriiieeennd.*"

The blind man smiled. "Indeed, little one. Friend." He straightened. "I am Darian, and this is my companion, Jagger Cross. I followed the Song of Death to you, and I can help you."

Mavian gaped at him. *I'm dreaming. This is all a strange dream brought on by exhaustion.* He pinched himself, but he didn't wake up. He looked to Merick, still standing like a statue. "What did you do to him?"

"I directed him," Darian replied. "He is free to do as he wishes now."

Indeed, Merick strode back to his station, unfazed by the appearance of these two strangers. But Mavian was not so easily convinced.

"What magic are you using?" Mavian asked. He pointed at his chest, where the tugging had diminished into a whisper. "What did you do?"

The blind man smiled, a fae grin that gave no answers, only more mysteries. "I think you know the answer."

Mavian chafed at that, and asked again, "What do you want?"

"Same as you, I expect. But surely it would be easier to sit and talk by the fire?"

Without an invitation, the blind man and the giant moved past Mavian and plopped down by the fire. Ekkar returned to his blankets. Feeling as if he had no choice, Mavian finally went back to his seat.

Mavian watched the blind man closely. He didn't quite know what he was watching for, only that the man's blank gaze sent shivers down his arms. He noted that Darian's eyes always stared past him, but somehow keenly landed on Merick or Ekkar. *Why?* This strange arrival was a mystery that would normally send Mavian rushing to his books, excited by the possibility of new knowledge.

But too much had happened, and too much was at stake, for Mavian to feel anything but trepidation now.

Every once in a while, Mavian glanced at the blind man's companion. The giant Skal loomed over Darian, but had said nothing. Was he a guard of some sort? A companion?

From across the fire, Darian said, "I have news from D'Clet."

"Oh?" Mavian tried to settle on the dirt, but his body thrilled with too many nerves to stay still. He crouched on his heels instead, the strain enough to distract his nervous muscles.

"Cara has joined with Talnor," Darian said.

The color drained from Mavian's face. "How do you know?"

"I traveled with her over the passes. I tried to guide her, but she wouldn't listen." Darian rubbed his cane between his hands, his white eyes reflecting the red fire. "She killed Alex."

Mavian didn't respond, his mind emptied. *Alex? Dead?* He spluttered, "But they were lovers."

"Not anymore."

"Why'd she do it? What reason...?"

Darian shook his head. "Her friend told me the story. Talnor demanded that Cara prove herself by killing one of her companions. She chose Alex for his crime of being *fampir*."

Mavian shut his eyes. "I'm sorry to hear it." *That's exactly what Talnor would do, too. Damn her!* Another fearful thought spun through him. "Does that mean that Cara and Talnor are here in D'Clet?"

I don't stand a chance against either of them, and certainly not against both.

"They have returned to Stonetree through the dread portals."

"Ah." Mavian shifted uncomfortably. *At least I won't have to contend with them.* "How do you know all this?"

"The Song of Death carries throughout the world. All are touched by it. Those who are connected to the Underworld, like Cara, have the loudest Songs."

Songs? A thrill of anticipation went through Mavian. He asked, "Is this the music I read about? The magic used by Valder and his mages?"

Darian nodded, and Mavian straightened, all his tiredness and suspicion forgotten. He gesticulated as he spoke, "So it's true! There is another kind of magic in the world!"

"Sit, and I'll tell you."

Mavian sat, enraptured, as Darian explained the magic of the Songs. When he finished, Mavian rocked back on his heels, his mind exploding with questions and ideas.

"That's why Gwen's magic didn't work the same as mine," Mavian said at last. "She used the Songs without realizing it. I wish she were here now; all the things we could discuss..."

He trailed off. *She'd want nothing to do with me.* He had tried to coerce her into helping him, and his friendship must have seemed a lie to her. *Yet another regret in a lifetime of mistakes.*

Mavian whirled through a hundred emotions and hopes. If what Darian said was true, then Mavian could master more magic than he had ever dreamed. *If*, of course, being the most essential question of all. Mavian asked, "What proof do you have of these Songs?"

The blind man tilted his head. After a moment, he said, "Not all can hear the Songs. Some are more attuned to a certain Song over another. Most can only hear one or two, if they hear any at all. But I can try to help you."

With a careful hand, Darian placed his cane on the floor. Then he reached out and said, "If you wish to hear, take my hand."

Tentatively, Mavian obeyed. When Darian began to sing, Mavian at first heard nothing more. He listened to the blind man's soft voice, to the depth and pain within it. But he couldn't hear this magic.

Then Jagger kneeled in front of him and put his hands over Mavian's eyes. Mavian understood and shut them.

Somewhere, deep inside his bones, a note resonated. It tolled like a novum bell, sonorous and low, echoing in his chest. Mavian gasped, astounded at the feeling within him. It didn't feel like any other magic, didn't have the grime of the Underworld stuck to it.

With a jolt, Mavian realized he'd felt this sensation before. It had infused him every time he used the white gem.

"The gem was enchanted with Valder's interpretation of the Song of Death," Darian said, somehow knowing the question before Mavian could ask it.

Darian withdrew his trembling hand. Mavian looked at him with concern. "Are you alright?"

"Sharing the Song can be difficult," Darian said. "It is taxing for me."

For a few minutes, Mavian wrapped himself in thought as the blind man nibbled at some food and drank the water the giant offered him. When Darian appeared to be in better shape, Mavian dove into his next question.

"What about Ekkar? What do you hear in his Song?"

Darian laid a hand on the prowler's head. Ekkar had curled up beside him, and Mavian couldn't help but feel a pang of jealousy. The blind man said, "He is but an animal, lost in his instincts. He knows the comfort of shelter and fire, and sees you and Merick as his pack-mates."

"Is there anything left in him of who he once was?"

"Traces. Imprints of a lost soul, echoes of language and thought. That is why he speaks the tongue of the Dead." Darian stroked Ekkar's hair, and the prowler burbled happily.

"Do you know who he used to be?" Mavian asked.

"Of course. His spirit still wanders Earda." Darian placed a finger between Ekkar's eyes. "But you don't need me to tell you who he was."

"So he is Verdon," Mavian breathed. He had believed it, but the confirmation sent a wave of relief through him. "What do you mean, his spirit wanders Earda? I thought the souls of prowlers went to Purgatory."

"A good guess, but incorrect. When Verdon and Sura Gellder conceived, it ripped Verdon's soul. Part of it went into Cara, the part that connects her to the Underworld. The rest, however, detached from his body with nowhere to go. So it wanders."

"And this happens with all prowlers?"

Darian nodded gravely. "A world filled with ghosts longing for release."

"Can we cure them? Reunite soul and body?"

Darian's expression was unreadable. "Perhaps. But only with a powerful Song."

Mavian retreated back into silence. Every answer Darian had given him resulted in even more questions. He stared at the strange pairing of blind man and giant, the scarred man as attentive to Darian's needs as a mother would be to her child. *How did they come to travel together?*

But more pressing were his questions about the Songs. Mavian longed to learn everything he could, to hear those notes once more. Yet he kept coming back to the same question, for Darian's earlier answer had not satisfied him.

"Who are you really? Why did you seek me out?" Mavian asked.

The blind man rolled his cane between his palms. The silence stretched on for a long breath before he said, "I am a guide only. I have failed in my attempts at securing the connection between Autorus's realm and Earda. You are my last hope."

"How am I supposed to help? I'm a failure and a traitor."

Those milky eyes reflected the firelight, red dancing over white. "That may be so, but you know the Underworld far better than most men. Together, I believe we can stop Cara and Talnor. And, yes, even find a cure for the prowlers."

"But you know the Song of Death!" Mavian protested. "Why would you need my help?"

Darian gave a small shrug. "If you'd rather I leave you to your misery, I can go and take my knowledge with me."

"No," Mavian said immediately. "I didn't mean to imply that. Only it seems that you have power beyond what I could muster. I don't understand how I can be of use."

"Trust me," Darian said. "I cannot tell you my purposes yet, but trust that I cannot do this myself."

Somehow, Mavian did trust this man.

"Very well," Mavian said. "When do we get started?"

CHAPTER ELEVEN
Seanna

"My father would be furious if he knew we were meeting," the elf maiden said. She floated as she moved, her hair trailing almost to her feet in a cloud of fine nut-brown strands. Unlike her father, the elven princess Ulalia was not stern. She threw back her head in a silvery laugh before she swayed to the music played by her personal minstrel, her diminutive feet carrying her in a dance all her own.

Seanna had asked for a private audience with Ulalia, and the maiden had come herself to accept. They sat now on a balcony built onto a high, sturdy bough, the floor under their feet shifting ever so slightly with the movement of the tree in the wind. Other than the minstrel, who played merry tunes on his citole, they were quite alone.

"Does he have to know everything?" Seanna inquired. "All daughters keep secrets from their fathers."

Ulalia paused in her dance, her small lips in a frown. Then a smile broke out on her cheeks. "You are right, of course. I have kept many secrets from him."

"Like what?"

The elf maid put a finger beside her nose and winked. "If you are trying to pry my secrets from me in order to curry favor with my father, you will not be successful."

"I would never break the bonds of friendship," Seanna said. She sipped at a fruity cordial, savoring how it splashed into her mouth. "I came to you because I believe you can help me."

"With what?" Ulalia began to dance again, her hands swaying above her head.

"Aremo Teru is your betrothed, correct?"

Ulalia made an annoyed sound, though even that was beautiful. "Unfortunately so."

"Have you written to him at all? Or received letters?"

"I have." Ulalia paused again, her hands lifted and her skirt coming to rest around her ankles. "Why?"

In her life before the war, Seanna would have lied to the maid or given only half the truth. Now, though, she knew that honesty may be her only approach. She leaned forward conspiratorially, her cup forgotten on the table. "Neither of us want to see him as a ruler. We can't face him with an army, but we can use whatever knowledge we have against him. You, being his betrothed, have access to him. It could prove useful."

Ulalia stroked her delicate chin. "If he loses this war – and maybe his head – I won't have to marry him."

"Indeed." Seanna pressed her advantage. "We women are no experts in the affairs of war, but we are experienced in court and politics. Surely we can discover a secret that would destroy Aremo."

The elf maid's smile broke through, a bright dawn after a long, cold night. She swooped down and hugged Seanna, who froze a moment before returning the embrace. A shard of ice broke inside her and melted away, one of many worries that she had carried ever since Henrik's death.

Before they parted, Seanna wiped away a tear that threatened to spill. *We are not alone*, she reminded herself. She stepped back and appraised the maiden.

"Write to Aremo," Seanna said. "Use whatever wiles you can. Ask him what he will do for you, his queen. Ask how he will prove his worthiness to the kingdom. Be subtle; it may take more than one letter." Seanna thought back to her first encounter with Aremo, at a party she had thought incredible. His paramour had been there, paraded about as if she were his wife. "And write to his paramour, Edlyn. Invite her here. No doubt Aremo plans to keep her on even after your marriage. We can learn plenty from his lover."

Ulalia nodded vigorously, her long hair bouncing against her legs. "I will start at once! And I will revisit his old letters to see what I can glean from them."

"Excellent." Seanna gave a pointed look to the minstrel, who hadn't stopped playing. "Can we trust him?"

"With all my heart," Ulalia said immediately. Though Seanna would have rather purchased or frightened him into loyalty, she accepted the girl's answer.

The next candle was spent perusing letters and helping Ulalia compose notes to both Aremo and Edlyn. Seanna found little of use in Aremo's original messages: his writing came across as utterly arrogant, but otherwise gave no new insights into him.

When Ulalia finished her letters, Seanna read them over and nodded approvingly. "These will do nicely. Send them out, and tell me the moment you receive any response."

Just as the women settled down to truly enjoy the spread of fruits and bread, Belrose walked onto the balcony. He gave a low bow and said, "Your Grace, the ranger you sent for has arrived."

"Thank you, Belrose." Seanna put aside her plate and wiped her hands. "If you will excuse me, Ulalia, I have another meeting today. I would be honored to dine with you again soon."

Seanna followed Belrose into the tree and down a few twists of the winding staircase before they came to a small chamber with broad windows. Inside, Ropaz waited beside a tall elf. His brown-green skin was darker than other Rengu elves, his eyes grey and wary. Unlike many other elves, he had shorn his hair completely. He was armed and armored, everything clean but well-worn.

"Captain Tzuriel," Seanna said as she entered. She held out her hand, and he kissed her palm. He said not a word, and Seanna hesitated before she continued, "You and your Rangers are wintering here in Rengu, if I'm not mistaken."

The captain inclined his head slightly. *It seems I shall have to drag this elf's words from his mouth.* Seanna said, "Have you been watching the Lofalin armies? Their movements and camps?"

Another nod. Seanna tried to pry more, "Tell me what you know."

The elf lifted his hands, then flashed them in a series of gestures too quick for Seanna to follow. Her brow wrinkled in confusion. "I'm sorry, what are you doing?"

Again Tzuriel's fingers flew in various motions, each one clearly deliberate yet completely unknowable to her. Seanna looked again at Belrose. He was watching Tzuriel with a slight frown. He said, "I believe he's using a sort of language, Your Grace."

"With his hands?"

"Indeed," Belrose said as Tzuriel nodded. The elf finally gave a small smile.

Frustration made Seanna's head hurt. She forced herself to think clearly. "Do we need a translator? Or can you write?"

Tzuriel indicated the table, and Ropaz brought over ink and parchment. The elf dipped a quill, then began to write. Ropaz read over his shoulder, "*The Lofalins have few camps set up outside the major cities. Little movement in the winter.*"

Seanna thought this over. She asked, "Would it be possible to infiltrate their camps?"

Tzuriel wrote, "*Yes. It may take some time to find the right opportunity.*"

"Of course." Seanna swelled with renewed satisfaction. With Ulalia working from one angle, and the Rangers another, she could circumvent Voclain's orders and still fight back against Aremo.

But Tzuriel kept writing, "*Has Ameer Voclain approved this action?*"

Ropaz gave Seanna a pointed look. For a moment, Seanna kept the lie on her tongue, wanting to let it free. But she swallowed it and said truthfully, "No."

"*What if I refuse? Voclain is my leader, not you.*"

Seanna's fingers bit into her palms, but she kept her voice steady. "I don't think the Rangers want Aremo and his Lofalins to rule any more than I do. I know that Voclain is nervous, and he is right to be. But I cannot stand by and allow my kingdom to be so easily conquered. You can understand that, can't you?"

It was a long moment before Tzuriel responded. In those seconds, Seanna felt her satisfaction slipping away. *It was foolish. I should let go, as Voclain asked. I should be a mother first.* But then Tzuriel rose, nodded, and put a fist to his heart. He bowed, and Seanna rebuilt those walls that had threatened to crumble. *I am the queen, and my duty is to my people.*

After they had agreed on Ropaz meeting the Rangers to further plan their mission, the captain departed. Seanna sank into a chair, her legs trembling. "Am I doing the right thing?"

Ropaz's hands shook as he poured a chalice of wine. He gave it to her, but didn't meet her eye. He said, "We are safe here. Voclain has found villages willing to take in our refugees. Every day, there are fewer of us remaining in the tree. Other than our soldiers, the rest will move on with their lives. They are done with war, starvation, and fear."

"So you think we should be, too." Seanna held the chalice, but didn't drink.

"I don't see how we could win. Aremo and his armies are too powerful." Ropaz kneeled in front of her, and this time it was she that avoided his eyes. He said, "I am tired, Seanna. I want to rest. I want to enjoy these winter days with my sister and my remaining friends. My duty as High Predicant was to protect the spirituality of our people. But what is left of our religion? I am powerless now."

"That's not true," Seanna interjected.

Ropaz shook his head. "Some of the greatest wisdom is learning when you cannot win a battle, be it personal, spiritual, or political. This is a battle that we have no chance of winning."

Seanna was silent a moment, her heart locked in a feud of its own. She desperately wished to give it all up, to simply rest. But her people deserved more. She asked, "What does you believe, Belrose?"

"We should fight." The wizard clenched his fists. He had labored for days and days to forge an escape from the city, and he would not rest now.

Seanna nodded, her decision made. "I'm sorry, Ropaz. I

must continue on. If you and Portia wish to leave and start a new life, I will not begrudge you that decision."

"Portia won't leave you," Ropaz said. "And I won't leave her."

"Then you'll stay?" Seanna reached out and grasped his hand. "I need your help, my friend. We will need a spiritual leader before all this is over. Will you stay and help us?"

"For now," he said. He drew his hand back. "At least until the winter is out."

He left without another word, Belrose following close behind. Seanna fell back into her chair, all excitement at her earlier victories draining out of her. She knew she should be planning her next move, but Ropaz's words resonated in her bones.

I am tired, too. Seanna pushed herself to her feet and went to the bedroom she shared with Portia. The girl was holding the baby, and Seanna wordlessly took her child and settled down for him to feed. She stroked his fuzzy head, amazed at how much he had already grown. *I am doing this for you. For all my people. I cannot give up now.*

CHAPTER TWELVE
Druam

The brush pulled smoothly across the canvas, leaving behind a wet streak of glistening paint. Druam dipped it again and dragged its bristles over the dried colors, then stepped back to assess the effect. A portrait of Gwen stared back at him.

More brightness in her eyes. He wiped the brush clean and mixed his colors on the palette, focusing only on the task at hand. Like his brothers, he had spent his immortality honing those talents which most appealed to him. He had apprenticed under a skilled artist three centuries ago, then learned to garden from a Rengu elf. Working with his hands had always calmed his mind and steadied his rampant emotions, breathing a stillness into his eternity. He had painted the portrait of his mother, Imira, that hung in a dining hall in the abandoned wing of the palace.

If he could cry, a tear would have come to his eye at the thought of her. The last time he'd seen that painting, Gwen had called forth the image of his mother, her flowing hair and sweet smile, the scent of the plains after the thunderstorm which had always been her favorite smell.

Druam shook himself and turned his attention back to his painting. *I meant to move that portrait into the main palace long ago. I suppose I forgot sometime in the intervening years.*

A soft knock sounded at his door, and in sauntered Cairn Steel-Eyes, the Corsair Queen. Or, as she was known by only a few, Sura Gellder, the mother of the *sulpari*.

"Sura," Druam said in greeting, not looking up at her. He dabbed at the painting's eye.

She came to stand beside him. "It's a pretty piece. Is that your wife?"

He nodded. "Usually I commission a portrait by an artist far more skilled than I. This time, I'm afraid, the only reference I have of her is in my head."

He didn't mention the two conflicting memories of his Gwen. The first was the image of her at the palace: beautiful and poised, her hair perfectly plaited and pinned atop her head, her shoulders graced with a fine gown. But the last he'd seen her, she had utterly transformed, covered in animal skins and with ferocity in her eye. As he painted, he found himself conveying both: her hair loose and curling around her head, her dress green and brown, the landscape behind her an untamed tangle of vines and ferns.

Sura turned away from the painting. "My ships are in place, and my scouts have reported that the Lofalin fleet in Con Salur has weighed anchor. They're coming, Druam."

The brush quivered in his hand. He set it down, careful not to smudge the paint on the canvas. As he wiped his hands, he stood and paced over to the window.

"We're as ready for siege as we can be," he said.

"The people actually left?" Surprise tinted her voice.

Druam nodded. "Many did. I sent them to estates that can hold them, and can only pray that Rask will direct all his ire at Riverfen alone. But others refused to leave. This is their home."

Sura joined him at the window. "They are brave fools."

He frowned at that. "Is it so foolish to raise up arms against an enemy? This is their city as much as it is mine, and I will not force them to leave it."

"Then you're a fool, too. When the trebuchets lob boulders at your walls, your people will die. When the soldiers fight their way through the gaps, your people will die. When you're forced to surrender, your people will die."

"Your confidence is assuring," Druam said dryly. "The winter has given us time to ready for the attack. Avallune has found a way to repel the trebuchets. We can hold out against Rask and his army."

"Remember our deal," Sura said. "I guard the seas. None of my men will help you on land. If I feel that the odds of victory are against me, I will take my fleet and sail away without a second glance."

"Then you'd better return my gold."

"Ha."

"I know you, Sura. You will honor our deal. If the walls have fallen and we raise the flag of surrender, sail away. But as long as the city stands, your ships will remain."

"Fine." Sura waved a hand at him and walked away.

She had only taken two steps when Druam said, "Cara is with Rask's army."

Sura froze, her hand straying to the dagger at her belt. She turned slowly, her eyes hawkish. "What?"

"My scouts only just confirmed it a few days ago. Cara marches with Rask's army." Druam stared levelly at her, a challenge in his tone. "She murdered my brother."

Sura's jaw tightened. She didn't say anything.

Druam continued, "Sura, your daughter has chosen to make enemies of us. I do not wish to see harm befall her, but we cannot–"

"Enough." Her sharp tone sliced through him. "If I have to choose between my daughter's life and the safety of this city, you know damn well which one I'll pick."

"We are at war," Druam said. He loomed over her, letting a flash of *fampir* red into his eyes. "Do you wish me to command my soldiers to let her carve through them without raising a hand in their own defense? Do you wish me to sacrifice everything I have built over centuries for the life of a single woman?"

"What if it were her?" Sura said, pointing at the portrait of Gwen. "Would you allow your loved one to be swallowed up by battle?"

"I would do what must be done," he said. "Even if it meant I'd lose her forever."

The portrait's eyes burned into him, and he forced himself

to look away. *I have already lost her*, he thought. *Just as I lost all that came before her.* The grief in his chest longed to be released, but he had no outlet for it. He could not cry no matter how he wished to.

First Verdon, then Gwen, then Alex. It should be me instead. Druam turned his impotent rage on Sura. "Your daughter *murdered* Alex. He loved her, he tried to change for her, and she slaughtered him. His hands were bound behind his back, did you know that? He was defenseless, and Cara butchered him like a pig."

Sura glared at him, tears sparkling in her eyes. Her knuckles were white on her dagger's hilt. She said through gritted teeth, "As if you haven't slaughtered your way across the centuries. Cara is my daughter and your niece. We should both be trying to save her."

"Then tell her the truth," Druam said. "Tell her who her father is. She despises me; do you think she'll take pleasure in our familial bond?"

"She'll see reason," Sura said, a plead in her voice. "When she arrives in Riverfen, I'll talk to her. I'll make her see that she can still choose a better path."

Druam started to argue, then closed his mouth. *She is a scared mother.* Beneath the veneer of a corsair, beneath all the steel and infamy, was a woman afraid of what could happen to her only child. He could not reason with her, just as she would not be able to reason with Cara.

He sighed and said, "I will do all in my power to protect her. However, Sura...don't meet with her expecting forgiveness. Don't let your heart attach itself to a peaceful reunion."

"I think you have a painting to finish." Sura swept out in her usual fashion, though this time, Druam thought he saw a slight rounding to her shoulders, her head held just a little lower.

His emotions flurried through him, grief and anger and a tense waiting. Rask would soon come, and Druam knew that his city may not last the spring. He picked up the brush, wet it, and pushed the bristles onto the canvas, hoping that his turbulent thoughts might finally quieten.

CHAPTER THIRTEEN
Jagger

"Come on!" Mavian shouted at Jagger. He had his fists up, though they were held all wrong: fingers too loose, thumb tucked under where it would surely break, wrists bent. Jagger rolled his eyes and settled into an easy stance, his fists held lightly but firmly.

Been too long since I beat up a poncy lad. Jagger smiled. It had also been too long since he had a good scuffle.

His smile slid into a frown as he remembered the events in D'Clet. If he'd been there when Cara had murdered Sandu's friend, he wouldn't have hesitated to fight back against her. He understood why Sandu – one-armed and grieving – hadn't even tried, but he still wished that he could have fought her. See how well Cara sucked down someone's blood with a knife stuck in her jaw.

Mavian swung hard, and Jagger only just dodged. He shook himself. *Can't get caught up in your own head. That's how you got yourself here, isn't it?* The spindly noble threw another fist, and Jagger easily caught it and threw it aside, sending Mavian reeling.

Apparently, without his magic gem or dark powers, Mavian thought it best that he learn to defend himself in hand-to-hand combat. Jagger had only been too happy to oblige.

Merick and Ekkar watched the fight. The prowler whined and scuttled about, clearly wanting to help Mavian but held back by the wight's heavy arm. The wight stood entirely still, only his eyes moving to observe the combatants.

Jagger wasn't sure what to make of that one. The wight had been raised from the dead, just like him, but only traces of its personality were left. It had an eerie grace, like all that remained in it was restrained violence. To be perfectly honest, Jagger was glad that he was on the same side as the creature. He didn't relish the idea of trying to take it down.

He focused his attention back to the fight just as Mavian's fist connected with his cheek. It was a weak hit, barely a slap, and Jagger didn't flinch. He gave a wolfish grin, delighting in Mavian's face going pale.

Time for the offensive. Jagger moved with a dancer's grace, his body going exactly where he wanted it to go. He rained blow after blow on Mavian, hard enough to sting but not to injure. *Might have some bruises in a few candles.* Jagger watched with a practiced eye as Mavian floundered away, his arms held up to protect his face, but held in such a way that he could easily break past them.

Jagger stopped and signed for Mavian to do the same. Though Mavian had been practicing the unspoken language throughout the winter, he still struggled with some of the gestures. Jagger tried to only use the ones Mavian was most familiar with, but he missed the ease with which he communicated with Sandu.

Hope the lad's alright, Jagger thought. At least Sandu's father was with him, and would hopefully keep Sandu alive long enough to find his children again.

Mavian dropped his arms, panting, and wiped his brow. His weak shoulders trembled, and he gulped from his waterskin. Jagger squatted and watched him with amusement. It had been a long time since he'd sparred with a man who was a green fighter. Training others had been his favorite job with Fauste's Shiv. No murder or blackmail, just good physical back-and-forth.

"Gods," Mavian muttered, "you're fast."

Jagger signed back, *"You're getting better."*

"Not quickly enough." Mavian made a frustrated noise.

Jagger shrugged. *"Some people just aren't meant for battle. No harm in that."*

Mavian dragged his fingers through the dirt and slumped with his back against the cave wall. He said quietly, "I relied too much on that damned gem. If I'd learned other forms of magic, I wouldn't be quite so useless."

Jagger rocked back to his bottom and crossed his legs. He waited for Mavian to continue.

"I don't even know who I was trying to prove myself to. Druam, perhaps, or Renna. Part of me wonders if she would ever have loved me without my darker side. You were married, right? How did you know what she truly thought of you?"

Memories came like dark wine to Jagger's mind, both sweet and bitter. The day he'd met Raven, their wedding, the smell of her hair and the smoothness of her skin. The day he'd lost her. He fiddled with a knife, twirling it between his fingers. After a moment, he signed, *"At first, I didn't want her to know what I really was. I hid myself for a long time. The lie couldn't go on forever, and I told her the truth before she found out for herself."*

His fingers stilled as he dwelled on that memory. He had been so frightened that she'd see him as a monster. He closed his eyes and remembered that horrible moment after telling the truth. He knew she would abandon him, but then he felt her hands on his cheeks, her soft voice promising that she wouldn't leave him.

He signed, *"It was when she stayed with me that I knew she really loved me. I did my best not to fail her, but, well, life has a funny way of showing us all our mistakes. She died before I could take her out of that hellhole and give her the life she deserved."*

Mavian nodded, his green eyes fixed on his hands. He said, "All I wanted was to shower Renna with everything she desired. Instead, I trapped her in dreams and spurned the man who raised me. How do you even come back from that?"

Jagger let out a low chuckle. He knew that guilt. It was lodged in his own heart, poking and prodding at him every waking moment. Once, Raven's voice had silenced the demons. Now, he had no one to shield him.

"I killed an entire Valadi family," Jagger signed. "I left one girl alive. When I met her again, she screamed and they chased after me. I will never receive forgiveness from them, and that's for the best. What I did was unforgivable."

"So we're both bound for purgatory," Mavian said. "We two sinners."

"Redemption isn't about forgiveness," Jagger signed. "It's about doing better. Being better. I've murdered enough people to fill a graveyard, and nothing I do will bring them back. But what I can do is help others now. Maybe it'll be enough. Maybe it won't."

Mavian's eyes drifted over to Merick and Ekkar. He said softly, "Do you think helping the prowlers is the right thing?"

Jagger nodded.

Mavian asked, "What about Merick? Keeping him here...that has to be selfish."

Jagger shrugged again. "Depends on what he thinks. Could be he likes it. Could be a constant torture."

"And what about the Songs? Magic that powerful must be corruptible." Mavian stared at his hands, and Jagger realized the true reason why he wanted to learn to fight.

"You're afraid, aren't you?" Jagger signed. "Terrified that if Darian teaches you the Songs, you'll use them for evil."

Mavian shifted and averted his eyes. He was quiet, then let out a long breath. "Yes. Fighting with my fists, I can only hurt one person, and probably not very well. But the Songs...I could do awful things with them. Worse than I've ever done before."

"And that's why you should learn them," Jagger signed. "Look, none of us knows what the veck we're doing. But you're no fighter, and maybe the Songs will do more good than bad in the end. No way to know but to try."

Mavian swallowed, then nodded. He got to his feet and put his hand out to help Jagger up. Jagger took it and bounced to his feet.

"I'm ready to try again," Mavian said, raising his fists up.

Jagger mirrored him and thought with a smile, I think I'm going to like this one.

Chapter Fourteen
Sandu

"We can't afford any of these places," Sandu said. He and Cadel stood outside a run-down bunkhouse, its shutters hanging from the windows and its door spattered with mud.

"But it's a sty!" Cadel protested. "Surely it can't cost that much?"

Sandu gave a half-hearted shrug. "It seems everyone's coming to the capital for the trials. Since they're public, people want to be there. Even this place raised its prices; not like they're hurting for customers."

Cadel ran a hand over his brow and sighed. "So what next?"

Sandu hefted the coin purse. *Just like the old days: lighter than feathers.* "We rough it. There's a forest just outside the city; we'll stay there. I can set snares and cook over a fire. It won't be easy, but we can manage."

"We'll freeze," Cadel said.

"Don't worry, Da. It's warmer here than Dotschar in winter. We'll survive." Sandu pulled his father out of the way of a hurrying merchant, then set off down the street. Cadel followed, still sulking slightly, though his mood visibly cheered as they entered the forest.

It was quiet and serene beneath the bare boughs, with birds trilling in the distance and foxes peering from their dens. Sandu took a deep breath. The air was clean, the trees creaking in the breeze and the needle-carpeted floor soft under his feet.

They plunged further into the forest, searching for an

adequate campsite. Eventually, they settled on a smooth area beneath two large pines, with a stream running nearby and a large boulder beside which they could build a fire. Working together, they erected Sandu's tent and made a ring of stones. A pang of sorrow went through Sandu as he surveyed their little camp. It reminded him of the many nights he'd spent with Cara on the road. He remembered how she had laughed one night when he'd accidentally snared a frog.

He shook away the memories. She was an enemy now; a murderer.

Yet as he started cooking, all he could think about were their conversations and stories around the fire. *How did she become such a monster?* She had fought with her inner beast, but she had never been wicked.

Lost in his thoughts, Sandu startled when Cadel shook his shoulder.

"What is it?" Sandu asked.

Cadel didn't say a word. He pointed at the branches of a tree, his mouth set in a grim line. Sandu nearly yelped as he caught sight of a massive wildcat perched there. Its fur was blacker than the night sky, though red shone in it from the firelight. Its great green eyes blinked slowly. At the end of its tail twitched a scorpion's stinger.

Sandu swallowed hard. "It's not possible."

"I've not gone mad, have I?" Cadel whispered.

Sandu shook his head, his stare glued onto the creature. *A nightcat.* They were creatures of myth, not flesh-and-blood. Perhaps he'd hit his head earlier and was now hallucinating.

"What do we do?" Cadel asked, his voice low.

"I don't know," Sandu answered. He reached toward the fire and pulled a piece of meat from the spit. He tossed it toward the nightcat, hoping that the food might distract it. The creature yawned and stretched, then gracefully leapt from the branch to the forest floor. It was massive, its back reaching to Sandu's hip. It smelled the meat, then lapped it up with its pink tongue.

Not daring to breathe, Sandu held as still as possible. The nightcat regarded them a moment, then sniffed the air. It crept closer and closer, and he leaned back. Sweat dripped down his arm, terror clogging his throat.

The nightcat paused in front of Sandu. It sniffed his hair, its massive nose blowing moisture onto his forehead. Sandu closed his eyes and swallowed. *So this is it. I finally die as a meal for a creature that shouldn't exist.*

A sandpapery sensation swept across his cheek. Sandu peeked from one eye as the nightcat gave him another lick. His mouth was dry, his mind racing. *Do I taste good? Oh gods, what if it toys with me?*

Then the nightcat purred, a deep, rumbling noise that reverberated through Sandu's chest. It stepped back and sat on its haunches. There was something strangely friendly in its eyes, a message that Sandu couldn't understand.

Slowly realizing that he wasn't about to be eaten, Sandu reached out a tentative hand to the creature, ignoring Cadel's hissed warning. The nightcat didn't snap at him. It didn't move as his fingers brushed the fur of its cheek.

"Incredible," Sandu breathed.

The nightcat allowed him to touch it for a minute longer, then stood and padded toward the fire. It reached to the spit and delicately grabbed the remaining meat from it. Sandu bit back his frustration; they wouldn't have another meal until morning at the earliest.

It chewed its stolen dinner, then slunk back into the trees. Not even its green eyes were visible in the growing gloom. Sandu's stomach growled, but he sat back and took a deep breath. His father wore a similar expression of confusion mixed with relief.

"Never thought I'd see one of those," Sandu tried to joke.

Cadel merely shook his head. "You're mad, my boy. Utterly mad. We should go back to the city and take our chances on the streets."

"I don't know, Da. I don't think it'll hurt us." Sandu watched the woods where the nightcat had vanished. "When I touched it, I felt a sense of...kinship, somehow, deep in my chest. Like it knows me."

"Don't be foolish. We should pack up and leave come morning."

Not up for an argument, Sandu only nodded his head. He put out the fire and crawled into the tent. Sleep did not come for awhile yet, but when it did, his dreams were full of mythical beasts.

✳

Dawn brought with it a cold frost that coated the ground and trees with white. Sandu rubbed his stump and tried to build up a fire. After many frustrated attempts, he finally had a blaze hot enough to combat the chill that seeped into his bones. Finally warming, he took a look at his surroundings, hoping to maybe catch a glimpse of the nightcat.

A bundle near the edge of the clearing caught his eye. He went toward it, then paused, astonished. There was a pile of small animals, squirrels and rabbits and even a muskrat. Each had been neatly killed, with dried blood caked around their throats.

"What's that?" Cadel called as he emerged from the tent.

"Food," Sandu said in amazement. "It brought us food."

He gathered up the pile of animals and brought them back to the fire. All that day, he and Cadel worked to skin, gut, and cut the meat into slices. They hung these from the nearby trees, letting them dry so they could last a little longer.

That night, the creature did not return. Nor the next, or the next after that. Sometimes, as he lay awake, Sandu thought he heard a low keening on the wind, or a growl, or a purr. But each time he poked his head from the tent, he saw nothing.

It was over a quinn before the creature next returned. By this time, they had used up their supply of meat, and Sandu worked hard to set various snares in the woods before it was fully dark. His fingers had adjusted to the work using only one hand, and he improvised with using a foot to help tighten knots. Just as he finished his last snare, he heard a grumbling noise.

The nightcat sat and watched him; he hadn't even heard it

approach. Braver this time, Sandu held out his hand. The nightcat bumped its forehead into his palm, and he scratched between its ears.

"You're beautiful," Sandu said. "What are you doing here of all places?"

It didn't respond. Of course, he hadn't expected it to. But then something curious happened: it padded a few feet away, then glanced over its shoulder as if expecting him to follow. Sandu stood and took a few steps. The creature made a huffing noise, then continued into the forest. He followed it, astounded that it moved slowly enough for him to keep up.

They traveled through the forest, ducking hanging boughs and skipping over streams, until they came to a patch of briars. The creature made a strange noise, almost like a humming purr, and the briars parted for them. Sandu crawled, wary of the thorns to every side, until they emerged into a hollow within the briars. Inside the hollow was a small pool of water, a nest of broken pine bows, and a woman.

The woman sat cross-legged, running her fingers through the water. At first, she appeared entirely fae, out of the same legends the nightcat had emerged from. Yet the more Sandu gazed at her, the more he knew her. Beneath the layers of wildness, he recognized a figure he had met before, one that had been etched into his memory through her kindness and magic.

As the nightcat prowled toward her, the witch smiled at it. She hummed, and the creature responded in kind. Sandu's awe grew. *Are they...communicating?*

The nightcat curled up at her side, its giant head in her lap, and blinked slowly at Sandu. The witch's violet eyes bored through him.

"Come and join me," she said.

Sandu sat as close to the briars as he could without being pricked, nervous to go too near this strange woman. He said, "Are you the sorceress? The one who knows magic of other places?"

She tilted her head, regarding him with an animalistic stare. "I am a witch, though I have been called sorceress in the past."

A smile broke out over Sandu's cheeks. He scooted closer, all apprehension gone in his excitement. "You can help me find my children!"

The nightcat purred. The witch said, "You are their father. Eaton and Elvy."

He nodded vigorously. "Yes! You know them? Where are they?"

"They lived with me during the height of winter," she said. "In the Woods where I dwelled for many long years. But I cannot return easily, and I don't know how to guide you there. I'm sorry."

"But Darian said–"

The witch's lips narrowed at that name, and she cut Sandu off. "Even if I knew the way, I cannot leave Demarren now. I must stand trial."

"But you're out here! Surely you can easily escape." Sandu reached toward her, and she flinched back. He pulled his hand back into his lap. "Please. You're the only hope I have of seeing them again."

The witch shook her head again. "Lintem brought you to me because you smelled familiar, as you are the children's father. I wish I could devote myself to your cause. But I must try and heal my country. If I escape, that may only bring more strife. I must stay and see this through."

Grief and anger made Sandu choke on his next words. "You helped me once. In the Cascade Palace, when you were still Gwendolyn Strilu. When you still had a heart."

She didn't react with anger, nor with shame. She simply stared at him, and he felt as if she were poring over the contents of his soul. He shifted uncomfortably, nervous that he had been too offensive. After a long, long moment, she said, "You have suffered greatly. Your Song overflows with pain. But I must stay. My trial will be at the start of spring. Perhaps after that..."

Another thread snapped in Sandu's already-worn heart. He didn't stop the tears that flowed into his beard. He buried his head in his arm.

"Lintem will help you if you remain in the forest," she said.

"I can give you money for supplies. But I cannot help you right now, even if I wished to. I don't know if the Woods would answer my call."

Sandu didn't answer her. A gentle hand descended on his head, and a feeling of peace flowed through him, warm as the hearth in winter. Gwen gave him a rueful look.

"Do not let anguish overcome you, for you are more than your pain. I vow to you, once my trial is concluded, I will help you. Until then, survive. Live in this forest. Find peace within your soul." She kissed his forehead.

Sandu no longer felt his despair, but also knew that it still lay buried in his heart. He nodded. "I will see my children again."

Her hand lingered on his head a little longer before she pulled away. "Lintem will guide you back to your camp. If you call for him, he will hear you."

Sandu took one last glance at the woman. He didn't know whether she was still Gwen or was wholly a witch, and didn't know which he preferred. Walking back to camp, though, his steps grew lighter. *I found the sorceress across the sea. Now all I have to do is survive until she keeps her oath and brings my children back to me.*

CHAPTER FIFTEEN
Cara

Thousands of feet pounded the dirt into mud. The column of men stretched as far back as Cara could see, banners waving over the grim-faced soldiers marching to the drumbeats. Camp followers and suppliers came behind them, with wagons upon wagons of food, weapons, cloth, metals, and more. The *fampir* prisoners that had been captured were held somewhere in the column. Riding near the front of the army, Cara couldn't help but glance continuously behind her at the mass of people. At Stonetree, where the men had spread out through the keep, village, and fields, she hadn't quite understood the sheer numbers headed now to Riverfen.

The battle during the Masque seemed a pittance compared to this impending siege. Cara wondered if Druam had mustered any more forces after losing so many at Stonetree. *He will see that he has no choice but to surrender. We outnumber him.*

One night, as the spring sun sank into the green horizon, Talnor came into Cara's tent. Though smaller than Rask's command tent, it was large enough to hold a bunk, table, and chair. Cara sat cross-legged on the bunk as Talnor folded her long legs across the chair.

"Is it time?" Cara asked. Excitement thrilled through her.

Talnor nodded and held out a flagon. Blood swished inside it, still warm. It should have reviled her, but Cara trembled with anticipation.

"The blood can help you discover your abilities," Talnor

said. "Drink."

Cara obeyed. The blood slid down her throat: *fampir*, she thought. It coated her mouth and stained her lips red. Talnor brought the chair forward so that she could hold Cara's hands.

"Close your eyes. Breathe deeply," Talnor instructed. "Feel the blood in your belly, the power it holds. Focus on it."

The blood swilled in Cara's belly, both incredible and nauseating. She swallowed and breathed carefully, holding each inhale before letting it out slowly. The beast rose up into her head and chest, and in its heat, she sensed it: power. The black fire she had once used lay at her fingertips.

Rather than calling it up, she honed in on the source of the power. It nestled in a hidden place near her heart, pumping with similar intensity.

"Good. Now explore the other pieces inside you."

A similar vein glowed by her kidneys. Cara reached for it, feeling a new power flow through her hands.

"What does it feel like?" Talnor asked.

"Cooler than fire," Cara said. The sensation flooded through her, pure turning to copper, life becoming death. "Water into blood."

Talnor exhaled. "The power used by the red-headed fiend. I have seen it and marveled at its potency. Search more. Find the last."

Cara delved through her body, watching for that glow. This one she found beneath her stomach, worming its way around her intestines. It felt of rot, a pestilence inside her that threatened to turn her organs black. It made her sickened and excited all at once.

Cara opened her eyes, releasing the pull of all three powers. They settled into their respective areas, burning at her, desperate to be brought forth. The beast went less readily, its howl curdling in her veins.

"How do you feel?" Talnor asked.

"Strong," Cara replied, flexing her fingers. "Like I have magic of my own."

The *fampir* grinned, and Cara couldn't help but smile back

at her. Talnor said, "You are learning what immortality should be."

Cara almost didn't want to ask, but found herself saying, "And what's that?"

"The power to do as we please."

✳

Cara had left Riverfen a fugitive, fleeing from the earl. She returned now at the head of a great army, with the knowledge of the ancient *sulpari* flowing through her veins. She overlooked the mighty city from the top of the dam as soldiers marched dutifully across, their helmets flashing in the sunlight. Unlike her first time coming to the city, the dam and roads were empty of rustics. The people had all retreated inside the city, and even the temporary camps outside its walls had been emptied. The Cascade Palace shone in the afternoon light, a distant beacon at the top of the plateau.

"The years have been kind to it," Talnor remarked. She sat easily on her horse, shading her red-tinged eyes. "And we will destroy it."

"Only if Druam refuses to surrender," Cara said. "It will be his own foolishness that determines Riverfen's fate."

"Do you see the ships on the waters?" Talnor asked. She pointed to the glittering bay. "Cairn Steel-Eyes' fleet. The Lofalin ships have no way to aid us."

"Do we need the ships?" Cara asked.

"They can stop Druam and his people from fleeing, and provide some support in the siege."

"Can't the Lofalins destroy the enemy fleet?"

"Their ships were made to carry soldiers for a long voyage, not for sea warfare." Talnor shook her head. "Their ballistae can hit a city's walls easier than a moving target like another ship. And from what Rask has told me, Steel-Eyes' ships are too nimble to catch."

Cara narrowed her eyes at the distant sails. "Perhaps I can do something about them."

Talnor said, "Wait."

Cara paused.

Talnor pointed at the city. "There's something shimmering in the air."

Though difficult to see in the harsh afternoon sunlight, Cara saw it. All around the city, small sparkles of light appeared randomly in the air.

"What is it?"

"A protection of some kind. Come, Rask will be expecting us."

Cara touched her heels to her horse's flanks and began the long ride down to the fields outside the city.

Rask and the generals were already in the command tent when Cara and Talnor entered. The men leaned over a table, which held a map and wooden markers, and conversed in low tones. At Talnor's entrance, Rask bowed. He gave a cursory nod to Cara.

"The elves will take the walls on the north side of the city, on the other side of the river," one of the generals said. "Unfortunately, it seems Strilu was ready for them. His men harried the elves all the way from the mountains and destroyed the trebuchets."

"How long will it take to construct more?" Rask grunted.

"Deshes, if not longer. The earl's men also torched or cut down the nearest forests. It'll take days to find suitable wood."

"Hm." Rask prodded the map with a finger. "The fleet?"

"Outside the blockade. Steel-Eyes has too many ships for them to attempt to break through."

Rask nodded to one of his mages. "And the city?"

The mage, eyes huge behind thick glasses, trembled as he said, "Your Distinction, it seems that Avallune Martill and the other city mages have devised a new ward. Even with the trebuchets, most attacks will be easily rebuffed. Nothing can get through the barrier."

"What about the men?"

The mage shook his head. "It's meant to defend against all attacks, magical and physical. I'm afraid we'll have to figure out a way to undo the spells before we can attack."

"How long will that take?" Rask's glare could melt a candle.

"I...I don't know. It's a completely unknown working. It could take us months–"

Rask silenced him with a wave of his hand. "Damn Strilu. He's had all winter to plan for this."

Talnor stepped forward. "The *sulpari* may be able to breach the barrier."

"How?"

"Her magic is from the Underworld. I doubt the mages' spell will be able to defend against it."

Rask's glare moved to Cara. She stood tall beneath it, unafraid of this old man.

"What will you do? And how long will it take?"

Cara let the beast rise into her just enough to briefly warp her features before pushing it back down. "I will cause havoc in the streets."

"How long?" Rask repeated, completely unmoved by her words.

"A deshe," Cara said. "I must practice and prepare, and ensure that what I do will affect the entire city."

"Good." Rask turned back to the generals. "In the meantime, keep the men in fighting shape. We can intimidate them even if we can't yet breach the walls. Send a message to Cairn Steel-Eyes. Perhaps we can reach an agreement with her."

The meeting concluded, and Cara left as soon as she could. She stared out over the city, wondering whether it would fall before the soldiers could burn it down.

After dinner and meditation, Cara walked through the camp. She passed Talnor's tent, but paused as she heard her own name.

"...Cara?" Talnor was asking.

Rask's papery voice answered, "It depends. Do we need her for the Ossuary?"

"I'm afraid so. Valder used a *sulpari* to trap my kin. I believe only another *sulpari* can free them."

Cara looked around, but no one was paying any attention

to her. She sidled closer to the tent, pretending to adjust her bootlaces, and listened closely.

"Ah." Rask gave a watery cough. "But you are sure you can subdue her?"

"She will not be a problem for us," Talnor murmured in that sickeningly sweet tone.

"Good. Now...you are sure the Ossuary holds the spell we need?"

Cara leaned closer, listening intently.

"I am sure," Talnor said. "With the king's blood, you will regain your youth. With mine, you will never fear death again."

So that's what he wants. Cara glared at the canvas as if her gaze could penetrate it. *Immortality.*

Before she could be caught, Cara slipped away, chewing over what she had learned. Rask feared her – as he should – but he and Talnor needed her. More and more, though, Cara was less sure she needed them. *After this siege, we'll see where we stand.*

Though her mind was awash with plans, Cara fell asleep as soon as she lay down in her bunk. She woke to a frantic knocking on one of her tent poles.

"My lady," a soldier said, panting. "You're wanted in the command tent."

"Why? What's happened?" Cara demanded. *Do they know what I heard?*

The soldier said, "Cairn Steel-Eyes has sent word. She'll negotiate with us...but only if you're the one who does it."

CHAPTER SIXTEEN
Seanna

Seanna touched her ears yet again, feeling the familiar roundness beneath her fingertips. In her mirrored reflection, pointed ends poked out from underneath her hair. Her coppery skin had a tint of green to it, and her hands sported an additional finger on each. She appeared like a Rengu elf.

"Incredible, isn't it?" Ulalia beamed. She turned Seanna's head from side to side, making satisfied noises. "Yes, I think this will do."

"How long will it last?" Seanna asked. It disturbed her to see an elf looking back at her, one that shared her nose and eyes and lips, yet with eerie differences.

"A couple of candles," the elf maid said. "And it won't work against those who know you."

Seanna pulled away from the mirror. "Then we don't have long. We should go to her now."

Arm in arm, Seanna and Ulalia strode up one of the spiraling staircases until they came to a chamber built within the tree. It was lit with the glowing fungi, and had small windows that opened out on the Minwood's inner structure. Inside, a beautiful elven woman waited for them. She was just as Seanna remembered her: bronze skin that shimmered in the light, golden eyes, jet-black hair that was worn in a thousand tiny braids. Bracelets clinked on her arms, and long necklaces adorned her graceful throat.

"Edlyn!" Ulalia came forward and kissed the other woman's

cheeks. "I am so delighted that you came."

Though Edlyn returned the gesture, Seanna noted that it held no affection. Indeed, it seemed that Edlyn inspected Ulalia as a cat would a mouse, hungry and contemptuous.

"This is my dear friend Serena," Ulalia said, gesturing to Seanna. Though they had only met once, Seanna thought it prudent to give herself another name, just in case Edlyn saw through the illusion.

Edlyn inclined her head to Seanna, but didn't offer her cheeks. She regarded Seanna a moment. "You seem familiar."

Seanna gave a small laugh. "I'm sure we've met at some party or another. Perhaps in Dedaria?"

"Hmm." Edlyn turned back to her host.

Seanna settled on a settee as Ulalia and Edlyn sat together on a low couch. Ulalia poured wine for her guest, then said, "Tell me all about Con Salur. Has it changed much since the siege?"

Edlyn played with her goblet, but didn't drink. "It is quieter now. The people stay in their homes, and soldiers patrol to ensure that curfews are followed."

"Ah." Ulalia glanced at Seanna.

Sensing the maiden's unsureness, Seanna said, "I have heard that the Silver Keep survived the destruction. Is it still a thing of beauty? Do you live there now?"

"It was mostly untouched," Edlyn answered. "But Aremo has not taken up residence yet."

That surprised Seanna. She pressed, "Why not? Surely he would savor his victory."

"Not while the queen and her child live. Only then will he be truly triumphant." As Edlyn spoke, her lip curled. Something irritated her about the whole issue, but what?

Ulalia said, "You don't sound pleased with his decision."

Edlyn shrugged. "The city is ours, the queen likely dead or fled entirely from D'Ehsen. I think we should celebrate."

"Indeed," Ulalia said. "He did put our marriage on hold due to the war. I had thought he would want me now, but..." She put a small simper into her words, as if she were truly upset at the postponed wedding.

Edlyn smirked. "Don't sound so petulant. Enjoy your days without him."

Seanna perked up at this. Ulalia stroked the rim of her goblet and asked, "Why? I know you have been his paramour for a long time, and I would not dream of coming between you, but I had hoped we could be friends. All I want is for his happiness."

"And that will ruin you," Edlyn said. She put her cup down and leaned back into the couch. Her golden eyes were not unkind. "I don't envy your betrothal to him. He and I have given each other many pleasures, but..."

The silence stretched on, and finally Ulalia asked, "But what?"

Edlyn sighed, and Seanna saw past the composed façade to what lay underneath. This woman was hurting. Seanna scooted forward on the settee and said in a low voice, "You're unhappy with him."

In the elf woman's eyes, Seanna knew the same pain she had lived with for so long in her own marriage. She reached forward and took Edlyn's hand. "He's not here now. Believe me, I have known the heartache of love gone sour. Can you tell us what's the matter?"

The façade broke completely. Edlyn let out a small sob, though no tears cascaded down her cheeks. Even in agony, she was incredibly composed. She held Seanna's hand tightly, and said after a deep breath, "He has changed. He was once affectionate and warm. But he's so cold now...and when he does want to be close, he demands more and more. I am no stranger to exotic love-making, but what he wants has become so extreme. Beyond that, he is never satisfied. He has taken Con Salur, but now he wants the queen dead. Once she's gone, I'm sure he'll turn to Demarren or Skålland. He will never be happy, and so neither will I."

Edlyn trembled, staring at nothing. Her grip on Seanna's hand was so tight, Seanna's fingers began to ache. But Seanna didn't pull away. She said gently, "I am so sorry, dear one. What a tragedy it must be to see one you love transform into something unrecognizable."

"I want to leave, but I'm terrified," Edlyn said. "He won't let me. Once he has something, he never lets go of it."

Seanna stroked Edlyn's hair with her free hand, not speaking while she figured out the best course of action. She should tread carefully, for she didn't know this woman's temperament. Encouraging her to leave Aremo could make her dig her heels in further. But saying nothing might make her withdraw, losing any possibility of gaining information.

After a little contemplation, Seanna settled on targeted comfort. *Let her talk herself into whatever she really wishes to do.* She said, "My poor dear. It must have been terribly difficult to live with him these past months."

At Seanna's nod, Ulalia scooted closer to Edlyn, wrapping an arm around her shoulders.

Edlyn's lip quivered, and she said, "I never know how he'll behave. Some days he's giddy and sweet, others he rages and blames me for some small thing or other. No matter how I try, he is never appeased."

"I see why you warned me away from him," Ulalia murmured. She rubbed small circles on Edlyn's back. "If I take your place, would you be free of him?"

"I could not ask it of you." Edlyn wiped away another tear before it could fall. Seanna admired the woman's composure. It reminded her of Cairn Steel-Eyes.

"Could you go to the Lofalins for help?" Seanna asked gently. At the mention of the Lofalins, Edlyn stiffened. The elven woman's gaze darted about the room as if the fungi were listening in.

"It is safe here," Ulalia said. "You have nothing to fear."

"Without Aremo's protection...I fear what would happen to me," Edlyn whispered.

"Why?" Seanna asked.

Edlyn took a deep breath before she said, "They are zealots. They wish to cleanse all of D'Ehsen of vice and blasphemy. They see it as a sacred country corrupted by mankind. If it is purified, they will make way for the resurrection of their god."

"And you are a practitioner of those vices," Seanna said grimly. She remembered the terms the ambassador had brought to Con Salur so long ago. Would he have been willing to allow grace for her people?

But what of Aremo? She knew that the elf had no qualms about living in corruption. How had he convinced the Lofalins to look past his indiscretions?

Part of her cautioned that she should wait to ask such questions. Pressing Edlyn now could break her or cause suspicion. But what choice did Seanna have? Winter had come to an end, and springtime could bring yet more bloodshed if Aremo chose to pursue her.

"Edlyn," Seanna said. She shifted so that she held both of the elf's hands. "Aremo is no saint. Why are the Lofalins even working with him?"

"I don't know," Edlyn said. "They know what he is. They know what he's capable of. Yet the Lofalin generals fear him; they won't speak against him."

"What of the Lofalin priests? Some of them traveled over, yes?"

"They despise him. Either they were kept ignorant, or Aremo has blackmail against them. I never dared ask." Edlyn sniffed and relaxed her shoulders a touch. "It doesn't matter, though. Aremo will win. You and I will both be trapped in his clutches."

"Don't think of that now," Ulalia assured her. "Stay here as long as you please, as my guest. Perhaps time will give us answers."

Seanna pulled away from Edlyn to grab the elf's goblet. As she handed it over, she noticed Voclain through the door. He stood at a distance, though fury was plain in his expression. Quickly, Seanna made her excuses and went out to him. Before he could speak and ruin their ruse, she pulled him away.

"What are you doing?" Voclain demanded. "I told you—"

"I could not stand by and allow Aremo to win!" Seanna hissed. She darted a glance back at the chamber, but it seemed Edlyn hadn't noticed. She pulled Voclain a little farther away.

"You were right, we cannot defeat him on the battlefield. But perhaps we can be more subtle in our victory. Edlyn is a fount of information."

"You cannot trust her! *Think*, Seanna. Why do you think I never invited the Lofalins or any of Aremo's inner circle into my home? They are all snakes, smiling even as they plunge a knife into your back." Voclain's grip turned the flesh of Seanna's arm white. She tried to pull away, but he didn't let go.

"She was hurting, Voclain. If she believes us to be friends–"

"She will still bring the wolves down upon us. As soon as my daughter departs, I am sending that foul woman away."

"Don't," Seanna pleaded. "I saw beneath her veneer. She is a woman filled with pain. If she trusts your daughter, she could reveal a secret that can bring down Aremo."

"She's a fine actress," Voclain said. He shook his head. "I thought you more clever than this, Seanna. A weeping woman brought down your guard. I speak as a friend: you cannot trust a word from her poisonous lips."

Seanna finally pulled her arm from his grasp. She rubbed at the tender skin and glared at him. "I have been in politics a long time. I know what I saw in there."

Voclain sighed deeply and pushed his fingers against his temple. "It does not matter what you believe. I am sending her away."

"Please, Voclain. If we could just have more time–"

"No." He slashed the air with his hand. "She is going. You will not see my daughter; I cannot have you filling her head with hopeful nonsense. And if you try to defy my commands again, I will not hesitate to cast you and all your people out."

"You wouldn't dare," Seanna said. Her old pride flared up, and she drew her shoulders back. "I am the queen of Dotschar. You would not send me away."

"I will if you do not stop. Accept defeat, Seanna. You are queen of nothing now." Voclain did not allow her a response. He swept past her, his head held high.

Though she longed to scream at him, Seanna held her composure. She took a steadying breath, forcing her fingers to unclench. *Belrose can help me.*

As she walked toward the wizard's chambers, Seanna came upon Portia. The girl held Landin in her arms and bounced him while she hummed. When she noticed Seanna, she paused and bowed.

"Would you like him?" Portia asked.

Seanna almost took him. But he was sleeping soundly, and she didn't wish to disturb his rest. She shook her head. "Let him sleep." She stroked his head, not meeting Portia's eye. *I am doing all of this for them and my people. I cannot give up, no matter what Voclain says.*

"You look tired," Portia commented. "I can prepare the bed if you'd like to lay down."

She's so thoughtful. Not like me. Again Seanna shook her head. "That is very kind of you, Portia. But I can't rest now."

Portia reached out and touched Seanna's shoulder. Seanna stilled, her breath quickening at the touch.

"We all care for you," Portia said. "You should rest before you burn yourself into ashes."

Seanna was so, so tempted to give in. Why shouldn't she allow herself to fall into Portia's arms, or take Landin for walks and spend her days as a mother instead? Her heart yearned for that simple life, for the knowledge that only a family relied on her.

For a long moment, Seanna savored the touch. Then she carefully removed Portia's hand. "I need to see Belrose."

Her heart fractured at the hurt in Portia's eyes. Seanna turned away before she could do more harm. *See? You would damage her, and she is too good for you. Focus on the kingdom. They need you now.*

Yet as she lay in bed that night, listening to the soft breathing of Portia and Landin, Seanna wished that she could have all of it.

CHAPTER SEVENTEEN
Mavian

Mavian's teeth chattered in the cold. He pulled his cloak around his shoulders, wishing he had a pair of mittens to warm his hands. He envied Ekkar's apparent immunity as the prowler bounded through the snow with many a chirp and burble. He and Darian sat a distance away from the cave while Merick and Jagger stood nearby, equally mute guards.

"Did you resurrect Jagger?" Mavian asked. He had only managed to bring his beloved back through a complicated spell made by ancient mages, and even then a *fampir* had stolen the body. He couldn't fathom how Darian had managed it.

"I did," Darian said.

"How? What working did you use? I've researched–"

Mavian's tumble of words were cut off as Darian raised a hand. The blind man shook his head and said, "All spells were created from the Songs. But they are weaker, less flexible. I used the Song of Death."

"But *how*? Could it be done again?"

Darian's voice was calm and soft. "I have known the Song of Death my entire life, and even I could only achieve such a thing once. It came with a cost: Jagger's voice. I could not repeat it if I wished."

Mavian peered at the blind man. "Is that why your eyes...?"

Darian hesitated, then nodded once. He did not elaborate, and Mavian pondered who brought this man back to life. Mavian decided to veer away from the subject and said, "Can you show me more of the Song?"

"It is most powerful when you discover it," Darian replied. "You are surrounded by the undead: Ekkar, Jagger, and Merick. Lose yourself in the moment. Listen to the wind."

Mavian shivered. Did he really wish to learn this powerful magic? The man he had been before the Masque would not have hesitated. *But I've changed. I don't know if I'm worthy of such a gift.* He glanced to Jagger, but the silent man didn't meet his eye. He thought back to the words they had shared.

He was no fighter; the bruises that adorned his arms were proof of that. He was no mage, for he had never been able to cast higher workings without the gem. These Songs could help him be something more, yet he feared them. Mavian said, "I don't know if I can do it."

Darian replied softly, "I would not teach you unless I thought you would use this Song wisely."

How long had it been since someone else had put faith in Mavian's goodness? He thought bitterly about Druam, who had always seen the potential in him. *Druam would want me to do it. For Verdon.*

At last, Mavian said, "Alright. I'll try."

"Good. Sit comfortably. Close your eyes. Think not only of what these men are, but who. Who are they? Their experiences? What gives them strength, and what takes it away? Focus on the one you know the best."

Mavian looked from prowler to wight to Jagger and back again. He knew Ekkar and Merick, but only as undead. He had barely known Verdon in life – he had only been a child when the man vanished – and he had only seen glimpses of the real Merick.

Finally, Mavian settled on Ekkar. He had heard enough stories from Druam and Alex to gather some knowledge of his cousin. He pulled from his deepest memories:

When I first came to Riverfen, Verdon walked with me in the gardens. He asked me about what I was learning and told me about lantern faeries. On another visit, Verdon gave me sweets and had me recite my letters. One time, in the dead of night, I couldn't sleep and went to Druam's chambers for comfort. I heard them arguing, Verdon insisting that he must return to Mott at once. I remember being afraid. Then he came out, noticed me, and embraced me. That was the last time I saw him.

As Mavian pieced together the truth of who Verdon was, he realized that he must also acknowledge what the man had become. He thought of Ekkar's idiosyncrasies, how the prowler sniffed at his meals or leapt ahead while traveling. Every little noise that Ekkar liked to make, every tiny joy or animal despair.

Then, in the midst of his musings, he heard it: that low, sonorous note. But this time, it came from Ekkar. It tolled through the prowler, rich and strong. A chorus of bells rang throughout the music, high and clear, notes of purest happiness and contentment: chasing a bug as Ekkar, the sweetness of blood, the love of a woman, notes that echoed all his lives, mortal and *fampir* and prowler. Yet beneath them, that note repeated, over and over, with the finality of a cold grave in the barren ground.

Mavian gasped and opened his eyes. The music encompassed him, sucking at him like molasses. He forced it out, astonished at the power that lay within one man's Song.

"I heard..." Mavian couldn't find the right words to convey everything in that Song.

"I know," Darian said.

Voices sounded through the bare forest. Jagger and Merick stiffened, then together drew their weapons. Mavian and Darian sat as still as they could. Even Ekkar, sensing trouble, crouched underneath a bush.

A trio of soldiers tramped through the woods, close enough to hear but still indistinct. Their voices carried, complaining about patrol and winter and other mundane realities. Mavian's breath caught in his chest as the soldiers walked parallel to their hiding spot. He didn't move again until they were gone and the echoes of their voices had faded into silence.

"Chadron's men," Mavian said when it was safe. "They're patrolling farther out than I expected."

"You need allies," Darian said.

"If you can Sing up an army, it would be greatly appreciated."

"Surely others wish to depose Chadron."

Mavian threw up his hands. "And who would that be? Even if there are lords who hate him, they loathe me even more. None of them would listen to me."

Darian said, "Then what do you plan to do?"

Mavian puzzled over this. He had lost the scholars and his workshop. Even if he heard the Song of Death, he didn't know how to use it. Deep down, he knew that Darian was right.

He needed allies.

*

Mavian paced the old mill, his steps sending up tiny puffs of dust. Occasionally, he paused and glanced out from the shuttered window before resuming his walk. He felt terribly alone, for only Darian had chosen to accompany him on this foolhardy task.

"They're not coming," Mavian said for the hundredth time. "Or they're sending their soldiers after my head."

"Peace," Darian said smoothly. "They will come."

Despite the day's chill, sweat gathered under Mavian's arms. He clenched and unclenched his fingers, wishing he could feel the hard gem between them.

"This was foolish," Mavian said. "What was I thinking? These lords wouldn't betray Rask even if they hate Chadron."

"You said yourself that these lords were the ones left behind when Rask marched on Stonetree. They were snubbed," Darian pointed out. "If they weren't invited to partake in the glory of battle, there must be some resentment."

"Or they were chosen to stay and safeguard Rask's province," Mavian countered.

"Then leave," Darian said. "Find a way to defeat Chadron on your own."

Mavian didn't respond. A trio of horses trotted up the path toward the mill, each leading a retinue of men-at-arms with poleaxes and banners. Mavian's mouth went dry. *They're here.* His feet could have been nailed to the floor for all he tried to move them. His body had gone numb, his mind emptying.

It's too late to run.

The three men on horseback dismounted, waving for their soldiers to wait for them. They strode up to the mill and knocked once. Darian put his hand on the knob. Mavian finally managed a nod, and the blind man opened the door. It swung slowly, hanging slightly askew from its hinges, and admitted the lords.

Lord Ravenhill led the trio, his wide shoulders swathed in furs. Behind him came the small Lord Whitecave and then Lord Roseway with his bright red cloak. The three men paused as they caught sight of Mavian.

"Ah," Ravenhill said. "Lord Fareyes. I am genuinely surprised."

They hadn't yet drawn their swords, and they stood at ease as Darian shut the door behind them. Mavian took a deep breath, willing himself to put on the courtly personality he had once worn in Riverfen. When he felt ready, he gave a small bow. "Thomas, how good to see you again. How is your wife?"

"Pregnant again," Ravenhill muttered. His gaze went to Darian. "Who's this?"

"A friend," Mavian said. "A rustic with some command of magic."

Though he hated speaking about Darian like that, Mavian knew well the mannerisms lords expected of each other. He drew the ghost of Lord Fareyes around himself.

"Hmm." Ravenhill directed his attention back to Mavian. "Your letter intrigued me, I must say. As did your choice of meeting place." He scrutinized the dusty mill which contained only a few pieces of battered furniture and moth-eaten cloth.

Mavian made a friendly gesture. "Sit, and I will tell you our plan."

The lords' eyes glittered as they sat around a rickety old table. It seemed the other two were content to let Ravenhill speak for them, for he said, "I'm surprised you're here, Strilu. I thought you were Rask's dog through and through."

Mavian licked his lips. "I, er, departed Rask's service after the siege of Stonetree."

The lord's look was inscrutable. "Why?"

Here is where we know their true loyalties. Mavian took a deep breath, then said, "Rask has allied himself with an ancient *fampir* who seeks to wreak havoc on our world. When I realized this, I sought help from Earl Seastone and allied myself with him instead. It is my hope to take D'Clet from Sir Chadron, and from there counter Rask's plans."

A terribly long moment passed, the silence pressing in on Mavian's nerves, a dark ocean through which he could not yet see the light. At last, Ravenhill said, "Are we truly to believe you? You, a practitioner of the dark arts, whose foul prowlers killed our friends and family at the Masque?"

Mavian opened his mouth to defend himself, then closed it. He could not deny Ravenhill's accusation. Instead, he tried a different tactic. "Rask wished to expose Druam Strilu and cause chaos. I was but a means to that end. Clearly, he did not value you or your families enough to warn you."

He waited, his heart beating hard against his ribs, hoping that this manipulation would work.

Ravenhill regarded Mavian for a long, long moment. The lord's hand strayed to his hilt. Mavian wetted his lips, but said no more.

Ravenhill said at last, "I hold no love for Egil Rask or his family. When he raised his levies for his campaign against Stonetree, I objected. I sent him the bare minimum, as my duty requires. My friends here can attest to the same."

The other two lords grumbled and nodded, but their looks were still deeply unfriendly. Whitecave whispered in Ravenhill's ear. Ravenhill nodded, his frown growing. He said, "The gods do not judge kindly upon those who consort with the undead."

"We are at war, my lords," Mavian said, doing his best to keep his voice level. "Would you object to Earl Seastone's aid?"

His eyes dark and appraising, Ravenhill leaned back. The other two lords whispered in his ears, and he nodded sagely. He said, "Earl Seastone is a blight upon this world. We would not work with him, nor do we approve of Rask's consorting with undead. If they kill each other in this siege, the world would be better for it."

Mavian licked his lips, his heartbeat roaring in his ears. *I should not have come here.* He said, "I understand, my lords. I–"

"You led Rask into heresy," Ravenhill interrupted. His brows drew down, hooding his eyes. "You used dark magic."

Mavian blanched. He could deny nothing. He glanced to where Darian had been standing, but the blind man was gone. Mavian was alone.

"We despise Chadron and his frivolities," Ravenhill continued smoothly, "but we will not work with a blasphemer."

"Please..." Mavian said. He stood and backed away, his hands held feebly before him.

Ravenhill and the two lords pushed their chairs back. They loomed over him. Mavian remembered Jagger's lessons and put up his fists, planting his feet in what he hoped was a good stance.

The lords laughed and advanced. Mavian threw a fist and managed to catch Ravenhill's cheek. The lord spit; he was not laughing now.

"You'll pay for that," Ravenhill said. He swung a meaty hand. It slammed into Mavian's chest, sending him sprawling against the dusty wall. Mavian coughed and struggled to stand. The lords closed in on him, raining blows against his arms as he tried to protect his head.

Mavian gave up. He collapsed to the floor, his arms shaking and blood dripping into his eyes. He didn't resist as the lords hauled him out into the sunlight, didn't fight back as soldiers clapped irons around his wrists and tied the rope to the saddle of Ravenhill's horse. Blinking through his tears, he looked for Darian, but the blind man had utterly disappeared.

Mavian stumbled as the horse dragged him into motion, his mind gone utterly blank. He had failed. *Will they kill me now? Or wait until they've had their fun?* Somewhere in the wind, he heard the low, sonorous note of the Song of Death.

CHAPTER EIGHTEEN
Gwen

Gwen's trial was tomorrow, and she could not sleep. The bed held no comfort, and the twinkling lights below were not the colorful ones she longed for. She had no one to speak for her and no idea how she could bring peace to a country which harbored such hatred for her talents.

As she walked onto the balcony for the third time that night, Gwen thought of Druam. What would he say? With all his wisdom, would he have found a solution that brought harmony instead of discord?

Without really thinking about it, Gwen drew upon the scrying spell. She no longer needed the bowls of rosewater and incense; the Songs that composed the spell were intricately woven, yet simple in their melodies. She Sang them, her voice floating out over the city. *Let me see Druam again.*

With a blink, Gwen found herself in the Cascade Palace. She stood in the familiar study, the lanterns twinkling below. *He made it home.* That, at least, was some small comfort.

"I've waited every day for you," Druam said from behind her. Gwen turned slowly to face her husband. He was thin and pale, his eyes bright in a gaunt face. His clothes hung loosely on him, his hair dull.

"So it wasn't a dream," he continued. "I've lain awake many nights wondering if you had been a phantom of my fatigue or an illusion sent by my enemies."

"I went to Autorus, as I told you I would," Gwen said. So

much had happened since their last, brief meeting, and she looked at him with new eyes. She had grown into a woman, and her heart did not know whether to love him. All the questions she had wanted to ask him were forgotten now that she was confronted by reality.

"He released you?" Surprise colored his voice.

"I was never his prisoner," she replied.

Druam reached for her, and his fingers passed through her shoulder. He stared at his hand as if it would poison him. "You're not really here."

"No." Gwen noticed a painting behind him. With a start, she realized that it was a portrait of her. The art was finely made, yet she couldn't fathom that such an image really echoed her. *I am no longer that porcelain doll.*

"This isn't me," she said.

"I could only work from my memory." Druam stood close to her, his eyes devouring her.

"It shows what I used to be. Not what I am."

"To me, you will always be the beautiful girl from Demarren."

It should have been a compliment, and she knew that he meant it as such, but she bristled at it. "Am I not beautiful now?"

"You're...different."

When she had first married him, she had been barely out of childhood. If he had spoken like this to her then, she would have railed and raged, overcome by the seething emotions inside her. Now, though the comment stung, she had enough self control to measure her response before she spoke.

"I have grown older in the Woods. Perhaps even older than you."

"That's not possible." A spike of emotions punctuated his Song. Gwen reached to it and found a cauldron of feeling within him, always close to boiling over.

She smiled. "I lived in the Woods for lifetimes. They are not of Earda, and their time is not ours. I have grown older, and though your face is the same as it was centuries ago, your heart has grown younger."

"Yes." Sadness spilled through the melodies within him, a melancholy that flowed into every note. "But I still love you."

"You love her," Gwen said, gesturing to the painting. "You don't know me anymore."

"Then come to Riverfen and let us learn to care for each other once more. Gwen, not a day has gone by when I haven't thought of you. Didn't you remember me when you were in the Woods?"

"No." Her answer brought a wave of despair to Druam's Song. Gwen said, "I forgot everything of my life on Earda. Even my own name." She brushed her hand against the painting's face, her fingers going through the canvas. "I was only a child when I first came to Riverfen. I knew nothing of the world. You took advantage of me."

"How?" Druam's grief blasted into anger, flashing through his Song like wildfire. "I gave you protection and love, I let you explore your magic even though I was afraid of it. I gave you everything."

"I was a *child*," Gwen said again. "Only seventeen. You could have done all that without binding my heart to yours. Now I know that you are centuries old, I wonder how you could have entered into such a marriage. Did you fear my growing older and falling in love with someone else? Did your lust override your common sense?"

Though his expression was carefully smoothed, Gwen heard the consternation that burned within his Song, the notes so hot they could have scorched her. She hadn't intended to confront him, but she could not fathom the decisions he had made.

"You wouldn't understand," Druam said through gritted teeth. "You don't know half of what my life has been."

"Because you didn't tell me," Gwen said. "You hid the truth of yourself, and now you expect me to understand you?"

Despite her placid countenance, Gwen's anger built inside her chest. Before she went into the Woods, she had trusted Druam with her entire being. *And he lied to me.* He had taken the trust of a vulnerable girl and twisted it for his own selfish desires. How long would the deception have lasted? Five years? Ten? Her entire lifetime? If she hadn't taken her destiny into her own hands and traveled to the Woods, she may never have learned the truth, both of herself and him.

They had each changed in the intervening time. With a sudden sense of clarity, Gwen knew that she could not trust Druam to solve her problems. Somewhere in the centuries, he had lost his wisdom. Every thought, every action, was tainted with surging emotion. He was incapable of seeing beyond it.

"I wish you luck in the coming siege," Gwen said.

"Gwen, wait!" Druam called, but too late. Gwen released the scry spell and returned to her corporeal body. She shuddered, a burst of emotion threatening to overwhelm her. She pushed it down. She would not be like Druam.

In the Songs, Gwen knew the answer she sought. She had always known; she simply hadn't wanted to acknowledge it.

She returned to the bed and slept soundly until the soldiers woke her. She was ready for her trial.

✳

Flanked by soldiers, Gwen entered the amphitheater, a huge outdoor space where all could come hear the debates of the Great Council. It sank down into the earth in concentric rings that descended to the lowest point at the center. Councillors, guildsmen, and rustics crowded around, the people from the upper edges pushing to catch a glimpse. Olfrick Kron was seated in the central space. As soon as Gwen entered, his eyes narrowed, his lip curling. Gwen sat opposite him, her expression neutral.

The councillors occupied the ring closest to the center. The Skals, their robes trimmed with fur and bells braided into their blonde beards, clustered on the eastern side, while the Demars, dressed in loose breeches and tunics, their skin decorated with tattoos, sat on the western. They eyed each other with as much suspicion as they gave to Gwen.

The council marshal tottered to the center, his weak frame

held together by ancient sinews, and said in a voice as thin as the papers he carried, "We gather today for the trials of Councillor Olfrick Kron and Princess Gwendolyn Zaman. Kron stands accused of treason and regicide, Zaman of the use of illegal magic. Councillor Daghorn, if you will please step forward."

The pale man stepped forward, his fingers caressing his long mustache. Daghorn gave a mock bow to Gwen, then turned to the marshal. "I represent Councillor Kron as his advocate, and speak against this filthy creature." He waved a hand at Gwen.

"We will focus only on Kron to begin with," the marshal said. "Habib, I believe you speak for those whom Kron wronged?"

Habib stepped down into the center, standing across from Daghorn. The two exchanged a contemptuous look. Habib bowed to the marshal. "I speak for the people."

"Very well. Daghorn, what is your defense?"

Daghorn rolled his shoulders and swept his arms out. Charisma dripped with every word, "My fellows, Demarren has long been under the rule of invaders. Conquerers who destroyed the peace of the Skals who have dwelled in these lands for innumerable years. Is it not justice to seek freedom? To pull ourselves out from under the heels of Demars? Kron did what was in the hearts of every Skal!"

The crowd murmured, some nodding along, others frowning. Gwen stayed utterly still, allowing herself to tune into the Songs that drifted through the air. What she found frightened her. Many of the Skals had felt downtrodden and inferior for years; they would not condemn Olfrick for attempting to lift them up.

Daghorn continued, "Wullum Zaman was a tyrant! He could have helped the Skals in his country, but he chose to ignore them. He furthered the divides between our peoples, and harbored a witch in his own household." Daghorn sneered at Gwen. "Magic has been forbidden in Demarren for generations, and for good cause! Mages and witches bring chaos, corruption, and death. Did Kron not bring justice against those foul creatures? Did he not save us from the tyranny of a selfish man?" He paused, allowing his words to sink in. "I argue that regicide in the name of justice is not murder. It is righteous, and so Olfrick Kron must be reinstated as Liegelord."

The crowd shifted and whispered, and the marshal waved for quiet. Habib stepped forward. Unlike Daghorn, who strutted about, he stood still, his hands behind his back, and spoke quietly, "Olfrick Kron swore to protect Liegelord Zaman. He made a sacred oath, upon this land and its people, to obey. Could he have pushed for equality without violence? Could he have hanged witches without also condemning hundreds of innocents? Could he have convicted Zaman without also murdering the man's wives and son? Kron had many avenues open to him, and he chose the one which would bring the most harm to our people. Daghorn may argue that Kron's actions were righteous, but there is nothing defensible there. Kron is a traitor and a murderer, and he must be hanged for it."

The Skals grumbled, and a few of them booed. The marshal called for order. When he had command of the amphitheater, he said, "Daghorn, please present your evidence."

The trial settled into its rhythm of witness, questioning, and debate. Daghorn argued that Olfrick only wanted to uphold the most sacred laws of their land, pointing to Gwen as evidence of magic in Wullum's court. Habib responded with fierce defensiveness, claiming that few who were hanged were actually guilty.

Gwen kept the Songs in the background, a constant reminder that none of these men were her friends. Her gaze, however, stayed only on Olfrick. His Song beat against his ribs, fear and confidence in waves as councillors either raged against him or rallied for him.

He was afraid. Beneath the confident veneer lay a man who knew that his life could be much, much shorter than he'd wished.

For a moment, pity stirred within Gwen. He had done what he thought was best for his people, shortsighted and cruel though he may have been. They both wanted peace in

Demarren, but had drastically different views on how to accomplish such a thing. *Is there no good answer? No matter if a Demar or a Skal occupies the throne, there will be strife.*

Not only must the two be united in common cause, they must have leadership who understood the various needs and desires of the differing communities. And how could one leader hope to accomplish such a task?

There should be no throne at all. The thought struck Gwen, a tempest that shook her to her very core. No throne? But every kingdom had a ruler. Every kingdom needed a ruler. Was that not a part of life, coded into language itself? There could be no kingdom without a king.

Yet Gwen could not shake this monumental idea. It frightened and fascinated her. If not a king or Liegelord, who would rule? How would power be passed on?

Built into the rings was a stone throne. The councillors sat a distance from it, as if fearing the implications of being too close. Gwen shifted her gaze to the throne, staring at it as the trial dragged on. She stopped listening to the debates and the Songs, her attention wholly fixed on that symbol of power which was the cause of so much discord.

If Olfrick were set free, he would sit upon it. She could not allow that to happen.

Gwen met Olfrick's eyes. She rose smoothly to her feet and strode to him. *I will have to prove his guilt to them.* As she walked, she hummed a Song that blazed through her, fiery in its righteousness.

The council watched her. Their music faded to a buzz in her head, crowded out by the consuming Song that coursed in her. Daghorn attempted to stop her, but she pushed him aside.

Gwen put a hand on Olfrick's head. He protested, but then the Song hit him. It flowed from her, heating him until his skin glowed. Gwen spoke, her voice raw with power, "Tell them why you started the Trials."

Olfrick gaped at her, his eyes lit with the fire of the Song of Truth. He could not lie under her hand; he could not resist answering her.

"I wished to rule as Liegelord. I knew the populace would kill for fear of magic."

"Did you hang innocents?"

"Yes."

"Did you measure the cost of victory?"

"No. I did not care that innocents would be killed."

"Even if they were Skals?"

Olfrick swallowed heavily. "Yes."

"Even if they were children?"

"Yes."

"All for the pursuit of power?"

"Yes."

Gwen lifted her hand, satisfied. She turned to the rows. "He confesses his own guilt. He did not wage a campaign against the Gifted for the sake of the country. He did it so that he may rule."

For a moment, utter silence dominated the space. Then the council burst into a tornado of sound. Skals shouted that Gwen had forced Olfrick to speak, Demars defended her. Gwen returned to her seat, waiting for them to calm down.

Eventually, the marshal regained order. He asked for final arguments from the advocates. Daghorn muttered something under his breath, and Habib remained silent. When it was clear he'd get no more from them, the marshal said, "Without a Liegelord to pass judgement, we councillors must vote."

One by one, the councillors filed down to the center. They placed a stone in a bowl, white for innocent, black for guilty. Olfrick watched the whole process, his eyes wide, his skin still glowing from Gwen's spell. Gwen shut her eyes. No matter the outcome, she knew what she must do.

The marshal tallied the stones, and the whole crowd held an expectant breath. At last, the marshal lifted his head. "By vote of the Greater Council, Olfrick Kron is found guilty. For the crimes of treason and regicide, the punishment is clear: he must be executed."

Olfrick slumped. He raised a shaking hand to his eyes and covered them. A rustic coughed, and the Skals and Demars all looked at each other as if unsure what to do next. The verdict had been made, the sentence proclaimed. Slowly, all of them shifted their gaze to Gwen.

The marshal shook himself and said, "We will now move on to the trial for Princess Gwendolyn Zaman. Daghorn, please–"

Gwen stood. The marshal's words died, and her flesh crawled with so many eyes on her. She said, "There will be no trial."

Her legs shook. She licked her dry lips and swallowed. She knew the Songs, knew nature and death and humanity, but that had not prepared her to heal a wounded country.

They must be united.

"I am guilty," Gwen said. She pointed to Olfrick. "You witnessed my magic this very day, and you could not throw a stone in the streets without finding someone who saw me enchant guards and summon winds. I am a witch."

The crowd sat stunned, as if they hadn't fathomed anyone freely admitting to such crimes. Gwen raised her eyes to the awestruck rustics at the very edges of the amphitheater and said, "I am not your savior. I am not your new Liegelord. I am a witch, and my duty is done. I hold no obligation to you."

The crowd surged and roiled, with shouts of anger echoing over the stone. The councillors looked nervously about, and a few soldiers edged toward Gwen. She lifted her arms, and they halted with fear in their eyes.

"Demarren needs no Liegelord," Gwen said. She pointed a hand at the throne, calling upon the Songs laced within the rock. With a mighty *crack*, the stone broke apart, shards flying every which way and dust rising into the air.

From within the choking debris, Daghorn cried out, "Kill her! She mustn't be allowed to escape!"

From above, voices cried out, "Kill Kron!" "Kill the witch!"

The Songs thrummed over Gwen's skin, and she smiled. She called out, "No man will lay claim to me!"

Whatever fear or awe had held the crowd back now broke. Rustics surged past the soldiers. Councillors cried out as they tried to flee.

The amphitheater erupted into pandemonium.

CHAPTER NINETEEN
Cara

The black waves slipped against the beach, sprays of mist coating Cara's face. She pulled her cloak around her. Though the spring days grew gradually warmer and warmer, the nights still held onto winter's chill.

Cairn Steel-Eyes' boat clipped over the waves. The lights of the blockade twinkled above the water, echoing the glittering lights of Riverfen.

"Why you?" Rask had growled the moment Cara had come into the command tent. She'd shrugged, unsure herself why a corsair captain would want her. Over a candle of arguing later, she had found herself waiting by the bay to meet with Cairn Steel-Eyes.

The longboat rowed closer. Cara rubbed her sweating hands against her breeches. She knew how to fight and had been taught arithmetic and history, but no one had ever schooled her in diplomacy. Rask had been thorough in his coaching: what demands to make, what concessions to allow, when to push and when to give up. His words rattled through her head, and she wondered if she'd be able to speak them at all.

The boat lifted from the water, hauled up by the corsairs. They pulled it up and over onto the sand, and Cara stepped shakily forward. She nodded at her soldiers to stay. They regarded the corsairs warily, their hands close to their weapons.

One of the corsairs bowed to Cara. "The Queen o' the Seas, yer ladyship."

The rest of the corsairs leered at Cara, their eyes hooded in the dim light. She glared at them, safe in the knowledge that she had a *fampir*'s blood in a flask at her side should she need it. *These cretins have no idea of my power.*

A woman stepped between the corsairs. She wore a velvet coat and had jewelry crowding her fingers, but Cara didn't care for the grandeur. She hadn't seen this woman's face in years, and could never have expected to encounter it again here.

Cara walked briskly to the tent that had been erected on the shore for them. Her belly turned with the beast roiling inside it, begging for release. *Not yet.* When the other woman had entered the tent, Cara let the flap fall and turned to face her.

"Mother," Cara said coldly. She waited for her mother to speak. When she didn't, Cara said, "So you're Cairn Steel-Eyes. A better name for a corsair than Sura Gellder."

Sura's gaze ran over her, too guarded to read. In the years since Cara had last seen her, more grey had graced her hair, and a few more wrinkles marred her forehead. But her mother still had that aloof look and calculating posture, each motion made with purpose.

"It's good to see you, Cara," Sura said at last. "You've grown into a beautiful young woman."

With a casual wave, Sura indicated one of the chairs. Cara didn't sit, and neither did Sura.

"So this is why you abandoned me," Cara said. The beast was hot inside her. "For a life at sea. People always ask me where my mother found the money to educate me and hire Merick; I guess now I can answer them."

"This was no life for a child," Sura murmured. She gripped the back of her chair, her knuckles white. "Too dangerous. Too unstable."

A thousand emotions tumbled through Cara. Relief and a tiny joy at seeing her mother again; anger at being abandoned so long; grief that they should meet during war on opposing sides; another flare of anger that her mother should be allied with Druam Srilu; curiosity at her mother's life. Cara took a deep breath to rein herself in.

Business first.

"What do you want, Sura?" Cara asked. Her mother winced at the use of her name.

"I wanted to see you," Sura said. "Is that so bad?"

"I'm here to negotiate on behalf of Earl Rask." Cara bit off the words. "If you wanted to discuss personal issues, you should have visited more often."

Sura winced again. Her short nails dug into the upholstered chair. "I'm afraid there's not much to negotiate. I have been paid well to defend Riverfen's harbor, and I don't plan on betraying Druam."

"Rask will double what Druam has offered."

"I doubt that." Sura raised a fine eyebrow. "Druam has had many lifetimes to accrue his wealth. Even if Rask emptied his coffers, it could not match what I'm being paid now. And besides the coin, Druam and I have enjoyed a long-lasting alliance."

Cara hissed between her teeth. She leaned forward, planting her hands on the table. "Druam does not deserve your loyalty. He is a foul beast."

"Remember, Cara," Sura said quietly, "I had a child with a creature such as him. I have no ill will toward *fampir*."

The beast tugged at Cara, and she resisted it. She glared at her mother. "You birthed a monster."

"We all choose what we do with the paths laid before us. I chose the sea. If you are a monster, it's because you elected to be." Sura sighed, her eyes dropping from Cara's. "I knew what you would become. Your father and I desired you. We could not have done it without a sorcerer's help. It was deliberately done, and I wouldn't take it back."

"Then why didn't you ever tell me what I am?" Cara almost tried to steer the conversation back toward negotiations, but her desires won out. For the first time in her life, she could ask her mother anything.

"You were too young. The years slipped by. Next time I saw you, I would have told you."

"Bit too late for that."

"I know." Regret scored Sura's voice. "I'm sorry for that. I wanted you to be innocent for as long as possible. Maybe have a boy in town that you liked, or friends to explore the forests with. I didn't realize how young you'd be when it started to affect you."

"But you still left me, even after you knew." Cara watched her mother carefully, trying to read past her warded expression.

"What could I have done? You are what you are. Nothing I said could have changed that."

"Why did you even have me? Why did you risk setting a monster on the world?" Fear stirred inside Cara. *Did she know the whole truth of what I am?*

"I wanted to have a child with your father," Sura said simply. "I never intended you to be a hero or a great warrior or to fight in the wars of nobles. I hired Merick so that you could defend yourself against a harsh world. I hired tutors so that you'd have opportunities beyond what I had. Mostly, I tried to give you what your father would have wanted for you. The sea has always called to me, and he knew I'd return to it eventually. But he would have had you to love and raise, a little piece of me to hold onto."

A tear sparkled in Sura's eye for a single moment. She blinked, and it vanished.

Cara stood frozen. Her mother had never spoken so honestly before. In that moment, she felt like a child again, and she half wished for her mother's arms around her.

"Who is my father?" Cara asked. She had asked it many times before: to Merick, Druam, and Laris. None of them knew. She told herself that the answer didn't really matter, but her pounding heart and sudden sweat betrayed her desire.

"I don't think you'll like it," Sura said.

"Tell me."

"His name was Verdon Strilu. He was Druam's trueborn brother."

The answer hung in the air between them, a truth finally freed from its cell. Sura watched her closely, but Cara stared past her, turning it over in her mind. *Verdon Strilu.* One time, Alex had told her about his brother: a scholar and peacemaker who spent more time at Mott's university than in Riverfen. He had disappeared long ago. *Around the time I was born.*

Conflicting feelings surged through her. She let out her breath, the truth beating in her head: *Verdon Strilu.* That made Druam her uncle, and Alex...*at least he wasn't Druam's true brother. He was brought into the family long after Druam and Verdon became* fampir. She hated this familial tie to Druam, whom she so loathed. Yet she also respected and admired the tale of the man she now knew as her father. Remorse burned in her as she thought about Alex. He had told her more of her father than anyone else without even realizing it, and she'd slaughtered him. *How many more stories could he have told me?*

Cara looked at her mother, at the pain hidden in her eyes. Sura stood still, waiting for Cara's reaction.

Emotion roiled throughout Cara, and the beast tried again and again to claw up her chest, to take her over in her moment of weakness. Cara clutched the table edge and pushed the beast down. *I will deal with this on my own.*

At last, Cara asked, "Did Druam know?"

Sura shook her head.

Cara took in this information as well. Druam had not lied to her; her hatred for him would not increase. But she still mulled over her father's name and station, everything she knew about him. Could she ask her mother for more stories?

No. Cara swallowed her pain at the decision. *She kept this from me for twenty years. Knowing more about him won't change the fact that he's gone. It won't change what I must do.* Her hatred for Druam, her need to find the Ossuary and make the world right once more, outweighed her childish wishes.

"Cara?" Sura asked. She reached for Cara, her expression finally open. Motherly.

"This changes nothing," Cara said. She took a step back. "What would convince you to take your ships away?"

A hardness covered Sura's vulnerability. "Nothing."

"I could burn your fleet," Cara said. She assumed a mask of strength. "You may not believe me a monster, but you are mistaken. I can and will destroy you if you don't leave."

"With what ships? The Lofalins' galleys are too large and clunky. They could never catch mine." Pride laced Sura's words.

"I don't need ships." Cara let the beast in at last, and red lit her eyes as fangs protruded onto her lips. Her mother blanched.

Sura recovered quickly, reassuming her confident posture. "You forget that you are a diplomat for Earl Rask. If you harm me, you forfeit all rights to negotiation."

Cara lunged for her mother, too quick for Sura to react. She pinned her mother against the floor, her claws wrapping around Sura's throat. Sura swallowed, her neck bobbing beneath Cara's fingers. She reached for a dagger at her side, but Cara was too quick. Cara grabbed her hand and pulled it behind her back, wrenching her shoulder.

"You are Cairn Steel-Eyes," Cara hissed. "Not my mother. You chose the sea over me. I choose revenge over you."

With the beast's strength, Cara hauled Sura up and pushed her toward the tent flaps, holding her wrists behind her back with one hand. She kept the claws of her other hand around the corsair's throat. They moved slowly out of the tent.

The corsairs lunged into action at the sight of their captain's distress. They drew their weapons, but stayed back as Cara bent her fangs to Sura's neck. Cara's soldiers tensed. All of them peered from Sura to Cara and back, waiting for their orders.

"Tell them to get into the boat," Cara said.

"All hands to the longboat," Sura said through clenched teeth. The corsairs moved begrudgingly, their hands tight on their weapons.

"Tell them to row into the water," Cara said. Sura obeyed.

The corsairs followed their queen's orders. Worry and anger shone on their faces, and Cara nearly laughed. *Should never have let your guard down, Sura.*

The longboat bobbed in the water, and the corsairs watched Cara warily.

"Taking me prisoner won't stop the fleet," Sura said. Cara spared a glance at her, then shoved her at two of the soldiers. They quickly held Sura's hands as Cara reached for the flask at her hip. She swallowed the cool blood, reviled at how slowly it moved down her throat. But then she felt the power that dwelled by her heart, swelling as the beast grew hot inside her, ecstatic with the promise of violence.

Cara said, "I want to show you what you're dealing with."

Cara focused on the corsairs' longboat. All the different powers coursed through her, but she wouldn't release the others yet. All she needed was her black fire.

It burst from her hands, black on the black waves. The corsairs barely had time to cry out before their vessel ignited. The black flames crawled up the wood. Screams filled the night air. The smell of burning flesh curled over the shore.

Cara smiled and turned back to her mother, the screams of pain and death floating over the water like music. She let the beast fade back down, its work done.

"Keep her as a hostage," Cara said. The soldiers quickly bound Sura's wrists. None of them could look at Cara.

Perhaps now her mother would regret birthing a monster.

CHAPTER TWENTY
Seanna

"Seanna, wake up!" Someone jolted her shoulder, shaking it like a child's toy.

In her grogginess, Seanna shifted on her bed. It felt like the floor was moving, like she was back on a ship. She blinked and rubbed her eyes, disoriented by her surroundings. If the floor moved, she should be seeing timber walls and a porthole, not a delicately carved chamber and glowing fungi.

Beside her, Belrose gripped her shoulder tightly. He had a grim countenance.

Rengu! Seanna finally shook her confusion. *I'm in the Minwood tree.* The floor continued to shift, the entire tree groaning as it moved from side to side. High winds buffeted the trunk, blowing it this way and that.

"What's happening?" With Belrose's help, Seanna eased to her feet, which threatened to slide out from under her. She held tightly to Belrose's arm.

"Aremo's mages," he said. "They're trying to bring the tree down."

The wind howled as it beat against the swaying tree. Seanna and Belrose slipped and slid to the door.

"Where's Portia? Where's my child?" Seanna said, fear digging into her belly. Was Landin afraid? Did he know what has happening?

"Everyone's trying to get out before the tree falls," Belrose said. "I haven't seen her in the chaos."

Seanna's fright echoed in his face. They clung to each other as they started down the spiraling steps built into the tree's inner trunk. All around them, elves dashed haphazardly, some shouting, others tight-lipped in stoic determination. The lifts couldn't be used, the platforms swinging wildly with the tree's creaking movement.

"Seanna! Belrose!" Ropaz waved at them from one level below. He clutched a railing, his knuckles white with the effort. Belrose and Seanna made their tentative way down to him, grabbing at the railing whenever a particularly hard gust blew into the tree.

They made it to Ropaz's platform just as a scream sounded in the tree. An elf tumbled from the stairs above them, flailing his arms as he toppled through empty space. Seanna cringed away, unable to watch his descent.

"We have to leave," Belrose said, his eyes on the space where the elf had plummeted. "If this tree falls, none of us will be safe."

The tree listed and swayed, groaning with a thunderous roar. Elves all around them wailed and moaned, and as the tree's terrible lurches grew larger, more and more people dropped to their deaths. Seanna held tightly to Belrose and the railing, her fingers sore with the effort. Behind her, Ropaz kept one hand on her shoulder as if assuring himself that she was still upright. Together, they made their careful way down the endless stairs. Seanna couldn't tell in the dark and chaos how far they still had to go.

And, with every step, worry gnawed at her for her son and Portia's safety. Had Portia taken Landin for a walk to soothe him? Had she escaped? Or did her corpse litter the ground with the others, blank eyes staring up?

Get them out alive, Seanna prayed to whatever gods could hear her. *If you don't spare me, spare them.* She didn't allow herself to dwell on Aremo – who no doubt waited for them in the forest below – didn't allow herself to wonder how he had known to attack Rengu.

Belrose's hand became her lifeline. She focused all her

energy on maintaining her grip on it. If she didn't let go, all would be well. As long as she still held him tightly, she would survive. It was the only thought that let her put one foot in front of the other.

"Keep going," Belrose's calm voice encouraged her. "That's it, keep going."

She nodded, unable to trust her own voice. *I'm safe, I'm with Ropaz and Belrose. They survived the siege with me, we'll survive this, too.*

An enormous creak grated through the air, making Seanna's ears ring. The entire tree listed dangerously to one side, and didn't sway back. It paused a moment, hanging in limbo, then began to fall.

Seanna's feet swept out from under her, the stairs tilting until she could no longer maintain her grip on them. Empty space yawned under her. Ropaz yelled and grabbed at her with one hand while he desperately scrabbled at the railing.

Belrose was not so lucky. He fell into the air, his arms twisting. He met Seanna's eyes, and she saw desperation as he plummeted away from them.

"Belrose!" Seanna screamed. She reached for him, but her fingers brushed only empty air.

Belrose raised a hand and sent a wave of magic at her and Ropaz. It enveloped them, cocooning them as Ropaz lost his grip. The expected mad tumble did not come. Magic held them safely in place, secure against the trunk, as the tree slammed into the other trees below it, crushing them beneath its mighty weight.

Before his limp body was dashed against the far side, Seanna could have sworn Belrose smiled.

"Belrose," Seanna sobbed. She clung to Ropaz, her arms around his neck, her wet face staining his robes. He held her as the tree finally stilled around them, settling into its final resting place on the forest floor. The magic holding them gently disconnected from the wall and floated them down, setting them on the newly-made ground.

Seanna shook, not trusting her body's signals that

everything had ended. She clung to Ropaz, her only lifeline, and murmured, "Belrose, Belrose," his name a prayer on her lips.

Slowly, she regained consciousness of the world around her. Elves wailed and moaned, their bodies bruised and battered, some with their limbs broken, others unmoving forever. The stairs and walls all were sideways, creating a strange impression of not-rightness that made Seanna's head spin. Still holding tightly to Ropaz, she looked around at the devastation.

"My gods," was all she managed to utter.

Her eyes landed on Belrose's crumpled body. At last she tore herself away from Ropaz as she dashed to her wizard's side. She rolled him to his back and shook his shoulder, not believing that her stalwart friend was gone. He had saved her from Henrik's assassin, he had found the caverns that allowed their escape from Con Salur, he had been by her side when they fought through cold and starvation to this safe haven. He couldn't be dead. He just couldn't.

"Ropaz! You have to do something," Seanna shouted at him. "Please, bring him back. Heal him!"

Ropaz tried to gently pull her away, murmuring a truth that she refused to hear.

"You saved others, you can save him, too," she said, desperation making her cling to Belrose all the more. "He's not gone. I won't allow him to die."

"Shh, Seanna," Ropaz murmured. He finally managed to extricate her fingers from Belrose's clothes and pull her up. She resisted, but Ropaz didn't let her go. "There's nothing I can do, Seanna."

"Yes you can, I've seen you–"

"Seanna." He spoke firmly, like a parent to a child. She pulled her gaze away from Belrose. Ropaz took her chin in both hands, forcing her to look into his eyes, and said, "He's dead, Seanna. I cannot revive him."

"No." Her heart couldn't take any more loss. "You're wrong, you can–"

"Seanna," he said again, using her name like a prod, forcing her back to reality. "We have to get out of here in case the trunk crumbles. We have to find Landin and my sister. They could still be alive. Your son needs you to be strong, Seanna."

At the mention of her child, her mind finally allowed that awful truth inside her. *Belrose is dead. Landin needs me.* Seanna nodded, her tears splashing onto her feet.

"Come on, there must be a balcony or window nearby that we can use to get out." With one arm around her, Ropaz led Seanna away from the wizard's corpse.

After a little bit of hunting, he found an archway that allowed them to escapes the confines of the tree, and they stepped out into the ruins of the forest. Elves gathered in small groups, huddling together as if closeness would ward off their terror.

Ropaz guided Seanna to a small patch of ground away from the collapsed Minwood tree. There he deposited her. She sank to the loam, her legs unable to support her any longer, and lay her head against a tree trunk.

Her whole body trembled, her stomach churning even though she hadn't eaten in candles. Her hands shook too much to do anything with them. Her breaths came short, rattling through her throat. She realized that Ropaz was talking to her, and shook her muddled head to dislodge the buzzing that had built up inside it.

"What?" she asked.

"Someone has to find Landin and Portia," Ropaz said again, speaking slowly, as if she were dull. He continued, "I'm going to see if I can organize the elves into search parties, especially any Rangers that survived. We need to determine the dead and the wounded, and find healers to treat those still alive. Can I leave you here? Will you be alright?"

It took a moment for his words to sink in. She wanted to object, to force him to stay with her, but he was right. Someone had to take charge, and she was in no condition to do so. She said, "Yes. Do what you can. The moment you find Landin..."

"I'll bring him straight to you. I swear it." Ropaz brushed her hair from her cheek in a brotherly gesture, then straightened and set off toward the nearest group of elves. Seanna watched him passively. Her whole body felt as if it had been smoothed under a rolling pin, every muscle aching and every nerve alight. Tears rolled down her cheeks, and she hugged herself.

She desperately wished that Belrose were there to help her. He'd know what to do.

✳

Dawn light trickled through the forest canopy, casting shadows on Seanna's face. She opened her eyes and realized that she must have fallen asleep sometime after Ropaz had left her. Her body objected when she tried to sit up, and she fought past the aches and tightness until she had straightened enough to look around.

The fallen Minwood appeared even worse in the light. Parts of the trunk had caved in, and the silver bark was stark against the darker trees around it. Even the sides of the fallen Minwood were as tall as its still-standing neighbors. Seanna shivered. She wondered vaguely whether Belrose's body had been moved, or if it still lay there, alone in the dark, limbs akimbo and eyes open.

As she moved, an elf came into sight. She let out a relieved breath when she recognized him.

"Captain Tzuriel," she said. "You survived."

He made a series of gestures, then helped her to her feet. Seanna swayed a moment before finding her balance. She peered around; there wasn't another elf in sight.

"Where is everyone?" she asked.

The captain pointed. They threaded through the forest, around fallen trees and over torn branches. Occasionally, Seanna glimpsed a party of elves retrieving limp shapes from within the Minwood.

It didn't take long to arrive at the base of the tree, where the mighty roots had ripped from the ground and stood high in the sky. Many of them were gnarled and torn asunder, evidence of the wind's great power in upheaving the mightiest tree in D'Ehsen. The sight made Seanna's throat tight. *Aremo did all this,*

147

and for what? For revenge? To make a point?

Fury fueled her steps now. She didn't care that she had no army and no crown. She would not allow that elf to frighten her.

A circle of firelight and rumble of angry voices led her to a small copse of unaffected trees. When she stepped into the copse, she stopped short, taking in the scene before her:

Voclain Etrila lay on the ground, blood coating his head, his eyes closed. Ropaz kneeled beside him, tending to his wound as a Lofalin elf stood over both of them, spear leveled at Ropaz. Other Lofalins circled around, each armed, their eyes on their leader.

Aremo stood a few steps away, watching the other prince with a hateful gleam in his eye. And in his arms...

Seanna nearly screamed. Aremo held her baby, her only child, in his terrible grasping hands. It took every ounce of control inside her not to rush at him and tear Landin away. Her clenched fists shook at her sides.

The Lofalin guards noticed her and Tzuriel and pointed their spears at the intruders. Seanna raised her head high and stepped forward until the spearpoints nearly touched her chest. She called out, "Aremo Teru!"

The elf prince's smile widened as he turned his dark eyes on her. She tried not to shiver under that black gaze, but she couldn't help but dart a look at her child. Disgust roiled in her at seeing her child in the arms of her enemy.

"Ah, Seanna," Aremo said, her name hissing from between his teeth. "Ropaz here said he didn't know whether you survived. A simple misremembering, I'm sure."

The Lofalin guards raised their spears, and Seanna stepped into the circle, feeling as if she had just walked into a trap. Ropaz gave her a quick glance, then returned to his work, his bloodied hands glowing with healing magic.

"Give me my child," Seanna said, not caring for preamble.

"After I went to such lengths to get him?" Aremo purred. "It was not easy for my men to infiltrate the tree and grab him from your nursemaid. She put up quite a fight from what I heard."

Seanna dared a glance at Ropaz. He didn't meet her eye,

and her heart twisted in her chest. *Please, gods, not Portia, too.*

Aremo continued, "She eventually gave in when she realized how horribly outnumbered she was."

"Where is she now?" Seanna asked.

The elf shrugged. "Alive."

Seanna sent up another quick prayer, then said, "How did you know I was here?"

"Isn't it obvious?" Aremo tickled Landin's chin, and Seanna resisted the urge to grab a spear from a guard and throw it at him. The elf said, "A little bird told me."

It was then that Seanna noticed Edlyn behind Aremo. The woman trembled like a leaf. Aremo paid her no attention and continued, "She recognized you and came immediately to tell me. Such a good little pet, isn't she?"

Rage clouded Seanna's heart as she glared at the elf woman. She gritted out, "Indeed."

Edlyn gave a tiny shake of her head, her large eyes wet with tears. "I thought maybe..."

"Hush," Aremo whispered. He didn't even glance at his paramour. "She still disobeyed me in coming here, but we'll deal with that later, won't we? Now, Seanna. To business."

Seanna forced herself to look back at Aremo, fearing that she would break if she focused on the bundle in his arms. "What do you want?"

Aremo smiled. "I want Rengu. As soon as your little priest revives Voclain, the prince will cede control of the forest to me, and you will be taken to Con Salur to be hanged." Aremo shifted and waved a hand at Seanna. "Now do be a good girl and allow my men to bind your hands."

Seanna quickly stepped forward, and Tzuriel came between her and the Lofalin guard. She said, "I will not be taken prisoner today. What harm can I do to you, Aremo? I'm a woman bereft of kingdom and crown."

His dark eyes glittered. "I think we both know that you're still dangerous."

Any further words were interrupted by a dry cough from Voclain. The elderly prince slowly sat up with Ropaz's help, blinking blearily at the scene before him. He said slowly, "Aremo...why are you here? What happened?"

Ropaz murmured in the prince's ear, and Voclain's eyes widened. "My daughter...my people...how many are safe? Where are they?"

"In due time, Voclain," Aremo said. "Did you like that little display? The mages of Lofaliri are experts in elemental magic."

"You vile–" A coughing fit interrupted Voclain's curse. Ropaz put a hand to the elf's chest.

"He needs to rest," Ropaz said. "It's a miracle he survived at all."

Aremo ignored him. He crouched in front of Voclain and shifted Landin again. He said, "I am not unreasonable, Voclain. Send your daughter to Con Salur with me. Upon the consummation of our marriage, you will step aside and let her take control of the forest. If you refuse, well...wind will only be the start of your woes."

Seanna bit her tongue to keep from interfering. She didn't know how to wrest Landin back from the crazed elf prince, nor did she have an easy resolution to Voclain's plight.

Though covered in blood and dirt, his hair tangled, bags under his eyes, Ropaz stood tall, exuding a calming presence. He and Tzuriel exchanged a tiny nod. Ropaz said softly, "You forget why Rengu will not easily fall. Look up."

Aremo tilted his head. Scores of elves perched among the branches, each with an arrow nocked, ready to draw back and release on command. The Lofalin guards moved restlessly, assessing this new danger.

"The Rangers have defended these woods for centuries," Ropaz continued. "If you threaten their prince, they will strike you down."

Aremo stepped away from Voclain. Seanna could almost see his mind working, unraveling this new twist.

Then he laughed. It was a high, strange sound, like a murder of crows circling over their heads, waiting for them to drop dead. Aremo held up the baby, his eyes wild. "You would dare shoot me while I hold your king? What if an arrow goes astray? What if I *happen* to slip and let him fall? No, you wouldn't risk it. You're bluffing."

"The queen would still live," Ropaz said. Seanna trembled. *He wouldn't let anything happen to Landin...would he?*

Voclain finally managed to make it to his feet. Though he quivered under the weight of his own body, he stood as straight as he could. He said, "Give the child back to his mother, Aremo, and I will send my daughter with you. I will cede Rengu to you without a fight."

Aremo's gaze darted between them all, and he licked his lips. Seanna couldn't tell what was going on in that mad mind of his. Would he give in so easily? Would he try to call Ropaz's bluff? Did his spite for her outweigh his desire to own all the lands of D'Ehsen?

Her heart went out to Voclain, too. He had just sacrificed his daughter and country in order to bargain for Landin. She tried to catch the old prince's eye, but he was entirely focused on Aremo. She finally allowed herself to look again at Landin.

Her child fussed, his little face red and his fists waving. Every time Aremo adjusted his grip on the baby, she wanted to tear out his throat and grab her child back from him. Every nerve in her spiked with fury, and it was all she could do to keep from screaming at the smug elf.

"No," Aremo drawled at last. "A king in my arms is worth more than a wife. I will take Rengu with fire and force."

"No!" Seanna screamed. She lunged at Aremo, but Tzuriel grabbed her arms. She twisted and fought, desperate to reach her child. "He's mine! How dare you touch what's mine?"

"Temper, temper. Don't new mothers enjoy when others fawn over their babe?" Aremo's eyes danced at her anger.

"Give him back to me!" Seanna shouted. She freed one arm from Tzuriel, but Ropaz rushed to her and took it. She screamed at them, "Let go of me!"

"Come now, Seanna. You'll be with your child soon if you just surrender," Aremo said. "Be good and–"

"Now!" shouted Ropaz.

The archers in the trees focused their aim on the Lofalins

that surrounded Seanna. Their arrows loosed, and the way out of the copse was clear. But Seanna didn't care that she could escape. She kicked and screamed, fighting against Ropaz and Tzuriel as they tried to drag her away.

Aremo lifted a dagger and plunged it into Voclain's chest, then wiped the blood on the baby's blanket. He shouted at his soldiers, ordering them to advance.

Arrows flew down, blocking the Lofalins. More elves came to assist in pulling Seanna away. They lifted her legs, carrying her from the copse. Seanna twisted and shouted, trying to glimpse her child.

"Landin!" Her screams turned into ugly sobs as the group hurried her off. She hung limply in their arms. "He has Landin. That monster has my son."

"I know," Ropaz said. "I know."

"Let me go back!" Seanna pleaded. "Let me get my son back."

"He'll kill all of us," Ropaz said. "We need you to survive, Seanna. We need a queen."

"I don't want to be the queen. I just want my son," Seanna said.

She was carried deeper into the forest, farther away from the fallen tree and her only child. If her fury and grief could take form, it would be a fire that would burn down everyone who stood in her way. She would raze the forest if it meant she could have her child back.

When the elves eventually put her down, Seanna immediately tried to run back. Multiple pairs of hands held her firm, and she glared at Ropaz. "Let me go."

"Seanna," he said, gripping her shoulders. "I understand. I do. He has my sister, too. He has Portia. Do you understand? You aren't the only one grieving. But right now we must be strong. Voclain is dead, Rengu is lost. We must retreat and regroup."

Seanna ignored him. Her legs trembled, her arms shaking from so much effort. Her tears dripped to the loam, her heart shredded.

"He has Landin," she whispered.

"I know," Ropaz repeated. "And if we want to get him back, we must find a new haven. Come on, Seanna. You must be strong. For all of us."

"There's nowhere left to go," Seanna whispered. "We're all doomed."

Ropaz shook his head. "That's not true. We will find somewhere safe. We must."

But Seanna didn't want to find somewhere safe. She wanted to be with her son. *I should never have neglected him. I should never have put my duty above all. Now I've lost both the kingdom and my son.* Her chin quivered, and sobs broke from her chest. Her breath heaved into wails, and the elves finally released her. Seanna collapsed to the forest floor, her nails digging into her arms.

Ropaz stood back, allowing her to weep. When her energy was spent, Seanna coughed and gagged, her heaving making her want to vomit. She scrubbed at her face. Ropaz kneeled beside her.

Seanna looked up at him. "Where do we go?"

"I don't know," he said, "but we'll find somewhere. And we'll rescue Landin and Portia. We'll bring them home."

No more did Seanna wish to liberate her country from Aremo. That no longer mattered. She would tear him limb from limb for taking Landin from her. She would burn him and throw him from the red cliffs.

But her heart could not be tender if she wished to bring her son home. It would be walled, invulnerable against all attacks. The mother would have to be set aside until she held Landin once more. Only the unflappable queen could remain.

Seanna stood up and straightened her shoulders. "We go north."

"North? Why?" Ropaz stared at her like she had lost her mind.

"We have no allies left. But we will take D'Clet and make it our stronghold." The plan formed in Seanna's mind as she spoke. "We are done running."

CHAPTER TWENTY-ONE
Mavian

The shackles chafed Mavian's wrists and ankles, pulling at his limbs, making his shoulders slump. He straightened, though his muscles strained and complained at the effort. His feet ached from the long walk back to D'Clet, and his belly rumbled with hunger. The Song of Death sounded steadily, day and night, unescapable and terrible, a quiet music that filled his every waking moment.

I am going to die. Mavian knew it in his bones. He had put his faith in Darian and Jagger, and they had fed him to the wolves. Had that been their plan all along? And he so desperate that he fell for it?

I hope Merick and Ekkar are safe.

The keep loomed over him, the ravine plunging below its base. People on the bridge stopped to stare at him, and whispers followed his path: "That's Mavian Strilu," or "That's what comes from using dark magic."

Mavian focused forward. They were right, of course. He did deserve all of this. He had used dark magic, and look where it got him. No one would mourn him, and his body would be cast into a dark pit and forgotten by all save the maggots.

Ahead of him, the three lords laughed heartily. Ravenhill guffawed and slapped Whitecave between the shoulders, Roseway took a swig from the flagon passed between them. They paid no heed to the rustics that darted from their path.

They entered the courtyard, and Chadron waited on the

steps. He stood as proud as ever, a dark blue cloak thrown over his shoulder and the hook at the end of his arm flashing in the sun. His smile did not touch his eyes.

"My lords," Chadron said. "I had not expected you."

Ravenhill staggered from his horse and made a small bow. "We bring you a gift, Sir Chadron. An offering of our loyalty."

He beckoned, and one of his soldiers detached Mavian's chain. The soldier pulled him forward, and Mavian went without resistance. He stumbled a little. Pure glee lit Chadron's expression.

"What a pretty sight," Chadron said. "Where did you find this scum? Hiding in some mausoleum somewhere?"

"He came to us," Ravenhill said with a broad grin. "He wanted us to help him overthrow you."

Though the lord spoke with arrogance, Mavian caught the look sent up at Chadron. Ravenhill held no love for the knight, and Chadron clearly did not trust him, either. Belatedly, he wondered if he should have sat back and allowed them to kill each other off. *Ravenhill is nothing if not pragmatic. He would only have struck at Chadron if he were completely assured of his success. I couldn't have afforded to wait for him to make a move.*

Chadron circled Mavian slowly, smugness oozing from every step. "You've done well, my lords. Go and rest; tonight we shall feast to celebrate the enemy's capture."

"What'll be done with him?" Ravenhill asked. His eye glinted with malice.

"We need entertainment, don't we?" Chadron answered. "His execution will be the height of the evening."

The Song of Death grew louder yet.

✳

All around him, jollity prevailed. Lords and knights feasted together, mead and wine sloshing from their cups and scraps falling to the floor for the dogs. Women leaned on the men's arms or splayed in their laps. Musicians played from the corner, the drum keeping a merry rhythm while the flute and viol danced their way through complicated melodies. It was a feast of raw pleasure, with none of the elegance of Druam's palace nor the stoic severity that Rask preferred.

And Mavian sat in the middle of it all, staring at nothing. They had tied him to a throne, a mockery of the heights to which he had once aspired. His skin was wet from the food and drink tossed at him, his feet scraped by the tongues of passing dogs. He was stripped of his clothes, leaving only a loincloth to lend him a false sense of modesty. He shivered despite the blazing fire and tried not to count the minutes as they slowly passed by, waiting for the moment of his own execution.

How would it be done? They could hang a rope from the beams above and hoist him over the assembly, the most gruesome chandelier imaginable. They could behead him, letting his blood spill across the floor. Yet somehow, Mavian thought that Chadron would not be so traditional in his methods. The knight might open up Mavian's chest and draw out his organs, leaving him to scream as the dogs fought over his still-beating heart.

No, don't dwell on it. Mavian forced away his imagined demise, yet the Song of Death continued its awful rendition in his head. It had grown unbearable, making his ears ring and his jaw twitch with its force. Mavian would almost welcome his end if it meant the Song would go away.

A shape filled his vision, and Mavian raised his tired eyes. Chadron stood over him, stripped to only his shirt and breeches. The knight had a manic gleam in his eye and held his sharpened hook high. The hall quietened, every eye on the spectacle before them.

"No one's here to save you now," Chadron murmured. "No wight, no prowlers, no one. No magic to call upon. At the end, you're only a worm. A weak, pathetic worm who should never have ventured above his domain."

Mavian licked his lips. "At least I dreamed of more than pretty women and jousts."

The hook sliced Mavian before he could react. It cut deep into his cheek, sending ruby droplets flying. He gasped at the sudden pain. Chadron grinned and withdrew, his arm shaking.

"You're nothing!" Chadron cried. He cut again, this time digging into Mavian's left shoulder.

Mavian hissed between his teeth, pushing his head back against the velvet cushion. He tried not to look at his own blood dripping from the steel point. The Song of Death drowned out all else, bashing against his skull, rushing through his head. He could no longer hear Chadron's words, though he felt the hook's every bite. He cried out, and his own voice was lost in the midst of the Song.

Chadron struck again and again, cutting into Mavian's flesh, carving his chest and arms and face. Mavian screamed and sobbed, blood mixing with tears in his lap. He begged for mercy though he knew he would receive none.

In the throes of his pain, Mavian reached into the Song of Death. Maybe he could end it himself, stop the torture early and be done with it. Darian's words echoed in the melody: *Focus on the one you know the best.*

A thread of music gleamed suddenly, bursting in front of his eyes like a sunbeam through the clouds. Mavian nearly choked, amazed at what he saw.

The dam had burst. More and more threads of the Song of Death appeared before his eyes, twisting and curving. They were dark around Chadron, connecting the two of them in a mortal dance. Yet it was not this connection that Mavian latched onto. A melody twisted away into Autorus's domain, the melody that had infused his white gem. He reached for it, and it curled into him, an old friend finally reunited.

Now that Mavian held it, he didn't know what to do with it. Darian had hummed the music into magic, but Mavian had no sense of melody or pitch. He could not produce it.

His gaze slid to the musicians.

"Wait!" Mavian cried. "Please, stop a moment. In mercy's name, please."

As if it knew what he intended, the Song of Death calmed for a moment. His ears echoed with the music, but he could finally hear again. Chadron paused, his hook still held aloft for the next strike. "What is it, worm?"

"A last request," Mavian said. He thought quickly, reaching for a melody that captured the feeling that he held in the Song. "Would you grant it?"

Chadron scoffed, "Why would I do such a thing?"

"A final courtesy," Mavian said. "A demonstration of your kindness to your vassals. Please."

For a long moment, the knight contemplated this request. At last, he gave a curt nod. "I was getting bored of you anyway. What's your wish, that I may fulfill it and kill you?"

"Have your musicians play the Lament of the Forsworn," Mavian said. Chadron clicked his fingers, and the musicians struck up the music.

It was an old song, written centuries before during a long-forgotten war. Its minor chords echoed the melancholy of the Song of Death, and its lyrics moved between hope and despair. Mavian listened to it as long as he dared, still cupping that thread of Song.

I cannot sing, but perhaps this will be enough. Not really knowing what he was doing, Mavian willed the thread into the shape of the Lament, urging it to take form. At first it resisted, and worry leached into his marrow.

As Mavian listened to the musicians play, he unconsciously began to hum in time with their melody. The Song wove itself into the Lament, shaped by Mavian's intention and made into magic by his humming.

At first, nothing happened. But then, slowly, Mavian called upon the magic he had used so often before. The Song grew, eager to do his bidding. The floor began to shake, first in tiny trembles, then greater and greater. The chandeliers danced and clinked, the mugs on the tables bouncing to the floor.

Cries of alarm filled the room. Chadron stepped back, his eyes wide. He raised his hook.

Mavian's hum grew louder, and though the musicians stopped playing, he had bonded with the Song. He knew what he must do. With his old confidence, he reached out into Autorus's domain and pulled forth a Dread Portal.

The floors shook, sending people crashing to their knees. Chadron stumbled, his arm still raised to strike. The smell of rot and decay filled the room, and even the dogs gagged. Pressure built, grinding on ears and tightening chests.

The Dread Portal burst into existence in front of Mavian, twice as tall as a man and thrice as wide, its black-and-purple essence pulling at him. He kept humming, beyond the point of caring if he was on pitch or accurate. It was his music, and he had called forth this abomination.

From within the void crept the black tentacles. Mavian directed the Song, and the tentacles moved in accordance. They wrapped around Chadron.

The knight twisted. He slashed at the horrors, but they would not release him. The tentacles drew him back into the void, and in his final breath, Chadron met Mavian's eye. The knight did not scream, did not resist.

Chadron vanished into the darkness. Mavian's lips hurt from humming, but he continued his Song. Ravenhill and his friends tried to shove their way to the door. At Mavian's command, the black tentacles thrust aside all obstacles and grasped at the three lords. Like Chadron, they disappeared into Autorus's domain, their cries silenced by the overwhelming noise.

At last, Mavian released the Song. The Dread Portal snapped out, leaving traces of its awful aura behind. His ears popped and bled, his mouth still buzzing with power. Everyone else had fled.

His arms and legs were still bound to the throne. Mavian slumped over, exhaustion filling him. It had always been tiring to summon the Dread Portals, but doing so without the aid of the gem had completely drained him. He doubted he would be able to walk even if he could escape his bonds. His eyes fluttered, his heart beating weakly.

He had no strength to savor his victory.

✳

Mavian must have slept, for he opened his eyes to guttering candles and a dark room. Not even the dogs had returned to clean up the scraps; every bite of food and cup of wine had been left where it fell. He stretched, then paused. His limbs had been freed, the ropes broken on the floor.

His legs shaking, he stood and took his bearings. With tentative steps, he made his way to the door. The corridor outside was empty, though light flickered beneath a door on the far end. Mavian stumbled to it, holding himself up by clinging to the wall.

When he finally reached the door, he found it unlocked. He thrust it open, expecting a blade to come rushing at him. Instead, he found a comfortable room with a chair in front of a blazing fire, complete with a side table that held a plate of food and decanter of wine. Mavian's stomach grumbled, and he dove into the food. He didn't bother to sit in the chair. He curled up in front of the fire, warming his cold limbs and eating until he felt he would be sick.

Mavian had nearly dozed off again when the door opened once more. Merick and Ekkar were there, the prowler bounding in to sniff Mavian. Merick inclined his head, then took up a station on the far wall. Behind him came two more men.

Mavian's gut churned at the sight of Darian and Jagger. He watched them warily, unsure if they were there to help or harm him. Jagger stayed on the threshold, but Darian came closer. The blind man seated himself on the rug across from Mavian and laid his cane over his knees.

His throat raw from first screaming and then the Song, Mavian managed a painful rasp, "Where were you?"

Darian ran a hand over the cane's smooth wood. "You needed to find the Song yourself."

"I almost died."

"It would have been a shame." There was no remorse in Darian's voice. "It will not be long before Cara finds the Ossuary. We are on the brink of devastation. There was no time to coddle you. I saw an opportunity to force you into joining with the Song, so I took it."

Mavian glared at him. "You should have told me something. Anything. Given me a chance to prepare."

"Then the fear of failure would have overwhelmed you. It had to be done this way." Darian gestured at the wounds that traced Mavian's body, all of them sore and some still bleeding. "Let's take care of those, hmm?"

Mavian reluctantly allowed Darian to clean and dress the many cuts that Chadron had inflicted on him. He flinched at the stinging poultices, especially the ones on his face, and ruefully examined all the bandages that crisscrossed his body. *I will always have these scars. I'll be even more a pariah among the people.*

"There," Darian said as he finished up. His hands had been gentle, and Mavian marveled at how well he had been able to complete the work without sight. He sat back. "Now, we should discuss the ramifications of Chadron's death. What will you do with your new city?"

Mavian reeled a little. He had honestly forgotten the political consequences of his Song. In the throes of his panic and pain, he had only thought of ending his own suffering. He thought on it for a moment. "We need to make sure the guards are on our side, be it through fear or persuasion. Rask took most of his council with him, but those remaining will not be pleased. There's a lot of work ahead of us, I fear."

Darian gave a small smile. "Fortunately for us, there is a scholar in the keep willing to help."

"Ronan?" Mavian's head snapped up. "He's still around?"

"And he saved many priceless scrolls and manuscripts. But all that can wait until morning. You should rest."

Mavian leaned back against the granite stones next to the fireplace, relishing their warmth. He nodded, another yawn creeping up his throat. Even with a full belly and warm limbs, he was injured and sore and fatigued.

He allowed himself to be taken up to his old room, where Merick stood watch as he slept. In his dreams, he heard the Song of Death. No longer did it frighten him; he walked alongside it, taking solace from its steadiness. It had not claimed him that day, and that alone brought more than a little comfort.

CHAPTER TWENTY-TWO
Demarren

"Lot of people in the streets," Cadel commented. He and Sandu had come into town to restock their dwindling supplies. Even with Lintem's gifts of meat, they still needed salt, vegetables, and other sundry goods.

"The trials," Sandu said. His heart sank. He didn't know what to expect from the crowd. Would they side with Gwen, or try to kill her themselves?

And was there anything he could do about it?

For a brief moment, Sandu debated turning back to the forest and leaving Gwen to fend for herself. After all, she had powerful magic and he had none. Her only request of him was that he survive, and he could do that much better if he stayed away from the crowd.

Yet even as he thought it, Sandu knew that he couldn't just leave her. She had promised to help him, and he couldn't well expect her to keep this promise if he didn't assist her in return. His mind made up, he took Cadel's arm and followed the crowd.

The swell of people funneled them to an outdoor amphitheater. Sandu had to shove and push his way to the front, and even then he was nowhere near the center. Rows of seats, filled with the wealthy and influential, lay between him and the defendants.

Gwen sat with her head held high, seemingly unfazed by the procedures. Meanwhile, a pale-skinned Skal strutted about proclaiming Olfrick Kron's innocence.

The sun overhead burned into Sandu's skin. He sweated and shifted, only able to hear a few words from the proceedings below. Around him, the crowd grew restless. Hawkers moved about with kebabs and candied nuts, treating the trials as if they were sport. A few people debated quietly what they believed the verdict should be.

At long last, Olfrick Kron was declared guilty. Sandu let out a small sound of relief. Some of the crowd was furious, their brows furrowed and their arms crossed over their chests. Many, though, gave triumphant cries and hugged their neighbors.

"Not a popular man, was he?" Cadel commented.

As the marshal announced the next trial, the crowd quietened once more. Even the hawkers grew still, listening intently.

From below, Gwen's clear voice rose up: "There will be no trial."

Murmurs grew in waves. People looked at each other, confused. Sandu sought Cadel's arm and held it firmly. He could feel the tensions rising quickly, the storm that could break at any moment.

"We should go," Sandu said. But his feet remained rooted, his gaze fixed on the figures below.

As Gwen spoke, announcing her own guilt, the murmurs grew into cries of rage. Skal and Demar alike bayed for blood. Somewhere behind him, a fight broke out between two men.

Then Gwen pointed a finger at the stone throne, and it broke with a noise like a tree crashing into the ground. Dust was flung upward, coating Sandu's nose and throat. He and others around him all coughed, their eyes watering.

The people closest to the rim howled and surged forward. A few ran back, but most pressed inwards, crying for the witch's blood, for Olfrick's, for anyone's. The crowd pulled Sandu and Cadel to and fro, and they were helpless to resist it. Councillors and merchants tried to force their way out, but the bloodthirsty rustics slammed them with rocks and fists.

From inside the amphitheater, Gwen rose on a wave of air.

Her voice carried in a beautiful yet terrible Song, one that reached into the very fiber of Sandu's being. He let go of Cadel for a moment, distracted by the sight before him.

In the space of a few breaths, Sandu realized that Cadel was nowhere near him.

Da!" Sandu shouted. His voice was small in the melee.

He couldn't see his father. His throat clammed up in fear. Heat scoured his back, and he twisted as flames rose from a shop behind him. People poured around him, carrying him toward the violence. Sandu tried to pull back, tried to resist, but he couldn't.

Then his foot slipped. One moment, Sandu was upright, fighting against the flow of people. The next, he fell hard to the ground, his elbow smashing into the pavestones. He tried to catch his breath, but someone stepped on his stomach. Another boot found his leg. Sandu curled into a ball, trying to protect his head.

No one helped him. No one noticed him. The crowd, too enticed by the promise of blood, trampled him further into the ground.

Sandu prayed to every god he knew, the memory of his children held firmly in his mind. *Dream or Woods or some figment of truth, I will find you again.*

Then he was lost in darkness.

✳

The wave of Songs from the rioters crashed into Gwen, carrying anger and resentment, guilt and blame, hundreds of melodies building upon each other in a cacophonous tsunami. She maintained the Song holding her aloft and called out to Lintem, *Come to me! I need your help.*

Distantly, she heard his reply, *I'm coming.*

A spear whizzed past her head, and Gwen refocused on the turmoil below her. Men of status tried to flee, but could not get past the mass of rustics that rushed into the amphitheater. Soldiers gathered into cordons around their leaders, but rocks flew at them from all sides. One group of guards hefted their spears, aiming for Gwen.

With a Song, she sent a burst of wind at them, sending them flying back into the mass. Her keen eyes searched for Olfrick and found him lying prone underneath an onslaught of rustics. They beat him with their fists and feet, and his blood spilled onto the stone. She could hold no pity for him, though. If she did not leave soon, she would meet the same fate.

The crowd's Songs grew to bursting. Gwen attempted a calming melody, but it was too faint against the anger of so many. Some of the crowd fought with each other. One man got too close to a nervous soldier and found a spear in his side.

Rioters threw torches into the buildings around the amphitheater while looters forced their way inside and came back out carrying stolen goods. Gwen flew to the nearest fire. *If this spreads, the whole city could go up.* She Sang the fire down as heat scorched her face and arms.

All around her was chaos. Guards fought citizens who fought each other. The Songs thrummed with energy, threatening to catch her in their vortex. Her strength began to ebb, for maintaining the Song keeping her aloft while fighting the fires was too much.

Her skin turned grey with ashes. Her lungs coughed with the smoke, her voice growing hoarse. The ashes seeped into her throat, blocking her Song. Gwen coughed, trying to dislodge it, but nothing came up. Her eyes watered as she desperately tried to clear her mouth.

A rock thudded into Gwen's back. She cried out in pain, and her Song ended. She fell to the ground, only just saving herself from crumpling. With as much force as she could muster, she sent a blast of wind to push the rioters away from her. They stumbled and shouted, retreating from her.

"Help!" A man's voice called from the crowd. "Someone help us!"

Gwen scanned the crowd until she saw its source: an old man waving his arms. She pushed through until she reached him, and found that Sandu lay still on the ground.

He only had to survive. That's all.

The old man grasped at her arm. "Please, my son was trampled. I can't lose him again!"

Gwen coughed up ash and cleared her throat. She bent by Sandu and rolled him onto his back. His breath came slowly, slowly. He didn't have long.

Gwen choked out, "Lintem!"

The crowd screamed as Lintem rushed through it, finally there to help her. The nightcat crouched by her side. With the old man's help, Gwen lifted Sandu onto Lintem's back. Together, the trio tried to escape the crowd. It was hard to tell which way to go or where was safest. Openings were filled as soon as they were made, and fire spread from roof to roof.

Rain, Gwen thought. *We need rain!*

The skies were clear and blue, nary a cloud in sight. In the Songs of the Sky, Gwen detected a far-off cloud that carried water within its belly. She hummed to it, calling for it to come over the city. The effort made her dizzy; she had never tried to summon rain before.

"This way!" The old man pulled her through a gap in the crowd and into a blissfully empty alley. They all paused to gain their breath.

"My son," the man said. "Can you help him?"

"I can try," Gwen gritted out. She lay her hands on Sandu's chest, digging for his Song. It was faint, threaded with the Song of Death. *We could be too late.* She was so tired, her lungs screamed at her, her mind a bleary fog that tumbled every which way like a ship in a storm.

Overhead, grey clouds blocked the sun. The air grew cold and threatening.

Gwen took a deep breath and Sang.

✳

Sandu stood at the campfire. It was as he'd seen it twice before: a starless sky over a dark forest. A wagon with peeling paint just at the edge of the clearing. The campfire beckoning, cozy and warm, and beyond it...

"Hello Mumma," Sandu said. "Hello Nan."

His mother and grandmother lounged on logs on the other side of the fire, mugs of hot tea in their hands. Mumma sighed as he approached, and Nan picked up her switch threateningly.

"I told you to go and live a happy life," Nan said.

"I don't think it was ever happy," Sandu said. He gritted his teeth. *Did I really just say that to the ghost of my grandmother?*

"Dear son," Mumma said. She didn't move, but her eyes reached out to him. "I'm so sorry. I wanted you to be happy."

"It's not your fault," Sandu said quickly. "It's mine. I'm a coward, and I think I've run away one too many times."

"Don't be foolish," Mumma said. "You just didn't know where to go yet."

"I'm dying, Mumma," Sandu said. He thought he could feel his breath leaking from his lungs, the weight of a hundred people constricting his chest. "And Darian's not here to help me now. If I just sit with you, is that the end of it? Will I be dead and free?"

"Freedom is never what you think," came a male voice.

Slowly, Sandu turned.

A figure stood behind him, its form shrouded in darkness. Spots of light and color came like lightning in the mist, sporadic and mesmerizing.

Sandu wanted to ask the question, but didn't quite know how. "Are...are you...?"

"I am known by many names, but I am he who guides the dead to their rest. I have built shelters in Death, places for the dead to stay before they move on to Lyael, and punishments for those souls who have hurt others in life. I am Autorus," the being said. Its voice echoed with ancient knowledge, its tone slow and methodical. Somehow, it sounded familiar, like an old friend come to meet Sandu after many years apart.

Sandu gave a small bow, unsure of how else he should greet the Cythra of Death. He said, "Thank you for caring for my family."

The being had no smile, no eyes or mouth to convey feeling,

but Sandu thought he sensed a warmness coming from the Cythra. Autorus said, "It has been my honor."

Sandu nodded. He said without thinking, "Why do I keep going back? Why not just keep me here?"

"Because you have always been on the cusp, not truly dead. I had no claim on you unless you sat by the fire." Autorus tilted his head.

Sandu edged closer to the fire. "It would be easier to stay. It's warm, at least."

"But you'd never see your children grow up."

"They have Frederick." The words broke Sandu's heart, but he had to speak them. *My children don't truly need me.*

"And no mother. Wouldn't they benefit from two loving fathers instead of just one?"

Sandu shrugged. He was so tired, and the logs so inviting. "Why do I keep coming back?"

"You resisted the first time. That was when I knew that you might be someone special. The second time, I dared to hope, and again you resisted. Now, Sandu, you have the choice a third time. Will you stay, or will you return to Life?"

"Why should I go back?" Sandu asked. "My life is misery and pain."

"Because you will have thrice defied Death. In a way of speaking, you will have thrice defied me. That is powerful indeed, and could give you the strength you need."

"Strength to do what?"

"What must be done." There were no hints in the shroud around Autorus.

Sandu sighed. Did he really expect a Cythra to give a straight answer? He appealed to Mumma and Nan's familiar wisdom. "What should I do?"

"As I've said before," Nan said primly. "Go back and don't return until you're grey like me."

"Da is still there, and the children," Mumma said. "You can make the world better for them."

The starless sky engulfed Sandu's vision. He stared into it, wondering if he'd be truly dead the next time he saw it. He had fought for so long to reach his children, he had found the sorceress and rescued his father. As he reflected on it, he realized that he wasn't quite done yet.

At last, he turned to Autorus.

"Take me back."

*

With Lintem guarding them, Gwen focused all her energy on Sandu. Her voice was a raw whisper as she Sang. With her hands pressed against his chest, she used Songs to soothe his injuries and breathe air into his lungs. But there was the darkness inside him, that part of his Song that spoke only of agony. She could do nothing to alter that Song, and it could kill him.

Cadel hovered over her, murmuring a prayer under his breath. She tuned him out and did her best to ignore the chaos not far from them. *Only Sandu matters now.*

The Songs flowed from her, knitting together his broken bones and mending his bruises. *I could not save my country, but perhaps I can save him.* Her own skin took on his suffering, becoming sore and pained. If she had more time, she could use Songs that would not harm her.

By the time she finished, her voice was barely audible. Sandu lay there, physically healthy but still in that place between Life and Death. Gwen sat back. She had no more Songs in her, even if she wished to use them. If the mob found her here, she would be helpless.

In that space of utter weakness, a Song curled around her. All other Songs grew silent, and Gwen held her breath, listening. Its melody hissed in her ears, dark and terrible. It spoke of corruption and the ending of all things.

The Song of Unmaking.

It filled her soul with a greasy feeling, as if she couldn't wipe away the sludge of such horror. Unmaking was not as simple as Death: it could take away one's memories or ambitions, it could steal time, it could even remove the Gaiar from a person, leaving them empty but still alive.

It could remove the power of the *sulpari*.

Gwen held her breath as the Song soaked into her bones, and when Unmaking ended, leaving its stain inside her, she finally released it. She sucked in a new breath of clean air.

At that moment, Sandu opened his eyes. Gwen stood back, still reeling from the Song that befouled her, and allowed Cadel to come beside his son. The old man gripped Sandu's hand. "You shouldn't worry me like that, son. I thought I'd lost you again."

Sandu gave him a wan grin. "Wouldn't dream of it, Da."

Then Sandu looked at Gwen. She breathed heavily, her shoulders slumping and her back rounded. She gave him a nod, which he returned. While the two men spoke softly, she asked Lintem, *How is the city?*

Loud, he answered. *Dangerous.*

We need to get them out, Gwen hummed. Even that small usage of Song drained her. How could she hope to escape the city without her magic?

Lintem growled low in his throat, and Gwen's head snapped up. A trio of soldiers stood at the alley's entrance, their spears lowered at her. The one in the middle swallowed and said, "Witch, you are pronounced guilty. We are allowed to kill you if you don't come peacefully."

Gwen snorted, then grimaced at the pain in her throat. She said as loudly as she could, "I'll be killed either way. I'm not going to make it easy for you."

The soldiers exchanged wary glances. None of them moved forward.

Lintem crouched in front of Gwen, his tail twitching. *Can I attack?*

She put a calming hand on his flank. *Not yet.* She said, "If you leave now, no one will know that you found me. Don't risk your lives for men who care nothing whether you live or die."

One of the soldiers backed away and fled. The other two trembled, but stood their ground.

"But you're a witch," the leader said. "You have to be killed." He did not sound certain of his words.

Lintem bent low, his haunches twitching. That was enough to scare off the remaining soldiers. They scrambled away, leaving Gwen feeling empty. *Did I unite my people? Or did I drive the wedge further?*

She didn't have the time to remain in Demarren and find out. She would never again be welcome in its streets, much less its court. *I can only hope that the people find common ground.*

Gwen said, "We have to leave the city. We'll have to travel across the country to the mountains and cross over into Dotschar. From there we find a safe haven until we know how close the *sulpari* is to the Ossuary."

Sandu swallowed, but nodded. "How do we get out?"

"The old-fashioned way. We run, hide, and run some more." Gwen didn't relish the prospect, but she doubted they had time for her to recover and use the Songs. "Can you move?" At Sandu's nod, she said, "Lintem will scout for us. Stay with me, and we just might make it out alive."

Just like the last time Gwen left Demarren, she departed in secrecy. She didn't hide in a grocer's cart, but slunk through the alleys and across the streets like a common criminal. Her heart ached as they drew further and further from the castle, knowing that this time, there was no hope of returning.

CHAPTER TWENTY-THREE
The Siege of Riverfen

Cara crossed her arms and glared at her mother. Sura sat with her arms bound around the tentpole behind her and gazed coolly back. Next to Cara, Rask and Talnor assessed their new prisoner. Rask walked slowly around Sura, his cane poking at her.

"So this is Cairn Steel-Eyes," Rask said. "I'm underwhelmed."

Talnor said, "Taking a hostage wasn't part of our agreement."

"I cut off the fleet's head," Cara said. "Without her, they'll flounder."

"We can't be sure of that," Rask said, coming back to stand in front of Sura. He put his cane under her chin and forced her head up. "This one is clever. She'll have lieutenants who'll enforce her orders. Tell me, Steel-Eyes, why did you wish to meet with the *sulpari*?"

Sura didn't answer. She met Rask's eyes without emotion, as relaxed as if she were at a dinner party. Rask looked over to Cara. "Well?"

"She's my mother," Cara spat. She didn't see a reason to lie; it wasn't her weakness, after all. "Maybe she thought I'd be more favorable to her."

"Heh." Rask let out a low chuckle. "The great Cairn Steel-Eyes, scourge of the king's navy, a mother? Pity she's not as invincible as she thought herself."

"So what do we do with her? She won't talk," Talnor said. "I say we kill her."

"And deprive ourselves of a bargaining chip? I think not," Rask said. "Keep her here under guard. Perhaps Druam will listen to reason when he knows that his only ally is under our control."

Talnor shook her head. "The fleet's still out there. It's dangerous as long as she still lives."

"Then get rid of the fleet." Rask's watery eyes turned to Cara. "That's why we brought this one along, isn't it? I think it time for her to demonstrate her power."

Cara nodded. Rask departed, and Talnor asked, "Are you ready?"

"Yes. But I can't destroy every ship; there's too many of them."

"We only need to send a message." Talnor took Cara's arm. "Remember, every power is augmented by being close to its source."

"Build a bonfire on the shore," Cara said. "I will start when it's at its height."

Talnor left, and Cara was alone with her mother. For the first time since her capture, Sura spoke, "Don't do this, Cara. You can still choose a better way."

Cara crouched down so that she and her mother were eye-to-eye. "Druam chose this path for me when he murdered Renna. I'm only seeing it through."

"What would your father think?" Sura asked. Desperation lit her face.

"I wouldn't know," Cara said. "Thanks to you, I'll never know him."

Before her mother could protest, Cara stood and left the tent.

Two candles later, Cara and Talnor stood by the seashore. The heat from the bonfire licked against their skin, blazing hot even at a distance. A *fampir* huddled behind them, drawn and pale from her prolonged imprisonment. The waters shone blue and clear in the sunlight, with rays of glistening gold in the waves. Black silhouettes showed Sura's fleet strung out over the waters like a row of soldiers. Cara surveyed them with apathy, then turned to her captive.

The *fampir* pleaded and struggled, but Cara held her down and drained her blood. It was so easy now, such a routine task. The beast rose in her, swollen with the life she stole. Cara dropped the body and licked her lips. Her whole being thrummed with power, and she wondered if this was how Laris felt after he had stolen energy from her. She smiled at the memory of his death.

The blood rushed into her belly, its power heating her veins and making her fingers tremble. It gave her a heady feeling, better than wine or love-making.

Cara stepped toward the fire. It reached for her, hungry. The beast echoed its ferocity, two chaotic forces desperate to be unleashed. The power in her heart glowed red within her, and she coaxed it from its hiding place. It poured into her hands, lighting her skin with an inner fire.

An instinct deep inside her urged her closer to the fire. Cara edged forward until the heat became unbearable. It wanted to scorch her skin, its hungry flames licking over the air in front of her.

Before she could doubt herself, Cara thrust her hands into the flames. She screamed in pain before the beast overwhelmed her, drawing the blood from her belly to protect her. Cara blinked past the tears in her eyes and focused on the distant ships.

She had no incantations nor chants to speak, no working or spell to cast. Only the power in her and the screeching fire around her. The beast roared to be released.

Burn. Heat and desire poured from her hands and ignited the energy in the bonfire. *Send the black fire over the sea. Ignite the fleet that defies us.* Wave after wave of energy coursed from her, turning the bonfire from orange to black. It roared, higher and higher, a column of dark fire that reached its smoky tendrils to the sky.

Belatedly, Cara wondered if this power would steal her own

life essence. She desperately tried to draw back, but the beast overthrew her. It reveled in the blood and power, delighted in the atrocity it caused.

Cara collapsed to her knees. The column of fire moved across the water in a tornado of flames. It was high and wide, encompassing the first ship it encountered. Screams carried over the water, and Cara smiled grimly.

Ship after ship fell to the fire. It grew as it consumed. Ships toward the end of the line lowered their sails and skimmed away, vanishing over the horizon as they escaped. Over half the ships that had patrolled the bay burned into ashes, their timbers crumbling into black dust that filled the sky.

As the column whirled itself into nothingness, its duty complete, the heat that had filled it slammed back into Cara. The beast roared within her as the pain of fire raced through her veins. Cara screamed again, every nerve feverishly hot. She shook and fell onto her side, convulsing.

Talnor raced up beside her, but her words were lost in the roar that filled Cara's ears. Someone dumped cool water over her, but it did nothing to dispel the fire that ravaged her body.

Cara couldn't hear her own cries. She opened her mouth, her eyes wide and desperate. Her own thoughts burned up, leaving nothing but the sensation of pain. Voices whispered in her head, strange voices that she'd never heard before. Grey shapes flitted at the edges of her vision, translucent and strange.

Talnor shouted something, but Cara couldn't respond. Her body jerked back and forth uncontrollably. Talnor bit into her own wrist, then gripped the back of Cara's head, forcing it still. Talnor held her bleeding arm up to Cara's mouth, forcing the blood onto her tongue.

It washed over Cara, cooling the fire that raged inside her. Cara sucked at the blood, her fear and desperation overriding her caution. Talnor cried out and tried to pull back, but now Cara held her fast. The *fampir's* sweet essence tamped down the fire inside, and Cara could not stop herself.

Strong hands pulled her away. Cara hissed and swiped, her talons drawing blood from the poor soldiers who held her. Two more men piled onto her. She struggled and growled, but as the fire faded away inside her, so too did the beast retreat to her belly.

Weakness filled her limbs where once flames had raged. Cara sagged against the soldiers, breathing heavily. Talnor stood over her, rubbing her wrist ruefully and shaking her head.

"Will you live?" Talnor asked at last, her words dripping with apathy.

"Will you?" Cara asked, making her words as mocking as possible. She wrenched her hands from the soldiers and gestured over the smoldering bay. "I've brought a plague of fire to my mother's fleet, and you're afraid of a little cut on your wrist?"

"You could've sucked the life out of me," Talnor spat.

"Don't tempt me," Cara returned. She finally straightened and examined her hands. She had expected them to be blistered and raw, but they were as whole and healthy as ever. *Blood is indeed powerful.*

"I need to rest," Cara said.

When she returned to her tent, she found a quivering guard waiting for her. She cast a condescending eye on him. "What is it?"

"It's your m-. I mean, Cairn Steel-Eyes, my lady. She's escaped." The soldier shivered under Cara's glare.

"How?" Cara demanded.

"She must have cut the ropes somehow, and she slit the guards' throats. I only found them when I came to relieve them." He flinched as she raised a hand. Cara rethought her ire and brushed her hand through her hair instead.

"Fine. Get out of my sight."

If she hadn't just unleashed the black fire, she may have had the energy to search out her mother. Instead, Cara collapsed into the bed. Those voices that she'd heard on the beach slithered into her head, and she shut them out as well as she could.

Am I going mad?

✳

Far across the bay, black smoke billowed into the sky. Druam stood at the window and watched, his heart sinking with the ships. Beside him, Sura Gellder leaned against the doorframe with her arms crossed, her face impassive as she watched her life's work crumbling into ash.

"Do you think any made it out?" she said quietly.

"I have my hopes," Druam replied. "Your captains are clever and your crews fast. At least a few will have escaped the inferno."

"Then I must meet them at the cove. If any made it out, that's where they'll go."

"I understand." Druam faced her. "You did what you could."

"I made a fool of myself," Sura said, throwing herself away from the wall and slumping into one of the chairs in front of his desk. "I thought I could help her see reason. But you were right. Damn you, you know her better than I do."

"We are all fools around those we love." Druam settled heavily in his chair. "Where will you go now?"

"Home to my city to repair and rebuild. Aremo knows where it is; I can only pray he leaves us be until we're ready."

Druam nodded and held out his hand. "I wish you the best of luck, Sura. May your sails find guiding winds."

Sura took his hand and shook it, her grip firm. She gave him a wry smile. "Try not to die, won't you?"

Then she departed, like smoke over the water, and Druam smiled sadly to himself. *I doubt I'll ever see her again.* He allowed himself a brief moment to contemplate their tumultuous relationship, then turned to the business at hand. Avallune required more energy to maintain the magic shield over the city, one district needed another supply of rations to hand out, and on and on.

Riverfen was a city with many needs, and though he was only one man, Druam set out to fulfill them all. Below, the lanterns were slowly lit, still shining even in the midst of the siege. *As long as they shine, we will hold hope.*

*

Red light filtered through Cara's eyelids. With tremendous effort, she cracked open her eyes. She blinked, disoriented by the lights and people around her. Blankets and blankets had been piled on her, and a fire burned in a brazier.

"You're awake," Talnor said. She stood over Cara, not a kind, nurturing figure, but a pragmatic one.

"Y-yes?" Cara's lips struggled to form the words.

"It's been a quinn."

Five entire days? Cara squinted at the light, which seemed so bright after the grey land of dreams. She coughed a little and tried to sit up in her sheets. A camp curate hovered behind Talnor.

"Did it work?" Cara mumbled.

"What's left of the fleet has sailed away," Talnor said. "Druam hasn't surrendered yet, but I can feel the fear in the air. It won't be long." She leaned down. "Rask has ordered you to do more as soon as you're able."

Nausea swelled in Cara, but she pushed it down. She nodded. "Bring me one of the prisoners. I'll recover faster."

The curate bustled forward and checked Cara over. He clucked and muttered, but didn't object when Cara sent him away. A few minutes later, a soldier arrived with a gaunt-cheeked man. The man stared blankly forward, clearly resigned. He didn't fight as Cara sank her teeth into him.

His blood greatly rejuvenated her. She felt warm again, and the beast stirred contentedly in her. She nodded to Talnor. "I should be able to do it now."

"Excellent. What preparations do you need us to make?"

After sending the soldier to collect the needed prisoners, Cara stepped out into the camp. Clouds scattered over the sky, and she set off across the fields. Talnor followed her, strangely quiet.

As Cara walked, she reached to the power that lurked near her stomach. This next plague would be far more subtle, yet more powerful in its own way. Yet would it harm her the same as the first had? Might she slip into dreams and never wake?

The beast uncoiled and spread through her, assuring her with its warmth. She would not let her own power defeat her.

A cool spring wind lent a bounce to her step, and Cara walked quickly. She crested a hill and looked out toward Riverfen. The once-glittering city sat quiet and still, as if ashamed by the filth which drifted aimlessly in its harbor.

Cara found an orchard with slender blossoming trees. Weeds and vines had grown up around the trees in the absence of caring hands. As instructed, soldiers waited there with two nervous prisoners: one *fampir* and one human.

Cara quickly killed the prisoners. The beast rose as the blood flowed into her belly, its heat washing over her. Her near-empty stomach churned, nausea rising with the amount of liquid swirling within it. Cara tamped it down. She stepped between two flowering trees and put her hands to their trunks.

Beneath her hands, she felt the tree's life, slow and unencumbered. The beast drew forth the power inside her, and she released it.

This time, it did not tear away from her. It flowed, steady and strong, into the trees. Their branches withered and dried, the flowers rotting on their stems. A harsh wind blew up around her, carrying the tendrils of death into the city.

Cara released more and more of her power. The orchard died around her, the rot of each tree flying into the determined wind. Brown specks filled the air, a thousand minuscule particles that soared up and away, whirling inexorably to Riverfen.

Though this use of power had not dragged at her, still Cara stumbled as she withdrew her hands from the trees. Dizziness overtook her, a headache pounding in her temples. She put a hand to her head and watched the last of the rot as it dwindled from sight.

Over the next few days, all the greenery within Riverfen would turn brown and rotting. Fruit and vegetables would mold, trees would grow pale and sickly, grass would wither. Even with rationed stores of food, the people would soon feel the constriction of empty bellies.

But as the rot carried on its dreadful mission, voices assailed Cara's mind. They wailed and whirled, high-pitched and unnerving. Grey shapes crowded the edges of her vision, pushing in on her. *The owners of the voices?* Cara swatted at them, her hands going straight through. She shut her eyes, blocking out the translucent images. Yet the voices still crowded in, a mob of fear and despair.

Cara fell to the ground, her mind overwhelmed with the cries that would not leave her. She opened her eyes to Talnor standing over her, but then blackness seeped in, and she knew no more.

✳

The fruit rotted in Druam's hands, its mold spreading more quickly than was natural. All around the small orchard, fruit fell diseased to the ground. In the neighboring garden, vegetables crumbled and stank. Even the trees and shrubs which did not bear food were turning grey and losing their leaves.

Druam gazed at the conservatory. The greenery that had lived within its glass walls loomed dark and foreboding. *I must see it for myself.*

The air inside the conservatory tasted of death. Trees which had grown tall enough to touch the roof were shriveled, their branches dry and barren of leaves. Grass wilted underfoot. The lovingly pruned bushes drooped, their leaves curling and spotted with black.

Druam wandered his treasure in a daze, touching the dying plants without comprehending. The roses that he had brought from Con Salur lost their petals, the mighty willow in Gwen's sanctuary tipped over with the weight of its dead branches. The animals of the conservatory whined and ran from him, their nostrils overwhelmed with the scent of decay.

What will the dragons eat?

When Druam came to the orchids, he fell to his knees, unable to bear the hurricane of grief that crashed over him. All the orchids he'd cultivated for Gwen's wedding dress, every last one, was unnaturally rotted, the stems bent with the weight of dark-spotted heads.

Soft footsteps tread the pebbled path behind him. Druam didn't look back. His heart had dissolved in his chest, soaking through his stomach and over his liver, then sliding into his shoes, as dead as the plants around him.

"It's all over the city," Avallune said softly. The wizard sat down next to Druam and crossed his arms over his knees. "All our fruit and vegetables, everything that was green and living. It's all dead."

In all his years, Druam had never known such loss. He said, "It took me six centuries to cultivate these gardens."

"The people are scared, Druam. They need your guidance."

"That oak came from Belleslye," Druam said, pointing to an ancient tree with veins of sickly ink running through its bark. "I nurtured it from a sapling."

Avallune shook Druam's shoulder. "We need to figure out our food supplies and rations. The council is waiting for you; you must lead us through this."

Druam ignored him. "Life is so much more difficult to create than death. Lifetimes of work snuffed out in a few days. How could she have done this, Avallune? How did this curse go through your barrier?"

The wizard sighed. "Her magic is not known to me. I had no way to prevent it."

"Some of these plants were dead in the wider world. I had the only specimens left in existence," Druam said. "My animals needed them to survive. Now they, too, will die."

"Some of the councillors are speaking of surrender," Avallune said. His tone had grown frustrated, and Druam knew that he should attend to his duties.

What's the point when Cara will destroy all that I love?

"Will you surrender?" Avallune asked.

Druam shook his head. He didn't know what to do, only that he couldn't surrender. Not yet. *Let the lanterns shine a little longer.*

"Then what do I tell the council?" pressed Avallune. "They need to know what our course of action is. Will we retaliate?"

Druam nodded. "Yes. Raids, or magic, or some such. Find a way to get back at her."

The wizard clambered to his feet and held his hand out. Druam didn't take it. He stayed on his knees in the dirt, staring at his orchids.

Even the sight of scourged Belleslye had not hurt his soul this much. When he had seen the beloved city of his youth razed and burned, he had written a song to heal his heavy heart. Now, he had no words left.

✳

A cool sensation washed over Cara. She forced her eyes open, but her limbs didn't respond to her mind's wishes. She tried to turn her head, but only her eyes moved. As she blinked, the world slowly came into focus around her.

She was back in her tent with the curate standing over her with a damp cloth. He smiled down at her. "Finally awake."

Cara cracked open her lips, but no sounds emerged. She swallowed.

Talnor leaned over her. She caressed Cara's cheek. "It's been over a deshe, sweetling. We thought you'd never wake."

"Can you move?" the curate asked.

Cara tried to shake her head, but managed only a tiny movement. No words escaped her dry throat, but a soft whine eased from her lips. The curate frowned.

"I feared that might be the case," the curate said. "I'm not sure the cause..."

"I've sent the guard to find a drink for you," Talnor interrupted him, leaning over Cara. She held Cara's hand, but Cara could barely feel it. "You'll be fine again soon."

Will I? Could the beast have done this to me?

The beast slumbered inside her, nearly cold with how distant it felt. With a strange desperation, Cara pulled at it. It flowed sluggishly up into her chest, warm but not hot. Even with the beast in her limbs, Cara couldn't move. Panic surged through her. How could she defeat Druam like this? How could she use the Ossuary? Then there was the future beyond that: some part of her had envisioned being a powerful ruler in her own right, protecting the rustics and casting out the wicked. Or maybe a great warrior who traveled the world bringing justice to those who didn't know they needed it. Once the undead were destroyed, she could have done anything she wanted.

All of that turned to ash if she couldn't move.

A tear leaked from Cara's eye, and the curate wiped it away. She whimpered, her treacherous tongue still unmoving against the roof of her mouth. The curate made soothing sounds, but she resented his pity.

Even in her despair, she didn't regret the powers she had used. Burning the fleet to ash and rotting the crops of Riverfen had made her feel alive like nothing else. If she ever found the strength to move again, she would use the third and final power without any doubts.

After an interminable time, Talnor brought a human prisoner into the tent. She ushered the curate out, then carefully cut the human's throat. As blood poured out, she filled a mug with it and held it to Cara's lips. Cara drank, grateful that she needed no help in swallowing. Cup after cup refilled and went into Cara's body. Slowly, she felt a tingling through her extremities. She tried to move a finger, and it twitched on the bed.

Talnor muttered, but Cara didn't catch the words. The blood warmed Cara's body, and the beast stirred faintly. With great effort, Cara whispered, "More."

It took another human and a *fampir* before Cara's fingers and toes wiggled properly. She spent the better part of a candle experimenting with her legs and arms, and finally maneuvered herself to sit up. Inside her, the beast hummed contentedly, and Cara felt a stab of unease. *In the past, I healed rapidly with blood. But...what if the beast has stolen that energy from me?*

Talnor had stood by her the entire time. Her hands were bloodied and her expression impatient. After Cara sat up, Talnor said, "Better now?" with a twinge of irritation.

Cara said slowly, "Do you...do you think the beast is taking the blood's potency from me?"

"The beast *is* you," Talnor said. She crossed her arms. "What heals you heals it. Now, how long before you're ready for your final task?"

Cara glared up at her. "Weren't the first two enough for Druam to surrender?"

"Afraid not. The barrier's still up. The ships are lobbing ballistae at it, more for show than anything else. Rask is getting impatient. How long will you be?"

"A couple of days," Cara said. "I have a plan for the final power. Tell Rask what he must do if he wants his army still standing by the end of it."

When she had finished explaining her idea, Talnor left with parting scorn, and Cara settled in to heal. By the end of the day, she felt well enough to stand and walk around the tent. The beast yearned for more blood, and she resisted it. She would drink more for the final plague, but for now, she wanted only to regain herself.

Cara's estimate proved true. Two days later, she felt strong once more, and she set out across the camp with her retinue in tow. The soldiers watched her apprehensively, and she knew that they both admired and feared her. If this final power proved successful, Cara would have forced the city to surrender without a single battle. No doubt, though, that the men wondered if she'd ever turn her power against *them*. She cast a disdainful eye over them, and some cowered from her glare. *Good. They won't risk betraying me.*

They traveled a good distance away from the city, to a small hamlet on the other side of the dam. Cara stepped into the silent village, and empty houses greeted her. A stray dog barked at them before running off, and a few chickens pecked around in the dirt, searching for food that had long since been eaten. Overhead, grey clouds cast a despondent shadow over the earth, and a wind that still held the breath of winter blew cold across their faces.

Talnor stayed a few paces behind her as Cara made her way to the top of a waterfall overlooking the lake and dam. At the zenith, Cara turned around. Riverfen glinted across the water, its thousands of lanterns glittering in the evening light. Even in war, those damn lights were still glowing. But they would do nothing against Cara's final plague.

For this task, Cara had all her remaining prisoners brought to her. She killed each one quickly, draining them with ruthless efficiency. The beast lolled inside her, hot and ready. Cara paused a moment, marveling at how far she'd come. *How could I have feared this power?* She flexed her taloned hands, those claws now friendly to her.

As the wind whispered around her, Cara stepped into the river. The freezing waters tried to chill her feet, but the hot beast flushed through her. She went to her knees and placed her hands below the surface. The shiver that went down her spine at the breathtaking cold had barely passed before the beast's power filled her with heat.

As she touched the water, she searched for that source of power hidden near her kidneys. It was colder than the fire or rot, chilling her fingers even as it lit the water around her hands. Cara shut her eyes.

Send the blood rain over the lake. Fill it to the brim. A bright glow flew across the water. A mighty storm rolled over the plains. The glow in the water shot into the air, imbuing the clouds with dark energy.

Thunder rumbled as lightning danced through the sky, bursting through with a black light instead of white.

When it felt that she would be torn apart, the power finally left her. It leaked out of her fingers, its last vestiges fleeing through the water and up into the clouds. Cara shook in the water, finally feeling its chill.

Dark clouds circled over Riverfen like a maelstrom. Red coated the sky as blood poured into the lake above the dam. Black lightning scorched the earth, its thunder shaking Cara to the marrow.

The ground rumbled as the dam shook, its stones loosening

with the weight of the blood rain. Rask's soldiers had filled the spillways with debris, preventing any safe escape for the growing waters. Though her limbs shook with cold, Cara stared out at the dam, praying that her plan would work.

With a tremendous sound of cracking stone and rushing waters, the dam burst. The ground shook as it exploded outwards, sending the lake pouring toward the defenseless city. A wave of water crashed through the barrier and into the walls, painting red over the white. Cries of anguish drifted over the miles as the water scourged through the lower parts of Riverfen, washing over the poorer districts and tearing homes from their foundations.

I hope Druam watches his city drown.

Cara felt empty, as if her own blood had leaked out to fuel the plague. Weakness overtook her, feeling like her muscles had withered away and she hadn't eaten in days. Her wrists gave out, and she fell into the water. She wavered, her vision blurred for a moment.

An incredible pain wracked her. Cara doubled over, a scream escaping her lips. Talnor rushed to her side, but her hands only made the agony worse. Cara pushed her away as she collapsed, her whole body burning with some unseen force. It was worse than Laris's experiments, worse than cracking the bone of her leg, worse than after the black fire.

Vomit crawled up her throat as the agony ravaged her. Cara spat up bile, for there was nothing in her stomach to purge. She crawled to her hands and knees, gripping the earth with her fingers, praying for the agony to end. Was this how her black fire had felt to her victims? Every nerve, every muscle, every organ, every inch of skin blazing?

Cara's arms shook, her legs giving out from under her. She fell back into the river, her scream muffled by the water. Tears burned down her cheeks. Where was the beast? Couldn't it help her?

Another sensation frightened her. She couldn't feel the beast. Not hidden away, not in her head or chest, not in her limbs. It simply wasn't there.

At last, the pain eased away. First her hands and feet, then her legs and arms, and finally, the rest of her stilled. Phantom traces of agony fled through her before finally, blissfully ceasing. Cara lay, too afraid to move, feeling the changes that had come over her body. In the absence of heat, she felt cold. Deathly cold. Her hands were still taloned. She felt her face, the ridges and fangs. She still looked *fampir*, but the beast was nowhere inside her. She called for it, but it remained silent.

Yet, in its absence, came a strange yearning. The pulse of a nearby soldier pounded in his neck, so loud and enticing. Where once Cara had felt the beast's desire, now that desire was her own.

Slowly, carefully, Cara eased to her feet. Her clothes were soaking wet, and the wind whipped strands of her dirty hair into her face.

"What happened to me?" Cara asked. Her voice was husky and low, the way it was when the beast turned her.

"You became one," Talnor said. "You and your beast. You are truly awakened."

Cara stared at her hands, absorbing her words. Her heart still beat, and her stomach still ached for food. "Am I...am I *fampir*?"

"No."

Cara let out a sigh of relief.

"You are a true *sulpari*. What weakens *fampir* has no effect on you. Blood makes you stronger, yet you are not dependent on it. Everything that made you powerful when the beast overtook you is now always at your fingertips."

Cara breathed deeply. She could smell the men's sweat beading under their armor, the scent of their cologne. She caught sight of a hawk swooping on its prey on the other side of the village. Though faint, she could hear the cries of panic from Riverfen.

She took another deep breath. The world slowed to molasses, as it had in battle. She let time resume its normal pace.

But when she blinked, she gave a sharp gasp. Grey shapes emerged all over the hillside. They whispered, their voices still soft. The ghosts converged on Cara, murmuring too quietly for even her sharp ears. Talnor didn't notice as a ghost passed in front of her.

"Come," Talnor said. "And perhaps tomorrow, we will celebrate our victory."

As Cara followed Talnor, the ghosts pursued her, relentless in their whispers.

*

None of the lanterns came on in the city below. Either there was no one to light them, or the red waters had carried the glass and paper into the sea.

All day, trickles of people had come up the plateau, seeking shelter after their homes had been destroyed. Some districts on hills had been spared damage, but everything by the canals and rivers had gone under. The bay was a mess of debris and bodies. Fins circled the waters, searching out an easy meal from the bloated corpses of people who could not escape in time.

No one knew how many had died. No one knew how many survivors were alone and afraid, unable to make it to help until the waters receded. The stewards in the Cascade Palace recorded the names of all who came there and offered food, water, and a room to sleep. Soldiers had gone into the city on boats, searching for those who needed aid, or, more frequently, bringing bodies to be stacked and numbered.

I should have surrendered after the rot. Druam locked himself in his study, refusing entry to all, even Avallune and Eigbrett. He rooted himself to a spot on the balcony where the cold wind teased his hair.

The blue-and-white of his magnificent city had been colored red.

He had no more room in him for grief. For the first time in centuries, no emotions bubbled to the surface. No anger heated his blood, no melancholy soured his mouth. His entire body felt like parchment erased of its ink. He knew that something should be written there, but he couldn't remember what. All the experiences of his life had slipped away, washed out by the moment the dam had burst and flooded his city.

Surrender. Of course. He would tell his council to send word of surrender. What choice did they have? Cara had singlehandedly sent plagues upon his beloved Riverfen. She was a scourge who could not be stopped.

And she will kill me soon. If only Druam had known to take an extra moment to gaze upon his lanterns the night before. *They are gone forever now.*

The painting of Gwen stood, finally complete, on its easel. The flickering candlelight cast shadows over her face, and he saw judgment in her eyes. *She will not care that I am gone. She despises me, and for good reason. I never deserved her.*

Carefully, Druam took the portrait and hefted it. Moving slowly, he went to one of the shelves in his library and twisted a knob hidden behind a book. The bookcase shifted to one side, revealing a small room lit with glowing golden orbs. It had shelves from floor to ceiling, and each shelf held a series of portraits. Most had been painted by artists, the forms evolving over the centuries as paints and techniques changed. A few, the only ones similar to each other, had a style like the one Druam held now, for they were the paintings he himself had created.

His past wives stared at him, silent and complacent in their frames. They spanned in age, some young, some old. Some were beautiful and graceful, others plain but with a wittiness hidden in their smiles. All were extraordinary in some way. After all, hadn't each of them caught his eye?

Druam walked with his newest portrait until he reached the end of the room. He placed Gwen solemnly down among her fellows, then stepped back.

Last time he had spoken to Gwen, she had scorned him and blamed him for using her. He doubted she would want to see him now, a failure to his city. He drank in the smooth lines of her face, painted with care and love, and he touched the ruby of her lips.

Goodbye, my love. Druam walked out of the room. He shut the bookcase with a final click. *Perhaps their legacy may be preserved, even if mine is not.*

His feet lead, his soul hollow, Druam went back to the window. He hoped to spot at least one colorful, shining light, one last reminder that there could yet be hope.

All was dark below.

＊

The surrender came at dawn. A steward bearing the grey flag appeared at the gates, with Druam's message scrawled on a piece of parchment. The magic barrier came down at noon, and the conquering army thronged into the city.

Cara and Talnor rode at the front of the army, just behind Rask. Talnor smirked down at the surviving city populace. Cara kept her eyes forward. Whenever she turned her head, she saw ghosts in the crowd. They stared at her mournfully, many of them children. How many had been killed during this very siege?

But the living moved away from her in fear. She looked like a monster to them, a creature from legend come to destroy them.

No one cheered as the army marched through. The lanterns overhead remained dark. Wails and cries of pain echoed through the streets. Rank after rank of soldiers passed over the still-wet cobbles. The waters had receded enough for the army to travel the higher roads, but the lower districts were still flooded.

Druam's surrender had been clear: no looting, raping, or burning. Rask had accepted the terms gleefully, but Cara knew that the soldiers would go wild within days. Who would stop them?

The column went steadily through the city and up the plateau. Cara gripped her reins, excitement flooding through her. Druam would surrender officially, and then he would be executed. Her enemy would finally be finished, and she could search for the Ossuary.

Druam and his advisors stood on the steps of the Cascade Palace, their expressions grim. Rask rode up to him with a wide smile and said, "Not a single man lost from my army. A resounding victory, no?"

But Druam gazed past him at Cara. His voice was dull. "You let loose a monster. War is for soldiers, Rask. Not for the innocents who drowned in blood."

Cara raised her head, conscious of the ridges on her forehead and fangs that poked through her lips. "You should have surrendered, Druam. You brought this upon your people."

Druam shook his head. "So what's it to be, Rask? The headsman's axe?"

"Oh no," Rask smiled. "I believe my lady Talnor has claimed you. You may have escaped last time, but you will pay for each stolen day tenfold."

Druam did not react, and Talnor's grin faded. Cara frowned, gripping the reins tightly. She wanted to see him dead.

The soldiers swarmed around Druam and his retinue, clapping them in chains and leading them into the palace. Before Talnor could follow, Cara gripped her arm.

"Let me kill him," she hissed.

"Where's the fun in that?" Talnor said. "He trapped me for centuries, and I intend his punishment to last just as long."

"I won this city for you," Cara spat. "I deserve to kill him."

Talnor shrugged her off and walked away. Cara watched her, resentment festering in her heart. *Soon,* she promised herself. *As soon as the Ossuary is mine, I will kill her.*

With nothing better to do, Cara drifted into the palace and found her old room. It was just the same as she'd left it. She caught sight of herself in a mirror. She snarled at her *fampir* features, her hazel eyes tinged with red.

A flash of silvery grey caught her eye. She whirled, expecting to see a ghost from the night of the Masque.

Her breath caught in her chest. A man sat comfortably in a cushioned chair, his ghostly legs crossed. He had Druam's long nose and high forehead, with dark hair tied at the nape of his neck. His clothing was quite old-fashioned and scholarly.

The man's gaze was melancholy. He opened his mouth, but only inaudible whispers came out. He seemed familiar, like a memory lost until that moment. Something about him made her heart ache, and she couldn't look at him anymore.

"Go away." Cara shut her eyes.

When she opened them, she was grateful that he had vanished.

PART TWO

CHAPTER TWENTY-FOUR
Sandu

The green fields stretched out, full of new growths and budding plants. Past them, the mountains rose up, tall and terrible, their peaks glistening with snow. Those mountains were the border between Demarren and Dotschar; reaching them meant some degree of safety.

And some memories I'd rather forget. In his travels as a peddler and bounty hunter, Sandu had gone all throughout those mountains, from Daggenhelm to Kell and everywhere in between. Every road was tainted by the knowledge of what he'd done to earn some coin.

Sandu shook himself and reached out to help Cadel over the muddy track. Gwen and Lintem strode ahead of them, her with her back straight and head high, and the nightcat twitching his ears every which way.

"She's an odd one, isn't she?" Cadel commented in a low voice.

"She's not the same girl I met in Riverfen," Sandu said. "I barely recognize her now."

Cadel paused to take a long breath. "Don't suppose she can magic us up some horses? I'm not a young man anymore."

"I'll ask." Sandu strode forward and caught Gwen's arm.

She came to a sudden stillness, her gaze focused on the near distance. She said, "Your father won't make the journey on foot. And you're worried about the mountains."

Sandu gaped at her for a moment. "How did you know?"

"I heard it in your Songs." She looked at him. "There is a Song calling to me from Dotschar. We must reach it, and soon."

"What do you mean, you heard it?" Sandu pressed. "There's no music. We're not making any noise."

"I will try to explain later. For now, I will find us transportation."

"No," Sandu said. "You're conspicuous. Every town in Demarren will have heard what happened in Lordstown and be searching for you. I'll go and find us a wagon, unless you can produce one from thin air."

She regarded him a moment, her violet eyes guarded, then nodded. Before Sandu could turn his feet toward smoke rising from a nearby town, she began to hum. Somehow, he could feel her melody coalescing in the air around them. The sensation vanished, and he was left more than a little dazed.

Gwen pointed. "An old farmhouse in that forest. We should find a wagon there."

Sandu shook his head, but kept his doubts to himself. He didn't need to voice them, though, for she said, "The Songs showed it to me. Come."

Though he followed her, Sandu's skin crawled. He despised how she seemed to read his thoughts and feelings.

To his surprise, Gwen was right. There was an abandoned farmyard within a candle's walk, with a broken-down wagon lying in the ward. The wagon's wheels were cracked and bent, its bed covered in moss and dirt. Rust blighted every bit of metal on its surface.

"This won't do us any good," Sandu said. "It's beyond repair."

Gwen stroked a hand over the wood. "It only needs to remember its former shape." With that, she began to Sing, her voice carrying over the weeds and broken walls.

Before Sandu's eyes, the wagon transformed. The rust flaked away to reveal shining metal, the dirt and moss filtered through cracks until the wood was clean. The wheels straightened and repaired themselves. Where once there had been a relic, there now stood a perfectly fine wagon.

But Gwen didn't stop her music. She lifted her head and Sang louder, weaving some spell that Sandu couldn't fathom. When she finished, she said, "Check for reins and other supplies."

Sandu didn't question her this time. He kept looking back at the wagon as he followed her instructions. Cadel helped him to bring out a variety of blankets, leather straps and harnesses, and whatever else they could find that was suitable for a journey. Most of it was moldering or broken, but again, Gwen mended it all through her magic.

"Remarkable," Cadel whispered as they watched her pass her hands over the harnesses, restoring the polished leather.

Sandu had no words. He only shook his head, his tongue completely in knots. He had seen Laris's magic and Darian's healing, and while those were equally incredible, something about this new magic intrigued him.

He was not surprised when a pair of horses trotted into the yard. They were well-kept, with brushed manes and smooth flanks. When Cadel questioned it, Gwen said, "I asked, and they came."

They could get no more answers from her, and so decided to keep their questions to themselves. They loaded the wagon bed, and Sandu helped Cadel to climb up in the back. Sandu sat on the seat and took the reins while Gwen pulled herself up beside him. The nightcat's tail lashed back and forth, and he took off into the trees.

"He will find us at nightfall," Gwen assured Sandu, again answering something he had not asked.

The horses pulled the wagon out of the farmyard and onto the road. As the sun continued its slow pace through the sky, Cadel's snores rose from the back of the wagon. Sandu glanced at Gwen from the corner of his eye.

Her unwavering gaze was on the road ahead. Her hands were held loosely in her lap, and she matched the wagon's movement with an ethereal grace, almost as if she were a part of the wood itself.

Sandu had never been one to keep his thoughts to himself,

but now he found it hard to form the words. After a few moments of struggling, he asked, "Where are we headed, exactly?"

"D'Clet," came the answer.

"Why?"

"There is a Song that calls me there."

"How do you know? What does that even mean?" Sandu gripped the reins, his knuckles white. Would this woman's words be as cryptic as Darian's?

Gwen explained the Songs to him, speaking without inflection. He didn't understand all of it, but nodded along anyway. When she finished, he had a hundred questions. However, only one of them truly mattered to him.

"What happened when you vanished from the Masque?" Sandu had only seen her twice in Riverfen, so many months ago. The first time was when she'd healed him after his mind betrayed him. The second, when she disappeared in a haze of magic from the ballroom, leaving her distraught husband behind her.

She said, "I went to the Woods."

"Yes, but where are they?" Sandu pressed. He needed to find the Woods if he wanted to see his children again.

"I don't quite know. Somewhere beyond Earda, I imagine. The Witches brought me there and showed me visions of the past and present. They taught me to use the Songs." She stared out at the trees, an ancient melancholy in her eyes. "I dwelled there for many long years before I met your children. I had lost my humanity, and they helped me to find it again."

"But how did they get there? They're not magical...are they?"

Gwen blinked slowly. "They had an innocent magic to them, as all children do. I think most of us lose that spark when we grow older. As for how they came, Autorus sent them. The Witches are his sisters, and he knew they would keep the children safe."

"But why?"

Gwen gave him a contemplative look, as if considering how

much she should say. Before the silence stretched too long, she said, "Autorus knows that your role is not yet completed. I need you to help me find Cara's Song. If your children remained on Earda, you would be too distracted to do what must be done."

"So he sent them off to the Woods," Sandu said. If he ever met Autorus again, he had half a mind to deck the bastard. "What right did he have to take them away?"

"You'll have to ask him," Gwen said with a shrug.

Sandu frowned at that, but decided not to go further down that line of thought. Instead, he said, "So you've been to the Woods. Can you send me there?"

She reached out and lay a finger to his cheek. He froze. She frowned slightly before withdrawing her hand.

"What was that?" Sandu asked.

"You're not ready," she said. "Your Song is disjointed, contradictory. You are one thing and yet see yourself as another. Until you acknowledge the full truth of yourself, your Song cannot guide you to the Woods."

"I want to try anyway. I need to see my children," Sandu insisted.

"And if you fail?" Her violet eyes bored into him. "What then?"

"Then I'll keep trying until I succeed." Though his words were confident, a hole dug into him at the thought of yet another failure.

She nodded. "We can try when we've rested."

✳

As the sun started to dip toward the mountains, Sandu turned the wagon off the road. Gwen hopped off and headed into the trees, her nightcat appearing beside her. Sandu and Cadel followed until they came to a trickling stream bordered by moss.

Sandu began to prepare his blankets, but Gwen held up a hand. She touched the moss and Sang, a beautiful sound that carried through the trees and wriggled into Sandu's ears. The moss grew and grew, spreading over the dirt until it was a large enough space to accommodate all three of them. When Sandu put a hand to it, it felt springy and soft.

"Wow," he whispered under his breath.

Apparently, though, Gwen was not done. Her Song changed, and a warm bubble formed around them, reaching to the edges of the clearing and stopping where the trees grew too closely together. The magic switched again, and tubers sprouted from the ground.

With a satisfied smile, Gwen sat down and plucked the tubers from the earth. She magicked a fire into a circle of stones and began to roast the vegetables. Sandu sat down beside her, his bottom oddly comfortable with the moss beneath it.

"I suppose we won't starve," he said in as carefree a tone as he could manage.

"No," she agreed. "Nor freeze. The Songs will keep any late-season frost from us."

They ate in silence, and when the final crumbs were cleaned up, Sandu turned to Gwen. "Show me the Woods. Please."

She sighed, "Very well. I suppose your father would want to go, too?"

Cadel looked between the two of them. "If it means seeing my grandchildren..."

"Then take my hands. Lintem, lend me your Song."

Sandu and Cadel took her outstretched hands as the nightcat lay his head in her lap. Gwen took a deep breath, and Sandu did the same. He held the air in his belly, then released it. *I am ready.*

"Think of the children," Gwen said softly. "Their laughter and smiles, their tears and anger. All the good moments and the bad, the details of their personalities. Hold them in your hearts. I will think of the Woods."

This Song was unlike the others Sandu had heard. Those had been peaceful or turbulent, gentle or strong, but this one had all those and more. It tugged at his heart, pulling at the threads that held him together.

It frightened him. While Cadel smiled, Sandu wanted to run. All he heard was terrible discord. Flashes of memory came to him: the children crying as he swatted their bottoms, Tambrey calling him a coward and a layabout, Da being forced into the wagon that would take him to prison.

Sandu was overwhelmed with negative memories. He could not think of all the good and bad with the children. Dread consumed him.

"What is this?" Sandu gritted out. His hand shook in Gwen's.

Gwen stopped Singing for a moment, though the nightcat's purr kept up her music. She cocked her head at Sandu. "That is your Song. To reach the Woods, you must acknowledge all of yourself. Search deeply. Find your core."

Sandu tried. He dug deep into himself, but all he found were ghosts and shattered dreams. Tambrey's last breath, quiet in reality but thunderous in his memory; the loss of his arm, stumbling about through the world with no idea what to do; failing everyone he had ever loved.

Cadel inhaled sharply. He stared at a spot in the trees, his eyes wide in amazement, his mouth hanging open. Cadel breathed, "It's beautiful."

Gwen looked not at the trees, but at Cadel. Sandu noted a deep, raw pain in her expression, a small representation of true emotions at last.

"I can see red grass and grey trees," Cadel said.

"The Woods," Gwen said. Longing filled her voice.

Sandu strained, but even with the Songs audible around him, he saw no portal or door, nothing that showed him his children. "Why can't I see them? What's wrong?"

"Eaton! Elvy!" Cadel cried. He let go of Gwen's hand and took a step forward. Then he frowned. "Don't you see them, son?"

Despair clogged Sandu's heart. He shook his head.

"His Song is complete. He knows himself," Gwen said. "The Woods know his surety and have opened themselves to him."

"Da!" Sandu cried as Cadel took another step. "Da, don't leave me!"

Cadel didn't look at his son, his gaze locked on that

invisible doorway. "They're calling for me. They need family, son. I need to go to them."

Sandu opened his mouth to protest, but Gwen squeezed his hand. "Let him go. He will be safe there, and will care for them until you know your own Song."

Cadel turned his head to Sandu, his face swathed in golden light. His wrinkles were more shallow, his stance stronger. He smiled. "I'll watch the children for you, son."

"Da, please," Sandu pleaded.

His father took another step and vanished into the air. The Songs slowly dissipated, leaving Sandu empty. His beard was salty with tears.

"Why couldn't I follow him?" Sandu asked.

"You were not ready yet," she answered. She took a shaky breath, and Sandu could have sworn her eyes sparkled for a moment.

"Why didn't you go?" Sandu asked.

"The Woods will not allow me to reenter," she said in a small voice. Despite the wisdom in her gaze and the power in her magic, she appeared a young girl again, lost in a world that held no place for her. "I had hoped...but no. I cannot go back."

They sat there for a long time, the last rays of sunlight giving way to inky blackness, their hands still entwined in mutual support. Lintem purred in a comforting rumble.

"He's gone," Sandu said, breaking the silence at last.

"He's with the children. He'll be happier there," Gwen said.

"I know. I just wish..."

She gave his hand another squeeze. "I understand."

He truly believed that she did. Somewhere beneath the grime and animal skins, her heart still beat. She was not entirely gone from humanity.

"I don't want to go back to D'Clet," Sandu said softly. "I don't think I can face it without him."

Her expression was sympathetic. "It was not easy for me to return to Demarren after the Trials. But I went because I had to resolve the fire that threatened to consume me. Now I can move forward with a clear mind. D'Clet did nothing to harm you;

Cara did. And it is her, not that city, that we must steel ourselves to meet."

She gently disengaged herself from him and left the clearing, Lintem padding softly after her. Sandu hugged his knees and stared into the fire. He prayed that Da and the children were safe, but did not pray for himself.

All that night, the visions that haunted him flitted in and out of his head, mocking him with their faint laughter.

CHAPTER TWENTY-FIVE
Mavian

"There is enough coin left in the coffers to pay the guards' salary for one more month," the treasurer said, his fingers sliding over the numbers written on the parchment. Like all the rest of the councillors that remained in D'Clet, he fearfully stammered through his report. "I'm afraid Chadron and Rask's campaigns have drained our resources."

Mavian's head ached. He rubbed his temples as he scanned the pages. "And I suppose they've already bled the lords and rustics dry?"

The treasurer nodded. "Collections were sent out just last month. Rustics have only recently planted the fields; more taxes will cause unrest."

"Do you have any suggestions?"

"Find more money, and soon," the treasurer said.

Very helpful. Mavian murmured his thanks. The treasurer bowed and swept up his papers, then departed in a rush. Heaving a great sigh, Mavian leaned back in the large chair in Rask's old study. It was a simple room, with clean granite walls and a mighty fireplace. Shelves behind the desk housed reports and ledgers, while a glassless window opened out over the ravine and city beyond.

A knock came at the door, followed by Ronan's soft footsteps. His arms were piled high with manuscripts and scrolls which he deposited on the desk. "These were all I could save, I'm afraid."

"Thank you, Ronan," Mavian said. He took a quick peek through the pile. Many of the tomes were older, some useful, some not so much. Not one of his own journals or notebooks remained. With another sigh, Mavian shifted in his chair and wondered how much he could trust Ronan. He said, "Are the rest of the scholars situated?"

Ronan bobbed his head. "They've set to work restoring the old library."

An awkward silence filled the room. Mavian played with a quill while Ronan sat staring resolutely forward. At last, Mavian said, "You were right to leave me. I didn't have a plan."

The scholar gave a small shrug. "Yet you still ended up with Rask's seat."

Another silence, which Mavian broke by asking, "Why did you work for Chadron?"

"It's best to keep one's enemies close, and easier to sabotage that way, too," Ronan answered. "I saved those papers, didn't I?"

"You did," Mavian conceded. He pushed the quill tip into his finger, withdrawing it before it could prick his skin. He glanced up at the scholar. "I'm not going to keep this seat for long unless I have help. The coffers are running dry, the people fear me, the guards only stay for their salary. What would you do in my place?"

The scholar ran a hand over his tonsure, his lips pressed in thought. He finally said, "I would find allies. Rask is aligned with the Lofalins; no doubt they'll turn their attention to you now."

"Hm." Mavian rubbed his brow, his headache worsening. "Aremo Teru sits pretty in Con Salur. With the spring upon us, he may decide to claim D'Clet before Rask can return."

"Unless they don't know that it's fallen to you," Ronan said.

"Word spreads quickly. I doubt–"

"The couriers were always sent by the guard," Ronan interrupted. "Leaving on Chadron's orders and his alone. Unless you told them to inform Aremo of the change in leadership..."

Mavian leaned back in his seat, a plan forming. "We're sure no couriers have left the city?"

"I spoke with the captain of the guard just this morning. All of his men are here and accounted for."

"But rumors still abound," Mavian pointed out. "If a courier hasn't informed the Lofalins, word will have spread by the merchants and travelers."

"Then we head them off. Put out official notices with Rask's seal, lie to the people if you must. Send a courier with a forged letter telling the Lofalins that all rumors are false."

"Then do it. We need time to gather allies."

"I will draft the letter immediately," Ronan said. He stood and gave a small bow. "For what it's worth, I am glad it is you and not Chadron that I serve now."

Mavian didn't answer as the scholar backed out of the room, closing the door behind him. He dug his finger into the skin behind his ear and slowly opened his mouth. His jaw popped, and he winced. He'd been gritting his teeth in his sleep every night since he had summoned the Dread Portal.

It didn't help that he'd been hearing Merick's Song louder and louder with each passing day. Melancholy and anger filled each note, haunting Mavian day and night, the last echoes of the crimes he had once committed.

His headache worsened, and Mavian buried his head in his hands. *No more.* His decision made, he pushed his chair back and threw open the door. He had to speak to Darian.

Mavian found the blind man on the terrace, standing with his hip pressed against the stone railing, the only thing keeping him from a deadly drop into the black ravine. Darian was motionless, his cane laid on the stone, his hair lifting gently with the breeze.

Darian spoke without turning, "You and I have walked alongside the dead for a long time. Some of those willingly went with you. Others did not."

Mavian shifted. "I need to release him."

"Yes."

"Do you know how?"

"No." Darian's fingers drummed an inaudible beat on the weathered stone. "But you do."

"That's not true," Mavian protested. "I have barely any idea how to repeat what I've done before, much less a new endeavor. I need your help."

"In the future you will. For this moment, no. You know what to do."

Mavian waited for more elaboration, but none came. Frustrated, he stalked back to his chamber. Merick waited for him there, as still as always, no breath filling his barrel chest.

For a long moment, Mavian contemplated the wight. Could Darian be right? Was Mavian past the point of guidance?

With a tilt of his head, Mavian indicated for Merick to follow him. The wight stepped smoothly into place, and together they descended to Mavian's old workshop. It had been ransacked, with glass on the floor from vials thrown against the wall, chalk ground into dust, and ripped pages strewn over the toppled table. Mavian picked through the mess. He had already gone down to see if anything could be retrieved; nothing had been salvageable.

With Merick's help, Mavian swept part of the floor clear and sat down. Merick moved to stand against the wall, but Mavian called for him. With a little hesitance – unusual for the stoic creature – Merick clumsily sat across from Mavian.

After a deep breath, Mavian said, "I'm sorry."

The wight didn't respond.

"I should have done this a long time ago. Well, if I can do it at all, that is." Mavian paused, forcing himself to stop his rambling. *Just do it.* "I'm going to try and release you."

Again no response. Mavian had hoped for a glimmer of recognition or even the rare spoken word. But Merick simply stared at him.

Mavian cleared his throat. The cold ground was hard against his thin buttocks, and he suddenly wished that he'd done this in his more comfortable chambers. For a moment, he contemplated changing locations, but then he stopped himself. *You're searching for a delay. Do it now.*

In that quiet, familiar place, Mavian centered himself. He allowed the Song of Death to flow over him, a waterfall of music that caressed his soul. In the waves, he searched for Merick's individual melody.

It wasn't hard to find. The wight's melody stood out, black against the swirl of colors, its notes tainted with the sickly purple hue of the Dread Portals. Mavian flinched as he mentally touched it.

What do I do now? Mavian held Merick's melody firmly in his mind, but went no further. For awhile, he merely listened, hearing the wight's undeath from its own perspective. Then, faintly, a harmony caught his attention. It touched the black, then dipped away, then came back at infrequent intervals. Intrigued, Mavian tugged at this complementary sound.

He jolted when he realized that every time the harmony touched Merick's melody was when Merick had spoken or acted strangely in his undeath. The harmony was softer, kinder, more understanding. It flowed more easily toward Death, though never quite reached Autorus.

Without second-guessing himself, Mavian followed the harmony. It pulled him forward, and he blinked. His eyes were suddenly heavy, his limbs weighted with sleep. He felt himself tugged into dreams, and did not resist.

Mavian opened his eyes to the grey land of dreams. It was disorienting, no clear up or down, no ground to settle his feet and no sky to gaze toward. Sounds came muffled to his ears, and silhouettes flitted through the grayness, never quite solidifying. The harmony came stronger now, and Mavian followed it as he would a lifeline, clinging to that shred of humanity within the void.

He did not know how far he walked. It could have been one mile or a hundred, for time and distance had no place in that burdening fog. Occasionally, a dreamer would call out to him, or a face grow clear for the span of a breath before vanishing back into the mist.

Just before Mavian gave up to return to the waking world, a tree materialized from the gloom. Between its roots there grew an array of blooming flowers, each more radiant than the last. An indistinct figure sat cross-legged among the stalks. As

Mavian drew closer, the figure coalesced into a familiar form: Merick.

But this was not the undead wight Mavian had known; there was ruddy red in this man's cheeks instead of the grey tint of undeath. Carefully, Mavian sat across from him. The large man opened his eyes, which were a warm brown, and regarded Mavian.

"Hello," Mavian said weakly.

"So you're the Hooded Man," Merick said.

Mavian nodded, not trusting himself to speak.

The old mercenary plucked a flower from beside his knee. He held it up, its blue petals bright against the grey. "This is where they put me to rest. Not where I'd pick, really, but I suppose they didn' have much of a choice."

A lump formed in Mavian's throat, and he swallowed hard. "I'm s—"

"Shoulda made it to Riverfen with Cara," Merick continued. "Shouldn' have hidden my pain. Too proud to admit that I was hurtin', though. And I paid the price." A faraway look entered his eyes, as if he weren't quite seeing Mavian. "She comes here, now an' then. I call for her, but she can' hear me. An' I can't leave this spot. Every now and then, I hear or see things from the waking world. I saw you, you know. An' that bastard. What was his name?"

"Chadron," Mavian managed.

"That's right. Some knight he was. Didn' deserve the title." Merick looked up into the tree branches. "I miss her. My Cari."

"I'm sure she misses you, too," Mavian said. He didn't know if such a wicked person could hold those feelings, but didn't think it the right time to express his doubts.

"Did she find Renna, at least?" Merick asked.

"She did," Mavian said. That lump came back again, larger and more painful. It clogged his throat with grief.

Merick peered out into the endless grey, his eyes moving back and forth. When Mavian turned, he saw nothing.

"I'm sorry for what I did to you," Mavian said. "I'm sorry that I...I murdered you, raised your body, and trapped your soul here. I was foolish and selfish in those days."

Merick didn't answer, his gaze still locked on something that Mavian couldn't see.

"I'm here to release you. To send you on to Autorus."

Mavian squirmed as Merick's gaze shifted to him, those eyes holding a terrible depth of grief.

"Are you now?" Merick asked, his voice a low rumble.

"Yes," Mavian said. "I'm sorry that I ever did this to you."

"I've grown used to the grey," Merick mused. "It's peaceful, you know. Don' know what I'll face with Autorus."

"I'm sure you'll have earned your place in his Halls," Mavian said. "Please, let me rectify my mistake. Let me release you."

The silence of the grey land weighed on them for a long time before Merick finally said, "Alright. One more adventure can't hurt."

Before Mavian could act, Merick reached out and grabbed his arm. Even in dreams, his grip was strong. The mercenary leaned down, his nose nearly touching Mavian's. "I know Cari isn' who she used to be. But if you harm her again, I'll hunt you down from the afterlife. I'll escape Autorus and haunt you to the end of your days. Understand?"

Mavian swallowed and nodded. Merick released him, then sat back up and closed his eyes. "I'm ready."

The Song of Death showed Mavian what to do. He hummed an off-key tune, but his intention guided the music. Merick's Song disconnected from Earda, and the mercenary faded away, his melody finally bringing him to Autorus.

Mavian opened his eyes to the color and smells of his workshop. Opposite him, Merick's body slumped to the floor, truly lifeless. Mavian reached over and shut those black eyes, a part of him grieving for the companion he had held so dearly these past months.

It was the right thing to do.

With all his strength, Mavian rolled Merick's body to its back, straightened the legs, and folded the arms over the chest. He would have to ask someone's help to carry him up to the cemetery and bury him. But for now, he would mourn alone.

Mavian sat for a long time in that darkness, grappling with what he had done and what he still had yet to do. Despite making this sin right, his guilt still crushed him. He put a hand on Merick's huge knuckles.

"Nothing will ever be enough to redeem me," Mavian said.

No response came from the wight.

CHAPTER TWENTY-SIX
Gwen

High peaks rose all around them, sheltering them from wind and sun. Most of the low passes were clear of snow, but whenever the road brought them up into the clouds, Gwen had to Sing away the icy glaciers that blocked their path forward. With so much traveling and Singing, she could feel herself waning. Earda did not sustain the Songs the same way the Woods did. She grew tired more easily, and her longing for the Woods encapsulated her mind, that distant music always on the edge of thought.

Sandu was a quiet traveling companion. He did not sing or whistle, nor did he comment on the weather or the towns they passed through. When they made camp, he did his part in cooking or cleaning, but was otherwise listless.

In his Song, Gwen heard his grief and fright. He missed his father and children, he mourned his wife, he feared D'Clet and Cara. Once, she had tried to talk with him about it. He had only turned his back to her and refused to speak more.

What do I do for him? Gwen hummed to Lintem one day as the wagon creaked along a hard-packed dirt road. She sat with her legs dangling over the rear while Lintem trailed behind, his tail swishing back and forth. His bright green eyes were focused on a bird flying overhead.

Give him time, Lintem purred.

Gwen frowned and twisted to look at Sandu. He slumped over the reins, his shoulders rounding to his ears. She called to him, "How far to the city?"

"A few days," came the monotoned response.

He can't be in this condition when we reach D'Clet. We need him ready to face whatever comes our way, Gwen hummed. Lintem didn't answer, his gaze still sharp on that bird. Gwen ran a finger over the rough wagon wood. What could this broken man do against their enemies?

He knows her. That was the simple truth. And Gwen had let Sandu grieve for a long time; who knew how long they had before Cara found the Ossuary? She must use him to learn more about her enemy.

That evening, after she'd Sung a wayfarer's pine into shape around their fire, Gwen said, "Put your hand in mine." She reached out, and Sandu nervously put his fingers on her wrist. Gwen said, "As I Sing, I want you to picture Cara."

"Why?"

"We're going to see her."

Sandu shook his head. "I can't do that."

"Sandu, before I face her in the Ossuary, I must know her Song. I can glean bits and pieces from you and the others who have known her, but her Song is strongest within herself. I must see her to examine it. All you have to do is show her to me. Once we're there, you may let go of my hand and return here."

"She'll kill me," Sandu said.

"Our bodies will remain here. She cannot harm us."

Sandu swallowed. Fear flared within his Song, but resolve slowly worked its way in. At last he gripped her wrist and said, "I'm ready."

As Gwen Sang, his Song fixed on Cara. Melodies came to Gwen's consciousness: Cara and Sandu's days of traveling together, the night in the tower when Cara mourned Merick, how afraid they'd been before the Masque. The murder of Alex kept intruding into Sandu's music, and Gwen squeezed his fingers. *Focus on the Cara that you knew.*

Gwen blinked, and the woods around them were replaced by a beautiful room in the Cascade Palace. She and Sandu were on a chaise, and Cara sat at a small table, her back to them. Her short hair had grown a bit longer over the winter, still as curly as ever. She wore a battle-aged sword at her hip.

The sight of her sent an ache through Sandu's Song. She'd been his closest friend for so long, and he so desired them to be close again. Yet Alex's death loomed between them, a chasm that he couldn't hope to cross. Gwen sent a wave of warmth through their connection, urging him to be brave.

Sandu made a strangled sound, and Cara whipped to face them, red in her eyes and sharp points over her lips. Sandu let out a small gasp. Cara drew her sword as she whirled, and it cut through the air where Sandu and Gwen's heads were. Gwen winced, but felt no pain. The sword went through her as if she were air.

Cara paused, her eyes widening in recognition. She slammed the sword in its sheath and crossed her arms. "What are you doing here, Sandu?"

"Well...I'm not really here."

"I figured that out for myself."

Gwen sat still, letting their conversation play out. As they spoke, she reached for Cara's Song. When she touched the melody, she shivered.

What she heard greatly disturbed her.

Sandu licked his lips. "Cara, you don't have to do this. You don't have to be this person. I know you – the real you – is inside there somewhere. You can still leave that devil-woman and do the right thing."

"The *fampir* are evil," Cara said. "They have to be eradicated."

Sandu darted a look at Gwen. Cara's gaze followed his. "Who's she? Someone else to burden with your woes?"

Though Sandu flinched at that, he said, "This is the Lady Seastone."

Cara snorted. "Very funny, Sandu."

Gwen said pleasantly, "It's true. We've met, actually."

Cara's eyes grew hard. "Yes. When your husband murdered my lady."

"Only because she and Mavian were trying to kidnap me."

"Don't twist the truth. You're a *fampir's* whore, and that's enough for me." Cara's hand twitched on her sword.

"Cara, please," Sandu started. She snarled at him. Sandu yelped and dropped Gwen's hand. The scry spell rippled as Sandu vanished from the chamber, leaving Gwen alone with Cara.

Gwen regarded the other woman curiously.

Cara hissed, "I thought you'd vanished for good."

Gwen tilted her head as Cara loomed above. She said, "I was gone for a very long time in my perspective. Yet I returned during the same winter that I had departed."

"I don't care about you or your magic."

Gwen cocked her head and peered once more into Cara's Song. It was full of contradictions: an attachment to life, yet connected to Death; a desire for goodness and grace, yet willingness to commit murder; a childlike need to be desired, yet stubborn resistance to any who may guide her. Deep within the Song lay an ever-present undercurrent to the Underworld, layered with deceit, self-loathing, and terror.

The beast. Sandu had spoken of this presence inside Cara before, his tone both fearful and reverential. It had haunted her and aided her, both a boon and a curse. And its tie to Cara was as strong as any bonds in nature, completely united with her soul.

Only the Song of Unmaking can separate the two, Gwen realized.

"What are you doing?" Cara demanded. Her sword was out again, leveled at Gwen's chest.

Gwen broke from her reverie and met Cara's eyes. She said, "I'm sorry."

"For what?"

"For how much you despise yourself." Gwen couldn't imagine hating her magic so much. It was a part of her, as twined into her being as the beast with Cara. *Could Cara have found its Song and made peace with it? Is it too late now?*

"You don't know anything about me," Cara said. Behind her brash tone, Gwen heard discord in the Song.

"I once thought my magic was evil," Gwen said. "I wished it had never come to me. The Song of Vengeance almost consumed me, as it's doing to you."

"I don't know what you're talking about." Cara edged away, her Song a staccato beating of fear and truth.

Gwen listened a little more, the veracity of her words ringing throughout Cara's Song. She recognized other Songs entwined with Cara's, one of which echoed with lost potential. *The Song Darian wanted her to hear.*

With deliberate slowness, Gwen uncrossed her legs and stood to face Cara. The other woman waved her sword, but Gwen had nothing to fear from it. No harm could come to her body. Though she stood shorter than Cara, Gwen raised her head high and met the other's eyes.

"Darian was wrong," Gwen said. "There's still a chance for you. I can teach your Song to you. You can turn back."

"I can't." Sorrow lurked behind Cara's eyes. "I killed Alex. I drank the blood of others, and I enjoyed it." Sudden anger flashed in her red eyes. "I slaughtered the people of Riverfen while Druam watched."

"My brother was murdered in front of my eyes. His people were turned against him, and after he fell, they executed his wives and his eldest son," Gwen spoke flatly. "My nephew was not even a man when they killed him. I know the pain of unjust loss. I know the fury of vengeance. Its Song called to me before I ever knew its name."

Gwen took a step, closing the gap between them. Cara's eyes were wide, bordering between fear and furious. Gwen said, "Your conflict is clear in your Song. Once, you were driven by compassion and love. Find it again. Hold onto it. Don't fall into the mire laid at your feet."

Cara swallowed, her gaze darting between Gwen's eyes as if hoping to find an answer there. A long moment passed. Cara said quietly, "The beast has become one with me. Can you still remove it?"

Gwen hesitated. The Song of Unmaking was the only course, yet what destruction would it require in return? It was a final option, the last resort before calamity. She could not wield it yet.

Cara stepped back, Gwen's silence stretching too long. She shook her head. "Empty promises. That's all magic can give. You're just like Darian and Laris: you'll say whatever you need to get what you want, but you'll never deliver."

As she spoke, a black flame flickered between her fingers. Its heat reached for Gwen, wanting to sear her, and it took everything in her not to end the spell. She stood firm.

"If you try to stop me, I'll kill you," Cara said. "The Ossuary is my birthright, and I'll take it no matter the costs. I'll make sure no one has to deal with the undead ever again."

Darian was right after all, Gwen thought. A melancholy path stretched in front of her, bleak and unforgiving.

Gwen hummed, pulling herself back to the bower. Sandu shivered in a ball on the moss, his hands pressed over his ears. Though she was emotionally drained, Gwen reached out to Sandu's Song. She found the dark discordant chords that pressed down on his melody, and muted them. It would not cure him, but at least he would be able to recover for a time.

When Sandu was able to straighten, Gwen stepped out of her magic bower and into the forest. Songs flowed on the breeze, sweet and tantalizing, the sounds of nature and life and death all intermingling. She took a deep breath, her heart aching for the simplicity of the Woods.

That familiar Song drifted from D'Clet, calling out to her. She closed her eyes and listened, assuring herself that she was doing the right thing. *Druam must deal with his choices on his own.* Part of her wished she could again become that naïve girl that had given her entire heart to him, but she knew that she could never return to her former ignorance.

I am a Woods witch, no longer the princess of Demarren, and no longer an earl's wife.

CHAPTER TWENTY-SEVEN
Seanna

"This is taking too long," Seanna muttered. She peered from the boarded-up window, the view of D'Clet obscured by tall pine trees. A dirt path wound toward the abandoned farmhouse they had chosen as their hideout. "He should be back by now."

The mute Captain Tzuriel didn't respond. He sat at the rickety table, his eyes closed. Somewhere out in the woods, a troop of his Rangers lay in hiding. Most of their company had remained in Rengu to secure the safety of its people after Voclain's murder, but a few had decided to come with Seanna. *Only twenty of them, with a mighty wall, a ravine, and over a hundred guards standing between us and Chadron.*

A bird's call lifted from the trees, and moments later, two shapes emerged from the dark green. Seanna let out a relieved breath at the sight of Ropaz, then inspected his new companion. The other man wore patched scholar's robes, his tonsure greying and his step heavy. Together, they came to the old house and entered.

"What news from the city?" Seanna asked immediately.

Ropaz gestured to the scholar, who stepped forward. The scholar bowed. "Your Grace, I bring an offer of truce."

"From Chadron?" Seanna asked, surprised. *Why would he send a scholar and not a soldier? Why would he even enter negotiations with me?*

"No, madam. From Lord Mavian Strilu."

Seanna gaped at him, her words lost. "Mavian Strilu?" she

finally managed. "The same Mavian Strilu who set his prowlers on me and murdered my father?"

The scholar nodded. His eyes were sharp, his tone measured. "He has defected from Earl Rask and taken D'Clet from Chadron."

All the men watched her, and Seanna didn't know what to say. Anger flooded through her, followed by grief, and then confusion. She merely shook her head, her tongue refusing to work. Ropaz kneeled next to her with concern.

"Can we trust him?" he asked.

The thought of looking into the eyes of the man who caused her father's death sickened her. Yet now he held the very city she needed in order to fight back against Aremo. She drummed her fingers against the table.

"I don't know if I can face him again," Seanna said, her voice quiet under the cobwebbed ceiling. "I've had to bury so much anger and grief these past few months. I feel hollow, like there's nothing left in me. But if I have to see him again, I fear that that emptiness will fill with hatred. It'll burn me up inside."

Ropaz put a warm hand on her shoulder, his eyes soft. "You are the only one who can let go of that pain. If you cannot do it for yourself, do it to save your child. Let yourself feel all the fury and melancholy that you've hidden away, and then let it go."

"I don't know if I can."

"It will hurt," he said. "And believe me, your grief will never truly fade. Not while you still hold love for those you lost. But you will be able to see past it, especially if you focus on what needs to be done."

Somewhere deep in her heart were all the emotions she'd bottled up, swirling inside her, beating against her skin. Seanna took a steadying breath and forced herself to meet the scholar's passive gaze. "Is Chadron still alive?"

"No," came the neutral answer.

"How did Mavian kill him?" Seanna asked, dreading the answer.

"With his dark magic."

The answer lay heavy in the air, a foul truth that she knew

she must recognize. *Can I ally myself with such a man?*

But she had little choice. The man who sat in D'Clet mattered not; the obstacles to reaching him were still in place, and her force so very small. If Mavian truly wished to negotiate, then perhaps she could use him. *Driving out Aremo and his army is the only thing that matters now. If we all survive this...perhaps then Lord Mavian Strilu will answer for his crimes.*

"Where would he like to meet?" Seanna asked at last. *You are the queen. You will look this snake in the eyes and use him to rescue your child.*

✳

The small abbey was nestled in a vale on the eastern side of the valley. It was an idyllic place, with a stream running through and trees lining the surrounding ridges. As Seanna rode in with her escort, she couldn't help but feel threatened. Night had fallen quickly, and she imagined prowlers hiding beneath the rocks and men in dark armor peering at her from behind the grabbing branches.

I can't believe I agreed to this.

As they rode into the abbey grounds, the abbess hurried out to meet them, her white face nearly as pale as her wimple. The woman bowed and said, "They are waiting in the dining hall. Please, I ask that all weapons remain outside."

Seanna gestured for the Rangers to wait, and Ropaz gave her a small nod. *Even without weapons, we are not weak.* Squaring her shoulders, Seanna entered the humble building and followed the abbess through small corridors until they reached a cozy dining room. It shared a fireplace with the kitchen and was filled with comfortable rugs and well-loved chairs.

Despite the cheery room, Seanna's heart plummeted when she saw Mavian. He sat, shoulders stiff, at one of the tables that faced the door. The scholar waited with him, but Seanna's eyes were drawn to the prowler that chewed bones under the table like a dog. Her heart thudded in her throat, and she swallowed with difficulty.

As gracefully as she could manage, Seanna went to Mavian and extended her hand. Though dressed in rustic linens, she would behave as a queen. Mavian gave her palm a quick kiss, his eyes darting away guiltily. Last time she had seen him, she'd caught her lover in his arms. When the formalities were concluded, Seanna sat opposite him, flanked by her allies.

Seanna said, "You're either ridiculously brave or foolish to ask to meet me. As I recall, you convinced my lover to betray me and soon after attempted to murder me."

Mavian winced, and the scholar gave him an apprehensive look. To his credit, Mavian met her eye and said, "If I could alter history, I would erase those events entirely. I have hurt many people, and I sincerely regret my actions. That is why I wish to move forward now and help you retake Con Salur."

Seanna mulled over his words. *Can I trust his sincerity?* She studied the prowler. "What of this creature? Its presence implies that you are still enmeshed in the dark arts."

"Ah." Mavian's eyes brightened. He leaned down and scratched the prowler's head. It burbled at him, and Seanna recoiled. Mavian said, "This is Ekkar. I found him in Stonetree. He's very important, you see. He's the very first prowler."

"How do you know?" Seanna asked despite her misgivings.

"Druam recognized him." Mavian explained it all to her while Seanna sat with nausea churning inside her. Every instinct told her that this was a bad idea, that she should order her men to kill Mavian and leave before he sank his claws into her. Yet something about him made her pause.

As he spoke, Seanna realized that she saw herself in him. She had once put herself above all others, damn her conscience. She had hurt people – including Renna – and been pleased with the results. Just as he now begged her forgiveness, she had once begged it from Druam and Henrik.

In that moment, she softened toward him.

When Mavian finished his story, Seanna inspected the prowler more closely. She didn't notice the Strilu resemblance, but then she hadn't seen much of any undead. She said, "If what you say is true, then we have an extraordinary opportunity in front of us."

Mavian nodded, his green eyes alight with passion. *I see why Renna fell for him.* But there was something that Seanna had to know before she would agree to work with this man.

"I wish to speak with Mavian alone," she said.

Ropaz appeared worried, but eventually left. The scholar departed with him, followed by the prowler. When Seanna was completely alone with Mavian, she said, "Did you mean to play with my heart?"

"Madam?" His eyes were wide and confused.

"You encouraged Renna to seek my bed," Seanna said softly. He opened his mouth, then closed it and gave a helpless little shrug. Seanna continued, "I cared deeply for her. I would hold her and imagine a life with her. But she only ever used me at your behest."

She paused, waiting for a response. When none came, Seanna said, "I mourned her deeply when she was killed, even though she'd broken my heart. I mourned, too, the relationship I thought we'd had together. And I hated you for taking her from me. I despised that she loved you instead of me." Seanna took a deep breath before her next words. "So tell me, Mavian: did she ever care for me?"

His answer took a long time. In those moments of silence, Seanna built a wall around her heart, determined not to let his words affect her. At last, Mavian said, "Renna did not love you. When you were together, she imagined it was me instead."

"Then she is a fine actress indeed," Seanna murmured. She quickly wiped the tears that had sprung to her eyes.

Mavian leaned forward and tentatively reached out a hand. Seanna thought about pulling hers away, but decided not to. He rested his fingers on top of hers and said, "It was a cruel trick to play on you, Madam."

"Seanna."

"Seanna," he corrected. "I allowed my spite and petty actions to guide me. I allowed love to blind me. As much as I love Renna, she brought forth some of my worst impulses. It was for her that I joined with Rask and dominated the prowlers.

It was for her that I attacked the Masque."

"My father died because of you," Seanna said, though there was no spite in her words. It was a simple truth.

Mavian shut his eyes. "Many loved ones died because of me. I understand if you will never forgive me, but I believe we must still find a way to work together."

Her heart had already been hardened by so much loss and war. When she had learned of her father's death, Seanna still had a crown on her head, a husband, and a family in Brin. Her pain had never gone away, but it had grown smaller and smaller through necessity.

"I may never forgive you," Seanna said. "But I trust that your goals are the same as mine. Now, if you don't mind, I've been sleeping on hay for most of the journey, and I would enjoy a bath and a real bed, even one made of stone."

"Of course. Ronan will escort you into the city and provide you with accommodations."

"Excellent." Seanna stood and held out her hand. "I pray that we find success."

Mavian kissed it and bowed. "I will do all in my power to make it so."

As she departed, Seanna wondered whether dealing with the devil would be the price of victory. *Anything to tear down Aremo,* she assured herself. *There is no right or wrong in war, only survival.*

CHAPTER TWENTY-EIGHT
Sandu

D'Clet rose over the landscape like a huge grey headstone, the clouds that hung low over the mountains an epithet that constantly reminded Sandu of Alex's murder. Had they bothered to bury his friend? Or had they flung his body into the ravine, leaving a feast for the wyverns that dwelled deep below?

In front of him, Gwen and Lintem crouched behind a scrub pine. The pair watched the valley, though Sandu didn't know what they were searching for. He shifted from foot to foot, his gaze flickering back and forth from the witch to the city. The waking nightmares encroached on his mind, pressing in with the closeness of those dark walls. Sandu took deep breaths, holding the visions at bay with all the strength he could muster.

Minutes dragged by until Gwen finally pointed to a cluster of woods east of the city. "That's where we'll find them."

"Who?"

"The ones whose Songs are familiar to me."

She talks in riddles almost as much as Darian did. Sandu wondered what became of the blind man and Jagger after they fled D'Clet. He hoped they'd found a cozy place to weather the winter and stay out of trouble. *Though that's unlikely with Jagger.*

They made their slow way toward the city, avoiding the main road, fearful of spies or soldiers from Chadron's forces. Sandu didn't mind trudging on animal paths. Green growths sprouted underfoot while trees sported bulbs and small leaves, the mountains finally preparing for spring. He breathed deeply of the sweet, clean air, his hopes renewing with the warmer days. And, in the cluster of green and brown, he couldn't see D'Clet. That, more than anything, lightened his heart and drove away the darkness in his head.

Murmuring voices ahead made him pause. Gwen's gaze was distant, and she seemed to be listening. After a moment, a broad smile swept over her cheeks. She met Sandu's eye. "Are you ready?"

No. Sandu nodded his head anyway.

Gwen peeled back the branches to reveal a sunny meadow. A brook cut its way through the grass, and birds wheeled overhead. Three men were in the meadow resting beneath a large oak.

Sandu's heart leapt as he recognized two of the men. "It's Darian and Jagger!"

But as he realized who the third was, his joy sapped into fear. The third man was Mavian Strilu. The last time Sandu had seen him, the bastard had set his prowlers on the Masque. The memory of their bites flitted across Sandu's skin, casting a shadow over his heart.

"What are they doing with *him*?" Sandu whispered.

"Mavian was my friend once," Gwen said in a low voice. "His Song echoes with remorse."

"I almost died because of him."

"The same could be said for Jagger, no?" Gwen said. "If you forgave one monster, surely you could do the same for another? I do not look forward to this meeting, but I know that it's necessary if we wish to stop Cara."

"Fine." Sandu crossed his arms and frowned at the men. "Let's get it over with."

Jagger noticed them first. He sprang to his feet, a knife appearing in each hand as his gaze swept over Gwen and Lintem. Mavian turned, his mouth dropping in a wordless gape.

Sandu stepped out from behind the witch and nightcat, his hands raised. "It's alright, Jagger. I'm with them."

Jagger relaxed only slightly, his glare still fixed on the nightcat.

Darian got to his feet and moved forward, his smile as bright as the sky overhead. "You found us at last. Welcome, friends."

Mavian came forward slowly. "You know these people?"

Darian nodded. "The young man is Sandu Crin, former companion to Cara Gellder. You may remember her." Mavian made a strangled noise as Darian continued, "And I believe you and Gwen are already well acquainted."

Mavian's gaze ran over her. He said weakly, "Gwen?"

"Hello, Mavian," she said. Her voice was neither pleasant nor tense. She spoke to him as if chatting to a neighbor one doesn't know particularly well.

"What happened to you?" Mavian asked.

Sandu joined Darian and Jagger to watch the exchange. In Jagger's steadying presence once again, Sandu allowed himself to relax. *My friends wouldn't ally themselves with Mavian unless it was necessary. I can trust them both.*

Gwen gestured at the nightcat. "This is Lintem."

Mavian shook his head, still staring at her in wonder. "I knew you were a powerful sorceress, but now...now you appear like something from the fae realms. Where did you go?"

"A story for later," Gwen said. She turned to Darian. "I knew your Song was familiar. Thank you for leading us here."

Darian inclined his head. "Come into the city, and we will all share our stories."

How do they know each other? Sandu glanced between them.

"The city?" Gwen peered at the imposing maze of stone. "What about Chadron?"

"He's dead," Mavian said. Beneath the veneer of confidence, Sandu heard a note of guilt in the man's tone. "The city is ours."

Darian and Gwen took the lead. Mavian walked slowly behind, still shaking his head. Somehow, Sandu ended up walking next to him. For a moment, he said nothing. The demons that lurked in his head pricked at him, and he feared that his mouth wouldn't work.

"You were at the Masque," Mavian said after a long silence.

Sandu could only nod.

Mavian continued, "I'm sorry. If I could go back and make it so the whole night never happened, I would."

Sandu didn't know what to say. His normal witty banter had dried up, and finally he said, "I almost died."

"I caused a lot of harm that night."

"Cara wanted to kill you. She hunted you all the way to D'Clet. She probably still wants you dead."

"Her and many others." Mavian watched Gwen. "How did you find her?"

"She went to the Woods," Sandu said. At Mavian's confusion, he continued, "I don't understand it well. All I know is that she can do things I never imagined."

"Why are you here? Not that I don't want more help, but Gwen and I didn't exactly part on good terms. And your companion, as you said, wants me dead. Surely you don't harbor any goodwill, either."

Sandu chewed his lip. *If Jagger trusts him, I can, too.* At last, he said, "Cara is going to enter the Ossuary. Some place of grand magic, I guess. If she has her way, she'll end any connection Earda has with the Underworld. Gwen means to stop her. I'm the one who knew Cara best, so I suppose that's why I'm useful. You know the Underworld, so you're useful, too. Gwen said that she can't do this alone."

Mavian nodded, his green eyes narrowed in thought. He said, "I don't think she's going to like what she finds in the castle. The queen arrived not too long ago; they hated each other."

"The queen?" Sandu stopped short. The phantom bites that lingered on his skin turned to unwanted kisses.

"What's the matter?" Mavian asked.

Sandu shook off the nightmares and resumed walking. He lied, "Nothing."

They drew many awestruck looks as they went through the city, most of the populace staring at Gwen and Lintem. She walked with her head high, ignoring the whispers. They wove through the streets and over the ravine, then into the castle. When they passed the threshold, Sandu shivered. He remembered the blonde demon standing at the top of the steps, the feel of the guards' hands on his arm, the sight of Cara sweeping the sword into Alex's neck–

Darian cleared his throat, and Sandu banished his memories. He breathed deeply and focused on Darian's words:

"We have much to explain and little time to do it. Gwen?"

The witch said, "When the queen is here, I will tell all that I know."

Sandu clenched his fists as they proceeded into the castle. *I don't want to see her.* He glanced around, and fear struck his heart.

A prowler crawled into the corridor, a dead rat caught in its mouth. Its red eyes gleamed as it padded forward. Sandu shouted in alarm and leapt back. *Why aren't the others afraid?* Sandu pointed at the prowler, but no sound escaped his dry mouth.

Jagger touched Sandu's shoulder, his hands flashing, *It's alright. Mavian's tamed him.*

Sandu shook his head. The prowler's eyes were latched on him now, its gaze curious and hungry. With a cry, Sandu tore his arm from Jagger and ran from the room, heedless of where his feet carried him. The waking nightmares flooded in, a hundred prowlers all leering at him from the shadows. His skin burned with their teeth and claws.

Someone called after him, but Sandu ignored them. His hands beat against his skull in a desperate attempt to drive out the howls only he could hear.

Sandu stumbled into a large dining hall. An array of elf and human faces greeted him, all blurring together in his panic. But one of them stood out clear, even from across the room. The queen was there, garbed in linen rather than silk, no crown on her braided hair, but he couldn't mistake her for anyone else.

His panic became shock. He was rooted to the spot, unable to think, unable to flee, his legs turned into molasses. The woman had haunted his dreams and nightmares, the kiss she'd forced on him weakening whatever resolve he'd once had. He was defenseless against the raw terror that ate up through his throat, gagging him. She was a monster, yet no one else could see it.

The others finally caught up with him. Jagger reached for him, and though Sandu's fright peaked as his friend touched him, he allowed himself to be led away. His breath ramped up again, a staccato rhythm in his chest.

Jagger led Sandu out into the light, away from prowlers and queens and shadows that writhed into memories. Yet the sunlight did nothing to dispel the darkness that clogged his soul, weaving a tapestry of fear and anguish over him.

A candle passed of sitting outside, the sun beating on his face, before Sandu found he could breathe again. His hands shook, and he gulped the water Jagger gave him. The only clear thought that came into his head was, *I can't do this.*

CHAPTER TWENTY-NINE
Seanna

The commotion at the archway startled Seanna. She glanced up from her meal, expecting a quarrel between the men. Instead, a strangely familiar face stared at her from across the room. The man had a handsome, if rustic, look about him, with a scraggly beard and unkempt hair. One of his shirt sleeves was tied over the stump of an arm.

Strangely, fear passed over his features. The silent giant came to collect him, and the young man was led away. Something about him stuck in Seanna's mind. She recognized him, but from where?

She realized with a jolt that that had been the Realm's Protector she had once called to her rooms in Riverfen. She had kissed him and known that a man's touch was never for her. Then, he'd been arrested for trying to murder her in the bathtub. Sir Eric told her he'd been released under the oath of Alexandro Strilu, and she'd later learned from Mavian that the Protector had indeed been innocent. It was Sir Chadron who had tried to assassinate her.

"Ropaz," Seanna said quietly, "What was the matter with that young man? I don't remember seeing him when we first arrived."

"He came with Lady Seastone," Ropaz said.

A sense of unease spread through Seanna. She hadn't expected to meet Gwen again, not after their disastrous relationship in Riverfen and the girl's disappearance during the

Masque.

I've groveled to so many people of late. I suppose one more won't hurt.

She didn't know what to expect from Gwen, nor what sort of welcome she'd receive. *She is still young, she will be amenable,* she tried to assure herself.

They went into a small antechamber lit with a merry fire. Seanna stopped short.

Mavian was there, of course, with his blind associate. A huge black panther – no, Seanna realized, a mythical nightcat – lounged on the stone floor next to a woman who appeared as if she had crawled out of a tree.

The woman watched Seanna, and she recognized Gwen's eyes within that stranger's face.

The words Seanna had rehearsed died on her lips. What could she say to such a creature? Was Gwen even human anymore?

"Your Grace," Gwen said. She dipped her head in the barest of nods, her locks sliding over her shoulders. "Thank you for coming. Let us begin."

Without further discussion, Gwen began to speak of magic and Woods and an Ossuary, things that Seanna could hardly fathom. She tried to keep up with the discussion, but much of it went over her head. She understood that the *sulpari* wanted the Ossuary, and that if she found it, she could do terrible things. How it all worked, Seanna didn't know, but at least she had Ropaz with her. *He'll explain again if I need him to.* He was nodding along as if he fully understood Gwen's speech.

When at last Gwen finished explaining, Seanna still felt horribly confused. All this talk of magic and Songs bewildered her, and she felt very small beside all these knowledgeable people.

To her surprise, Gwen said, "Let us walk, Seanna. Allow me to give you counsel."

The wild creature stepped from the room and Seanna hurried to catch up with her. As they strode side-by-side, Seanna examined Gwen from the corner of her eye. Yes, there was the same nose wrinkle and a similar tilt to the head, a slight rolling of the shoulders. Beneath all the wildness, this person was still Gwen.

The silence stretched longer. Seanna wondered if Gwen was having as much trouble finding words as she was. Finally, Seanna could bear it no longer and said, "I am glad you're safe and well."

"Are you?" Gwen's voice held no scorn or disdain. Seanna would almost have preferred her to yell and rage.

"Yes," Seanna replied. "Much has changed since our days in Riverfen. I wish I hadn't treated you so terribly, and I'm sorry for it."

"If it weren't for you," Gwen said, "I would never have learned magic with Mavian. You changed the course of my life."

"Oh." Seanna's voice was small. *She is simply being polite.*

"So much has happened since you ruined my standing with the court. Your sins were eclipsed, and my enmity for you faded." Gwen stopped, her gaze focused on the terrace below the window. Seanna followed her look and saw the young Realm's Protector sitting at the base of the railing, his head buried in his arms while the giant stood watch.

"Why did you wish to destroy me?" Gwen asked softly.

Seanna thought back to those petty, spiteful days. The reasons she'd used to justify her actions appeared faintly in her memory, ghosts of the woman she had been before the war. After she sorted through her remembrances, she said, "I was jealous of you. You were so young and beautiful and happy. You and your husband loved each other. I wanted a piece of that joy."

Gwen nodded. "If you wish for my forgiveness, you have it. I hear your remorse in your Song."

"So you can see into people's hearts."

Gwen smiled. "It is a weighty gift."

From the terrace below, the young man cried out. Gwen shook her head. "You hurt him deeply."

"I don't understand how," Seanna said. "We only met for less than a candle. He wasn't imprisoned for long, either."

"Fear is not a creature easily understood. Sometimes, we

face horrors and come out no worse for wear. Sometimes, a mundane strife can irrevocably alter our Songs and create a fright that haunts us forever. His Song is jagged with the edges of dread, prodding constantly at him, wearing him down until only a sliver of himself remains."

Seanna was aghast. She stared down at the poor man. "I didn't mean to hurt him."

"Intention has nothing to do with it."

"What do I do to make it right? How can I help him?"

Gwen's expression was somber. "There is nothing you can do. If he gathers the courage to confront you, show him your remorse. If he never does, do not seek him out. That will only make it worse."

A spark of anger flared in Seanna's breast. "Why tell me if there's nothing I can do about it?"

"Because at least now you know to leave him alone." Gwen's voice was cold. "He knows Cara better than anyone else. If I am to face her, I need him to help me understand her Song. If you constantly hound him for forgiveness, he will be powerless against his fear."

Seanna felt powerless in that moment. Since her capture by Cairn Steel-Eyes, she had slowly worked to redeem herself to those she'd hurt. But how could she show repentance if her victim panicked every time he saw her?

Gwen turned away. Seanna said, "Thank you for telling me."

The sorceress paused and said, "It was not done for your sake."

Then she departed, and Seanna was left burdened with a guilt she had never thought twice about.

CHAPTER THIRTY
Cara

Cara heavily considered burning down the door. She could hear Talnor on the other side, giggling like a schoolgirl as Druam grunted in pain. *I should be in there.* But the door was locked, and unless Cara wanted to force it down, she'd have to wait until Talnor emerged.

At long last, the handle jiggled and Talnor came out. Blood specked her porcelain skin and golden locks, a smile on her ruby lips. That smile faded as Talnor caught sight of Cara. She quickly closed the door behind her and locked it, slipping the key into a pocket.

"You're up early," Talnor commented. Wisps of dawn sunlight had only just started to filter into the corridor, lighting the dust motes in the air.

"I didn't sleep," Cara said. "You were in there all night."

"What of it? Mordecai and I have centuries to catch up on." Talnor began to walk away down the corridor, the hem of her dress sweeping against the marble floor.

"I deserve to be in there," Cara said. She didn't have to hurry to catch up; her long strides could easily outmatch Talnor's. "I deserve to see him dead."

"He entrapped me for lifetimes. He is mine."

Cara grabbed Talnor's arm, forcing her to a stop. Though the *fampir*'s eyes flashed red, her skin didn't transform.

"Let. Me. Go." Talnor hissed.

"Or what?" Cara leaned down, her own skin marred by the

beast's ridges and fangs. It was still difficult to face herself in the mirror every morning only for a monster to peer back at her. No matter how she tried, she couldn't change her features back to smooth human. The beast no longer dwelled in her stomach or whispered in her head. She was the beast, fully and completely, and her temper had grown hotter and hotter with each passing day.

"Rask worships me," Talnor said. "If you harm me, he'll make sure you pay the price."

Cara laughed at that. "Rask's an old man. I could kill him easily. Does he not remember who won this city for him, and with what powers?"

"You still need me to bring you to the Ossuary," Talnor said.

"Then do it," Cara spat. "I'm tired of waiting."

A long moment passed in silence. Cara subtly tightened her grip on Talnor's arm. The *fampir* glared at her, then finally said, "Meet me at the conservatory in a candle."

Cara curled her lip, exposing her sharp teeth, then strode away. *I'll play their game a little while longer. Just until the Ossuary is in my grasp.*

She meandered into the vast courtyard between the palace and gardens. It was not the pretty sight it had been on her first visit to the palace. Bodies were stacked on one side, each missing its head. In the center, the headsman labored over his work, efficiently executing each person that Rask had deemed traitorous or untrustworthy. All had been Druam's loyal nobles and councillors.

Heads were laid out in a neat line. Cara paused as she came to the two *fampir* that had loyally served Druam: Master Eigbrett and Shepherd Marin. Their skin was pale, their blank eyes staring into nothing. There was no sign of their undeath, no ridges on their foreheads or fangs over their lips. They appeared as normal men.

They deserved this.

In front of the headsman, the wizard Avallune stood tall and proud. Sweat dripped down his face, and he had been deprived of his fine robes, clad instead in a sackcloth. His hands had been chained behind him, his lips gagged with a leather binding. No magic would save him this time.

The click of a cane on stone announced Earl Rask's arrival. The old man coughed into a kerchief as he came up beside Cara. His watery eyes held great satisfaction.

"The headsman started early this morning," Rask said. "I don't think the sun had risen yet."

Only a few days had passed since they'd taken the city. Cara commented drily, "The trials must have gone quickly."

"Oh yes," Rask chuckled. "I didn't want any delay." He frowned as he watched Avallune. "I do wish that one had seen reason. He could have been useful to me."

"You would never have been able to trust him," Cara said. She watched as Avallune kneeled in front of the block, his eyes fixed on her. She didn't look away when the headsman's axe fell in a graceful arc and those clever eyes were dimmed forever.

For a short moment, guilt passed through her. That man had once helped her in her quest to find Renna. He had served the city faithfully, defending it until his end. He had not been *fampir*.

Cara nudged away the feeling, assuring herself, *Some innocents must die if the guilty are to face their sins.*

"Come, I wish to speak with you," Rask said, gesturing toward an open-sided tent on one end of the courtyard. It had chairs facing the executions and a table laden with food, a recreational spot for the victors to enjoy the fruits of their siege.

Cara walked slowly to match the old man's stride, then sank into one of the chairs. She picked at a piece of bread, but didn't eat a bite. Rask's thin hands trembled a little as he lifted a goblet to his mouth.

"I have you to thank for all this," Rask said, gesturing vaguely at the courtyard. "Without your talents, the city would likely still be under Druam's thumb, and we would have lost many more men in gaining it."

Cara inclined her head but didn't reply. Her gaze was stuck firmly on the blood-soaked axe as it sought another victim.

"However," Rask continued, "what concerns me now are

your loyalties. When we first met, Talnor had assured me that you were under control. I have begun to doubt her."

"Hm."

"I wonder if perhaps you will pin your ire on me." Rask's tone was calm, but there was a warning in his voice. "The danger with dogs, you see, is that you never know when one will turn on its master."

"I'm not your dog," Cara said.

"And therein lies the problem." Rask sighed and lifted a sweet pasty to his mouth. Crumbs dotted his lips as he smacked. He said through a full mouth, "I have always been able to tell a man's price. Sometimes I'm even willing to pay it. But you, Cara Gellder, are a mystery to me. You are a rustic, yet you seem to hold no taste for luxury. You are a warrior, but clearly desire more than the thrills of battle. What is your price? What must I do to keep you in line?"

Cara didn't hesitate. "Give Druam to me."

"You know I cannot do that."

She cast him a disdainful look. "Then you'll have to hope that my goals continue to align with yours."

"Surely there must be something else," he wheedled. "Land and a title, perhaps? Control of the city?"

Cara contemplated. Though her beastly emotions demanded immediate compensation in the form of Druam's death, she forced herself to slow down and think. Other than the Ossuary, what did she truly desire? Surely she could coax something out of this old man desperate to keep himself alive.

After a moment's thought, Cara said, "You will give all labor necessary to find and excavate the Ossuary. Even soldiers must put in their work."

His eyes narrowed. "Anything else?"

He was right to be suspicious. She would gain access to the Ossuary with his help or not, but she needed to know that she could trust him. She had overheard his true desires, but would he allow her into his inner circle?

"I want to know why you support Talnor. What will she do for you? Why did you want her raised?"

Rask let out a low grunt, his hands twined over the top of his cane. His watery eye never left her. He said, "The first request I will gladly grant. As for my motivations, those are my own, and not for purchase."

Cara leaned toward him, the red in her eyes glowing with the sunlight. A spurt of black flame burst from her hand, heating the tent and making him sweat. "You are but an old man, and I have the power that won this war for you. If you want my loyalty, you must give me honesty in return."

Rask popped a grape between his thin lips. "Then I call your bluff. You wouldn't kill me in front of all my guards. Talnor would seek your blood. If our alliance is to hang by a thread, then so be it."

I still need the Ossuary. Cara lowered her hand, and the flame sputtered out. Rask gave a short laugh. "I knew you didn't have it in you."

She stood without a word and strode away toward the gardens.

✳

"It's here," Talnor said. She stood in the center of Druam's conservatory, her eye roving over the blackened plants and neglected flagstones. Beneath her feet, a wyrm was carved into a stepping stone, curling in on itself in a spiral of scales and long wings.

"You're sure?" Cara asked. The overwhelming smell of rot and refuse made her want to gag, and she held down her breakfast with effort.

"Oh yes," Talnor said. "I remember, for I came just after Valder had destroyed my kin. His laborers were just placing this stone when I slaughtered them."

"So Druam built his entire palace around the Ossuary? It must be just below our feet." Cara shuffled her boots, imagining the ancient sorcerer's workshop not ten feet under her.

Talnor gave a scornful laugh. "Don't get too excited. The Ossuary itself is deep within the plateau, perhaps as low as the bedrock. There are many, many levels which must be traversed in order to reach it."

Cara frowned. "You never mentioned that."

"You never asked." Talnor gave a wistful sigh. "Valder was always careful with his research. Those of us who were allowed in were blindfolded and led down and down and down, spun around at intervals, even left to sit so we lost track of the time."

"How long will it take to excavate?"

Talnor gave a small shrug, and Cara rubbed her nose in irritation. Her heightened senses made it difficult to concentrate with the encompassing, awful smell around her. She longed to step outside the dead conservatory and breathe fresh air again.

Talnor didn't move. She ran the toe of her boot over the carved wyrm. "After centuries apart, I will see Galiyar again."

Cara paused, her mouth going dry. Talnor had barely spoken of her mate.

"He led the charge against Valder," Talnor said. "After he turned Druam and Verdon, he left me to care for them. I could feel Valder's Song even though it was too faint to affect me. It rattled my bones. Made me feel hollow."

There was an ancient grief in Talnor's eyes. "I abandoned my charges. They didn't matter. But Galiyar did. When I came to the River Valley, I saw them: *fampir* transformed to stone. Only one or two at first, then more and more the closer I came to this plateau. This entire hilltop was covered with them.

"I knew that Galiyar was at the heart of this place. I thought I could save him. But the stone was locked with a seal, and I could not enter." Talnor bent and ran her fingers over the worn runes. "I destroyed every *fampir* statue I could find on the surface. I don't know if it freed their souls. I dearly hope it did."

Cara stood spellbound. There was a wistfulness in Talnor's voice, an open wound that made the *fampir* woman horribly vulnerable. If Cara had walked upon a stranger in this condition, she may have put her hand to their shoulder and tried to comfort them. Instead, she held back, her twisted feral features stuck in a scowl.

While the moment lasted, Cara asked, "How did you and

Galiyar meet?"

"We lived in the same Minwood tree," Talnor said. "We married as young elves. But then the Dead's War came. Galiyar wanted to fight, but a wasting sickness took him. He shriveled in less than a year, turning from strong and hale to a walking corpse.

"That was when King Landin's sorcerers came asking for volunteers in a new experiment. They said it could grant Galiyar health and a longer life. How could we refuse?"

"Did you know what would happen? What they would do to you?"

Talnor's gaze was lost in memories. She said, "How could we? It was all so secretive. We went into those chambers mortal elves and emerged more powerful than we could have imagined. Galiyar became whole and strong once more, and I...I lost the child I'd been carrying."

Cara took in a sharp breath. She didn't dare move, both appalled at Talnor's emotion and intrigued by the story.

Talnor turned up those achingly familiar blue eyes, now tinged with red. There were no tears in them. "I had my revenge. I killed all those sorcerers, every last one of them. If we could not be happy in life, Galiyar and I could satiate ourselves in undeath."

Cara didn't respond, and Talnor stood, wiping her hands on her dress. She rolled her shoulders back, and any trace of the vulnerable woman vanished between her usual icy veneer.

"What do the runes say? How do we bypass the seal?" Cara asked.

"The blood of Valder Riesk and King Landin will open the seal," Talnor answered flatly.

"Blood of men long dead," Cara said. "There's no other way?"

"None."

"And you knew this." Cara's temper rose, flushing her cheeks. "You knew all along that we had no way into the Ossuary!"

Talnor started, "I–"

The clicking of a cane on flagstone made them both pause. Rask moved slowly toward them, his gaze as rotten as the surrounding leaves.

"What do you want?" Cara spat.

"So this is it," Rask murmured. He ran the end of his cane over the wyrm carved into the ground. "The Ossuary."

"But we can't undo the seal." Cara glared at Talnor. "Something our friend here forgot to mention."

Talnor cut in, "We need the blood of Riesk and the ancient King Landin."

"I don't see why that would be a problem," Rask said lightly. He coughed before he spoke again, "The line of kings has been unbroken since Landin's reign. I do believe the current infant king possesses the blood of his ancestors."

"Will it be enough?" Cara pressed. "The centuries have diluted it."

"The magic inside our veins is strong," Rask countered. "As you both well know."

Talnor said, "And what of Valder Riesk? I wasn't aware that he had any descendants."

Rask rubbed the wolfhead on top of his cane and stared down at the runes. "It was a closely guarded secret. He had an illegitimate heir that was but a child when he passed on. My family took that child in, and when she was of age, the patriarch married her."

Cara gaped at him, trying to understand his meaning. *It couldn't be this simple...could it?*

"You never told me this," Talnor said, her voice tinged with suppressed anger. "There could be no secrets between us."

"It wasn't relevant until this moment," Rask rejoined. "But now that we need the blood of Valder Riesk, I will admit that I am his direct descendant. It shouldn't take more than few droplets, hm?"

His quick return to business left Cara reeling. Her fingers wrapped around her hilt, her mind racing. *Rask wants immortality, but will admit it to no one. He holds all his secrets close...what else might he be hiding?*

Before she acted too rashly, Cara asked, "Must the blood of both be placed on the runes at the same time?"

Talnor shook her head. "As long as Rask's blood dries upon it, it should still work when we find the infant king."

Then we don't need Rask anymore.

Cara drew her sword and swung it in one fluid movement. Talnor cried out. Rask's eyes widened as the blade cut deep into his belly, his blood pouring onto the runes, which glowed an eerie blue.

Rask made a small noise, as if he couldn't quite believe it. He reached down to his stomach, his fingers coming up wet and red. He stared at them in surprise, his mouth working but no words coming out.

Talnor cried out and stepped forward. Cara drew her sword back and plunged it deep into Rask's chest, its tip coming out of his back slick with blood. The old earl made a strangled sound, then collapsed to the ground. Talnor fell to her knees beside him as he took desperate breaths. Cara pulled out her sword and watched them apathetically.

"How could you do this?" Talnor demanded, her hands on the old man's belly. "He's dying!"

"Good."

Rask sputtered and wheezed, his hands scrabbling at his wounds.

"You'll hang for this," Talnor said. "He–"

"Stop acting as if you actually cared about him," Cara said. She smiled as Rask grew still, his chest only rising the tiniest bit. "Neither of you had affection for the other. He wanted immortality and youth, you wanted Galiyar and revenge."

Talnor stood, her fingers closing around the gem at her neck. "Traitor! We trusted you–"

Cara laughed. "Did you? You didn't trust me, you used me. Now, either do as I say, or join him in the afterlife. Your choice."

Talnor glared down at Rask's corpse, then back up at Cara. "We were meant to rule as sisters."

"Don't think I'll fall for that again," Cara hissed. "I was a pawn in your games, nothing more. I'm done being pulled about by those who think they have more power than me. I will not yield to you any longer."

Talnor's eyes hardened. She muttered a few syllables, her fingers slashing runes into the air. A Dread Portal tore open the air behind her. The ground shook, throwing Cara off her balance. By the time she regained herself, Talnor had run into the portal, and it closed behind her.

Cara swore, then paused. Rask lay dead before her, and Talnor had vanished.

Riverfen was well and truly hers. *As are Druam and the Ossuary.* Cara's teeth poked over her lips in a broad smile as she stooped to clean her sword on Rask's tunic.

CHAPTER THIRTY-ONE
Sandu

In the quiet tower room, Sandu sat by himself. It was the only place he could find that didn't bring back memories. He could breathe easier there, where the open window looked out over the mountain instead of the city.

The door opened, and Darian entered. He joined Sandu at the window.

"The Songs are quiet tonight," Darian said softly.

"Good." In the darkness, Sandu couldn't see much of anything. He wondered if this was how Darian felt all the time. After a moment, he said, "I've felt so lonely lately. I have to watch where I go and who I'm with. I can't relax knowing that the queen could be in the next chamber over. What do I do?"

Darian's breathing was low and quiet, but in the room's silence, it was loud as bellows. He said, "Do you think confronting her will help you?"

"I don't know," Sandu confessed. "Sometimes I wish I could, just so I can see whether she feels sorry for it. But then I'm scared that she won't care. And I don't know which I'd prefer, honestly. Neither of those will change what happened."

"Can you forgive her?"

Sandu frowned. "I don't see how that would help anything."

"Forgiveness is not an act of mercy for the wrongdoer. It is acceptance for you. How can you ever let go and heal unless you acknowledge what happened?"

"She kissed me, is all. It only lasted a moment. I don't

understand why it haunts me."

Darian sighed deeply. "Did you want her to kiss you? Were you happy about it?"

"Well, no."

"Then she violated your person. She forced intimacy on you without permission, and therefore made you feel unsafe."

Sandu grappled with this. Was he ever really unsafe with the queen? He could have thrown her off if he wanted. *But I didn't. I froze.* He hugged his knees. "But I wasn't ever really in danger."

"No? Danger is not always life-and-death."

"But I've experienced so much worse," Sandu protested. "I've nearly died – three times! – and I watched my wife suffer before she passed."

"Pain is not rational," Darian said. "Just as we cannot predict what will give us joy or who we will love, we don't always know what will hurt us the most."

Sandu rested his chin on his hands and contemplated Darian's words. He said quietly, "Do you think I should talk to the queen?"

"Only if it will help you to heal."

Not like I'll get any more sleep tonight. Sandu pushed himself to his feet.

✳

Sandu stood under the archway with his arm tucked under his stump, warring with himself. If he took another step, he'd be in the same room as the queen. He'd gotten this far through dogged determination, but now that he was so close to her, fear had lodged itself in his throat. What could he possibly say to her? She was the queen, and he was nobody.

His gaze was stuck on her. She was seated on the far side of the chamber with her predicant, engrossed in conversation. They wouldn't notice him.

Before he could flee, Ropaz caught sight of Sandu. The predicant frowned and leaned toward the queen. She startled and stared at Sandu, the blood draining from her face.

Stiffly, the predicant stood and walked over. He appeared a kind man, though a serious one. Sandu was reminded of all the confessions he'd given to stern clothmen. *Never given a confession to a predicant, though.*

"Sandu," Ropaz said softly as he drew near.

"You know my name?" Sandu gaped at him.

"Seanna told me," Ropaz said. "She explained what happened between you."

"Oh." Sandu shifted awkwardly, his missing arm tingling.

Ropaz glanced back at the queen, then said to Sandu, "Would you like to speak to her?"

"I..." Sandu fought to put the words through his dry mouth. After a moment, he managed, "I don't know what to say."

"Would it be easier to speak to me?"

Sandu nodded. Ropaz said, "Wait here a moment."

He walked away to the queen. After a quick word, he summoned a steward and sent for privacy screens. Sandu shifted from foot to foot, staring at the walls, the ceiling, the floor. Anywhere but at her. When the steward finally returned with a pair of folded wooden screens, Ropaz positioned them against a wall about two feet apart. He then put three chairs out, one to the left, one in the middle, and one to the right of the screens. The steward bowed and left, and Ropaz gestured Sandu to come forward.

"Sit here," Ropaz said, indicating the left chair. Sandu peered around as Ropaz sat the queen to the far right, and then himself in the center space between the two screens.

"There," Ropaz said. "Pretend it's a confessional. Speak only to me. Perhaps it will be easier to explain that way. Please do not speak while the other is giving their account. Sandu, would you like to start?"

Sandu fiddled with the knee of his breeches and took a deep breath. *Pretend it's just any old clothman. That this is any old novum.*

"Shepherd," he said, "forgive me my affronts to the gods. I have gambled and lied, abandoned my family, and been a coward."

"The gods embrace you," Ropaz said softly. "Unburden your heart."

Sandu did. He told Ropaz everything, from his father going to prison, to Tambrey kicking him out, to taking jobs as a bounty hunter disguised as a peddler. He told what happened with Jagger and Fauste's Shiv, and taking the bounty for Cara and the events leading them to Riverfen.

"I was trying to be brave and loyal," Sandu said. "I went into the palace to find Cara. The Realm's Protectors hired me, and so I had good opportunities to search for her. Then..."

He faltered. *The queen is sitting on the other side of those screens.*

"Go on. It's only you and me," Ropaz said.

"Then I met the queen. She talked to me and took me to her rooms. I don't know why. Then she...she kissed me. It didn't last long, but I couldn't stop it. I didn't want to hurt her, but I didn't want her doing that, either. When she left, I couldn't move. I was dazed. Then I heard her scream, and I found her being drowned in the bath by another man. I tried to save her, and they threw me in the dungeons."

"Do you wish to share more?"

"Yes." Now that he'd started, Sandu grew lighter. He continued with his story, all the way up to watching Cara behead Alex. But he didn't mention the waking nightmares. Not yet.

"A tragic tale," Ropaz said. "Tell me, why do you think these events are affronts? Most were out of your control."

"Because of my cowardice. If I'd been strong enough, Da wouldn't have gone to debtor's jail in my place. I would have stopped gambling and faced my problems. Later on, maybe I wouldn't have betrayed Jagger. Or would have stood up to Cara."

"Why do you think you were unable to do these things?"

"I'm weak," Sandu said. He brushed his eyes with his sleeve. "I've always been weak. The past few months have only proved that."

"How so?"

"Most men could carry on and be strong. Not me. My own mind has turned against me. I see these...these waking nightmares. They're memories, of the queen and her knight and Cara and the prowlers, all around me, forcing me to relive those awful moments. I can feel the kisses and bites on my skin, and I lose control of my voice." Sandu's words stumbled and faltered, the panic threatening to rise in his chest. He pushed on. *I've explained it before, I can do it again.* The more he spoke, the firmer his voice grew. "I see things that aren't there. I feel like I'm going mad. And I can't help but think it's a punishment from the gods for my weakness."

Finished at last, Sandu leaned back against the wall. He rubbed the tears from his beard and took a steadying breath. After a moment, the predicant said, "You are not alone in your pain."

"I'm not?"

"I have met others who have experienced these waking nightmares, as you call them. Men who fought in battle, women who lost their children or were beaten by their husbands, people just like you whose minds could not heal from their suffering. I told each of them what I tell you now: it is not a weakness nor a punishment."

"Then what is it?"

Ropaz took a deep breath and said, "It is unfortunate. An unbalance of the humors, perhaps, or a cry for help. No matter the cause, even the strongest people can succumb. It says nothing about your morality or your goodness, only that you have suffered greatly."

Sandu thought about this for a bit. Somewhere, deep inside him, something loosened at the knowledge that he wasn't alone in experiencing this. That it wasn't some divine punishment or repayment for his misdeeds. He said, "Is there a way to cure it?"

"Some have overcome it. Some have not. It is not an easy road, but I will help you walk it if you wish."

"I'd like that." Sandu smiled even though no one could see him.

"Is it alright if I speak to Seanna now?"

Sandu had forgotten that the queen was even there. He said, "Yes. I think I'm ready for that."

"Shepherd," came the queen's voice, "forgive me my affronts to the gods. I have lied and gossiped, committed adultery and brought harm to others."

"The gods embrace you. Unburden your heart."

"My affronts are too numerous to list today, but I wish to dwell on one that has greatly hurt another." The queen's voice trembled. "I did not intend it, but my actions have brought immense pain to a man who did not deserve it."

Sandu gripped his knee and closed his eyes, forcing himself to breathe as regularly as possible. *Listen. Just listen to what she has to say.*

"Go on," Ropaz said.

"When I was in Riverfen, I met a maid. Her name was Maeria. Well, actually, it was Renna, but I didn't know that yet. I cared for her and brought her into my bed."

That surprised Sandu.

The queen continued, "But she betrayed me, and I learned that she was truly in love with Mavian. I was angry with her. In my jealousy and pain, I thought to try another man. I've never enjoyed my husband's arms, but I thought perhaps I hadn't found the right man. So when I met a handsome Realm's Protector, I decided to kiss him and see if it moved me."

Ropaz was silent. Sandu's arm and legs trembled, his panic bubbling below the surface. Still, he forced himself to wait and listen.

"It was selfish," the queen said. "I did it to serve my own purposes, and thought nothing of the Protector's dignity. I kissed him, and when I realized it did nothing for me, I left him."

"Did you realize then that you had scarred him?"

"No." A shaking sigh, as if the queen were breathing through tears. "I have lived these past months in ignorance while he suffered."

"Do you feel remorse for your actions?"

"Yes. If I could change things, I would. If I could speak to the young man, I would tell him how sorry I am. If there is anything I could do to make things right, I would do so in a heartbeat."

Ropaz said, "Even if the gods forgive you, I cannot speak for the Protector. Sandu, what do you say to her?"

Sandu startled. He hadn't expected to talk to her, even through Ropaz. His throat closed up, his phantom arm aching with pain. He opened and closed his mouth a few times, but nothing came out.

"Do not feel as if you have to give an answer," Ropaz said. "After all, Seanna has only confessed to me."

This time, Sandu spoke to Seanna. He didn't care in that moment that he was speaking to the queen, nor that his words were biting. He said, "I can't give you forgiveness yet. I want you to feel guilty. I want my pain to hurt you the way it's hurt me. If we all come out alive at the end of this, maybe I'll be able to reconsider. But right now, it's still too raw."

"That is your right," Ropaz said. The queen didn't speak at all.

Sandu pushed away from the wall and walked to the archway. *I need some fresh air.*

CHAPTER THIRTY-TWO
Seanna

The stone beds were no more comfortable to sleep on now than when Seanna first came to D'Clet so many months ago. At least she didn't have a child in her belly to impede her tossing and turning. When she could bear no more, Seanna slipped from between the heavy furs and pulled a robe about her shoulders. The nights were still too cold to remove the heavy stone block from the window, and she couldn't stand the impenetrable blackness of her room.

Holding aloft a candle in a sconce, Seanna slipped from her room, her feet sinking into the heavy rug in the corridor. Very few were awake; she heard little noise as she tiptoed through the castle.

At one juncture, she heard the tapping of tools from Mavian's workshop. She left him to his nighttime work. A shiver passed over her spine, and she glanced behind her.

Gwen's nightcat padded softly down the hallway, a limp rabbit hanging from his jaws. His gold-green eyes turned to Seanna, and as he passed, his scorpion tail flicked by her feet. Seanna jumped, but the nightcat paid her no more heed.

Her steps eventually carried her to the small novum built within the castle's walls. To her surprise, a faint glow came from beneath the door. When she creaked it open, she found Ropaz kneeling beneath the statues of the nine gods, his back to her.

"Who is it?" Ropaz asked without turning around.

"Only me," Seanna replied. She kneeled beside him and set

her candle on the floor. "You couldn't sleep either?"

"No," Ropaz said. "I decided to pray for Landin and Portia's safety."

A lump came into Seanna's throat, and she forced it down with a heavy swallow. "Then I will pray with you."

For a time, they stayed together in silence, each mouthing their own prayers for their loved ones. *Keep him safe. Keep him healthy. I will be with him again soon.* With Ropaz beside her, Seanna felt a twinge of guilt for praying about Portia. *Keep her safe. Let me see her again soon.*

Shame intruded into her thoughts. How could she pray for her own family when she'd done so much harm to another? She had given her confession to Sandu, but received no forgiveness for it. *Let Sandu find peace. Let him grow whole despite my harm.* A selfish part of her wanted to add, *So that I won't feel so guilty whenever I hear his name,* but she kept that in the back of her mind where it belonged.

When her knees had started to hurt from the cold stone floor, Seanna pushed herself to her feet and held a hand out for Ropaz. He took it, and she pulled him up. As he dampened the candles, Seanna said, "I wonder if Gwen could help us find our loved ones."

Ropaz grew still, his fingers trembling on the raised damper. "They are likely already dead."

"Aremo wouldn't give up his hostages," Seanna argued. "Gwen possesses magic beyond our imagining. If anyone could do it, she could."

Slowly, Ropaz lowered the damper over the flickering wick. With no more candles alight, the novum was dark and smoky. In the gloom, he said, "She isn't human anymore. Why would she see reason to help us?"

Seanna put a hand on his arm. "I knew her before. That Gwen is still in there, even if she's buried beneath the grime. What do we lose by asking her? The potential gains far outweigh the risk of rejection."

"You are putting far too much trust in old enemies. Gwen has cause to despise you, and Mavian attacked the Cascade

Palace. That blind man knows far more than he tells, and he travels with an assassin. Don't think I didn't recognize Jagger Cross's name and reputation. We are surrounded by liars and murderers, and you want to hand them our vulnerabilities?"

Seanna had never heard Ropaz speak so vehemently. She took a step back, wishing her eyes could adjust better to the darkness so she could see his expression. "Gavriel–"

"I will not lose you, too!" Ropaz's voice was low, but his words were forceful. "You're the only friend I have left in this miserable place."

That's what he fears? Despite the tension, Seanna smiled. She cupped her hands around his. "I know your loss and pain. You're the only person I trust here, and I could not bear it if something happened to you. But if we are to survive this and find Portia and Landin, we must be decisive now. We must allow the possibility of risk in order to gain rewards. You are strong and compassionate, but remember to save some of that for yourself."

For a moment, Ropaz stood still. Then he wrapped his arms around her and embraced her. Seanna nestled her head into his shoulder and rubbed his back. She murmured, "When was the last time you did anything for yourself? Took a long bath or savored a sweet pastry?"

"There's never been enough time to think of my own selfish needs." His words were coarse, their cadence laden with tears.

"You cannot care for others if you don't take care of yourself first. We will manage a few days without you; go into the city and drink or gamble, lock yourself in your chamber with a pile of books, whatever you need to find your strength once more."

"But the Lofalins–"

Seanna spoke over him, "I will tend to the war effort. This is an order from your queen: get some sleep and relax a little. Then, when you're ready, rejoin my council."

He leaned his cheek against her hair and didn't say anything for a few breaths. Then, finally, he murmured, "Thank you, Seanna. I think some days outside the city will greatly comfort my soul."

Before he pulled away, she clutched him and said, "I will do everything I can to bring our loved ones back. Even if it means working with those we don't trust. But I promise, I will watch out for myself. You won't lose me."

She released him, and he stepped quietly away. The door opened, and he gestured for her to follow. Outside of the smoky novum, the corridor air felt cool and light. Seanna breathed deeply and nodded to Ropaz. "Feel no guilt for doing what you must for yourself."

He hesitated, then nodded and strode away. After he disappeared around a corner, Seanna returned to her own rooms, and sleep claimed her at last.

❋

In the morning, Seanna sought out Gwen. She found the witch in a small courtyard lined with trees and shrubs, seated on the ground with the nightcat's head in her lap and staring up at the sky with a disturbed expression. When Seanna kneeled in front of her, Gwen blinked and lowered her gaze.

"Something the matter?" Seanna asked.

Gwen glanced up at the sky before answering, "The Woods are growing distant again. For a time, after I helped Sandu's father enter them, I could hear their melodies. Faintly, carried only on strong winds, but still there. Now I cannot hear them at all."

Seanna didn't quite know what to say to that. She eventually settled on, "I'm sorry."

"I took them for granted for so long," Gwen said. "I wish I had savored them more."

Seanna knew that feeling well. "I can understand that."

"Why have you come?"

To business, then. After shifting so that her legs were comfortably crossed, Seanna said, "I need your help. Aremo Teru has my child along with Ropaz's sister, Portia. Do you have any magics that could help us rescue them?"

The pause that came after her question was unbearably

long. Seanna wanted to reach out and shake Gwen into replying, but she forced her hands to be still in her lap. Her heart beat against her throat, and she oscillated between hope and despair. *She will help. She won't. She wants to. She can't.* Seanna's nerves thrilled with anticipation and fear, and she opened her mouth to again beseech Gwen's help when the witch spoke.

"I cannot rescue your child, but I can help you see him, if only for a short time."

"Can I hold him?" Seanna asked immediately. "Will he know it's me?"

"The scry allows him to see and hear you, but you will be ghostlike, not really there. You will not be able to touch him." Gwen's tone was kind, but her words were firm.

Seanna didn't have to think twice about it. "I'll do anything."

"Then hold out your hands." Gwen put her palms out for Seanna to take. But Seanna hesitated, remembering Ropaz's fearful words. She hadn't expected Gwen to perform her magic then and there; what if it hurt? What if it was dangerous?

"Have no fear," Gwen said. "I will be with you. Think of your child as I Sing."

Seanna swallowed hard and put her hands in Gwen's. The girl's skin was no longer soft and smooth; it was callused and rough from so long in the wilderness. Her fingers were not gentle and delicate, but firm and confident.

The witch's Song rose up around them, beautiful and haunting. Seanna closed her eyes, imagining Landin: his round cheeks and bright eyes, the patch of hair on his head, his giggles as she played with his toes.

When she blinked, she was home in Con Salur. The red cliffs rose above her, and seagulls wheeled in the blue sky. Still holding Gwen's hands, Seanna straightened and looked all around them. They were in the courtyard garden of some noble's compound in Midtown. The whitewashed walls were clean, the trees bright against them. Unintelligible voices drifted from the house, though the street beyond the wall sounded far more quiet than it should have.

And, over by the peony bush, was Portia holding Landin. She laughed as he lifted his little arms to a passing butterfly. Both appeared a little pale and thin. Seanna stared at them, transfixed. *Is this a dream?* She clutched Gwen's hand, not daring to let go for fear of losing the moment forever.

Portia caught sight of them and froze. Her mouth dropped open, and she shut her eyes as if she couldn't believe what she saw. Seanna took a few steps forward, still holding Gwen's hand, and said, "I'm here, Portia. It's me."

Gwen stayed silent, though she walked with Seanna. As Portia opened those lovely eyes once more, Seanna said, "I've missed you."

"How is this possible?" Portia asked. She was rooted to the spot, her arms clutched protectively around Landin. "Is this another trick?"

"A trick?" Seanna stopped short. "No, it's me, I swear it. What has Aremo done to you?"

At that, Portia gave a fearful glance to the house. "He's always watching. His mages fiddle with my mind, making me see things that aren't there or remembering things that never happened. This is another trick, I know it. I won't give in."

"Portia," Seanna said, reaching for her. Her fingers slid through Portia's cheek, ghostly and translucent. "How can I make you believe that it's really me?"

Seanna's heart broke at the distrust in Portia's gaze. Gone were her tender touches, her sweet smile and charm. Speaking gently, Seanna said, "When we came to Rengu, I asked you a question. You never gave the answer, so I will ask again: if you could leave all this behind you, where would you go?"

Some of the ice covering Portia's guarded expression melted away. Tears slid down her cheeks. "It really is you, isn't it?"

"I swear it, Portia."

"But how?"

"She is a powerful witch," Seanna said, gesturing to Gwen. "She brought me to see Landin. I had hoped you would be with him, and I could tell you both that..."

The words died in Seanna's throat. Portia watched her

expectantly, hope bleeding through her broken gaze.

This could be my last chance. Even if Seanna somehow gained an army, she might be too late to save them. Aremo was wicked; if he knew he might lose, he would not hesitate to kill his hostages.

Seanna swallowed. Her hand sweated in Gwen's, and she took strength from the silent witch. At last she said, "I needed to tell you both that I love you." She bent to Landin, stroking his head though her fingers did not truly touch him. "I love you, my son, more than life itself. You are precious and good, and I swear I will raise you with none of the darkness that has scourged my life." She raised her head to Portia, whose lips trembled, her cheeks wet with tears. "Portia, I'm sorry I never had the courage to say it before. I love you, for all the months you have traveled with me and stayed by my side. I love you for your compassion and kindness; you are a far better woman than I deserve, and I always feared I would hurt you. If we manage to find each other again, I will never let you go."

A shout rose from the house before Portia could answer, from an elf who had spotted them. Portia held out her hand to Seanna's cheek, but her whisper was lost beneath the clangor of armed elves rushing into the courtyard.

"We must go," Gwen urged.

Seanna blinked, and found herself once more in D'Clet, with Gwen sitting across from her and Lintem languidly licking his paws. Though her chin wobbled, Seanna did not cry. She inhaled sharply, held the breath a few seconds, and let it out.

I was a woman for a moment, but I must become the queen again.

Try as she might, though, she couldn't dislodge Portia's stricken expression from her heart.

"I need to speak to one more person," Seanna said, making a snap decision. *If one queen cannot help them, perhaps another might.* "Can you bring me there?"

Gwen's lips were pale, sweat sticking to her forehead. She took a long drink from a water bladder, then nodded. "We cannot stay for long, I fear. Bringing another with me is more taxing than going on my own."

"Then I'll be quick. I want to see Cairn Steel-Eyes."

Once more Gwen Sang, and as Seanna's vision cleared, the wide seas were around her, a tall mast with a white sail above, and a host of crewmen scurrying about. As she and Gwen popped into existence among the working throng, a hush fell over the ship. Seanna cast about, searching for the Corsair Queen, before finally catching sight of the woman at the helm.

The Corsair Queen was in her element: her hair loose and flowing with the wind, her cheeks ruddy with seaspray and her eyes sharp on the commotion below. She threw back her head and laughed at the sight of the two women who had come aboard her vessel.

"The Queen without a Throne!" Steel-Eyes crowed. "To what do we owe the pleasure?"

A corsair made to grab Gwen's arm, but his hand passed right through her. He stumbled back into his fellows. Steel-Eyes pursed her lips and made her slow, confident way down to the main deck. As she came before Seanna, she waved her hand through Seanna's cheek.

"Not really here then, are you?" Steel-Eyes said.

"Sura," Seanna murmured, low enough for the surrounding corsairs not to hear, "I need your help. Aremo Teru has taken my child and his nursemaid. Please, I beg of you...rescue them. Keep them safe in your fortress until I can defeat him."

Cairn Steel-Eyes's lips thinned. "I have already lost too many good men and ships to this war. Find someone else to do your bidding."

"You're the only one," Seanna pleaded. "Please, mother to mother. I don't know who else I can trust."

The word hung in the air, weighted with tension. Steel-Eyes said slowly, "Why would you trust me?"

"Because we both want our children to be safe." It was a gamble, Seanna knew, but she truly had no other choice. If not Steel-Eyes, no one would be able to reach Landin and Portia.

Steel-Eyes leaned in low, her voice almost too low to hear, "Bring my daughter back to me."

"I swear it."

Steel-Eyes nodded, then stepped back. Gwen finished her Song, and Seanna let out a low sigh of relief as the courtyard in D'Clet coalesced around her. She finally let go of Gwen's hand and slumped her shoulders, her body wracking with the sobs she wished she could unleash.

When she looked up, Gwen was standing over her, fury darkening her eyes. Seanna scrambled back as Gwen advanced. The nightcat rose, his tail twitching, his hungry eyes on Seanna.

"Gwen..." Seanna tried to say more, but her tongue refused to form the words.

"How dare you make such a promise!" Gwen shouted. "Cara is too far gone. She destroyed Riverfen, and you think you can bring her back from the brink? What will Steel-Eyes do with your child when you return empty-handed? Hm? She will dangle him from the bowsprit and throw Portia under the waves."

"I had no choice!" Seanna yelled back, finally unlocking her voice. She stood, only barely taller than Gwen. "You are not a mother, you wouldn't understand! I did what I must to ensure my son's safety."

"You truly believe him safer with a band of thieves? You did not hear their Songs, you didn't hear what they wanted to do to us."

"Oh, I can imagine," Seanna spat. "I was there, in that den of monsters, yet I came out the other side. And I would much rather bargain with Cairn Steel-Eyes, a woman with a price, than Aremo Teru, a madman with no sense of morals."

Lintem growled, and Gwen put a hand to his shoulder. She shook her head. "I should never have helped you."

She stalked away, leaving Seanna miserable. The witch's words had wormed into her head, making her doubt herself. *But I had no choice. I did what I must to save Landin.*

The memory of Steel-Eyes's cruel laughter rang through her head, and she wondered if she had made a promise she had no hope of keeping.

CHAPTER THIRTY-THREE
Gwen

The Song of Death blackened the caverns directly below D'Clet. As she drew closer and closer to Mavian's workshop, Gwen nearly gagged with the overwhelming flavor of it, decay left long trapped with no fresh air to blow it away. This Song was ancient, a relic from centuries past.

Gwen followed the Song through the workshop and down a labyrinth of tunnels, her way guided with glowing red orbs. Lintem padded silently beside her, his tail swishing as his large head peered side to side, searching for danger. *The danger has long left.* Yet its Song stained the corridors, a residue that would not easily wipe away. Pain and horror lay within it, souls forced into becoming *fampir* without knowing the costs.

And one undead, trapped in a sarcophagus, spending her lonely eternity dreaming up her revenge.

The room was much as Mavian had described it. The tomb in the center was bone white, matte and stark, drawing the eye to it. Blood splattered the floor, long-dried and brown. It cracked under Gwen's bare feet.

The Song of Death echoed so loudly in here that it hurt Gwen's head. It had a *fampir*'s melody, mournful and everlasting, but hatred lurked in its notes as well. A raw, terrible hatred, like Gwen had never heard before. Whoever this creature was, she despised the living, but she loathed Druam even more. His Song wrapped around this one, entwined through obsession, warped almost beyond recognition.

The Druam that this woman had known was cruel and fanatic, hunting her across the country and imprisoning her in the worst ways imaginable, his callous disregard for her pleas laced like a black string around the melodies that Gwen had known. For centuries, the *fampir* he had trapped here had been dominated by the all-consuming hope of revenge.

Deeper within the *fampir*'s Song, Gwen heard a lust for blood and an insatiable thirst. This woman had delighted in the pleasures of the hunt far more than any other undead Gwen had encountered.

And this is the creature that now whispers in Cara's ear and holds Druam captive. Within that dark, terrible Song, Gwen also heard a resounding truth: the *fampir* woman was crippled. Her undead nature that had given her power for so long was veiled from her, hidden away once she had taken a new body.

Body and soul are intrinsically wound together, Gwen realized. *Separating one from the other is nearly as terrible as Unmaking. Monsters are made when that delicate balance is toyed with. This woman is a* fampir *soul in a mortal body, condemned to die like the rest of us yet haunted by Autorus.*

With a shiver, Gwen knew, too, that the *fampir*'s original body still lay within this sarcophagus, a husk that had once held a soul trapped within it. Using the Song of Stone, Gwen moved the lid. It fell with a crash to the floor and split in half. Dust rose into the air.

When it cleared, the husk within lay brown and lifeless. It had been an elven woman once, but now its skin was dried to its bones, its eyes rotted away, its hair fallen out in clumps.

There are hundreds of fampir *trapped like this within the Ossuary.*

Gwen stared for a long time at that body and the stone surrounding it. Scratchmarks covered the marble, deep remnants of desperate attempts to escape. *How long did it take before she succumbed?* The undead woman would not have needed food, water, or air the same as a human. Her torment could have lasted far, far longer before her arms fell to her sides, her legs stiffened, and she screamed inside a body that would no longer move.

Lintem growled low, and Gwen glanced over her shoulder. Mavian was at the entrance, his face pale as he surveyed the room. He swallowed and stepped inside, his eye roving over the traces of his last visit. He came beside Gwen and, after a moment of hesitation, peered down into the sarcophagus.

"So that's Talnor," he said. "She's shorter than I'd imagined."

"Do you think she ever dreamed in there?" Gwen asked.

"I don't know if *fampir* dream the way we do," Mavian said. "One of many questions I never had the chance to ask Druam."

A heavy silence loomed between them. Mavian took a shaky breath. "I don't like this place. I can hear music, like a nightmare put to sound."

"Talnor's Song of Death," Gwen said. "She has infested this place with her melody."

"Is there any way to clear it?"

"In time it will fade." Gwen put her hand on Lintem's head. "This place is suffocating."

"Then we should go back up into the keep."

Gwen shook her head. "Not just the tomb. All of D'Clet. It's so harsh, stone and steel and endless streets leading to grey mountains. I miss horizons of trees and magic in the air."

"You miss the Woods." Mavian had always been shrewd.

Gwen's fingers curled in Lintem's fur. He purred and nudged her hip with his head. She said, "Everything in me aches to go back. The Songs on Earda feel stale and flat to me. They have no color, no spark."

"What do you mean? They're incredible. I've never felt magic so strong and encompassing."

"You did not hear it in the Woods." As Gwen spoke, the ache in her chest stretched out into her limbs, making her hollow inside and out. She longed to tread the twilight paths with her feet in the loam, to spring from branch to branch with coarse bark under her palms. She wanted to hear the whispers of the trees and to sleep where the Songs blanketed her.

"Tell me about them," Mavian said. He started walking out, and Gwen followed.

How to describe a dream?

"It is a place of quiet, yet there are endless sounds. Nothing is as it seems: the rocks are trees and the branches boulders, the animals' fur and feathers made of wood and jewels. The trees Sing to you, begging to be freed, and you must ignore them." As she spoke, Gwen warmed to the topic. She told him everything, speaking the entire journey back up through the tunnels and into the keep. They came out on the large terrace that hugged the mountain and bordered the ravine. A sharp wind slapped her cheeks and blew her hair, and Gwen raised her arms and laughed with its bite.

Mavian smiled with her, but there was something melancholic in his eye. Gwen lowered her arms.

"What's wrong?" she asked.

"I'm happy for you," Mavian said. "That you have lived and seen so much. I wish that I hadn't squandered so many of my own opportunities."

Gwen heard the regret in his Song, a steady tempo of loss and determination that beat throughout him. She said, "I can hear–"

"Will you stop that?" Mavian's hands lifted in frustration. "I can't have a normal conversation with you anymore. You're always peeking into my Song, using it to parse out what I'm going to say before I say it. It's infuriating. Don't you understand how invasive it is?"

Gwen gaped at him, taken aback. She'd grown so used to tapping into the Songs around her, she hadn't realized that it could be spying on someone's privacy. In the Woods, all creatures heard the Songs, and it was understood that the meanings conveyed were as open as a person's words on Earda.

"You never considered it, did you?" Mavian asked.

Gwen shook her head. "I'm sorry. Adjusting back to life here has been difficult, and I naturally want to use the Songs to help me. But I recognize how degrading it must feel. I will block out your Song from now on unless you give permission."

"Good." Mavian nodded. "But don't do that just for me. Everyone deserves the privacy of their own heads."

"I will try." The thought unnerved her. As much as she knew the compassion of Mavian's request, Gwen had grown used to reading others through their Songs, understanding their intentions and the truth behind their words.

But it is a crutch. She had once navigated social interactions without the Songs. She could do so once more.

With great effort, Gwen withdrew from Mavian's Song. It was woven into the threads of the music around her, and she had to disconnect it one strand at a time until she could no longer hear it. It was like blocking out one bird's call from a symphony of noise.

When it was done, Gwen asked, "Tell me what you want to do after this is all over."

"You're not listening to what's in here?" Mavian asked, pointing at his head. She nodded, and he said, "Honestly, I don't know what I'm going to do. I want to help the prowlers, but after that...my wife is dead, and I don't really want to go back to Fareyes and run the estate. I think someone else would do a better job. The scholars don't need my help in returning the university to its full glory. What purpose will I have left?"

"Perhaps you will find an answer in the Songs," Gwen said softly. In her heart, she suspected where he might go, but did not want to give voice to it. Not yet.

"Perhaps." He shrugged. "I should go. Darian wanted to teach me more of the subtleties of the Song of Death."

Gwen watched him leave. She couldn't help but empathize with his position. After all, what would she do if the war ended and the Woods were still inaccessible? All she wanted was to return to their comforting embrace and live out her days among the whispering trees.

The ravine called to her. Gwen stepped onto the wide stone railing which was all that separated her and a long, long fall. Holding out her arms for balance, she walked lightly on the stone, the black void on her left, the safety of the terrace to her right. Lintem paced beside her, a small note of worry in his Song.

What if we never go back? Gwen hummed to Lintem.

We will, he assured her.

But what if we don't? Will we find a forest and become hermits? Gwen wobbled a little, then corrected herself. *Technically, I am still Lady of Seastone. My duty would lie in that human city, surrounded by human Songs.* She shivered at the thought. She didn't know if she ever wanted to return to Druam, much less the city that he had thoroughly stamped with his ideals. Every cobble and lantern in Riverfen echoed with traces of his ancient Song. She could not escape him there.

What of Autorus? Could you take his place? Lintem asked.

The yawning drop beside her drew her eye. Gwen paused and stared into the depths. *I don't think so,* Gwen hummed. *Death has never been the strongest Song for me. Neither is Humanity. Nature calls to me, envelopes me. If I am to be a Guardian of the Songs, it will be for the Songs of Nature.*

Who will take care of the Songs of Death and Humanity?

Gwen glanced back at the door where Mavian had disappeared. *Someone better suited for them.*

There are many more Songs outside of D'Ehsen, Lintem said.

I know. Someone else will have to discover them. All I want is a hut in a meadow where there are no human Songs to clog up my ears.

I want that, too.

Gwen smiled and hopped off the railing back onto the terrace. She rubbed Lintem's ears. *Come. We have work to do.*

CHAPTER THIRTY-FOUR
Sandu

"I want to try again," Sandu said. "I want to go to the Woods."

Gwen didn't turn away from the books and parchments laid out before her. "You're not ready yet. You don't know your own Song."

"How can you be sure of that?" Sandu pressed.

"Do the nightmares still plague you?"

"Well, yes, but—"

"While you are still healing, your Song is fragile. Malleable. You must find peace within yourself before you can go to the Woods." Gwen's voice was kind but firm. He would gain no ground with her.

Before he left, though, Sandu decided to try another tactic. He said, "The Songs can do most anything, can't they?"

Gwen sighed heavily. "The greater the task, the more exertion is drawn from the wielder. Why?"

"Can they bring my arm back?"

Gwen was quiet for a long time, and Sandu nearly bent under the weight of his own shame. *Shouldn't have asked. She's got too much to do to worry about one man's woes.* He clutched at the space his arm should be, the phantom limb tingling even though he knew it wasn't there.

"If you still had the detached limb, I could perhaps encourage the two to rejoin," Gwen said at last. "But the Songs cannot change nature's tendencies. They cannot force a new one to grow, nor can they change the past. I wish I had a better answer for you."

Sandu nodded, his mouth shut tight with grief. His arm had burned away, consumed into ash to draw the plague out from him. There was no going back.

"Someday," Gwen said, "we could try a prosthetic. One charmed to move at your will. But that is a mixture of science and magic that I have not explored, and I cannot do so right now."

He didn't respond. What could he say? There was nothing that could be done now, and she may never figure out a prosthetic. He would have to resign himself to a lifetime of uselessness.

As Sandu made his way to the terrace – a place he had often found himself, a quiet spot to think and dwell on his mistakes – Ropaz intercepted him. The predicant looked refreshed.

"When did you get back?" Sandu asked, surprised to see him.

Ropaz said, "Only a candle ago"

"Do you feel better after being gone?"

Ropaz shrugged. "Time will tell."

For a time, they walked together in silence, Ropaz appearing content to simply match Sandu's slow pace. Sandu hadn't spoken much to Ropaz since the night of his confession. *Why would he seek me out again?*

They reached the terrace. The sun shone brightly on the stone, and Sandu covered his eyes. *Too bright.* He turned around and meandered back the way they'd come, his steps even slower than before. The silent predicant paced alongside him.

Without realizing it, Sandu walked to the room where Cara had murdered Alex. Though the blood had long ago been mopped up, he imagined the red stains on the rug and the sneering woman by the fireplace, the soldier's grip on his wrist and Alex's head thumping to the floor.

"Sandu?" Ropaz spoke for the first time since they'd begun their walk.

"This is where it happened," Sandu said. The waking nightmares closed in on him, bites and kisses and claws and

Cara, ripping him apart and laughing as they did. His tongue sealed itself to the roof of his mouth, his hand rapidly clenching and unclenching at his side.

The predicant reached for him, and Sandu pulled away with a cry. But Ropaz didn't let go. His grip was strong, and he grasped Sandu's chin with his other hand, forcing him to meet his eye.

"Breathe deeply," Ropaz ordered. Sandu tried to do as he instructed, but his heart was going so fast and he couldn't keep up, he had to breathe faster in order to keep up–

"Look at me," Ropaz said. "Breathe in...hold...and out. There. Just like I am. Breathe with me."

It was the most difficult thing Sandu had ever done, but he managed it once. Then twice. Then a third time, and a fourth. As he kept on breathing deeply, his heart slowed. His hand relaxed. He watched Ropaz, all his being focused on the air coming in and out of his lungs. The specters faded away, back to the edges of his soul.

"Come now," Ropaz said. "Let us find a quiet place to recover."

Sandu followed, a docile lamb, as Ropaz led him to the small novum built into the castle. Candles were lit all around the tiny space, tainting the air with their faint odor. The golden light soothed Sandu, and as he sat down across from Ropaz, he managed to whisper a few words of prayer.

For a long time, Sandu didn't say anything to Ropaz. He stared at his knees, his phantom arm aching, and tried to form words around his stubborn tongue.

"W-why are you here with me?" Sandu managed at last.

"What do you mean?" The predicant's voice was kind.

"You just got back. Why did you come to me instead of the queen?"

Ropaz scooted his chair closer until their knees were touching. He said, "I have thought long about you since your confession. I have seen much suffering and tragedy in my days in the novums, yet something about you has picked at my mind. I believe the gods want me to help you."

Sandu glanced nervously around at the nine statues. "Do you really think they're listening to us? That they can see and hear everything?"

"There are many schools of philosophy regarding the gods," Ropaz replied. "Personally, I have always thought that they do not continually observe us. I think they set Earda into motion, then retreated to their sanctums to live out their eternities."

"Then why pray to them? What good does it do us?"

"Prayers are not only answered by the gods," Ropaz said. "Some are answered by the clothmen who hear the pleas. Some by the very people who made them. Even if the gods do not interfere, the very act of worship and prayer can be a balm for many people. It comforts them."

Sandu placed a hand on one of the statues. "I've never been very religious. Didn't have much time for it."

"No one is perfect," Ropaz said with a small smile.

Sandu's hand drifted to the empty space of his left arm before he caught himself and put it on his knee instead. He clutched at the fabric of his trousers as he said, "Why would you want to help me?"

"That's not the question you should be asking," Ropaz said. "I may be High Predicant, but my heart has always been with the rustic folk. They have always had greater need than the nobles."

"So..." Sandu didn't know what to ask. He wasn't in the mood to fish for answers.

"The 'how' is the important part here," Ropaz said. "As I told you before, you are not the first man I've encountered that dealt with such nightmares. I have developed a method to help people like you, but it will require effort, trust, and confronting that which you fear. We can start with the lesser fears, the ones that haunt only a little, then work our way up to the worst ones. What do you say?"

Sandu rubbed at his knee, trying to see the trap in Ropaz's words. He could find none. *What harm could it do? Not like anything else has worked.* He asked, "Does it involve magic?"

"It does. A form of healing magic which I developed."

Ropaz smiled again. "Your friend, Gwen, recently pointed out to me that I had managed to manipulate the Song of Healing without knowing it."

"Alright." Sandu mustered up the little courage he had left. "Let's try it."

"Good. I can start now, if you wish."

After Sandu assented, Ropaz reached out and began tapping Sandu's knees, alternating left and right. He said, "Close your eyes. Imagine one of your fears -- a small one -- and the cause of that fear."

Sandu obeyed. A flow of warmth trickled up his body from his knees, and he breathed slowly. *A small fear.* His stump shivered, and he decided to focus on that one. *I'm afraid of being useless without my arm.*

In his mind's eye, he saw himself as whole once more. But then his left arm vanished, and he was left unbalanced and awkward, always unwanted and unneeded.

"Tell me what you see," Ropaz said without stopping his tapping.

"I see myself," Sandu said. "I'm trying to find work, but no one wants me. I'm not useful to them."

He imagined himself going from door to door begging for work and being turned away from all. Bakers needed someone who could properly knead the dough, Protectors needed someone who could fight, and farmers needed laborers who could wield a scythe. None of them wanted him.

"I want to work so I can feed my children, but I only see myself becoming a beggar," Sandu said. His throat closed up, and he pushed past the blockage. "I'm even more of a burden than before."

The tapping stopped. Sandu opened his eyes, his body tight with fear and melancholy. Ropaz said, "Good. You're in a hopeless place now, but we need a way to bring you out of it. You can read and write, yes?"

Sandu nodded.

"You may never be a laborer or a Protector again, but you could be a scribe. Or a clothman. Or even a steward, with your quick mind and loyalty. I'm going to start again, and I want you to picture yourself as whichever one of those appeals most to you."

After another deep breath, Sandu closed his eyes once more. He saw himself again, one-armed and slumped. He tried to picture himself as a scribe, writing manuscript after manuscript without a left arm to hold the parchment down. *No, that's not quite right.* A clothman? But he wasn't religious, he wouldn't want to betray the people that put their faith in him. And a steward involved a lot of interaction with nobles. Sandu had had quite enough of nobles.

He spoke these quandaries out loud, and Ropaz said, "Clothmen are not always men of high faith. Many join in order to lend an ear and help those in their flock to find solace."

This time, Sandu imagined himself in a clothman's robes. Instead of preaching, he was in a confessional, giving advice and helping others. The idea didn't upset him. Instead, he quite liked the thought of it.

"I could help others who are dealing with the same demons I've known," Sandu said. "Counseling them through grief or bad decisions."

"Indeed." Ropaz again withdrew. "This was not meant to force you to decide upon a new career. It was meant to help you rethink your situation. Think about your arm. What do you feel now?"

Sandu wiggled the stump as he thought about it. "I feel like I'm still missing something. But maybe it's not all bad. Maybe I don't need it to be wanted or useful."

"Very good. The loss of your arm has changed you, but it has not damaged your soul. You are still Sandu, and you have much to offer this world."

Sandu left the novum feeling lighter than he had in months. His children would be so proud if their papa became a clothman or steward, and he could support his Da on such a salary. *Maybe there is hope for me when the war is over.*

CHAPTER THIRTY-FIVE
Mavian

Mavian's eyes adjusted quickly to the moonlit forest, the silhouettes of trees dark and mysterious around him. Leaves rustled in a faint breeze, and far off, the cries of prowlers echoed in the night. Once, Mavian would have set traps for them. Now, he would wait until he had the cure. He desperately hoped that Darian would help him with that tonight.

Across from him, Darian sat with his cane over his knees. The blind man stared straight forward, and though it was foolish, Mavian couldn't help but feel as if he were being examined.

Mavian's glance flicked to the others in the clearing. Ekkar was tumbling about with happy trills, while Jagger stood straight, his arms crossed over his chest, watching the woods for any signs of danger.

"Why isn't Gwen here?" Mavian asked. Darian had brought him here to study the Songs, but he thought that she should be helping, too. Didn't she know the musical magic better than anyone?

"She hears the Song of Death, but it is weaker for her than us," Darian gave that secret smile that Mavian could never quite read. He said, "Take my hands. If you wish to cure the prowlers, you must know Ekkar's Song."

Mavian did as he was asked. Darian's hands were cool and firm, barely a callus on the smooth palms.

"Listen to the Song of Death," Darian instructed.

Mavian obeyed. When he reached out, the Song came much quicker and louder, a familiar melody now. It strummed in a steady beat around him, the consistency of Death more predictable than the foibles of life.

"Good," Darian said. "Now reach through it. Unravel only Ekkar's Song."

One thread in the Song called to Mavian. He followed it to find Ekkar's melody, one he was well acquainted with. But this time, Mavian lingered, pushing back to the Song's earliest chords, delving through its many iterations and changes, all the way back to Verdon's Song, buried deep within the prowler's. He noted how Ekkar's melody was far simpler than Verdon's, a life reduced only to instinct.

When he investigated Verdon's Song, he found far more than he could have imagined. The Song touched many, many other threads, from Songs of Knowledge and Curiosity to the Songs of the Ocean and Love. These he could barely make out, only knowing them through the memories that Verdon related to them. Unlike Druam, who had mostly stayed in Riverfen for his eternity, Verdon had traveled much of D'Ehsen and even once to the Eadrion Empire, searching for clues of his kind and other undead that could exist in the world.

One thought echoed in Verdon's Song, a lonely idea that came again and again over centuries' worth of music: *We are solitary in our undeath.* The wights had been extinguished after the Dead's War, either sent back to their graves by their masters or destroyed on the battlefield. The *fampir*'s numbers had never recovered after the Ossuary, and they did not spread across the oceans.

As Mavian withdrew from Verdon's Song, he paused at the juncture where the man's soul split from his body. The main melody continued on in Ekkar, but there was a smaller thread, only faint, that stretched out far past the clearing, disappearing into the night, a bond connected to Ekkar's Song by the barest of threads.

"Verdon," Mavian whispered. His voice reverberated through the thread. Ekkar paused, then went back to his play-fighting.

The other Song, the one that belonged to Verdon, grew louder and louder. Mavian's eye darted about the clearing, but nothing was amiss.

The sonorous note that lay beneath Verdon and Ekkar's Song tolled persistently, calling to Mavian. He didn't know what to do with it.

"Look not with your eyes, but with the Song," Darian said.

Mavian took a deep breath. The Song sounded around him, as loud as before. He shut his eyes. Flashes of color burst behind his eyelids, vibrant with the music of the Songs. Fixing those in his mind, Mavian opened his eyes once more.

The color remained, overlaying the creatures in the clearing. Red and orange around Ekkar, a cool blue over Jagger, and over Darian...

A kaleidoscope of color, every note and whirl of Death, masking the shape of Darian's body with their bright light. Mavian nearly covered his eyes. As he blinked away the intense motes of color, he noticed another figure.

This one was translucent, his outline the palest blues and grays. Though his feet touched the forest floor, his whole body seemed light, like it was floating. He was just as Mavian remembered him.

"Verdon," Mavian said again, the name reverential on his tongue. He stood on shaking legs, his gaze stuck on his cousin.

The ghost regarded him with a kindly expression, but did not speak.

"Darian was right. You're not in Purgatory." Mavian didn't know what else to say. He had never imagined seeing his cousin again.

Verdon inclined his head. His gaze went past Mavian to Ekkar. An expression of deep sadness came over him. Ekkar tumbled about, blissfully unaware of the presence of his own soul not ten feet away.

"You recognize yourself." Mavian looked between them. "I'm sorry if it's hurt you to see what you've become."

Verdon only stared, the melancholy of twenty years deep in

his eyes. Mavian dared a step closer, and the ghost did not move. He said, "Can you speak?"

Verdon didn't answer, and neither did he seem to hear the question. He reached out to Ekkar, then withdrew his hand.

"How can I make you whole again?" Mavian stepped between them, forcing Verdon to focus on him.

Verdon spread his hands in a helpless gesture. Mavian turned to Darian. "How do I bring him back? How can I unite his Songs once more?"

As he spoke, the ghost of Verdon Strilu faded away, its Song growing softer and softer until it was only the faint wisp again.

"Wait!" Mavian cried. "Don't leave yet!"

But the Song of Death grew faint, and Verdon was gone. Mavian took a shaking breath, and realized that his limbs trembled with exhaustion. With an old man's carefulness, he sat down in the loam and tried to still his quivering hands.

"How did it feel to see him thus?" Darian asked.

"He appeared so...sad," Mavian said. He wished he'd never summoned the ghost. *What if I fail? What if he's stuck like that forever?* "I don't know how we can free him from this half-life."

"We must find a way to speak with Valder Riesk."

"But he's dead! He's been dead for centuries," Mavian exclaimed. "Even you can't speak with the dead...can you?"

"It will take a great deal of preparation and effort," Darian replied. "But it can be done."

Mavian lay back onto the ground. Ekkar crawled over and cuddled up beside him, and Mavian put his arm over the creature's shoulder. He took a deep breath and said, "Just tell me what I need to do."

CHAPTER THIRTY-SIX
Cara

Cara stood in the conservatory staring down at the sealed Ossuary door. Rask's body had been removed, but his blood still stained the glowing runes, drying now into a brown crust. She had allowed no one to clean it up.

Talnor had fled, no signs of her left in the city. Cara couldn't bring herself to care. The rest of Rask's advisers waited for her in the palace, no doubt plotting against her. *Let them shiver in their boots for a little longer.*

Once they were dealt with, she would go to Druam. Would she kill him yet? Or torture him, as Talnor had once done? His death had been well-earned, but its method might take her some time to develop. He was too foul for something swift.

Something moved behind her, and Cara whirled, her fingers gripping her sword hilt. She relaxed when she saw Gwen, the sorceress's form opaque but for shimmers that showed she was not truly there.

"You're too late," Cara said.

"I know." Gwen's expression was oddly reminiscent of Druam's: aloof yet curious, unknown decades hidden beneath a veneer of youth. The witch stepped toward a drooping plant, her hand wisping over the blackened leaves. "What did you do?"

"What I had to." Despite her brash words, Cara's heart thundered in her ears. Something deep within her feared this witch. *Can she see the truth of me?*

Though she knew it would do no good, Cara drew her

sword. Its weight comforted her, a solid, tangible thing that she could hold onto.

"Why are you here? To pester me? Try to *help* me, like some misguided saint?" Cara spat, acid tinging her words.

"You draw ever nearer the Ossuary," Gwen murmured. Her hand played over the plant's dead curves. "I cannot allow you to reach it."

"You can't even touch me," Cara sneered. "I brought Riverfen to its knees *by myself,* and you think you can stop me?"

"You are but a scared child," Gwen said.

Cara knew she should have turned heel and left. There was no point in debating with this witch, yet she couldn't stop herself. Her anger at the whole damned world flared in her, with nothing separating her and her beast.

"I have to do this!" Cara shouted. She pointed at herself with a trembling finger. "Look at me! I'm a monster because of Valder Riesk and his experiments, because of Talnor, because of Druam and my father. If they had all let the Underworld be, none of this would have happened. And I have to fix it. I have to be normal again."

Gwen watched her apathetically. Cara would have preferred her to be equally furious, to have another red-hot creature to battle. When no emotions rose in her opponent, Cara's anger heightened.

"Don't you have any feeling left in you?" Cara shouted. "You're not even human anymore, are you?"

"I am no less human than you," Gwen said softly.

Cara's body shook with bottled rage. Burning the ships hadn't been enough to appease it, neither had turning the plants to rot or flooding the city. Nothing in those months since Alex's death had worked to lessen the tide of self-loathing and anger that had built within her since the Masque.

But with the anger came fear. What if the beast was forever entwined in her soul? What if Druam was right, and she was wrong?

Cara shook herself. *No. I can't believe that.* If she did, she'd lose herself. *I have to stay the course and trust my decisions. The*

Ossuary will free me.

Cara's palm was raw with how hard she clutched the sword hilt. She loosened it with effort and glared at Gwen.

The sorceress said, "Sandu still believes in you. Did you know that?"

The name struck a blow against the shield over Cara's heart. He had betrayed her and abandoned her, but he had been her only friend.

"He's wrong," Cara said. She didn't meet Gwen's eye. "I'm not the woman he knew."

"You're lying."

Cara spat at the ground. "Get out of my head."

"I can't read your mind, Cara. Your Song is loud, pushing out from you. It circles around you, trapping you when it should be freeing." Gwen stepped forward, and Cara shrank back from her.

Gwen continued, "Don't pursue the Ossuary. Let the dead rest where they lie."

Moisture pricked at Cara's eyes, but none fell to her cheeks. The *fampir* in her would not let her cry, not now that the beast had overcome her. She said, "You don't understand. I've done terrible things. I must have done them for a reason...if I give in now, all those deaths will be for nothing." She turned her red gaze on Gwen and forced her grief down where it belonged. "Tell Sandu that all his hope is for nothing."

Gwen didn't reply. She faded away, leaving nothing but thin air where she had stood. Cara let out a breath and tried to force her shoulders to relax. *This air is too stale.* She marched out of the conservatory, and her cheeks were cooled by a spring breeze. The air was damp with rain not far on the horizon.

As she stood beneath the slate clouds, trying and failing to gain control of herself, Cara spotted a speck of color on the grey stones. She bent over a blue-winged butterfly.

Cara held out her hand to the delicate creature. Its wings shivered in the wind. Slowly, tremulously, the butterfly stepped onto her open palm, its wings opening and closing, their span nearly as wide across as her fingers. Cara stood and cupped it against her breast. She strode slowly, watching the butterfly, praying it would not fly away or be blown off. It clung on as she went into the palace and down the long corridors, her breaths shallow so as not to disturb the tiny creature.

She came to her rooms. Every movement as slow as a dance, Cara crouched down next to a flower pot and laid her hand on the dirt. The butterfly left her palm and nestled among the green sprouts which had come back after the rot.

For a long time, Cara just sat there, watching the beautiful thing. It was safe because of her. It had trusted her. Needed her.

Perhaps, if this small bug could trust me...perhaps I could be good again. The thought was tantalizing. Good again? Was she ever good? She had done everything for the good of the people, but it only led to the deaths of thousands. She had left a bloody trail behind her, but this creature trusted her, and she saved it. Was that all it took? A gentle hand, a careful walk? But it meant so, so much to this one tiny life.

Cara leaned her forehead against the table edge and breathed deeply. She had held her convictions for so long, she didn't know how to release them. Or whether she should.

I was so sure I was right about Druam and the fampir. *I felt the evil of the beast in me. I used it, and none of that power was good.* She thought of Talnor, of the hatred the woman had carried for centuries. *Will that be me?*

Even amid her doubts, Cara knew with a fervent truth that the connection between Earda and the Underworld was not right. It had been tainted by the creation of the wights and *fampir* in the Dead's War, the rot worsened by the *sulparis* and the prowlers. *None of us should exist.*

Cara watched the butterfly, its blue wings resting against each other as it hunkered in the pot. *Can things of beauty survive in a world connected to Death?*

Somehow, Cara thought that the answer lay in the Ossuary. No matter if she sought it to sever the Underworld from Earda or to shore up the connection, she must go into that tomb and find Valder's writings.

Her resolve reaffirmed, Cara pushed back from the table. As

she moved, she could have sworn she saw a ghostly figure bending over her and stroking her hair. But when she turned around, no one was there.

She stood and rolled her shoulders back. Rask's men waited for her, and she could not show weakness.

✳

The council room of Riverfen, usually airy and open to the sea breeze, was stifling and hot. Panels had been put across the gaps between pillars, and braziers churned out heat and smoke. Cara didn't understand the purpose of ruining the beautiful space until she saw the grim faces that sat behind the table.

I don't think they're pleased with the change in leadership.

As Cara stood before the great marble table, she noted the soldiers stationed silently all around the room. They regarded her warily, their fear tangible in the air. One Lofalin general sat among the men at the table, as stone-faced as the rest.

She remembered the last time she had been brought before a panel of wealthy, powerful men. She had been a nobody then, a weakling. Now, even though she stood below them, one woman against an array of generals and stewards, she held her head high, not a drop of shame or fright in her heart.

"Maid Gellder–" started one of Rask's generals. *General Stoddard, I think?*

She interrupted him, "A large guard for one woman. Are you that afraid of me?"

He ignored her. "You have committed the murder of High Earl Rask. Do you deny the charge?"

"No." Cara stared levelly at him. "I do not."

A few murmurs swept the panel. Apparently, none of them had expected her to confess so easily. Stoddard regained himself quickly and said, "Then we have no choice but to sentence you to death by decapitation."

"Try it."

Her challenge swept over them. The soldiers hefted their spears, the generals' hands drifted to the weapons at their sides.

Cara didn't move. The beast marred her complexion, its fury ever in her belly. She contemplated how best to kill them. *Fire? Or old-fashioned swordplay?*

"Let us not be hasty," the Lofalin general spoke. All heads turned to him. His golden eyes narrowed. "We all know what this woman did to conquer Riverfen. I, for one, would rather depart this room alive."

The human generals grumbled, and the Lofalin continued, "We Lofalins have never condoned the use of death magic. It is abhorrent to us, and we only agreed to aid Rask due to the lucrative trade deals offered during negotiations. Upon his death, those deals are rendered null and void. I refuse to serve a creature who not only practices the dark arts, but revels in them."

Cara waited for him to finish.

The elf continued, "Therefore, my troops and I will return to Con Salur. We will depart the city peacefully, and leave the River Valley unscathed."

"You can't abandon us to this monster!" shouted one of Rask's advisers. "You must help us maintain our hold of the River Valley."

The Lofalin looked only to Cara. "Do you permit us to leave in peace?"

She didn't hesitate. "Yes."

"Why even ask her? She's a traitor!" the other generals roared. One of them shouted for her arrest, another for her death. A few soldiers edged toward Cara, and she gave them a withering glare. They backed away, and she turned her attention back to the marble table.

Black flame burst into life above her open palm. The ruckus died down, and Cara leered for a moment at each general. "Gentlemen, you may run the city as you please. Divide the River Valley among yourselves; I don't care for land, title, or power. I want Druam and the Ossuary. Everything else is meaningless. By all means, allow the Lofalins to leave. They want nothing to do with me, and you do not need their armies now that Druam has been defeated."

General Stoddard said, "And if we choose not to serve under you?"

"Make one of yourselves king for all I care," Cara said. "Help me if I require it and otherwise leave me be. That is all I ask."

Stoddard crossed his arms. "And what assurances do we have that you won't destroy us?"

"None. I do as I please." *And I will not grovel to worms such as yourselves.*

"Then we have no reason to let you live." The general pointed at her. "Men! Bring me her head."

Cara sent the black flame rising toward the ceiling, its heat turning the room unbearable. The soldiers sweated in their armor, and the generals leaned back. Not a single spear lowered to face her. Cara let the flame die down to a flicker.

"Your men value their lives over loyalty."

Stoddard stood and drew his sword. The others didn't move. He wavered a minute, then slid the blade home in its sheath and sat back down. An awkward silence filled the room.

With a heavy grunt, the Lofalin general pushed to his feet. He had gone a few steps toward the stairs when a Lofalin soldier, dressed in a light courier's uniform, dashed nimbly inside. The soldier thumped his fist against his shoulder and spoke quickly in the elven tongue. The general's scowl grew deeper and deeper.

The soldier finished his report and stood stalk still while the general mulled it over. The human generals had come to the edge of their seats, and Stoddard broke the silence by asking, "News from Con Salur? Is all well there?"

"Aremo has lost the king," the Lofalin general said quietly. There was a sharp intake of breath from the marble table, and Cara furrowed her brow. *The king?*

"How?" Stoddard demanded.

"Cairn Steel-Eyes. She and her damned crew of corsairs scaled the cliffs, stole into the city, and took the child out from the guarded villa. Most of the navy is still here; Aremo has asked us to pursue." The Lofalin spread his hands in a helpless gesture.

"It seems our time together would have come to an end today no matter what decision you made."

Cara's mind raced with the possibilities. The infant king in her mother's hands? She could catch two fish with one net if she went with the Lofalins. *Kill my mother and take the infant. With his blood, I can open the Ossuary at last.*

"I'm coming with you," Cara announced. Though murmurs had crept up after the general's pronouncement, the room went utterly silent again. She raised her chin to the Lofalin. "I know Cairn Steel-Eyes, and I need the child."

"The king is the rightful property of Aremo Teru," the Lofalin said, though a hint of fear entered his eyes as she stepped closer to him.

"I only need his blood," Cara said. "Then I'll return him. Besides, Aremo is far away, and I'm here with you now. One of us could kill you in the next breath."

The Lofalin general swallowed heavily, then bobbed his head. "Be at the docks by noon. We catch the next tide out."

Cara inclined her head. "I will return with the king. Keep Druam under careful watch; I will leave instructions for his punishment before I depart."

No one argued with her, and she stalked off down the stairs, already scheming how to deal with her mother. Unlike those weak-willed men, Sura Gellder would not easily bend to threats of violence.

CHAPTER THIRTY-SEVEN
Sandu

Sandu paced behind Gwen, waiting for her to return from her scry. His steps carried him within inches of the sleeping nightcat, yet he found he had no more fear for the creature. It could kill him with one mighty paw, yet it had never shown any aggression toward him.

One less thing to be afraid of.

Sandu's heart had grown significantly lighter since his session with Ropaz, and he greatly anticipated the next one later that day. He was beginning to feel like his old self.

However, when Gwen had told him that she planned on scrying on Cara again, he hadn't been able to join her. The fear had crept up into his throat, raw and terrible, and he couldn't push it down. Instead, he waited as Gwen sat, cross-legged and perfectly still.

After interminable minutes, Gwen took a shuddering breath. Her hands moved from her lap, and she stretched her shoulders. Sandu came in front of her.

"Well?" he asked.

"Her Song is as turmoiled as before," Gwen murmured as she rubbed the back of her neck. "But she still cares for you."

"How do you know?"

Gwen gave a sad smile. "Because it hurts her to hear your name. She is wavering between the girl you knew and what she thinks she must become."

"Then there's hope for her," Sandu said. He couldn't help

the optimism that flared in him, a candle whose flame he had long thought extinguished.

The smile slipped from Gwen's face. Her violet eyes were serious. Remorseless. "Ask Darian how many went to Autorus because of Cara. Does she deserve life after all the devastation she has caused? Riverfen is irrevocably altered because of her. It will take decades for its people to recover."

Sandu shook his head. He had seen Cara do horrible things, but he couldn't dislodge the memory of her in that tower room after Merick's death, her vulnerability making her as fragile as a doll. The Cara he knew was impulsive and acted under her emotions, but she was still human.

"Did you hear remorse in her Song?" Sandu demanded.

Gwen didn't answer.

Sandu took a step forward, but Lintem growled, and he pulled back. He gripped his stump, holding it tight against his body. "You don't have to kill her. You spared Olfrick Kron. You can spare her, too. Look at the queen and Jagger, and how much they've changed. As long as there's still a little of Cara left in her, we need to find a way to help her."

"She doesn't want our help," Gwen responded. "If she reaches the Ossuary, she will use it to sever the tie between Earda and the Underworld. Have you thought through the consequences of that?"

"No," Sandu admitted. It was unfathomable, like forcing the sun to rise in the west.

Gwen said, "It would alter the very fabric of life. Perhaps we would all die and go to Lyael. Perhaps none of us would die. Ever. The prowlers and *fampir* are sustained by their connection to the Underworld. We don't know what would happen to them." She leaned forward, cupping Sandu's chin in warm fingers. "None of us could join our family in Autorus's domain, and they would still be there, waiting for you, far beyond the length of your lifetime."

Sandu swallowed, his eyes wide as he stared at the witch. *Cara wouldn't do such a thing...would she?* Then again, he had never thought her capable of cold-blooded murder until she had killed Alex.

Despite Gwen's chilling words, he couldn't let go of the hope flickering inside him. "Cara will turn back. She won't go through with it. I know her."

"Do you?" Gwen released him. "Speak to Darian. Ask him what he saw on your journey to D'Clet."

What is she talking about? Sandu backed away from her, searching for the lie in her gaze. He could not find it. He stumbled out of the room and down the corridor, disoriented as he tried to imagine what Darian could tell him. *Surely he would have told me everything by now? Surely he left nothing out?*

He found the blind man in the workshop below the castle, patiently answering questions lobbed at him by Mavian. As usual, Jagger lounged nearby, his ever-watchful eye on Sandu as soon as he entered.

"...in the chamber?" Mavian was asking while poring over a weighty tome.

"Don't focus on the books," Darian said in an exasperated tone, as if he'd said it many times before. "Craft it with the Song. Alter it to suit your needs."

"You keep saying that!" Mavian snapped. "That doesn't make it any clearer."

Before their argument could devolve further, Sandu stepped forward, his need for the truth outweighing common courtesy. He said, "Darian, what did Cara do on the road to D'Clet?"

Darian stilled, his back to Sandu. Jagger straightened, one of his hands making a gesture that Sandu didn't catch.

"What does this have to do with anything?" Mavian asked.

Sandu ignored him. "Darian. Tell me what you know."

Darian's shoulders raised in a deep sigh. His milky eyes stared in Sandu's direction. He said, "It is an unpleasant matter."

"I don't care. Tell me."

"You have enough weighing on your soul. You need not carry this burden."

"Don't tell me any vecking riddles." In that moment, Sandu wished he had two hands so he could use both to strangle

Darian. "I want the truth, plain and simple."

"Fine." Darian spoke flatly, as if describing his midday meal instead of atrocities. "She slaughtered a *fampir* farmer near Yilfer. She drank the blood of animals to heal her leg. After Laris's return, she massacred a coven of *fampir*, including the humans that lived with them, and Laris, who had followed her. She used the blood of man and *fampir* to wield dark powers."

Sandu reeled, his head full as he imagined Cara doing those things. *No. That can't be right. She wouldn't!* But it fit all too well: the way she acted after Yilfer, her leg, Laris's disappearance that Sandu had never thought to question. Sandu sank onto the floor, his legs too trembling to hold him.

Jagger kneeled in front of him and signed, *I didn't know it all, either.*

Sandu looked past him to Darian. "Why didn't you tell me before?"

"Your mind was already fraught with nightmares," Darian said gently. "I could not give you more."

"So Alex...that wasn't a fluke?" Sandu's fingers trailed over the floor, making small patterns in the dirt.

At a gesture from Darian, Mavian and Jagger departed the workshop, their footsteps fading into the darkness. Darian came over to Sandu and settled on the ground next to him. His presence was comforting, his shoulder warm where it pressed against Sandu's. He said, "Cara was not born wicked. She did not wake one day and decide that murder was right. Over many strifes and many inner battles, her perceptions became warped. She lost those she loved and blamed it on the beast inside. What could have been a boon became an enemy, one she could never rid herself of."

"Why couldn't I see it?" Sandu asked. "I was with her, I saw her beast, and I always thought that she was stronger than it."

"You cannot blame yourself," Darian said. "Even Cara did not know it was happening within her."

"So what do we do? Kill her? Try to save her?" Sandu buried his head in the crook of his arm. "She frightens me, but there's still part of me that wants to see her as the maid I knew before."

Darian rubbed Sandu's back, making small circular motions as if settling a child. "Maybe you will succeed where I failed."

"How did you fail?" Confusion made Sandu's head dizzy.

"I heard the discord in her Song. I met with her after she drank blood and murdered *fampir*. I tried to guide her into union instead of chaos. I failed." Regret laced Darian's voice.

Sandu regarded Darian for a long time, a question that had lurked inside him finally bubbling up to the surface. "Who are you, really? Gwen had to go to the Woods to even learn that the Songs existed, yet you've heard the Song of Death for years. You raised Jagger from the dead. Did you go to the Woods, too?"

Darian withdrew his arm and rolled his cane between his hands. His reply took a long time, and when it came, he spoke almost too soft to hear, "That is an answer I am not yet willing to give."

"But you're not just a man," Sandu said. It wasn't a question.

Darian hesitated, then nodded. "I'm not just a man."

Sandu let out a breath, then pushed himself to his feet. "Thank you for telling me about Cara. I should go see Ropaz."

He doubted the magic would work as well with his thoughts all akimbo. Try as he might to suppress them, all he could picture was Cara, her face stuck with the beast's feral features, laughing as she killed.

CHAPTER THIRTY-EIGHT
Seanna

Seanna stood on the terrace, her hips pushing into the railing, and stared into the ravine. It yawned before her, so long she couldn't see its ends, so deep she could not fathom where its bottom lay. *Has anyone ever traveled into its depths?*

The wind whipped at her face, pulling her hair from its braid and stinging her cheek. The city lay before her, the empty pass beyond it. *Did Steel-Eyes rescue Landin and Portia? Are they safe at last?*

In this peaceful valley, one would hardly know that a war had decimated the rest of the kingdom. Of all the cities, D'Clet remained untouched. *But if Aremo discovers our presence here, he will bring his army and turn the stone to rubble.*

*Unless...*Seanna trembled. An idea had played in her mind for days. *It would be unwise. Risky. We'd likely all perish.* Yet she couldn't dislodge it; it had become a sticky sap that even the most powerful of soaps couldn't wash away.

"What are you thinking about?" came Ropaz's voice from behind her.

Seanna didn't turn. "Even if Gwen is successful in preventing Cara from taking the Ossuary, we must still contend with Aremo. I think, while we are all still capable of it, we should strike now. Eliminate the lesser threat before tackling the larger one."

"Lesser than Cara, certainly, but it will still be no easy feat."

"Then we don't face him head-on." Seanna looked to Ropaz.

"We use his own deceptive tricks against him."

"You believe we should send an assassin after him?" Ropaz appeared dubious.

A small smile played about her lips. "On the contrary. Please summon a council of war, and make sure Gwen and Mavian are there."

In the intervening candle, Seanna returned to her room. She had not dressed in a queenly manner since Rengu. She had only a thin silver circlet to call a crown, along with gowns taken from the wardrobes in the castle. None of them fit her quite right, and she hadn't the time nor the inclination to find a seamstress to alter them. But now, she slipped on a sea-blue silk kirtle over her shift and let her hair down. She placed the circlet on her head and turned to the mirror.

The queen who gazed back at her was not the one she had known for so many years. Months of hardship and hunger had made her curves flatter and her skin dry. Her ribs stood out, her arms and legs lean from the hard winter months. She had barely any muscle to speak of, and her face was thin. Her hair hung in lank curls around her face.

When she had been held hostage by the corsairs, Seanna had wanted to become a better queen. Without even knowing it, she had transformed into a leader anyone might admire. She had led her people through war, birthed a king, and now she would save her kingdom from a tyrannical elf. *I have finally become the queen I always wanted to be.*

Seanna held that pride in her belly, buoying herself with its warmth. If she was to convince the others of her plan, she must be confident in it.

The council met in a cool chamber, its windows open wide to let in the spring air. A circular table dominated the small room, with six chairs placed evenly around it. Seanna seated herself and waited. Ropaz came soon after, followed by Gwen and Mavian. The scholar, Ronan, slid into a seat and readied his parchment for note-taking, while the silent Captain Tzuriel sat with his back ramrod straight, his observant gaze flitting about the room.

"You have a plan?" Mavian asked. *He's never been one for small talk.*

"I do," Seanna replied. She quickly laid out her stratagem, then sat back, waiting for the objections to come. Silence met her. She waited another moment, then asked, "Well?"

Ropaz spoke first. "You want to invite Aremo? Here?"

"Indeed." It was a protest Seanna had been expecting. "If we go to him, we will be in unfamiliar, enemy-controlled territory. If we bring him here, we'll have time to prepare."

"Preparations didn't save Riverfen," Mavian pointed out.

"They didn't know what to expect. We do." Seanna placed her palms on the table. The cold surface shocked her skin. "If he comes expecting to find Chadron, he will be less paranoid. Still cautious, but he may let his guard down a little."

"And what if he brings all the Lofalins?" Ropaz interjected.

"We must assume that he will."

"It's risky," Mavian said.

Gwen leaned forward, and all quieted. Her expression was inscrutable. "If this plan fails, we will be unable to stop Cara in the Ossuary."

Seanna swallowed hard. Those strange violet eyes disconcerted her. "Yes. I understand the risk. But now is the best time for it. Defeating Cara could leave us weakened, and Aremo will not hesitate to use that to his advantage."

The others at the table exchanged looks. Captain Tzuriel stood, clapped his fist to his heart, and bowed to her. Seanna gave him a grateful smile as he returned to his seat. The scholar scratched his chin with his quill, but said nothing else.

Ropaz said quietly, "I support the queen's plan."

Mavian spoke next, "I'm not sure we can succeed, but I agree with Seanna's reasoning. Aremo must be reckoned with before we go to the Ossuary."

All eyes turned to Gwen. The witch sat quite still, her gaze unfocused, a low hum coming from between her tight lips.

At last, Gwen said, "I will help you, but the Songs must always be balanced. You must be willing to give of yourself when the time comes."

The ominous words made Seanna's hands shake. She forced them to still. *A queen does what she must.* "Then I'll gladly do it. Ronan, draft a letter to Aremo."

"What should I write?" the scholar asked.

Seanna gestured to Mavian. "You know Chadron better than I. What reason would he give for inviting the elf?"

Mavian took a deep breath, his fingers rubbing his temple. "Rask is dead. Chadron, drunk bastard though he was, would know that his own alliance with Aremo would be tenuous as a result. He would ask Aremo to come and renegotiate terms, offering a feast and festivals to sweeten the deal."

"It may not be enough," Ropaz said quietly. "Aremo would simply send an ambassador instead of coming himself."

"What does he want above all else?" Gwen's soft voice carried across the table. Her eyes were on Seanna.

Fear settled in Seanna's heart. *No. There has to be another way.* But the truth was plain in front of her, unavoidable and terrible. "He wants me."

"No," Ropaz said immediately. "It's too dangerous. If he knows you're here–"

"It's the only way," Seanna interrupted. "He won't come for any other reason. But if he knows that 'Chadron' has captured me, he'll want to verify it himself. And then he'll want to kill me."

"We cannot sacrifice you," Ropaz said. "You are our queen!"

The old wound ripped inside of Seanna, and fury flooded through her. "I am Queen Regent, not queen by birthright. If sacrificing myself ensures my son's safety, I will not hesitate. This could be our only chance at getting close to Aremo. He'll think he's won, his guard will be down."

The rest of the council watched, not interfering in their argument. Seanna pushed back from the table. Ropaz reached out and grabbed her wrist. Seanna shot him a glare, but he didn't let go. He spoke calmly, as if to a wild beast, "Do not let your impulsivity overpower you. Try to be reasonable, Seanna. I know that you despise Aremo, and I do not blame you for that. But will personal revenge be worth it at the cost of your own life?"

Seanna dashed away the tears in her eyes. "He took my son. An infant, not even a year old, and he tore him from me."

"Landin is safe–"

"He is in danger as long as that elf lives," Seanna spoke over Ropaz. "I will not idle here, waiting for a siege that could doom us all, when an opportunity has been given to us. What other chance will we have to get close to Aremo without hindrance or battle? I know you disagree, I know you care for me, but I must do this. For months my allies have given their own lives to protect me and my people. It's my turn."

"Sending others to die is a ruler's duty," Ropaz said. "No queen in history would give herself up on a gamble like this."

Seanna gave him a small smile. "Then I will be the first."

He folded his hands around hers. "Think about those who love you: myself, your people, Portia."

Seanna bit her lip at that, but didn't interrupt. Ropaz continued, "You are not some distant figure on a pedestal to idolize. You are our friend. We don't want to lose you."

"That choice isn't always given to us," Seanna said. "At least now we have a chance to say goodbye."

He sighed heavily. "You are determined in this course?"

"I am." Seanna felt sick to her stomach, but forced herself to say, "Ronan, you and Mavian compose the letter. I trust that you'll word it well. Come to me as soon as you receive his answer."

The council dispersed, and Seanna sank into the hard chair. Her heart galloped in her chest, sweat dripped down her arms, and dizzy nausea made her want to curl up for the rest of the day. Her plan had been set in motion, but if it failed...

Aremo will slaughter us all, and I'll have been the sheep who brought him into the paddock.

Chapter Thirty-Nine
Mavian

The white sarcophagus lay in the cold stone chamber, its lid half-tilted against the floor. Mavian wet his dry lips as he approached it, his head full of that night when his pride had blinded him. *This was never a place to resurrect Renna. It was only ever a tomb.*

He peered into the open coffin, and a shiver passed down his back as he regarded the husk within. It didn't appear elven anymore, its skin taut against its bones, its hair more like straw than the lush curtain it once was. The body was smaller than he'd imagined, the only signs of its cruel nature the fangs that poked through desiccated lips and the claws of its clasped hands. *If only I'd destroyed it before it could harm Renna.*

Mavian turned away disgusted, though he wasn't sure if the feeling was more about himself or Talnor. Behind him, Darian had seated himself on one of the steps that rose around the sarcophagus.

"Death is strong here," Darian commented. "This will serve us well."

Mavian nodded and began to set up the materials for their spell-Song. Though the magic of the Songs was powerful, the components could ease the strain for the casters. Their endeavor of summoning the ghost of Valder Riesk required a great deal of energy, and Darian didn't want them to die in the effort.

As Mavian worked, a curious tingle crept up his spine. The actions of setting out candles, lighting incense, and drawing runes on the floor gave him pause, and he eyed the white sarcophagus.

He must have been still long enough for Darian to say, "Something the matter?"

Mavian shook himself and returned his attention to the chalk in his hand. "Nothing."

"I hear the lie."

Mavian ground the chalk against the floor with particularly vicious pressure. "Last time I performed a working here, I brought an ancient evil back to life and condemned my wife to a half-death in the world of dreams."

"Ah." Darian didn't say more.

When the rune was finished, Mavian sat back and wiped the sweat from his forehead. He said, "Other than us dying, what else could go wrong with this?"

"We could summon the wrong ghost," Darian said. "But as long as we remain conscious, there is no chance of that spirit escaping to wreak havoc on the world."

"And the odds of one of us collapsing?"

"Low."

But not impossible. Mavian reached into his pack and withdrew a handful of smooth round stones. They glowed faintly in his palm, imbued with the Song of Death, reminding him uncomfortably of the white gem he had once used to summon horrors from the Underworld. *It's the same process as Valder used,* Darian had told him. *Kill an animal – or, in the old times, a human sacrifice – and imbue the stone with the creature's Song as it dies.* It had taken a few tries to get it right, and though the castle cook had appreciated Mavian doing his butchering work, the process still didn't sit right with him.

Chickens and pigs will lend their energy to the spell, he reminded himself. He remembered the old dog he had killed to bring Renna back. The sacrifice had not fazed him then, but now the weight of the deaths hung heavy over him. He held each stone in his hand, whispering his gratitude before placing it on its proper rune.

Everything was ready, and Mavian guided Darian into position. But Mavian could not bring himself to stand in his assigned runic circle. He wavered at its edge, staring at the chalk lines on the ground. His hands patted nervously against his legs, and he took a deep breath to gather his courage. *It's to save Verdon and cure the prowlers. It's the right thing to do.*

At last, Mavian stepped into the circle. "I'm ready."

Darian started the Song, his voice low and steady and oddly beautiful. His tones wove perfectly with Death. Mavian listened for a moment before he remembered that he, too, had his part to play. His own voice wavered, but as he settled into it, he found that the notes came more easily.

The Song rose up around them, the chamber echoing with their voices. At first, nothing happened.

Then, in front of the sarcophagus, a pale light began to form. It was small at first, no larger than Mavian's nail, then grew and grew, rising to the ceiling above. It was a perfect rectangle, like a doorway, and from within its depths came the blue silhouette of a man.

Mavian slowly stopped his voice, letting Darian carry the weight of the Song, as the spirit of Valder Riesk stepped from the glowing doorway. Unlike Verdon, his limbs and clothes were fully colored, though blurred at the edges. The intense light behind him faded a little, allowing Mavian to see his face.

The spirit bowed to Darian, then turned to Mavian. "Who are you who brought me forth from Autorus's halls?"

Mavian swallowed, his throat dry from the Song. He said, "I am Mavian Strilu. I ask for your help."

Valder's spirit cocked his head. "How may a long-dead man help you?"

"Your Ossuary," Mavian croaked. "I need to know the knowledge it contained."

Valder shook his head. "I have given it once, and for that I am still paying the price."

"To whom did you give it?" Mavian asked.

The spirit didn't answer. Darian said quietly, "Remember your promise, Valder."

The question implied a familiarity between the two, as if Darian somehow knew Valder. *But Darian isn't* fampir, *he's not immortal.* Mavian's confusion only deepened when Valder replied in a language that he didn't understand. Darian replied in kind, and Mavian realized they were speaking High D'Ehsi, which he had learned to read but had never heard spoken aloud. The syllables didn't match their letters the way he'd always interpreted, and though he translated the odd word, he couldn't follow their conversation.

After a little back-and-forth, Darian struck his cane against the floor. Valder flinched, then bowed once more.

Why does an ancient ghost capitulate to Darian? Even Mavian's clever mind couldn't puzzle it out. More and more, he was beginning to believe that this strange blind man was more than he let on. A sorcerer, perhaps, like Gwen? Another person who had been to the Woods and learned its secrets? Another type of undead, one so ancient that even Valder's copied texts revealed nothing of his origin?

Before Mavian could ponder more on it, Valder said to him, "I did not make the Ossuary. It was a place of heavy magic where Autorus ascended from mortality into Cythric power. Landin's men created the *fampir* in D'Clet, while I used the Ossuary to harness dark magic. My gem, you see, was not the only one I created. Many more like it allowed my mages to create the wights and counter Landin's undead.

"It was not enough. The *fampir* were too strong after they turned against their master. Eventually, Landin and my own king, Erlix, made a treaty in order to combat the ever-growing population of undead. I spent years in the Ossuary finding ways to fight against them. During this time, a man I trusted developed a means of breeding *fampir* with mortals."

"The *sulpari*," Mavian guessed.

Valder nodded. "As they grew, they became an even greater scourge than the *fampir*. I had to put aside my studies in order to defeat them. All my gems save one were destroyed in the process. But in that endeavor, I discovered the Song of Unmaking. With the help of the last remaining *sulpari*, I lured as many *fampir* as I could into the Ossuary. But our combined efforts were not enough; rather than making the *fampir* mortal once more, we only managed to trap their souls in their bodies, turning them into living statues.

"I had thought all my work destroyed so that none may create such monsters again. But the traitor had made copies which survive to this day, and stole my gem from my corpse before he sealed away the Ossuary forever."

The records Mavian had found of the Dead's War had told him much of this story, but now the gaps were filled in. Now he knew the whole truth. He said, "Who was he? The one who stole your knowledge?"

"A man I considered as close as a brother: Boian Rask." Bitterness filled very syllable. "He raised my daughter in his vile ways, corrupting her and the people we had once served. My only consolation was that he died before finding the key to immortality."

"And his descendants never stopped searching," Mavian said. "I never questioned where Rask found your gem or the manuscripts he gave to me. His family waited for generations for a fool like me to free their mistress, hoping they would be repaid with her eternal gift."

Valder nodded. "Be wary. The Song of Unmaking is powerful, but taxing. Are you willing to give your life to Sing it?"

That was a thought Mavian didn't want to contemplate just yet. *Maybe Gwen will have found another way.* He changed the subject. "Did the birth of the *sulparis* create prowlers from the remains of their fathers?"

"The *fampir* men were killed after conception. They could not be trusted."

"So you don't know how to cure them?"

Valder's gaze was soft, his voice kind. "I have never tried. Perhaps it will require the Song of Unmaking. Perhaps not. Only the Song of Death will tell you the truth."

"Thank you," Mavian said. "I am sorry for bringing you from your rest. Go now in peace."

The spirit faded away, the door of light dwindling into nothing. Mavian blinked away the spots in his vision. When his head no longer spun, he turned to Darian, who sat as calm as ever, as if he had just finished a pleasant spring stroll rather than the summoning of an ancient ghost.

"What was that about?" Mavian demanded. "How do you know High D'Ehsi? Even the scholars I consulted at Mott didn't know exactly how it sounded. Who *are* you?"

Darian's lips curved in that smile that had grown frustrating. The blind man said, "Do you really have no guesses?"

"Some other kind of undead? Are you a *sulpari*?"

Darian shook his head. "I'm sure the answer will come to you eventually."

Mavian had half a mind to beat the answer out of him. He opened his mouth when a new, jarringly familiar voice interrupted them:

"Mavian."

Standing at the ancient stone door, her hair tinged with red from the magical orbs, was Talnor.

The white gem glowed faintly in her hand, the reek of Death still on her. Her eyes were wild, her features showing the shadow of her *fampir* heritage without transforming

"She killed him," Talnor said. Her gaze was beseeching, terror dripping from her words. "I couldn't stop her."

Jagger took a step forward, a knife flashing in his hands. Mavian gestured for him to stand down, then moved cautiously toward Talnor. "Cara killed Rask. That's what you mean?"

"She murdered him and turned against me!" Talnor's hands shook with such violence, Mavian half expected her to send the gem flying.

"It's alright, Talnor. She's not here. She can't reach you."

"Where's Chadron?" Talnor glanced around as if the knight had hidden himself in the walls. She took a deep breath, and the tremors in her limbs lessened. The air grew cold as she returned her gaze to Mavian.

"Chadron and I worked out a deal," Mavian lied. He edged closer. "He hates me, but he knows that I'm useful."

Her eyes narrowed, but she didn't back away. "He...let you

live?"

"The three of us must stick together," Mavian said. His mind raced, trying to figure out how to keep her calm long enough to create a plan. "We'll defeat Cara together."

She didn't answer, and doubt crept across her face. Mavian took yet another step closer. "I've missed you, Talnor. I never realized how wrong I was to leave you."

A flash of smugness entered her eyes. *Good. She likes to be flattered.* Mavian continued, "Chadron and I aren't wise enough to keep D'Clet going. We need a strong leader like you to guide us."

Satisfaction spread over her features, and Mavian used that moment to reach out to the Song of Death. It swirled around her in a tumult of sickly green; she was an aberration in its melody.

In the Song of Death, he also saw the thin thread that connected her to Dreaming and then beyond to Autorus's Domain. It was made of the same ghastly hue, its tendrils unraveling like a broken bowstring.

Could it be so simple? Mavian nodded mindlessly to Talnor's declarations of revenge as he felt along the thread, searching for a weak point. *Must it be Unmade, or only severed?*

Mavian chanced a glance at Darian, whose face was impassive. He would find no help there. To his other side, Jagger practically quivered, his fingers splayed. If Mavian didn't act, he had no doubts that Jagger would.

It would only be Unmaking if I sought to separate her and Renna, Mavian realized. *Killing her would send them both to Autorus.*

"Mavian," Talnor said, smiling benevolently at him. "Prove yourself to me. Kill the blind one and his dog."

"Of course," Mavian replied. He hummed the Song of Death, reaching a hand to Darian. But in his mind, he stretched toward that sickly green tendril, and ordered the Song to sever it.

Talnor let out a small gasp, her hand clutching at her heart. She fell to her knees, her porcelain skin turning ashen, the light leeching from her eyes. The white gem tumbled from her grasp and rolled across the floor, its facets reflecting the ruby-red orbs.

"Traitor," left Talnor's lips before she fell forward into the dirt.

Mavian inched toward her, then pressed her side with his foot. She didn't stir. He bent and rolled her over. The corpse he held appeared much as it had before he had tried the resurrection spell, its skin waxy and pale, its eyes an unseeing blue.

Slowly, Mavian lifted his fingers and shut those eyes. He would never attempt to open them again.

✳

"What do we do with her?" Gwen asked flatly. She stood over the body of Renna Nellestere, occupied no longer by the *fampir* Talnor. Darian and Jagger had disappeared, and now she and Mavian were alone together in that foreboding chamber.

"I don't know." Mavian slumped against the wall, the white gem sitting beside him. He did not touch it. "It happened so fast, I don't know what to do now."

Gwen crouched next to the corpse. "You've learned the Songs quickly, Mavian. This gem...may I see it?"

He didn't answer, and she went over and took it. As she held it, she made a little gasp. "Do you feel it?"

Mavian touched the gem. It felt as it ever did: cold, unyielding. As he held his hand against it for longer, though, he detected the swirl of Songs that lay beneath its deceptively clear surface. "I never realized its true potential."

Gwen peered into the gem's facets. "These Songs are tied to the Ossuary. Without them, its magic is wild. Untamed. Whatever Cara does there will spiral out of her control. Even I wouldn't be able to harness the Ossuary without this to help me."

Mavian barely stirred as she sat beside him, his eyes locked on the body.

"She's really gone this time," Mavian said.

"What do you want to do now?" Gwen asked.

Mavian was quiet for a long time. He didn't know the

answer to that. After an awkward pause, he said, "I've fought so hard to save Renna. Now she's truly gone, and no Songs can bring her back."

"I am sorry," Gwen said.

Another pause.

"We should do something with the body," Gwen said. "Do you want to bury her?"

Mavian shook his head. He had already mourned Renna; he didn't have the strength to put her into the ground, too.

"We can't just leave her here."

For a moment, Mavian considered putting Renna into the sarcophagus and sealing the chamber. But that also didn't feel quite right. "Maybe we should take her to Cara."

"You can't be serious." Gwen gave him an incredulous look. "Why would you do that?"

"I want Cara to know what happened," Mavian said. "I want her to know that she's lost the gem and her only ally. Maybe then she'll reconsider what she's doing at the Ossuary."

"Or it will drive her further into insanity." Gwen regarded Mavian intently. "Are you sure you want to kick the hornet's nest?"

"Yes." The more Mavian contemplated it, the more he became resolved. Renna had left this body long ago; it was not his duty to bury it. And he meant what he had said: if anything could sway Cara, perhaps it would be this.

"Very well." Gwen started to stand, but Mavian put out a hand to stop her.

"Wait." His tongue worked for a moment against the back of his teeth. When would he have another moment to say what he had longed to say since she had first returned? "I never apologized for what I did to you."

The weight of centuries burdened her eyes. He couldn't read the blank canvas of her countenance. She held his gaze for a long time, then said, "It doesn't matter."

Something in her tone made him pause. *She doesn't mean that. Beneath all the mystery and magic, she's still a person.* Yet he understood her stance now, as he hadn't understood Druam's before. *She carries the Songs on her shoulders. She cannot afford to be emotional or hold grudges; there is no luxury of time or space for her.*

With intense sadness, he realized that the girl who loved exploring her magic was gone. The woman before him had seen the depth and breadth of her own gifts, losing herself to gain them. No more would she while away an afternoon reading dusty tomes or practicing simple spells that made her laugh with joy when she got them right.

In that moment, he realized that she had not spoken of Druam since she had arrived. *Has she forgotten him, or is the thought too raw for her?*

"Don't you want to come with me to Riverfen? Bring Druam back with us?" Mavian ventured to ask.

She stared at him, and for a moment, the girl beneath the witch peeked through, violet eyes wide and frightened. Then the moment ended, the girl once more trapped within the magic.

"You should go," Gwen said, her voice flat.

"Of course." Mavian gathered himself and stood. Gwen stayed in place, lost in Songs he could not hear. With the little strength he had, he lifted Renna's body onto his shoulders, then opened the Dread Portal. He stepped through and into the Cascade Palace.

It was eerily quiet. No guards were stationed in the corridors, no nobles that tittered behind their hands. Not a soul walked the long halls.

Adjusting his grip on Renna's body, Mavian made his way through servants' passages until he reached the entrance hall. There, he waited until he was sure no one was coming before he dragged the corpse into the center of the room. Part of him wanted to go find Cara and show her himself, but he doubted he had the strength to fight her. She would kill him before he could utter a single word.

Instead, Mavian settled for scribbling a hurried note and leaving it on the body. One last time, he studied the woman he had loved, then left. He wavered, torn between wanting to find Druam and wanting to leave that miserable place. Knowing Cara, Druam would be under constant guard. There was no chance of Mavian breaking him free.

In a quiet, empty spot, Mavian summoned a Dread Portal to return to D'Clet. As he stepped through into Death, all he heard were Renna's screams.

Chapter Forty
Cara

Cara balanced on the ship's prow, her body swaying easily to the motion of the waves below. She loosely held a rope in one hand while her gaze rested on the mass of fog that lay before them. It rose from the waters and up into the clouds, an unnatural grey mist that imposed itself over the calm sea.

"You're sure she's in there?" Cara asked.

The Lofalin general nodded. "Before the invasion, I was the general who went with Aremo Teru to negotiate with the Corsair Queen. The captain must follow the lights to find her city within."

"We can expect resistance."

"Indeed. Her 'city' has cannons and a labyrinthine warren of passages. If I were you, I'd burn the entire place down as soon as I was in range."

"Mm." Cara didn't care what he thought. She called back to the helmsman, "Take us in."

The fog descended over them. *My mother is in there somewhere.*

The ship glided smoothly through the mist, following the lights as they twinkled in and out of sight. The sloshing of waves against the hull receded in the eerie silence. Shapes of grey ghosts drifted over the water, calling to her, their voices lost in the encompassing quiet. Cara closed her eyes, ignoring them. *I can't do anything for them until the Ossuary is mine.*

A long time passed before the ship emerged into sunshine

once more. Cara blinked at the sudden blue skies. Then she stilled, staring at the mass before her. It shouldn't have been possible, this child's arrangement of ships and wood, prows jutting out at all angles and sails acting like decorative curtains between the keelhauled ships.

Yet there it was, larger than she'd imagined, a terrible reminder of the power her mother had chosen over her own child. Cara's lip curled.

As she appraised this ocean city, Cara noticed something odd. There weren't any other ships floating freely in the water. Her heart dropped into her stomach. Had her mother fled? Were all the corsairs gone over the sea, spread across the four winds where she couldn't follow?

Cara cursed. "Bring us in carefully. It could be a trap."

The words had barely left her mouth before an explosion sounded across the water and a cannonball soared overhead, splashing into the sea just beyond the ship. The Lofalin sailors shouted in alarm and raced to and fro, messing with the ropes and readying their own cannons.

One of the sailors came too close to Cara, and she casually reached out and grabbed him. Her gaze didn't leave the floating city as she bore down on his neck and drained him. Power stirred in her belly, waiting to be released.

Cara dropped the lifeless sailor and held her hands out. Just before she unleashed her power, she paused. *I need the infant alive.* If she burned the whole place down with the child king inside, she would lose her only chance at gaining entrance to the Ossuary.

She directed her ire at a ship jutting out from the city, only attached by a few spare gangplanks. One of the newer additions, most likely. The black fire burned across the water and engulfed the ship, its flames reaching toward the greater city. A bell rang from somewhere in the labyrinth, and small shapes scurried to the burning ship, trying to stop the spread of the flames.

Cara's ship hove closer. She shouted across the water, "Cairn Steel-Eyes, come out or I will burn your city to ash. You've seen what I can do."

The whirr of cannonballs stopped. The city grew quiet save for those brave souls still fighting the hungry black flames. A voice shouted back faintly, "Hold! Our queen is coming."

Cara lowered her hands and waited. The deck tilted lazily under her feet, gulls cawing above. The sun pricked at her skin, almost too hot to bear. Finally, a familiar shape emerged from the city and paused on the dock.

The Lofalins lowered a longboat, and Cara rowed to the city. She climbed easily from the small vessel to the rolling docks and stood over her mother.

The woman who went by many names did not back down. She was Cairn Steel-Eyes, Corsair Queen and master of this city. Cara waited for Sura Gellder to emerge from under the icy facade, but the mother did not come. Cara wondered if she would ever see that side of her again.

"What do you want?" Sura asked.

"I want the child," Cara said. "I may even let you live after you bring him to me."

Sura spat into the water. "I sent him away. Somewhere safe."

"You're bluffing."

"Am I?"

Cara shrugged. "Then there's nothing stopping me from burning this city and everyone in it."

Sura's jaw tightened. "You only have one ship. We can easily overtake it."

"Not before I set this entire thing ablaze. All the wood above the water must be dry as kindling. Not to mention any oils or grease that will easily catch. Do you really want to play this game with me, Mother?" Cara spoke loud enough for the corsairs to hear. Sura flinched at the use of the endearment.

Sura's stoicism returned quickly. "What do you want with the child? He's nothing to you. Just an innocent."

Cara wavered over lying or telling the truth. She eventually settled on, "He won't be harmed. I give you my word on that."

"Ha." Sura's dry laugh bounced over the waters. "You took me hostage under a flag of truce in Riverfen. Why would I ever believe your word?"

Black flame appeared over Cara's upheld hand. She let it play over her fingers. "I'm not very patient. Either bring me the child or watch your precious city burn."

Sura scrutinized Cara, then the corsairs. Cara could imagine the wheels turning in her mother's head: give up one child to save her city and corsairs, or sacrifice the lot of them for an infant king? If her mother was as prudent as Cara suspected, the answer would be easy.

Then one of the corsairs nodded to Sura, and she turned back to Cara. "Then I suppose you'll have to burn us."

Frustration surged in Cara, and the black flame spiked. Sura took half a step back, a hint of fear creeping into her eyes. *No. I must not lose my temper.* Cara reconsidered her position. She still couldn't risk burning the entire city, not unless she was sure the child was elsewhere.

I can control it. Cara pointed her finger at one of the corsairs behind Sura. The black flame gusted from her nail in a small blast, hitting him and searing the skin of his throat. He choked and gasped as smoke burned his lungs, then fell sideways into the water.

The corsairs leapt back, and Sura cringed away. Cara pointed her finger at the next man.

"Wait!" the man cried. "The child's here! He's in the center of the city!"

Sura closed her eyes for a brief moment. She closed her fist, and the man crumpled to the ground as green marks scored his veins. Cara raised a brow. *How did she manage that?* It could be a useful tool in the future.

"A handy trick, Mother," Cara said.

Sura glared at her. "My men know the price of disloyalty."

"And now I know that you lied to me. Even if you refuse to bring the child, one of your men may decide that their life is worth more than an infant's. I wonder, can you dispose of the traitors fast enough?"

Sura heaved a great sigh, then said, "Laaravat, bring the child, please."

Cara grinned and lowered her hand as a corsair hurried

away. She settled her hands behind her back, bouncing on the balls of her feet as her mother stood stiffly with her shoulders hunched. It wasn't long before the corsair returned, a bundle in his arms. He came close and showed Cara the child's small, serious face.

Cara's breath caught as she examined the diminutive creature. It gazed up at her with intelligence, its tiny forehead creased with a frown. Suddenly, the weight of what she was going to do crashed down on her. Cara tore herself away and focused again on her mother.

She reached for the black flame, readying to unleash it upon the corsairs despite her earlier promise. But the memory of that little blue butterfly intruded into her head, a reminder that she had once wanted to be good. *I have what I need.*

"The next time I return, I will burn this city. I suggest you leave before I have the chance." Cara took the child, and was surprised at how heavy he was. She climbed back into the longboat and took one last look at her mother. "You gave me life. Today, I'm sparing yours. Don't expect such mercy again."

Then she rowed away, second-guessing herself with every stroke. *It's for the good of everyone,* she reminded herself. *I need to do this to save us from the undead.* The baby began to cry, and Cara couldn't block out its high wails.

CHAPTER FORTY-ONE
Seanna

"They've arrived." Ropaz stood at the doorway to the novum where Seanna prayed.

Quickly finishing her invocation, Seanna said, "Where are they now? Have they crossed the ravine?"

"Word came from the gate. Aremo and his retinue have entered the city and are making their way here." His lips were tight, his hands making fists at his sides. "There's no going back now."

Seanna stood and put a hand on his arm. "Then we pray that it all goes well."

The group that gathered in the entrance hall was somber. Mavian wore clothes that had once belonged to Chadron, tailored now to fit his slighter frame. He shuffled from foot to foot, his face pale and his eyebrows knitted. Ropaz was dressed as the steward, his somber robes exchanged for the grey-and-orange colors of Rask's house. His hair had been slicked back, his beard trimmed and styled. He carried himself with arrogant pride, holding himself in a way counter to his normal humble posture. Even Seanna had to look twice to remember that this was her stalwart predicant. A few more of Chadron's old advisers – the ones they could trust – had all come, and they worked to hide their stress.

Gwen strode into the room, unaccompanied by her nightcat. She stepped straight to Mavian, Singing under her breath as her hand traveled from the top of his head to his slick boots. In front of Seanna's eyes, Mavian transformed into Chadron: those green eyes becoming a steely blue, his right hand replaced with a silver hook.

"Incredible," Seanna breathed.

"An illusion only," Gwen said. Sweat broke out on her forehead. "I must seclude myself to maintain it. If I am disturbed, I could lose the spell. Try to complete your task before I must sleep."

With that, she drifted from the hall. A soldier came up to Seanna, an apology on his lips. "I'm sorry, Your Grace. Your hands, please?"

Seanna extended her hands, shivering as the cold irons were shackled around her wrists. It reminded her of the last time she'd been in shackles. Aremo had seen her at her most vulnerable, and it was only through the mercy of the Corsair Queen that she did not end up in his talons. Seanna glanced at Mavian and the rest of the men; it was only their deception that would save her life now. *Am I right to trust them?*

She didn't have long to contemplate the foolishness of her plan. The great doors swung open, and a troop of Lofalin elves marched in. They stamped in unison as they formed two rows facing each other, making a pathway for the rest of the entourage. A series of Lofalin generals swept in, their tabards decorated with gold trim and their bright eyes flashing.

Aremo came last. His long black hair swayed as he sauntered in, his thin mustache gleaming with the oils he'd combed through it. His robe was open down the front, revealing his shaved chest. Seanna shuddered to think that she had ever desired to win his favor.

As he came in, Aremo nodded to 'Chadron', but his gaze remained locked on Seanna. She didn't quail under the intensity of his look. Even in irons, she met his eye with all the pride she could muster. The elf stopped close to her.

"Welcome–" Mavian started.

Aremo held up a hand, and Mavian stuttered into silence. The elf stalked around Seanna, one finger reaching out to brush her shoulders. He breathed, "There is a queen under all that muck."

Mavian cleared his throat, and Aremo's attention finally left Seanna. Mavian said, "We welcome you to D'Clet. Rooms have been prepared for you to wash the dust from the road, and a feast readied on the terrace. As for the queen..."

To Mavian's credit, he perfectly captured the arrogant, compassionless gaze that Chadron had once possessed. "Let her join us for the meal. One final feast as queen. Then, I grant her to you as a gift. We can further negotiate on the morrow."

"Indeed." Aremo licked his lips. "I have waited this long. I can hold out a little longer."

As the stewards led the elves to their chambers, Seanna let out her breath. Once the echos of their footsteps receded, she nodded to Mavian. "Well done."

He said nothing as he retreated up the stairs. Ropaz came to Seanna and unlocked her chains, then walked her out of the entrance hall.

"Is everything prepared for the feast?" Seanna murmured.

"Yes."

She stilled her heart against the fear that threatened to rattle it. "Then we must move forward."

✳

The great stone table on the terrace had been laid with an assortment of food and drink. Lofalin wines had been sourced from Rask's vast cellar, while the cooks had done their best with the food remaining in the pantry. Few shipments had left the plains, and Seanna knew that the harvest would be low that year with the loss of so many laborers. *This may truly be my final feast.*

A group of troubadours struck up a tune as the elves mingled with Mavian and his fellows. Acting the part of the doomed queen, Seanna remained at her seat, poking at the plate before her. It wasn't difficult; she had barely any appetite anyway, for her stomach churned with nervous humors. Every time she glanced at Mavian, she was astounded at how much he appeared like Chadron. It was eerie, seeing a dead man brought to life through mere illusion.

To Seanna's surprise, Aremo also did not mingle. He stood in a circle of chatting men, but didn't participate. His eye was constantly drawn to her, and she could not read his expression. He appeared troubled, maybe even disappointed. But why? He finally had her in his clutches.

The nerves in her heart ate at her confidence in the plan. Did Aremo suspect anything? Was he playing with them?

The bell rang, signaling that the main course was ready to be served. Aremo gracefully swooped into his seat beside Seanna, his dark eyes malevolent. He didn't say a word as servants sliced meat onto their plates. Seanna fidgeted, barely touching her own food.

Partway through the meal, Mavian stood and held out his goblet. "A toast! To our continued friendship and the end of this war."

The guests lifted their own goblets, quaffing the wine and smacking their lips in appreciation of the vintage. Seanna dared a sidelong look at Aremo; he had not touched his drink. Mavian sat down rather abruptly, his fingers tapping at the table.

"Something wrong?" Aremo's silken voice startled Seanna.

"Of course," she retorted. "You're here."

"Ah, there's the wit I've so missed." Aremo leaned toward her, his finger running along her jawline. "Odd time for a toast, don't you think?"

"Chadron has never been one for propriety," she responded. Sweat beaded on her brow, her skin cold where he touched her. "Get your hands off me."

"Oh, don't worry, pet. I've never had anything so crude in mind for you," Aremo purred.

The question that had been bottling up inside her finally came out: "Why do you want me, then? You would have paid handsomely for me in the corsairs' court, you destroyed a Minwood just to reach me...why this obsession? Just kill me and be done with it."

He cocked his head, his black eyes disquieting. "Because

you escaped. So many have tried to kill you, and so many have failed. It became a game, you see. A game that I now have won."

Don't be so sure. Seanna ducked her head and returned her attention to her plate, her queasiness increasing with each passing moment. Aremo started in on a conversation with Mavian about Rask and the situation in Riverfen. Seanna barely listened. *Come on, it shouldn't be taking this long.*

But the rest of the dinner passed with no further incidents. The Lofalins grew more and more drunk, though Aremo had so far only sipped from the flask at his hip. Mavian had once again taken up the jovial act as Chadron, and insisted that the band play dancing music even though there were no women present other than Seanna. Just as the music restarted, servants brought out a magnificent platter filled with desserts: puddings and tarts, custard pies and marzipan cakes. The party fell to, and Seanna got up to take a piece for herself.

Before she could move a few steps, Aremo grabbed her wrist. He pulled her close and led her away from the table. His grip was worse than the shackles. He began to lead her in a dance, his eyes gleaming with malice.

"I think I deserve the first dance," he said. "After all, you will soon be my prisoner."

Seanna didn't dare glance at Mavian or Ropaz. The men they pretended to be would not save her, and she did not want them to give up the game. She forced herself to smile at Aremo. "What will it be, then? The rack? The cross? Beheading? A pyre?"

His forehead creased. "It will not be that simple, my dear."

A sudden burst of inspiration made her brave. "You don't actually know what to do with me, do you? You've spent so long plotting and scheming and hunting after me, and now that you've captured me, you have no idea what to do. Execution is too boring, imprisonment too long." She rose on the tips of her toes to whisper in his ear, "It's a game you never really wanted to win."

His hand clenched at her waist, and he bent down to whisper back, "Cara has your son."

Seanna stopped short, Aremo half-dragging her into the

next step. Her mouth was open, her ears ringing. "What? No. That's impossible."

"Is it?" His wicked grin was terribly honest. "One of the Lofalin generals in Riverfen sent word that he personally escorted Cara to Cairn Steel-Eyes's fortress. She emerged from the fog with a royal passenger."

"Steel-Eyes would never–"

Seanna's protest was interrupted by a series of gasps and groans from the crowd. Aremo, still holding her tightly, whipped his head up to see the commotion.

Lofalins clutched at their throats, coughing. Others sneezed, and blood spurted from their nostrils. Still others reeled, holding their hands to their heads as their eyes bulged. One of them collapsed, his goblet crashing to the ground. Then another spilled from his chair, and a third fell prone.

Aremo hissed and shook Seanna. "How did you manage it? I know this is your doing!"

Seanna smiled blithely. "Are you sure you don't want that wine, Aremo?"

His nails bit into her skin. "So it *was* the wine."

"And the desserts. And the meats and cheeses and vegetables. Everything on that table was poisoned." Seanna smiled at the horror that slowly spread over his face.

"But you ate! And so did Chadron." Aremo spun to look at Mavian and the other humans.

"It's marvelous how effective antidotes are when taken before a meal." Seanna tried to extricate herself from Aremo, but his grip only tightened. He whirled back to her, a droplet of blood leaking from his nose.

"You little..." Aremo coughed and stumbled into her, his fingers suddenly slackening. He fell to his knees and scrabbled at her dress.

Seanna leaned down, taking his chin in her hand. She relished his fear. "The difference between us, Aremo, is that I wanted to win."

She stepped back as he hacked and groaned, blood slicking the pavestones as he spat onto them. Aremo crawled toward her, and she took another step away from him. The other Lofalins tried to run or draw their weapons, but they could not hold out for long. They dropped, more and more of them, until the terrace had grown quiet.

Seanna stared down at Aremo's unblinking eyes, her heart in her throat. It took a moment for her to realize that she'd done it. She'd really won.

He will no longer threaten me.

But were his words true? Had Cara really taken her son?

Seanna fled the terrace, straight to Gwen's isolated chamber. *I must know the truth. I must know that all this wasn't for nothing.*

But as her feet pounded the corridors, she couldn't help but remember the strange honesty in Aremo's voice. She couldn't shake the feeling that, for once in their miserable interactions, he had been completely truthful with her.

✳

Seanna returned to her corporeal body. Gwen sat across from her, tender empathy in every line of her body.

"I'm sorry–" Gwen started.

Seanna stood up and walked away. Cairn Steel-Eyes had confirmed her worst nightmare, and now she felt numb all over. Portia was safe and sailing to land that very moment, but that thought brought little comfort.

I'm so tired, Seanna realized. *And even my victories are bitter.*

She walked through the abandoned, derelict corners of the castle, away from everyone and everything that would try to convince her that things would turn out all right. Some part of her had known that Aremo would not harm Landin; he wanted her too much to damage his only bargaining chip.

But Cara? Cara was a murderer.

CHAPTER FORTY-TWO

Gwen

The white gem was cold in Gwen's hands, its edges pressing against her skin. It glowed faintly from the inside with a cold light, and if she peered closely enough, she could see wisps, like clouds, skimming underneath the hard surface. The gem hummed with Songs, its power buzzing, barely contained.

"This isn't going to work," Gwen said. "When Alex was cured in the Whispering Woods, it required great power and materials that we don't have. All three Witches had to contribute to the Song to make it work."

Darian gently cupped her hands around the gem. "You know that you will have to use the Song of Unmaking soon. Using it now will mean greater success later."

"Or it'll kill me," Gwen retorted. "Why take the risk?"

"If we're successful now, there's a chance that you won't need to use the Song against Cara," Mavian said. "Her father will be with her in flesh and blood. That could be enough to sway her against using the Ossuary."

"No," Gwen said. "The Ossuary contains thousands of souls that we can pull from if we need the energy. We don't have that here."

Gwen knew that she was making excuses. All of their arguments were sound, but a shiver ran through her every time the gem pulsed with a beat from the Song of Unmaking. *What if it goes wrong?* She remembered well the Song of Unmaking in the Whispering Woods, how the ground shook and the sky darkened, the trees wailing at the reversal of powerful magic. Using the Song here could collapse the caverns or bring the castle crashing down into the ravine.

Darian's hands were warm around hers. Gwen sought answers in his milky eyes. He had not yet revealed his true nature to the rest, and she would not share his secret. As a man, Autorus appeared weak and mild, more of a scholar than the force of Death itself. Gwen had mostly avoided him, knowing that he would seek her out when he was ready to use her. She had hoped to have more time before this moment.

Gwen said softly, too low for Mavian to hear, "Are you sure this is the wisest course?"

Darian nodded. "Mortals have used the Song of Unmaking and survived. It is dangerous, yes, but you are strong. You know yourself."

"But Valder died trying to cure the *fampir*, and he was in the Ossuary with the gem and a *sulpari*'s power to guide him. This is an even greater task with fewer advantages."

"Close your eyes." Darian leaned his forehead against hers, and a flow of Songs came from the touch. They breathed through Gwen, kissing her with their soft music. "Valder did not know the Songs of Nature nor Humanity. He only knew Death, and it claimed him. Weave the beautiful Songs in and around Unmaking. Nurture it and soften it. My sisters, experienced as they are in the music, have long been separated from humanity. Their casting is not yours. You have many more advantages than you think."

Gwen opened her eyes and glanced at Mavian, worry festering in her heart. "You're going to take him, aren't you?"

Darian gave a tiny nod. "When the time is right."

"Will you tell him first?"

"When the time is right."

Gwen stepped back. "We should go where the Songs are strongest."

"The sarcophagus?" Mavian said.

She shook her head. "No. The mountaintop, where the wind carries Songs from all over D'Ehsen. I will need your help to cast it."

He paled. "I'm not ready for that."

"Neither am I." Gwen tucked the gem into a pocket and strode away. She would need a cloak to warm herself in the icy winds.

✳

The harsh wind whipped over Gwen's face, scrubbing her cheeks with sand from the distant seashores and hints of rain from the north. It buffeted her with Songs, too many to name. She heard notes from hundreds of different Songs, some Humanity, many Nature, and a few Death, both foul and comforting. For a time, she stood upon the rocks with her face pointed up to the clouds, reveling in the melodies that flew around her. None were touched by the Woods magic, all fresh with the distinctive sounds of Earda.

The others gathered behind her. They had brought no incense nor candles, no runes or charms to help with the casting. They were not purifying Ekkar's blood, as the Witches had done for Alex. They were searching for a soul.

Darian held Ekkar's claw, his face flushed from the climb up the slippery rocks. His hand shook on his cane, but he looked determined. Mavian wrung his hands together, his lips pale. A sheen of sweat covered his brow.

Gwen sat down on a flat rock, the stone cold beneath her crossed legs. She beckoned for Mavian to join her, and he sat across from her, their knees touching. Darian settled nearby with Ekkar, who chirped and burbled. Clouds covered the sky, protecting him from the sun's damaging rays.

"Do you know yourself?" Gwen asked Mavian.

"What?" His eyes were wide, his lips parted. Even without touching his Song, she could sense the fear in him.

"Are you confident in who you are?" Gwen asked.

"I'm ashamed of who I am," Mavian said. He licked his lips. "I've done terrible things."

"Good. Those are part of you. But you have good qualities,

too. Hold them all in your heart, each note that composes you." Gwen took a deep breath, centering herself. *I am Gwen. I am the Forest Witch. I am a Princess of Demarren, the Lady Seastone, wife of Druam Strilu and a sorceress. I am all of those and more.*

She began to hum Songs of Protection and Guidance. Her lips parted and her voice fled into the wind, which took her notes and swirled them around and around, creating a cyclone of music that encompassed the four of them.

Her first Song complete, Gwen reached out for Mavian's hands. He took them, his face still pale but his lips set in a determined line. *Connect your Song with mine*, she hummed. She could feel his resistance as her Song reached out to his. She prodded a little, and he gave in. Their combined Songs lifted up, soaring with the mountain's wind. Gwen's soul lightened, her joy heightening. If she closed her eyes, she could imagine herself wheeling like a bird through the sky.

But that was not her goal this day. Reluctantly, Gwen focused her attention back on the Songs around them. They were a symphony of sound, a bolstering force to draw on should she need them.

Sing Verdon's Song, Gwen urged. Mavian chanted, his voice more raw, less articulate. But the Songs didn't care for performance. Verdon's Song rang out, laced with Death. It stretched into the sky, colored with black and grey. But there were bright shades mixed in, shades of joy and scholarship and peaceful days. Love, too, shimmered in the Song that Mavian uttered.

Ekkar whistled and burbled, pointing to the Song as it shot through the air, off to find its master. The prowler hopped up and down, though Gwen couldn't tell if the creature was excited or afraid.

A figure emerged from the grey air. Gwen swallowed the sorrow that sprang into her. Verdon Strilu had his brother's looks, but also his melancholy, his posture, his calm gaze. *Remember yourself*, Gwen thought. *I am the Forest Witch. I am Gwen. I have made my decisions.*

The spirit peered down at Ekkar. The prowler stared back

up, suddenly still. The creature reached a claw up, giving Verdon the slightest touch. The ghost shrieked and Ekkar cried out, but neither of them drew back. They were trapped, barely touching, their excruciating pain bellowing in the Songs.

If Gwen waited too long, one or both could cease to be.

The Song of Unmaking haunted her mind, its melodies dark and foreboding. Gwen's hands tightened on Mavian's, and she hummed, *Focus on Verdon as you remember him. Whole, complete. His good parts, his bad. Everything that was him.*

Mavian nodded, his Song growing stronger as Gwen straightened. She wet her lips, then began the Song of Unmaking.

It pushed through her, its notes both wild and structured, ferocious and righteous. It had no master, and if she let it loose, it would Unmake all before it. It would force stones back into the earth, flatten mountains, turn back the clock on humanity until hundreds or thousands of years were erased in the blink of an eye.

Gwen set all her attention on honing the Song of Unmaking. She wove the Nature of man -- bones, ligaments, muscles, blood -- and Humanity -- Verdon, scholarship, leadership, brotherhood -- into it, calming its brute force.

The Song of Unmaking built and built around Gwen, growing in power not yet unleashed. She held it as she might a rabid dog on a leash, forcing it to her will. It did not want to succumb. Gwen's strength was running out. She reached into the Songs she had sent around them earlier, drawing from them, beseeching their help.

A thunderhead of Song shrouded her. Energy crackled like lightning within it. Her hands were sore from gripping Mavian's, and her sight was clouded by the Songs around her. Her mouth and throat were dry from the Song that ripped from her, but she couldn't let it go. Not yet. She could feel it worming around the other Songs, trying to find an escape.

Gwen felt the gem in her pocket. She let go of one of Mavian's hands, and nearly slipped away, the force of the wind around her trying to carry her off. She clung on to him with all her might as the fingers of her other hand searched for the gem.

She closed around it, and its power suffused her. She blinked, and the world changed.

Gwen was no longer on the mountaintop. The air was perfectly still, though it was not grey. It was full of color, all shades of the rainbow in a bubble around her, constantly eddying and flowing like a peaceful river. Gwen marveled at it before her attention went to two figures before her.

Ekkar and Verdon, though neither appeared as they had on the mountain. Verdon was solid, his skin and clothes their normal color. Ekkar stood upright, a white loincloth swaddled around his hips. The two regarded each other, alike in feature but clearly separate. Neither of them acknowledged her.

Trapped in that bubble of color, Gwen realized that the Songs she had woven had taken shape around her. Unmaking was no longer the most powerful; it was simply one shade among many.

But the longer she listened, the more she understood what would happen should Ekkar and Verdon touch in this Song-world. They would reunite, body and soul, but the Song of Unmaking would enact its price on the casters. She didn't know what that price would be, only that she and Mavian must pay it.

Forgive me, she hummed. She stepped between the two identical figures, raised their hands, and pressed their palms together.

The Song-world jolted, sending Gwen reeling. She staggered, and when she righted herself, she was returned to her body on the mountaintop. The Songs howled around her, Unmaking sending its energy into Ekkar and Verdon as they shuddered, their hands still touching.

Thunder boomed overhead and the ground quaked. Lightning struck, once, twice, thrice. Gwen threw herself onto the ground, covering her ears. Mavian shouted an alarm, and Darian cried out in pain.

The wind blew up, carrying away the remaining Songs that Gwen had constructed. The clouds settled into their normal grey, and the earth stilled once more. Gwen sat up, her head ringing. She reached to her ears, and her hands came away bloody. A high-pitched buzz sounded from all directions.

Mavian appeared beside her, supporting her elbow as she climbed to her feet. Across from them, Darian lay unmoving in the grass. Ekkar sat, perfectly still, staring into space. There was no sign of Verdon's ghost.

The buzzing faded a little, and Gwen said, "Are you alright?"

She had never been so grateful to hear her own voice.

"I think so," Mavian replied faintly.

Gwen stumbled over to Darian and rolled him to his back. He coughed and opened his eyes, and she sat back in relief.

A hand descended on her shoulder, and Gwen looked up at Ekkar. No, not the prowler anymore. He stood upright, and his face was no longer contorted in feral features. His eyes were soft and grey.

Gwen smiled faintly. "Welcome back."

CHAPTER FORTY-THREE
Sandu

"Breathe deeply," Ropaz instructed, his fingers making an alternating tapping rhythm on Sandu's knees. "Remember your mantra. Return to that place with those you fear. Say it to them."

Sandu swallowed and closed his eyes. In the past few days, he had conquered his fear of the prowlers and the gambling table. They did not trigger his waking nightmares, and the mantras he had made for them echoed in his mind, a shield against their wiles.

Now came the final test. Now came the moment when he must face the two women who still caused his mind to be overrun with memories.

In his head, Sandu conjured the images of Seanna and Cara. They stood before him, one all fangs and claws, the other tender, grasping lips. His palms sweated. He focused on Seanna, and then he was there again, below her on the couch as she straddled him and pulled him into a kiss, her hands tight on his cheeks.

But this time, Sandu shoved her off. He said, "You have no power over me."

The Seanna in his memory blinked at him. Through his deafening fear, he said again, "You have no power over me."

Seanna backed away, and Sandu stood. He said those words to her, over and over, until her specter lost all its terror. She was just a woman now. She could not hurt him if he did not let her.

"How are you feeling?" Ropaz said, his voice distant in the confines of Sandu's mind.

"I'm good. I'm ready to face Cara."

Sandu turned to the Cara in his head. Her face was contorted with her *fampir* heritage, her nails elongated into claws and her eyes tinted with red. She raised a sword and swept it through Alex's neck. Sandu flinched, his mouth going dry.

Then Cara turned to him. Sandu whispered, "You have no power over me."

She hesitated before her eyes flashed and she raised the sword once more. Sandu backed away, uttering the phrase again and again. She kept coming on.

Deep in his heart, Sandu knew that he didn't mean the words he was saying. Seanna he could easily rebuke, for she had already showed remorse for her actions. No such guilt came from Cara.

Sandu stopped suddenly, a wild thought coming to his head. He would never be able to stop Cara, not when she was determined. He hadn't the strength or the will. But he didn't have to fear the pain she would bring. It was *her*, not him, that would murder him. He had faced Death thrice and each time had been warm and happy. He didn't fear Death.

If I fear Cara, she has all the control. If I don't fear her, I can't stop her, but I will know that I died bravely. Sandu squared his shoulders and faced the memory-Cara. Her sword swung slowly. He could have ducked or sprang away. He could have cried out or pleaded for his life.

The sword swept into him, the imagined pain splintering across his mind and sending goosepimples up his skin. But as the sword's arc drew past him, Sandu looked Cara in the eye and said, "You have no power over me, for I do not fear you. I pity you."

The spell was broken. Cara gaped at him, her sword sliding from her grasp. She faded away into the recesses of his mind where she could do him no harm. Sandu breathed deeply and opened his eyes.

Ropaz smiled at him and leaned back. "You did well. What did you realize in there?"

"That I cannot control her. I can't fight her or stop her. But that doesn't mean she wins. I can face her knowing that she will never control me again. Yes, she could still kill me, but that is her failing. Not mine." A weight lifted off Sandu, the final shadows at the edge of his vision flickering into nothing. For the first time in months, he was content. "I will never be like Frederick, strong and stalwart. I will never be the man Tambrey wanted me to be. But I'm Sandu. I rescued my father from prison and I will find my children and bring them home. I just didn't allow myself to believe that I was worth something."

In that moment, Sandu heard his Song, fully and completely. In its melody came pain and loss, but great joy, too. It created images of his life as if a bard had made a ballad out of it. A low harmony sounded, and with it the memory of Da barreling mead. Then lilting notes as Sandu danced with Tambrey. High, trilling chords of his children laughing and playing. The music was both wonderful and haunting, for its truths could not be hidden.

Within the music, Sandu heard his cowardice and unfair rages, the pangs of his mistakes all laid out in bare detail. It broke into his soul, laying broad every doubt and scrap of remorse that had plagued him more surely than any disease.

This was the Song he had heard when Gwen had first tried to guide him to the Woods. But it was not complete, for with the terrible came good. For every mistake, there was a triumph. For every woe, a moment of joy. His life was balanced and whole. Sandu was no longer the man who gambled away his family's coin and sent his father to debtor's prison. He was no longer the man that Tambrey kicked out and who later betrayed Jagger for money.

Sandu had suffered and learned. His arm was gone, but in its place came a newfound determination to make his way in the world. His mind, once fragile and fragmented, was not perfectly whole again, but he now knew that it would heal in time. The ghosts were not gone forever, but he had learned to banish them.

As Sandu heard the entirety of his Song, a gentle light glowed in the wall beside him. He turned to it, but instead of hard stone, he saw a red-grass meadow and trees rounded down to the ground while stones lifted their rocky branches to the sky. He glanced at Ropaz, but the man didn't seem to notice anything odd.

This is for me, and me alone, Sandu realized. *The Witches have heard my Song and given me a gateway.*

Sandu stood, cutting off Ropaz's question by saying, "I can see the Woods. My children are there. I don't know if I can come back, but thank you. Without you, I never would have found the way."

He left Ropaz gaping after him as he stepped through the light and into the sunny meadow. Its breeze kissed his cheeks, carrying with it Songs he could not tell apart. In the distance, he heard the sweet sound of children's laughter and a man's low, booming guffaw.

Sandu ran, his lungs bursting with air, his heart leaping into his head. He vaulted over tangling roots and ducked beneath branches, his path never wavering. He crested a hill and saw them.

Elvy rode on Cadel's shoulders as Eaton chased them with a stick. All of their faces were flushed with joy, their hands dirty with the day's play. The twins' golden hair flashed in the otherworldly sunlight.

Sandu had never seen anything so sweet.

He dashed down to them, heedless of thorns and roots. He shouted and waved his arm, and the group below him paused. Cadel lowered Elvy to the ground, and she and Eaton raced to meet Sandu. They collided with him in a kerfuffle of arms and legs, all questions and laughter and high, fluting voices. Sandu let them carry him down to the ground, holding them as tightly as he could with his only arm.

He had been wrong. He could hug both at the same time, his lanky limb long enough to reach around Elvy, holding her in the crook of his arm as his hand wrapped around Eaton's tiny waist. His cheeks were wet with tears, his beard salty with their taste. Cadel stood over them and laughed.

"I found you again," Sandu said. "I finally found you."

"Grandpapa came!" Elvy shrieked.

"We learned magic from the Witches!" Eaton said. He pointed his finger at the ground, his tiny face screwed up in concentration. A small tuber exploded from the dirt, and Eaton handed it to Sandu. Sandu took a bite and delighted in the crisp flavor.

Eventually, Sandu sat up, one child on each of his knees. He ruffled Elvy's hair and smiled at Da. "How's it all been?"

"Never better," Cadel said. His eyes said all that words could not.

On the edge of the field stood the Witches. Sandu was surprised to see that their figures flickered as if they weren't entirely there. He levered the children off his legs and stood. He had business to attend to.

He strode to the Witches, Elvy clinging to his hand and Eaton gripping his breeches at the hips. The three women smiled at him, though one grimaced in pain. As he came closer, he noticed wrinkles on their once-ageless features.

"Are you alright?" Sandu asked them.

The tallest one said, "We are fading. Our Songs have been given to one who will guard these Woods after us."

Sandu shivered. He thought he knew who they meant, but he also knew that Cara could kill them all before Gwen ever had a chance to aid the Witches. "What if she dies?"

"Then the Woods will fade."

"Is there anything I can do to help?"

The middling one leaned forward and touched his brow. "Others have helped you find your way. If it is asked of you, pay that favor onward. You have your children now, but your work is not yet finished."

Sandu nodded though his insides twisted. He wanted nothing more than to settle down in a nice cottage with Da and the twins and never wander past his village's borders. *But they're right.*

"Can I take them back to Earda with me?" Sandu asked.

The Witches nodded, and the golden light that showed the gateway between places glowed in the meadow. They said as one, "We have watched them for you. Now, Sandu Crin, watch Earda for us."

With those cryptic words – a promise that should be fair, but rang ominously – the Witches vanished. Sandu smiled at the children. "We can't go home just yet, but how would you like to live in a castle for a little while?"

The twins whooped and raced to the gateway. Cadel followed close behind them. Before he went through, Sandu took one last look at the sunny meadow.

"Thank you," he said. Then he left the Woods behind him, knowing he would likely never see them again, and being slightly grateful for that truth.

CHAPTER FORTY-FOUR
Seanna

Seanna barely registered the busyness in the castle as Aremo and his generals were taken to be buried, and didn't acknowledge the victory that others cheered for as she passed. She slumped to her bed and stayed there the rest of the day. The next few days, Seanna went about her routine in a slow, instinctive manner. She ate when food was placed in front of her, slept when her body required it, and sat politely during meetings, her mind far away from the proceedings.

Cara has my son. The knowledge consumed her. She had seen the woman's power firsthand, and from everything the others had told her, Seanna knew that the *sulpari* had no qualms in hurting the innocent.

But why? The question dogged her, a query with no answer. Cara had never shown much interest in Seanna or Henrik. What had changed in the intervening months?

Seanna tried to ask Mavian or Gwen, but both were in seclusion after coming down from the mountain. Folks in the castle had seen the winds and heard faint music, but no one truly knew what had happened. The group had returned in the dead of night and hidden themselves away.

After an interminable amount of time had passed, Seanna couldn't wait any longer. She burst into Gwen's room, ignoring the growls from the nightcat stationed by the fireplace.

Gwen was not alone. She and Darian kneeled around a chair near the fire with a basin of water and a plate of bandages.

They were working carefully on someone hidden in the depths of the cushions. The man was breathing deeply, his eyes closed. He only wore a loose cloth on his lap. As Seanna drew closer, she let out a small gasp.

"Druam?" she said, for the man looked just like the earl. But after a moment, she knew that this was not Druam. There were subtle differences, though the familial resemblance was stark.

"Your Grace," Darian said pleasantly. "This is Verdon Strilu. I believe he was once the Lord of Mott."

Seanna sank into the opposite chair. She asked, "Is he asleep?"

"Not quite," Darian said. "But not quite awake, either. His body and soul have gone through much. He needs to rest."

"The spell on the mountains..." Seanna said.

Gwen nodded. "It brought him back." She dipped a cloth in the basin and wiped it on Verdon's chest, cleansing it of grime and fluids.

Seanna let out a small, disbelieving sound, but smiled, too. *Of course Gwen would find a way.* "Does Druam know?"

"I haven't been able to scry on him," Gwen said. Her tone was dismissive, evasive.

Seanna didn't press her further on that matter. Darian carefully felt over Verdon's skin for various cuts that had not yet closed. When he found one, he dipped a bandage in paste and laid it over the wound. As he worked, Seanna admired his deft hands.

"What did you need, Seanna?" Gwen asked, her attention still on washing her brother-by-law's body.

Oh. Right. Seanna had come for a reason. She said, "Cara has my son."

Gwen stilled. Her gaze flitted over to Seanna, then back to her work. "Your kingdom has its freedom now, thanks to you."

Seanna's nails dug into the chair's arms. "Everyone keeps telling me how wonderful my actions were. But I didn't kill Aremo for the kingdom. I wanted revenge for him taking Landin away from me. I wanted to hurt him."

"And you succeeded," Gwen said, her voice soft.

Seanna nodded numbly. "I thought Landin would be safe with Sura and the corsairs. They were so strong, so capable...I didn't imagine..."

After a long, burdened moment, Gwen stood and came to Seanna's side. Her strange scent, pine and mud and crisp fruity tang, wafted into Seanna's nose. The girl's appearance no longer startled her.

"We will get your son back," Gwen said. "Cara needs only a drop of his blood to enter the Ossuary. He is descended of kings, a direct line to King Landin of the past. If she has brought harm to your child, I will not stand in the way of your vengeance."

"Thank you," Seanna said. The last vestiges of her self composure failed, and she crumbled into vulnerability. She gulped air through her tears and leaned on Gwen's shoulder as she sobbed. Gwen held her, rocking her steadily. A heavy weight descended into Seanna's lap as the nightcat's head settled on her gown, his deep purr rumbling through her bones.

As Seanna's sobs eventually subsided, she straightened and ran her hands through Lintem's silky fur. "I never thought I'd cry into the Demar princess's arms," Seanna said with a little laugh.

Gwen smiled back at her. "This is what I had always hoped for us." Her expression turned serious as she glanced at Verdon and Darian. "He is fragile. I should return to him. But go to Sandu. He may not like you, but he understands your pain far better than the rest of us."

Seanna nodded and departed. She doubted she would follow Gwen's advice, and she went straight to the novum seeking Ropaz. He wasn't there. As she turned away, a child's laughter drifted through the halls. Seanna picked up her skirts and ran toward it, not truly knowing why she did.

She emerged onto the terrace. Sandu was there, a golden-haired girl holding his hand. Nearby, an old man and a little boy used sticks to play at swords. Sandu tossed a ball, and the girl ran out to catch it.

The happy moment was too beautiful to end. Seanna dawdled at the archway, watching them with envy in her heart.

She imagined Landin at that age, all arms and legs, his mop of dark hair falling into his face. He had Henrik's eyes and stern mouth, but Seanna's nose and bright lips. He would be brave, running along the tabletop on steady feet and leaping off into her arms.

Seanna sniffed and wiped her eyes. Sandu turned, the sunlight of his face darkening as he caught sight of her.

"I'm sorry," Seanna said before fleeing. She shouldn't have come, she shouldn't have watched those intimate moments.

The corridor was cool and dark. Seanna slowed and leaned against the stone wall, closing her eyes as she banished that lovely dream. *Even if I get Landin back, I am the queen, and he the future king. We will never have that freedom.*

Footsteps sounded behind her, and Seanna opened her eyes, expecting to see Ropaz.

Sandu stood there, his arm held awkwardly at his side. Something had changed within him, Seanna could tell. He stood straighter, his eyes no longer haunted by inner ghosts.

"You found your children," Seanna said. She forced a smile. "I'm glad for you."

"Yeah." Sandu ran his hand through his beard. After a moment, he said, "I heard about Cara. I'm sorry."

Seanna bit her lip and forced down yet more tears. "Do you think she'll hurt him?"

His silence was uncomfortably long before he said, "No. That's not her way."

"Even after the destruction of Riverfen? Your friend's murder?"

"Riverfen was distant and ruled by someone she hated. Alex...Alex was someone who betrayed her. Landin is an innocent child. I don't think she will hurt him." Sandu drew a little closer. He indicated a bench, and they sat down side-by-side. "I know how you feel. When the children went missing, part of my soul turned to ash. Every ray of sun had some shadows in it. I didn't think I could go on."

Seanna didn't speak. Sandu continued, "I tried to throw myself off a cliff. What was life without Eaton and Elvy?"

Seanna stared up at him. Every word he spoke hit a raw truth inside her. She knew that she would rather jump off the terrace than face the knowledge that Landin might truly be gone. She asked, "How did you push through?"

"Jagger pulled me back, for one," Sandu said. "He made sure I didn't do anything too drastic. Then Darian put some hope into me. He said that Gwen could help me back to my children. It was roundabout, but he was right. I had to make sacrifices, face my past and my fears, but I learned my Song. And then they were there." He saw the consternation on her face, and added, "Getting Landin back will be different. But you know that anyone going to face Cara is going to do all in their power to save him."

"I should go with them," Seanna said. But what could she do? Her influence held no spark against Cara's power.

"You'll know what to do in the moment," Sandu said. He stood and held out his hand. "Come and meet my children. Some time in the sunshine will do you good."

Her hesitation lasted only a moment. Then she took his hand and walked out onto the terrace. Though her chest still ached with envy, she masked it by knighting little Eaton, braiding Elvy's hair, then letting them chase her around the table, their giggles a balm to her pain.

CHAPTER FORTY-FIVE
Cara

The baby cried the entire voyage back to Riverfen. Although Cara had procured a nursemaid to care for it, she still had a pounding headache from its constant, incessant wailing. No matter where she went on the ship, she couldn't escape the child's high-pitched cry. It reminded her of a prowler's primitive screech.

When the city finally hove into view, Cara couldn't have been more grateful. She practically ran down the gangplank as soon as it was lowered, and walked hurriedly up the dirty streets to the palace, paying no heed to the debris and filth that had accumulated after her flood. The nursemaid and guards would follow at their own pace; she was simply glad to escape the infant for a little while.

Her steps were buoyed as they pounded the pink-stained cobblestones. Everything had come together smoothly: Riverfen's surrender, Rask's downfall, and now Cara had the blood of kings in a small, loud thing. *The Ossuary is almost mine.* Would she open it that very day? Explore its ruins and husks?

No, Cara decided. She would wait and savor her victory for a few days. She would enjoy Druam's defeat for a little longer before ending his reign on Earda. Had she yet enjoyed the spoils of war? She had been too busy planning and defending herself, she hadn't even taken a moment to sit in the splendor of the Cascade Palace and enjoy the knowledge that it was *hers*. Fully and completely. No longer could Druam's long reach bind her.

No longer did Rask or Talnor pull her strings. Cara breathed deeply of the rot-tainted air, and had never smelled anything so sweet.

Perhaps I'll bring Sandu here. I can show him how far I've come. She frowned at a lone dog scavenging from a pile of refuse. *But he's as blind as Darian. He can't see past the necessary evils to the good I've brought.*

Cara's footsteps slowed as she climbed up the plateau. A deep loneliness nestled inside her, an ache that made her heartbeats hollow. *All my friends are gone.* Renna was trapped, her body overtaken by a *fampir* that Cara despised. Merick's soul was bound to the dream world as his body walked empty. Alex was dead – Cara tried not to dwell on the details of how – and Sandu had abandoned her. No one in Riverfen was with her through loyalty. All followed her through fear alone.

But do I really need friends? Cara tried to convince herself that she was better off this way. Solitary, aloof, only holding regard for herself and her ends.

Unbidden, memories came to her. Renna, running along the creek and calling for Cara to follow. Merick in the training yard, his sword smacking against hers, his gruff voice both berating and encouraging. Sandu in the tower, his words soft as she grieved. Laughing with Alex and Sandu, enjoying their company as the stars twinkled overhead. The feel of Alex's arms entwined with hers, the murmur of his voice in the darkness of night's embrace.

Cara shook herself and pushed away the past. It would do her no good now. *I became a monster so I can save others. If they couldn't see it, that's their own fault.*

The idea of savoring her victory turned sour in her mouth. Perhaps, instead of gloating over Druam, she would sit alone in her room with a flickering fire and a decanter of wine.

As she mounted the steps to the palace, Cara assessed her grim-faced soldiers. They stood in perfect lines, staring straight forward. At the top of the steps, Rask's old steward waited for her. His expression was equally tight.

"What happened?" Cara asked immediately.

"Talnor," the steward said.

"What did she do?"

He shook his head. "We found her body. She's...she's dead. This note was left on her corpse."

Cara snatched the parchment.

Cara,

Talnor meant to betray you. She came to D'Clet to bargain with me, and I killed her. I have the white gem, without which you cannot control the powers of the Ossuary. You are alone and have not the means to achieve your ends. Let us make peace.

Mavian

Cara gaped at the letter for a moment, a rush of emotions battering through her. A quick grief, for though Talnor had not been a friend, she had been a steady presence. But that was quickly chilled by anger. Not the fiery fury she had once known, but a cold, icy knowledge that her enemies were ever plotting. How could she think to take any time for herself?

"Where's her body?" Cara demanded.

The steward led her to a small antechamber. Talnor's body lay in repose, draped with a white cloth. Cara lifted it. In death, the woman seemed more like Renna, her face smoothed and beautiful, her hands clasped over her chest. No hint of the *fampir* remained, and Cara knew that both had now gone to Autorus.

Cara gazed for a long time at the pristine corpse, and found that she could not mourn. She had lost Renna a long time ago. As for Talnor...well, Cara could only regret that she was not the one to deal the final blow. The *fampir* would have been useful in the Ossuary, but Cara could do without her. *One less loose end.*

Letting the cloth fall, Cara said to the steward, "Bury her."

"Should I arrange for a funeral?"

"No. There is no one left to mourn her." Cara walked away from the corpse.

She came to a window and watched the group moving slowly up the plateau. At this distance, she couldn't see the nursemaid holding the child. They would arrive soon.

Cara ran a hand over her brow. *I cannot afford to rest.*

But she was so tired, and the Ossuary would only drain her

further. She needed to sleep, to eat, maybe siphon some essence from another. More and more, she found herself turning to blood when she was fatigued. It rejuvenated her faster than anything else. *But the more I drink, the more I become like them.* Cara scowled. *When this is all over, I will never drink again. I vow it.*

To whom did she make the vow? She didn't know. The gods didn't matter, and her parents had no graves to swear on.

Cara's steps beat the familiar path to Druam's study. Something drew her to him, some need to be with another person. He had once treated her with kindness, and though she did not expect such things from him now, she found herself hoping to find solace.

Druam sat at his desk, his silent guards positioned in every corner of the room. He didn't look up as Cara entered. His hands shook, his hair falling around his face tangled and greasy. His skin, always pale, had taken on an ashy complexion, shadowing his face with grey.

This is not the proud man I first met, Cara reflected. And she had been the one to do this to him. She should feel a sense of remorse or shame, but she couldn't bring herself to care. *He has earned this for himself with centuries of deceit and murder.*

Cara sat down across from him, in the same chair she'd occupied during their first meeting. She stared at him, waiting. When he continued to gaze at his hands, she said, "I have the child."

He said nothing. All his pride and confidence were gone, snuffed away by defeat and despair.

"The Ossuary will soon be opened." Cara leaned forward, tapping the desk under Druam's nose. "You will accompany me into it."

He finally spoke, "Why?"

She shrugged. "It's an ancient den of evil knowledge, the birthplace of creatures like you. I may need you – or, more likely, your life – to complete my goal."

He gave the slightest movement, his gaze still stuck to the table in front of him. Cara took it as an affirmation.

She stood and walked away, not in the mood to play with

him further. She could not quite tell the feeling that flowed through her. Was it grief? No, she was well acquainted with that. She did not lie when she said that no one would mourn Talnor. Anger? No, for that filled her constantly, as innate now as breathing.

Satisfaction. That was it. After so long, after so much struggle, the end finally neared. It would all be over: all the *fampir* and prowlers scourged from Earda, her own beast finally gone from within her. The constant fear she had lived with for so long would be over, and she could at last breathe freely. No more wars, no more battles, no more masters.

A simple life and freedom at last.

Cara smiled. She would sleep well that night, and begin preparations on the morrow for entering the Ossuary.

CHAPTER FORTY-SIX
Mavian

Mavian awoke suddenly, snapping from unconsciousness to complete awareness in the span of a breath. He sat up straight in his bed. For a moment, he was disoriented in the darkness. His body and mind were sore from spell casting; had it been the resurrection spell for Renna?

No, that was months ago. This was different. Newer. In a flash, the memory of the mountaintop came back to him, the Songs gusting in the wind, the sheer power emanating from Gwen. His own fears that tried to bite at him, and the resistance against them.

Verdon is whole once more. Shivers traveled down his spine. *I did it. I cured a prowler.* But what were the costs? He felt fine and whole. He tested his senses, from speaking to listening to touching, and everything worked just as it should. *Did I even pay a price?*

As Mavian stood, his bones protested and his muscles ached. He washed his face, then looked into the mirror above the basin.

An older man stared back at him. Mavian's fine black hair, so carefully maintained, had gone grey at the temples. Wrinkles touched his forehead and the corners of his eyes, and skin spots had appeared on his hands. He felt older, too, not as spry as he had been only the day before, not as fit. He jogged out to find Darian, and had to gulp in deeper breaths.

A small price to pay. He didn't know how many years had

been shaved from his life, but he was sure it was worth it. He paused, though, a horrid thought coming to him. *Will this happen every time I cure a prowler? Will it kill me to make them all whole?*

Answers were needed. Mavian headed straight toward where he expected Darian or Gwen to be. They sat on the terrace, deep in conversation, the warm sun kissing their cheeks. And beside them...

Mavian stopped short.

Verdon had cleaned up, changing out his ragged clothes for a simple linen tunic and breeches. His hair was washed, and though his skin was still marred by scars and scratches, the worst of them had been rinsed out and bandaged. His skin, pale after so many years in the dark, glowed with health. He was thinner than Druam, his face less round, his nose more severe. But the resemblance was there, from the tidy dark hair to the way he held his hands behind his back. He stood slightly apart from the other two, his eyes closed as the wind brushed against him.

As Mavian approached, his gaze glued to Verdon, Gwen said, "You're awake. I was worried when you fainted after the spell."

"I'm fine," Mavian said. He pointed to his temples. "Only a little worse for wear."

Gwen's lips pouted in a little frown. She shook her head at Darian. "I can't hear it from him, either."

"Hear what?"

"The Song of Death," Gwen said. A deep sadness filled her voice. "I can't hear it anymore. The Songs of Nature and Humanity, yes, but not Death. Not since we cast the Song of Unmaking."

Mavian finally tore his eye from Verdon, who had remained still the whole conversation. "I'm sorry."

She gave a small shrug. "Magic has its costs. We will pay more in the Ossuary."

Mavian shivered. "That's actually why I came to find you. Do you think it'll kill us?"

Darian answered, "There's a possibility. Gwen and I have

been discussing it. We think we have a solution."

Mavian sank down into a chair near them. "I'm willing to hear it. But first." He turned to Verdon, drinking in his cousin as a thirsting man gulps down cool spring water. "How do you feel?"

Verdon opened his eyes. There was no hint of red in his iris. "I feel alive for the first time in eight hundred years. I have you and my fine sister-by-law to thank for that."

Mavian let out a small sigh of relief. Some part of him still thought that Verdon would only chirp and burble as Ekkar had. "You have no idea how happy I am to see you. And Druam! We have to tell him."

At that, an expression of regret passed over Verdon's face. He said, "I wonder...my brother and I have always been so different. Will he resent me for what I've done?"

"Don't you remember? When you – when your body was prowler, Druam saw you. He recognized you. I've never seen such hope and joy in him."

Verdon smiled fondly. "Ekkar did not gain memories the way we do. I remember impressions, smells, instincts. Nothing concrete, nothing solid. I remember his scent, faint and faraway. Was he really so glad to see me, even as a prowler?"

"Of course he was. We thought you were dead."

"When I was a spirit, trapped on Earda, I wandered for so long," Verdon said. He stared out across the mountains. "Those memories are even more faint. Wisps of images held together by mere threads. I spent much time with Cara, I think. I followed her, but I couldn't touch her. Couldn't speak to her. I remember her life far more vividly than my own."

A thousand questions came to Mavian's mind. He pulled them back before his tongue could form them, worried about offending Verdon or forcing him to relive an experience he might rather forget. Instead, Mavian forced himself to be quiet and listen. Much like his brother often did, Verdon spoke almost to himself:

"I could see, but not touch. I could sense, but not react. I drifted, aimless and lost, forgetting the names of people and places. But Cara...I always knew her. I could see her clearly, a beacon in those grey days. The voices of the others were muffled while hers was music. Their faces blurred, and hers a portrait. I didn't know why I connected so to her, only that she was an anchor in that horrid place between being and not."

Mavian shuddered. It was even worse than he'd imagined. *And all the prowlers are fated to this.* He said to Darian, "We need to speak to Autorus and find out how we can help the rest of the prowlers."

A look passed between Gwen and Darian that he couldn't read. Gwen stood up. "I will make preparations for what we discussed, Darian. Let me know when it's time." She turned to Verdon. "Don't be afraid to sleep. I will ensure your dreams are peaceful."

When she had gone, Mavian asked Verdon, "Your dreams?"

"When I tried to sleep after becoming whole, I felt terror. Things in the dark, watching me. Reaching for me."

"I didn't think *fampir* dreamed like that."

Without a word, Verdon reached across and took Mavian's hand. Mavian's question died on his lips as he felt the warmth of the other's skin, the steady pulse beating with an intensity that no *fampir's* could match. There were tears on Verdon's cheeks.

"You're mortal," Mavian whispered.

Darian said, "The Song of Unmaking is not a knife, neatly cutting and slicing. It is a hammer, crushing all in its path. In Unmaking the separation of Verdon's soul and body, it entirely severed his connection to Cara, and therefore, the Underworld. Remember, Mavian, Cara's beast was born of the tie between her father and Autorus. She took that connection from him."

"Will the process be the same for all prowlers?" Mavian pressed.

Darian shrugged. "It could be."

"Autorus would know. Tell me how we reach him."

"The Song of Death, of course. What other way could there be?"

"Do we summon him as we did Valder?"

Darian shook his head. "I don't think that will be necessary."

343

He turned to Verdon. "Go and rest. Your mind is exhausted after your ordeal."

Verdon quietly left, head bowed and hands clasped behind him, exactly as Mavian had remembered him so many years before. If it weren't for the incredible magic that lay before him, he would have spent long candles with Verdon, asking questions and enjoying the man as an equal rather than an aloof elder.

"Should we go down into the tomb?" Mavian asked, already half-standing.

Darian shook his head, a smile playing about his lips. "Just listen to the Song."

Mavian forced himself to slow down and be calm. He took a few steadying breaths, then closed his eyes and attuned to the Song. It came easily now, an old friend reaching for him. He took hold and opened his eyes.

As before, the Song's aura was bright around Darian, all the colors of Death: sudden and brutal, slow and peaceful, welcomed and feared. Mavian bent his own Song toward it, intending to follow Darian's connection to Autorus.

But when he touched Darian's Song, something parted. A secret long hidden between the notes and whorls, finally released. With a jolt, Mavian understood that Darian had purposefully kept it from him, his control of the Song so secure that he could keep Mavian from even glimpsing it.

The truth within the Song startled Mavian at first, before he realized that some part of him had always suspected. Darian had come from nowhere, had known the Song of Death more assuredly than was possible for any other mortal. He had mastered it, for it had created him.

"You're Autorus," Mavian breathed. Spoken aloud, the words rang with truth. "You've been here this entire time."

Darian nodded. Now, with the Songs around him, Mavian noticed that one of Darian's eyes had turned inky black, a perfect mirror to the milky white of the other. The man he had known was gone, replaced by an entity far older than Druam or Talnor.

"But...how? Why?"

"I have long been content to sit in my Halls and be a guide to the dead," Autorus said. "But the Songs have been in turmoil of late, and I decided to leave my peaceful domain and return to Earda. I took the form I had worn before the Songs claimed me, and have watched and waited, influencing those whose Songs thundered the loudest. The Ossuary, ever a place of power, was soon to be opened. I could not let that opportunity pass."

"What opportunity?"

"To go to Lyael." Autorus's mismatched eyes studied the sky, seeing something beyond Mavian's ken. "As long as I am tethered to the Songs, I cannot reach it. Are the gods beyond that gateway? A void? A new life? I do not know, and I desire to move on at last." His gaze returned to Mavian. "The Ossuary was a gift that I placed on Earda, a conduit for the Songs. Some used it wisely. When it became corrupted, Valder sought to close it forever. But his efforts, after nearly a millennia, have finally failed, and it will be opened again. When the Songs are used within it, a window of time will open. A window within which I may be freed, and the Songs may attach themselves to new guardians."

Mavian's thoughts buzzed against his skull. "I don't understand."

"I cannot move on to Lyael unless I am replaced. Without someone to guide the dead, all my work will vanish: Purgatory, the Waiting Place, the Halls. The dead will no longer have a guiding hand."

Mavian still couldn't wrap his head around it all.

Autorus continued, "Only a mortal can take up this mantle by sacrificing his own death. If imbued with all the Songs of Death while in the Ossuary, this mortal can take up my throne. Or, they can let it all crumble into nothing, casting the souls of the dead into Lyael."

Something clicked in Mavian's mind, a horrid realization. "You want me to be this mortal, don't you? You want me to replace you as the Cythra of the Underworld."

"Yes."

That single word carried the weight of centuries past and centuries yet to come, a chain around Mavian's neck that would pull him under and drown him. An eternity of harboring the souls of the dead, of maintaining the Halls he had never seen, of being forever apart from humanity.

It was not what Mavian had envisioned for himself.

Before he could react, before he could stop Autorus, the Cythra leaned forward and took Mavian's hands in an iron grip. Songs rushed to their touching hands. Mavian had time for a short gasp before they forced their way into him.

These Songs were not as he expected. He had heard them, strains or notes here and there, but never felt them. Not truly. The Songs of Death which he had used were a pittance compared to these. They blazed into him, hot as magma and cold as the far North, full of wonder and despair, teeming with the lives of all who had come and passed and all who still labored on Earda awaiting their time in Autorus's domain. Every death, every undeath, every brush with death, all penetrating his soul with nothing to stop them.

Mavian's body shook, his hands trembling. Sweat poured down his arms and off his brow, and his mouth opened in a silent scream. No noise could escape his empty lungs. He was caught, unable to resist, unable to tear away, staring into the remorseless eyes of a man he had once deemed his friend as all the Songs of Death scorched through him.

When it was over, Mavian slumped onto the ground, his throat raw from the cries that could not be heard. He shivered and moaned. His ears were deafened by Songs, as loud as trumpets next to his head. Clamping his hands over his ears, Mavian stared at Autorus.

No, not Autorus anymore. The inky black eye had turned back into white. The power around Darian had faded into a faint wisp, a tiny thread connecting him to the raw Songs he had impelled into Mavian. Darian swayed and collapsed, his breathing faint.

Mavian crawled over to him and shook him without thought, without care for the harm he could do.

"What did you do to me?" Mavian rasped. "What did you do?"

No answer came, and Mavian's poor mind could bear no more. Blackness consumed him.

CHAPTER FORTY-SEVEN
Gwen

Gwen could feel the surge of Songs, though she could not hear them. She closed her eyes in a brief moment of remorse. *He did what must be done.*

Only the power of Autorus could sustain the Song of Unmaking in the Ossuary. But Darian was not truly human; he could not wield the Songs on Earda with the same power as a mortal could. Just as the Witches needed the Woods for their greatest power, Autorus needed his domain. The Ossuary belonged to man, not to Cythra, and man must use the Songs within it.

I hope it did not hurt. Gwen wondered if Mavian had been happy to be chosen by a Cythra. She dearly hoped he had taken the Songs willingly, but Darian had been clear: no matter the cost, Mavian would become the conduit for Death.

Will he become Cythra when you give him the Songs? Gwen had asked on that terrace.

No, Darian said. *He will have all my power, but not yet my tether. Only the Ossuary can truly bind him.*

And if, in that place, he decides not to be bound?

I will have chosen wrongly.

Gwen knew she would have to speak with Mavian and comfort him. She knew the choice that lay before him, for it mirrored hers. If she did not bring the Woods to Earda, she could never see them again. And if she did, she could never leave them. The Song of Unmaking had made that clear to her.

In its music on that mountaintop, she had heard the variations and the costs. Repairing Verdon's soul had cost Mavian some of his mortal years, and it had deafened her to the Songs of Death. The requirements in the Ossuary were even more dire.

But she and Mavian could not do it alone. Her with the Songs of Nature, him with the Songs of Death, but someone else must hold the Songs of Humanity. A third soul was required, one to whom Gwen could give the Songs as Darian had just done for Mavian.

In Gwen's mind, there were only two possible choices. She could give the Songs to Gavriel Ropaz, a man who had seen much of Humanity and wielded magic of his own. But she thought the raw power of those untrained might serve them better. Who had lived through the worst sufferings of man, yet shown man's great compassion and perseverance? Who had been inundated with Humanity through the course of their experiences?

After Gwen helped calm Verdon into a magic, dreamless slumber, she summoned the two who best represented those ideals. If they did not volunteer, one would be forced to it. She had no other choice.

Sandu and Seanna waited for her in a small, sunny room. It was not the same tower room where Sandu had witnessed his friend's betrayal, but it was similarly cozy and round, its shelves lined with books, its windows open to let in the spring sunshine. A simple luncheon had been laid out for them, with tea brewed in a kettle and butter spread over fresh bread.

As Gwen entered, she briefly allowed herself to listen to the Songs of the other two. She heard some friction between them – a guilt and fear that time had not fully assuaged – but also a newfound understanding and respect. The knowledge gladdened her, and Gwen tuned out their Songs once more.

She would not invade their privacies during this conversation.

Sandu shifted nervously, his fist clenching at the knee of his breeches. Seanna appeared calm and poised, but one nail tapped against the arm of her chair, and the food on her plate lay untouched. Gwen sat smoothly across from them.

The others waited for her to speak. Gwen took a moment to gather her words, then said, "Cara will go into the Ossuary soon."

Sandu's jaw tightened. He glared at the floor.

Gwen continued, "Mavian and I can control the Song of Unmaking. We can untether her soul from the Underworld." She left out one of the costs. *Cara's will not be the only soul affected.* She said, "But she will need help to regain her Humanity. She had it once; you have both seen her act selflessly. That is why I need help."

Seanna assessed her with a calculating eye, something of the old, conniving queen residing in her features. "We are not mages."

"I will teach you the Songs of Humanity." *In so doing, I will sacrifice my tie to that music.*

Sandu's head jerked up at that. He gaped at Gwen, his right hand clutching unconsciously at the stump of his left arm. He didn't speak.

Seanna cocked her head, suspicion still in her eyes. "Why us? Why not Ropaz, who already knows magic and mankind alike?"

"Because you know Cara. He doesn't. And because you share a quality that humans innately strive for, a quality that surrenders us to our most basic instincts." Gwen paused. "You are parents. The Songs of Humanity bind us most closely to those we love. I have yet to meet a love that rivals that which you hold for your children. You, Sandu, have risked life and limb for your children. You conquered your traitorous mind in order to see them again. And you, Seanna, have sacrificed your kingdom and your safety for your son."

The words hung in the air. Neither of the other two moved. Sandu's gaze was glued to the floor and Seanna's hands clasped tightly in her lap. After a moment, Seanna said, "Cara still has my son. If learning the Songs will save him, I will do it. I would do it a thousand times over."

Her strong voice was undercut by Sandu's soft words,

"What price do we have to pay?"

Gwen bit her tongue and did not answer.

Sandu met her squarely in the eye, his gaze hard. "I know the price of magic. I've paid it." He gestured to his stump. "This sort of power doesn't come freely."

Gwen was quiet a moment. The air thrummed with tension. Her throat tightened, not wanting to let free the words. She said at last, "The price varies for each. For many, it is the loss of something precious. For a few, it is the burden of responsibility. If only one of you takes the Songs and follows me into the Ossuary, you could lose that which is most precious to you. If both of you go in, I cannot predict what would happen, but I know you would not lose your children."

A moment passed in silence. Then Sandu asked, "How do you know this?"

"I cannot know for certain," Gwen admitted, "but I have seen the patterns in the Song, and I know the two of you well enough to predict what pains you. The Song reaches into your very being, pulling out that which you hold most dear and using it against you. For me, it was my connection to the Songs – all of them – and so I lost that which made me stronger. For Mavian, it was time: years that could have been spent in research and study, taken from him in a single night."

Seanna stared at her hands, daintily folded in her lap. She was not the same as Gwen remembered. Her perfectly maintained appearance had become a simple, almost rustic style, with her hair brushed and braided down her back and hands callused instead of bejeweled. Her harsh, judgmental nature had been replaced by a soft kindness, shown in the way she held herself and waited to hear from others before speaking. The woman Gwen had met in Riverfen would not have had the strength to see this done. But the one before her now would not waver.

Seanna said, "I will do this for my son. Even if...even if I cannot stay with him, I will know that he is safe. And that is enough for me."

Both of the women waited for Sandu's response. Gwen

could sense the indecision in him. He had just recovered his children and his father and finally learned his Song, healing the broken threads of his heart and thrice defying death. He had given more than any man should. She could not blame him for denying her request.

Then Sandu took a deep breath. "Gods forgive me, but I'll do it, too. I want to help Cara find her way back to us." His expression was hard. "But if anything happens to me, you promise that my children will be taken care of. They'll never want for food or shelter or love. Even if that means bringing Frederick into some palace and treating him like a king."

Gwen nodded. She would pass his request on to Ropaz, who would see it done if she could not.

"When will we do it?" Sandu asked.

"Now," Gwen said. She sat on the floor and folded her legs, keeping her back straight. Closing her eyes, she took a deep breath. Then another. She thought of all the Songs of Humanity she had learned, using them in the Woods or casting them to aid her in Demarren. She would still be able to hear a person's Song, though only those melodies which tied to Nature. The ones which were solely human would be lost to her.

Gwen hadn't allowed herself to dwell long on the melancholy of giving up her wealth of Songs. If she did, she would have become mired in gloom and self-pity.

And now I must give them up. If this was to work, she could not hold any back for herself. She had to be selfless, wholly and completely. She shivered, remembering the Forest Witch she had been. Would she revert back? Or would she retain the parts of Humanity that made her Gwen?

She breathed deeply and held out her hands. If she waited much longer, she would lose her nerve.

Sandu took one hand, and Seanna clasped the other. Gwen warned, "This will be like nothing you've experienced before."

She tucked away the Songs of Nature, her last remnant of power, and pulled forth the Songs of Humanity. As she hummed, the Songs formed into colors and notes around her. Sandu and Seanna gasped, finally able to see their beauty.

Beauty which I must relinquish.

With a wave of power, Gwen sent the knowledge of the Songs into them. She did not parse through, did not hesitate. From her own Song, she wove the melodies into braids that she then roped around the other two. When she was ready, she let go of her own connection to them. As she watched, the Songs of Humanity sank into the Songs of Sandu and Seanna, intertwining and weaving as if they had always been there. As if they had always belonged.

Sandu fell onto his back and convulsed, his eyes wide as he stared at the colors above him. Seanna trembled and clutched at the furniture. As the Songs fused with them, they both fainted, collapsing to the floor as their bodies spasmed in reaction to the powerful magic.

Gwen's own body shook with exhaustion. She could feel the hole where the Songs of Humanity had been, like a spot in one's gums when a tooth has been lost. It felt odd, a gulf that would eventually heal but now picked at her, begging her to fill it.

It took all she had not to let the blackness overcome her. Gwen stumbled upright and staggered to the table where she drank clear water straight from the pitcher. It sloshed in her stomach, reminding her of that space where the Songs should be. She stuffed food down her gullet, feeding her body while her own Song still reeled.

When at last she felt steady, Gwen propped up the other two and called for someone to bring them to their beds. She slumped in the chair, wondering if Darian felt like she did: hollowed, drained. Empty of that which sparked the joy of her life.

At least I still have the Songs of Nature. Yet Gwen feared that those, too, would be taken from her when next she used the Song of Unmaking.

Before sleep claimed her, she remembered Mavian's words about Druam. She made a sudden decision: *When I wake, I will scry on him. I will lend him strength to face Cara and perhaps win us some more time.*

CHAPTER FORTY-EIGHT
Jagger

Darian's unconscious form was small in Jagger's arms. Jagger lifted him easily and carried him to their shared room, a small space with a clean-swept floor and two beds. He deposited his friend on top of the blankets and carefully arranged him so that he lay comfortably. Jagger pressed a hand to Darian's forehead; no fever.

Jagger didn't know what had transpired between Mavian and Darian, only that both men were now unconscious. That couldn't be good.

Hovering like an old maid would do no good. Jagger went out into the hall and down to the kitchens. He had seen Darian's work often enough to know what sorts of herbs might help ease his friend's illness. The cook skittered away from him, but Jagger didn't particularly mind. He pulled down bits of sweet-smelling greenery and filled a bowl with water, then heated that over the fire. Once it was warm, he stirred in herbs and took a few washcloths from the shelf.

With his implements in hand, Jagger returned to their bedchamber. Darian was still unconscious, so Jagger wet the cloths and laid them over Darian's forehead, cheeks, and forearms. Then he sat back and waited.

The minutes trickled by. Every once in a while, Jagger rewet the cloths or rearranged them on Darian's skin. He put a finger on his friend's wrist and counted the pulse beats. Darian's heart pumped slowly, sluggishly. Jagger frowned.

He was just about to get up and search for Gwen or Ropaz when Darian's eyes fluttered open. The blind man mouthed a little before a word came out: "Water."

Jagger held a waterskin to Darian's lips. He thought at him, *How do you feel?*

"Old. So very old." Darian smiled in that way of his, with a secret hidden in the creases of his lips. Gray tinted his dark locks, and spots grew on his skin.

Should I find someone to help?

"No," Darian said, his voice a faint whisper. "Let me sleep."

Jagger drew curtains over the gap in the rock, darkening the room. He sat back down on his bed, and though Darian's breathing came slower, Jagger did not sleep. He waited, his gut telling him that something important had just happened.

Darian next woke when the night was darkest. He moaned and thrashed, and Jagger held his arms down until he calmed. Darian's forehead beaded with sweat, his milky eyes staring up at the ceiling. A tear slid down his cheek.

"It's so quiet," Darian said.

Just rest. It's not morning yet.

"I can't hear them. It's too quiet."

Jagger made shushing noises and fluffed the pillow under Darian's head. Eventually, his friend returned to a fitful sleep. Jagger paced the room. It was the middle of the night, he should let the others rest...but with each passing candle, his worry grew. Something was wrong. Very, very wrong.

Jagger found Gwen first. She answered her door at his knock, but she wobbled as she stood and her eyes were bagged with exhaustion. Nevertheless, she followed him back to his room.

Darian lay perfectly still. Jagger drew back the curtain, letting the moon's faint light drift over his friend's face. Only the small rise and fall of Darian's chest showed that he was still alive.

Gwen held her hand over Darian's chest, her face tight with concentration. She sighed. "He is waiting."

"For what?" Jagger signed.

Gwen withdrew her hand. She said, "I don't know."

Jagger had been around thieves and criminals for long enough to tell when someone was lying to him. He loomed over her, his fingers flashing, *"Yes, you do. Tell me."*

"You will find out soon enough." Gwen drifted away. Jagger reached out to stop her, then pulled his hand back. He resumed his place and watched Darian.

＊

Three meals came and went. Every time Jagger studied Darian, his friend had aged a little more. A few wrinkles here, sunspots there, the grey hair overtaking the brown and then fading into white. Each passing candle, Darian seemed to age a decade until he was tiny and shriveled. Gwen returned every so often, but made no comment, nor did anything to stop it. When Jagger confronted her and tried to demand she do something, she merely shook her head and said, "He chose this. There is nothing we can do for him."

As sunset painted the sky with orange and pink, Darian woke again. He stared into nothing, his eyes barely open. His voice started weakly, though gained strength with each word, as he said, "I want to see Sandu and Mavian."

Jagger ran out, not wanting to leave Darian for more than a few minutes. He found both of them quite quickly and signed frantically until they followed. Sandu came without hesitation, but Mavian had some resentment in his gaze as he slumped after Jagger.

Sandu stopped short when he saw Darian, his confusion dying on his lips. Mavian crossed his arms and glared at the old man.

"How did this happen?" Sandu asked.

Darian's small, nearly translucent hand beckoned them closer. Sandu sank onto the bed, Mavian stood at the foot, and Jagger gently sat on Darian's other side, holding his fragile hand in his own. Darian's skin was papery and dry.

Darian's eyes roved in his head as he said, "Mavian, I am

sorry for what I have done. I beg your forgiveness. I gave you every scrap of the Songs I have ever heard; I am deaf to them now."

Mavian said nothing. Sandu leaned closer and said, "I don't understand, Darian. How could that turn you into...this?"

Darian's thin lips curved in a smile. He lolled his head toward the sound of Sandu's voice. "I am sorry to you, too, for my deception all this time. I lied to you and Jagger about who and what I was, but I think you are now ready to hear the truth."

Jagger squeezed Darian's hand. No revelation would startle him.

"I am Autorus," Darian said in a whisper. Sandu's eyes widened, and Jagger sat up a bit straighter.

Of course. It makes too much sense.

Darian continued, "The Songs gave me immortality and power. I lost my mortal form when I became Cythra. Even when I took shape in this body, I was still more Cythra than anything, for my soul resided in my Halls. But when I gave my Songs to Mavian, I became mortal once more. My body has aged, and soon I will dwindle into nothing."

"But the Underworld? You still rule it?" Sandu said.

Darian's head gave the slightest shake on the pillow. "When this body dies, I will go to Lyael. I can only pray that Mavian will take up the mantle I left for him."

Mavian turned on his heel and left, his expression a mask of fury. Jagger spared him only a glance.

"You're the one who sent my children to the Woods," Sandu said. "You're the Cythra the Witches told me of."

"Yes." Darian's other hand reached for Sandu's. "I knew you still had much to do, and they had to be kept safe if you were to accomplish it."

"So you can see the future."

"No. I can read the Songs, and I can predict the courses they might take. I truly believed I could sway Cara away from the path she is on. When I failed at that, I turned to you and Gwen as the ones who could stop her." Darian drew in a shaking, rattling breath. His pulse was a butterfly's wing under Jagger's thumb.

"But why me?" Sandu asked. "I'm only a simple rustic."

Darian coughed, a dry, wracking sound, then said, "You've heard your Song. You know you're so much more than that. I believed in you, and look how far you've come."

Sandu nodded slowly, his hand folded around Darian's. He was silent a moment before he spoke. "Is Tambrey at peace?"

"Your wife is at rest in my Halls, her soul joyous. I do not think she will move on to Lyael before she reunites with your children."

Sandu pressed his lips to Darian's hands, then stood. "Thank you for all you've done for me. I wish you peace in Lyael."

After a nod to Jagger, Sandu departed. Jagger brushed the white hair from Darian's forehead and directed a thought toward him. *Why did you choose me?*

"Why not? I heard your anguish and remorse." Darian's words were interrupted by another cough. "And you knew Cara and Sandu. It was a lucky thing that I found you, and that you agreed to come back."

I don't know what I'll do without you.

"Don't you? You have come far in your redemption, but there is yet more work to be done. And if all goes well in the Ossuary, there will be another who needs guidance. Who better to give it than you?"

Jagger frowned at that. *She won't listen to me.*

"You'd be surprised how much a person can change."

It was a truth Jagger couldn't deny. He thought, *How much longer do you have?*

Darian gave the tiniest of shrugs. "I will hold on as long as I can. Now that I can feel Death coming for me at last, I fear it a little. Strange, isn't it? I have known its embrace for an eternity, yet now that it comes for me, I wonder if it will be peaceful. There will be no Halls or Waiting Place for me. Only unknowable Lyael. A mystery."

Raven is there. She wouldn't go unless it was someplace good.

"Ah." Darian's secret smile was back. "I lied to you, my

friend. I am sorry for that. She has not yet moved on to Lyael."

Jagger's hands tightened over Darian's. Though his heart no longer beat, he could swear his chest tightened. His thoughts came frantically, spilling one over the other. *She's in the Halls? Or is she waiting? Does she know where I've gone? Will she still be there when I finally pass on?*

"Shhh, my friend." Darian patted Jagger's hand. "She is in the Halls waiting for you. I spoke with her, you know, after she died. She worried for your soul, that you would be in Purgatory for so long that she would have moved on to Lyael having never seen you again."

Why did you lie to me?

"I needed your help. It seemed the most convincing thing to tell you."

Jagger couldn't fault him on that. Gods knew he had lied many, many times, and usually not for any noble motive. And it had worked; knowing his wife was in Lyael would have spurred him to redemption far more readily than knowing that they shared the same Underworld, even if they were in vastly different afterlives.

"Jagger..." Darian's voice grew weaker, his eyes staring straight up. "Stay with me until the end. I don't want to die alone."

I'll stay with you as long as it takes, Jagger promised. He eased himself into a more comfortable position. If he had his voice, he would have sung to Darian, rough as his singing was. But all he could do was make a humming sound, not quite musical, not quite guttural.

In his head, Jagger sang the only lullaby he could remember his mother singing to him, a sweet melody about greeting Death as a friend:

When I walk that wintry path,
And summer fades behind me,
I shall find a friendly hand
Who leads me t'eternity.

CHAPTER FORTY-NINE
Druam

Druam almost preferred the simple torture he had received in Stonetree. It had been painful, yes, for Talnor knew how to manipulate the body to receive as much suffering as possible without the loss of consciousness. But it had been simple: loss of a tooth, ripping of nails, flaying.

The torture Cara ordered for him was different. It played with his mind, damaged his soul. She allowed him to sleep in his own chambers, if they could be called that. The soldiers guarding him clanged their shields or vigorously shook him at odd intervals, often when he had just entered his deepest sleep. Not a night passed without interruption of some kind.

Then there were the daily walks around the palace, dragged about by his guards. They forced him through the gardens, which may have been a peaceful venture were it not for the heads decorating a row of pole-arms. The guards made him watch the slow progression of rot.

I'm sorry, Eigbrett. I'm sorry, Marin. I'm sorry, Avallune, Druam said to himself every day. All had been extinguished far too soon. If only Druam had surrendered earlier, if only he had killed Cara when he had the chance; if only, if only, if only. The regrets and wishes beat constantly in his mind, a worse prison than any Talnor could concoct.

There were others, too, who lined the gravel pathway to the conservatory. Nobles, servants, soldiers, those that Rask had deemed too traitorous to live. Druam knew most by name, the syllables added to the litany of his misery.

The march continued into the conservatory, its once floral scents now moldy. The smell of death nearly overwhelmed Druam's greater senses. He was forced to walk the paths he had once groomed with tender care, past the trees and shrubs he had pruned, through the flower beds he had weeded with a lover's gentle touch. The winding paths took over a candle to meander through, and the guards, their noses and mouths wrapped with perfumed cloth to dampen the smell, made him take his time through every adjoining trail.

When they finally emerged back into the day, the guards sat him on a bench overlooking the city. This punishment held two purposes: the first, for Druam to weaken with extended time in the sun, and the second, for him to stare out over his ruined city, at the white walls now pink from the flood of bloodied waters, at the dead plant life that darkened the streets, and at the people, beleaguered ants far below that trudged over cobbles they had once proudly strode.

For the first time in his long life, Druam had no more feelings within him. He was drained, his soul an empty hive where once there had been thousands of bees filling him with emotion. Even his constant thirst brought barely more than a twinge, driven by instinct rather than passion.

I have failed Riverfen. I have failed my people. I have failed my friends and family. The mantra echoed in his head, a constant thorn that had shoved itself into him and could not be removed. He had been so confident in his foolishness, and would pay the price for the rest of his worthless existence.

One day, a thundering of magic shook the palace, then nothing. Silence. Druam waited for anyone to tell him the news, but no one came. No one would report to him anymore. He only heard through whispers passed between the guards that Mavian had come to return Talnor's body.

Even that bit of good news did not spark any fire within him. Druam lay awake, wondering if Mavian and the rest had forgotten him. His cousin must know that he was still alive; would they try to rescue him?

No, Druam decided. He was no use to them now. He had lost his power, his influence, his city. It was right of them to abandon him when he could offer nothing but futility.

Most nights, in the spare candles of sleep he managed to get, Druam dreamt of Gwen. She flitted between princess and witch, sometimes dressed in court gowns with braided hair and painted cheeks, sometimes beautiful yet terrible, her skin mottled with the paint of the Woods and her eyes filled with ancient knowledge. No matter what appearance she came in, she always said the same words to him:

You hid the truth of yourself. You took advantage of me.

Even in dreams, he did not know how to respond to her. She was right. He had stolen the remainder of her childhood.

One night after Cara had returned from the sea, Druam peered down at the city, hoping against hope for a single bright light to banish the darkness. He did this sometimes, when his despair allowed him to crawl from his bed to the window. He searched for one pinprick of red or blue, one shining spot of purple or green. One lantern, surviving when all the rest had been swept out to sea.

Like all the other nights, the city below remained dark. Not even a candle in a window to show that someone was alive down there.

Druam closed his eyes. Even if undead could weep, he hadn't the strength for tears. He turned away from the windows.

There, before him, like a beacon of hope, stood Gwen. Her silhouette was translucent at the edges, blurred just a little, and she shone with an inner light, an angel descended from the gods. His guards were nowhere in sight.

Druam dropped to his knees, too worn to do more. He stared up at the witch with her knotted hair and green-blessed skin, the clothing made by her own hands draping over her body. She stepped toward him, her expression impassive. It reminded him of himself, a closed book to all who didn't know the language within.

He no longer knew her.

She came closer and kneeled in front of him. She took his

hands, the sensation cool, a breeze caressing his skin. Druam desperately searched her eyes, a drowning man hoping for aid.

"What has she done to you, Druam?" Gwen asked, her voice soft and warm, wrapping around him.

"You're here," was all he could say. A tiny spark ignited in him, a flash of hope.

Beneath the witch's exterior, Druam saw Gwen's kindness and compassion, the sweet girl he had fallen in love with. She smiled at him. "I'm sorry, Druam. I should have come sooner."

"Are you going to take me away?"

The spark of hope burned out as she shook her head. "I came to warn you, Druam. Cara will soon enter the Ossuary. She has all she needs. If she takes you with her, she will use you to enact her terrible deed. You must do all you can to resist her. Can you do that, Druam?"

I can't do anything. Don't you know that?

The words didn't come. Druam was too fragile, too weak. He merely shook his head.

Gwen's ghostly hands gripped him tighter, cool water pushing against his skin. "Druam! Listen to me. If she begins the process, I will have to use the Song of Unmaking. It could sever both of you from the Underworld. Do you want that?"

I don't care. Druam froze. Cara stood in the doorway, her eyes flint. When he looked back to his wife, all he said was, "You were right to abandon me."

Cara strode to him and pulled him from Gwen's translucent hands. Gwen cried out, but she could do nothing. None of them could.

"It's time," Cara hissed at him. She glared at Gwen's scrying form. "You're too late."

Druam let himself be dragged from the room, his limbs too weak to fight back. He feebly tried to pull away, but it was no use. *I'm sorry, Gwen. I've failed you once again.*

CHAPTER FIFTY
The Ossuary

Cara stood over the Ossuary's stone sigil. The night was still. Expectant. Rask's blood painted the carving under her feet, dried now into stains that flecked from the edges. Cara lay a hand to the sword at her side, then shifted to grasp the dagger at her other hip instead. As she drew it, she turned to Druam.

The earl stood like a statue, staring straight ahead into nothing. He didn't examine his ruined conservatory; he'd seen it many, many times. In his arms, he clasped the infant. The child didn't move or cry; he stared out with wide eyes, his bottom lip quivering.

Druam startled as Cara drew close. He clutched the child close to his breast in a futile gesture. "What will you do to him?"

"Why should you care?" Cara reached for Landin, but Druam drew back. She frowned at his resistance. "Just a few drops of blood. He'll barely feel it."

"Then we leave him up here? There's no need to bring a baby into the Ossuary."

Cara ignored his question and reached out once more. This time, Druam didn't hold the infant back. Cara made a tiny cut in the baby's shoulder. Though his high cry pierced her ears and he wiggled away from the sharp edge, she managed to get a few droplets onto the knife. She turned and let them fall onto the sigil.

For a breath, nothing happened. Then the sigil began to glow, the intertwining limbs of the wyrm moving in their tiny circle. The creature's carved eye glinted a bright blue. Then the stone, sigil and all, vanished, leaving a hole where it had once been. A staircase spiraled down, down into the dark.

Holding a lantern aloft with one hand and gripping Druam's shoulder with the other, Cara pushed him toward the stairs. Together, they began the descent into the depths.

✳

Seanna stood at the window and stared out over the sleeping city. She had been unable to shut her eyes, and so she stood, gazing out over a place that had once reviled her. *What do the people think of me? Of all this?* Their master had changed, but she doubted their way of life would be much affected. D'Clet was the only city in Dotschar saved from the ravages of war. No children were torn from their parents' arms in the panic of invasion, no war horns had sounded across the valley. *They have no idea how lucky they are.*

A gentle knock came at the door. Seanna called, and the latch quietly lifted. *Ropaz, no doubt.* He had been staunch in his frequent examination of her and Sandu since Gwen had imparted the Songs on them, concerned about some adverse effect.

But the music that drifted into Seanna's ears – a strange sensation, hearing notes that weren't there before – was not Ropaz's. It was softer, sweeter.

"Portia," Seanna breathed. She smiled at the young woman, finally returned to them that very day. Like Seanna, Portia was dressed only in her shift, her bare feet peeking out below the white linen. Her hair was loose, billowing around her shoulders as she stepped into the room.

"My apologies for the disturbance," Portia started before Seanna cut her off with a quick gesture.

"Come look at the city," Seanna said. When Portia stood beside her, she continued, "When all this is done, D'Clet will be needed to help the other cities find their feet. So many people have lost their homes, their livelihoods, their families."

Portia had a slight frown, and Seanna's heart clutched. *Only bad news comes before the dawn.* "What is it?"

"Gwen says to prepare to leave," Portia said. "Cara is going into the Ossuary tonight."

"Tonight?" Seanna's voice squeaked. But she wasn't ready, she didn't really know how to use the Songs. If she wasn't ready, she would fail.

Portia's hand found its way into Seanna's. On a normal night, Seanna's heart would race at the touch. But now, she only had thoughts for the confrontation to come.

"When?" Seanna said.

Portia replied, "They're meeting on the terrace in a candle. Lord Mavian will transport you all."

Seanna nodded, her eyes still on D'Clet's warm yellow lights. A lump had taken over her throat, and she couldn't think past the fear that clutched at her chest. Portia squeezed her hand, and Seanna squeezed back.

"Thank you for everything," Seanna said. "I wouldn't have survived without you."

"Just come back to me," Portia said.

That jolted Seanna enough to turn her gaze onto the handmaid. All the untold longings and hopeful daydreams burst into her, and lightning tingled in the space between their entwined fingers. Seanna stared down at Portia, trying to find the truth in her eyes. Portia smiled.

"I know that you have had so much to contend with," Portia began "but I wanted you to know, before you left, that I care for you. Deeply. If you don't come back, I don't know what I'll do. I know it's not my place, that I'm a rustic and you're—"

Seanna put a finger to Portia's lips to stifle her speech. Her fingers trailed over the ruby curves, and Seanna nearly bent down. She stopped herself just before she closed the gap. Portia's breath hitched, and Seanna said softly, "I have longed so much to hear those words. I don't care what our stations are; it doesn't matter. But I've caused so much pain. I've not been a good lover or wife. I don't want to hurt you, too."

"You're a better woman now," Portia said. "Let me safeguard

my own heart. But if you left and I never told you how I felt, I'd never forgive myself. I want you, flawed as you are."

Errant tears made it to Seanna's chin before she brushed them away. With all the stress of motherhood and war, she had never dared to hope that Portia might share her feelings. Yet it came at the worst time.

Seanna grasped Portia's other hand. She rubbed her thumbs over their enjoined fingers. "I want to be better. I want to love again."

Portia drew closer. Their lips met, and the sparks that crackled between them grew into jolts that shivered through Seanna's body. She let out a soft moan and gripped Portia's cheek.

After a moment, Seanna broke away. She leaned her forehead against Portia's and said, "I will return to you."

"Good." Portia smiled. "Let's get you dressed."

✳

Mavian had never been one for praying, but as the time for departure loomed closer, he found himself in the novum. It was dark and quiet inside, the air tinted with incense and smoke from the few candles that guttered in their trays. His knees pressing against the cool stone floor, Mavian clasped his hands. He stared at the faceless statues carved on their pedestals.

"All my life I've wanted to be blessed with power," Mavian told them. "I wanted magic and knowledge. Now that it's been given to me, I don't want it anymore. Autorus tricked me. I beg you, please take this burden from me."

The statues said nothing. No wind blew through the cracked door, no light shone from above. No signs that anything had heard him.

The white gem hung heavy against his chest. It was cold, its hard edges pressing on his skin. It thrummed with power, the Songs of Death and the Song of Unmaking strong within its opaque surfaces. Mavian clutched at it, half-tempted to throw it into the ravine and be done with it. *The Ossuary can't change me if*

367

I never go.

His hand fell, and he sighed. The others would be waiting for him.

A late spring chill made him shiver as Mavian walked onto the terrace. He savored its breath across his skin. When was the last time he'd watched the snow drift across the forests and fields, or listened to the rain pattering across the flagstones? He had spent so much time buried in his books and scrolls that he hadn't truly enjoyed the pleasures of life.

All the possibilities of the future barraged him, opportunities that he would never have. Spending an entire day in the meadows and woods scouring for truffles or hunting for rabbits. Walking the streets of Brin during the summer festivals when pennants flew from every window and troubadours played on every corner. Finding love again, fathering children and watching them grow up.

Mavian bit down on his knuckle to keep from crying out. If he hadn't already seen Darian aged and dying, he would try to off the bastard himself.

Another presence on the terrace forced Mavian out of his reverie. He straightened and dropped his hand, brushing it against his tunic like a naughty child.

"Verdon," Mavian said. His cousin stepped forward and joined Mavian at the railing.

As Verdon leaned against it, he said, "I'm going with you. I want to see my daughter, to touch her like I never could before."

Mavian nodded. He had figured that Verdon would come with them into the Ossuary. He said nothing, though, for his thoughts were still mired.

"I am grateful," Verdon said, "for what you've done for me. I know it cost much. But if you manage it for the rest of the prowlers...so many souls will be at peace. They are wandering, lost and untethered. Many still have living families they could return to if you succeed."

"If I give up my own life," Mavian said bitterly. "That's the price. I free the prowlers, and Autorus claims me as his replacement."

Verdon shrugged. "I gave up my life for the promise of a child."

The others filtered onto the terrace, and Mavian pushed himself off the railing and away from Verdon. *He had centuries to live and enjoy life's pleasures. His decision was nothing like mine.*

Gwen, Seanna, and Sandu clustered by the door. Gwen kneeled and pet her nightcat, murmuring to him in Songs that Mavian couldn't understand. The creature pushed its head against her chest, then padded away, its long tail flicking as it disappeared into the dark corridors.

"Are you ready?" Gwen asked, straightening. Mavian nodded, not trusting himself to speak. Behind her, Sandu and Seanna were both pale but determined.

When he had first acquired the gem, Mavian had needed runes and chants to bring out its power. Now that he knew the Songs woven inside it, he merely tapped into them and Sang out a few lines to open the Dread Portal. The terrace shook as the purple gateway sprang into being, bringing with it the musty smells of Death.

Mavian held out his hand, and Seanna took it. They created a chain, each person holding the hand of the next. Gwen came last, gripping Sandu's shoulders so as not to lose herself in the gulf. *Five of us going into the void. How many will return?*

Mavian took a deep breath and stepped into the gateway.

✳

Sandu gasped and clutched his stomach. Even the beauty of the Cascade Palace, glittering in the nighttime, did not distract him from the roiling nausea from their short journey through the Underworld. He couldn't understand why Mavian had ever used it more than once.

One by one, their small party recovered. They were in the dark gardens around the palace. Not a sound interrupted the evening: no birds called, no bushes rustled. It was eerily silent, as if the world waited to see what emerged from the Ossuary.

Verdon led the way, guiding them into the conservatory.

Sandu trailed behind, his fear tight in his throat. He'd kissed his sleeping children and whispered a goodbye. Would he ever return to them? Would they remember him after he'd gone?

As the fears threatened to stop him, Sandu did as Ropaz had instructed. He took deep breaths and counted the fingers of his hand, first thumb to pinky, then pinky to thumb, counting until he felt better.

They came to the conservatory, and Sandu gagged with the smell of rotten plants. He held his tunic over his nose as he followed the rest into the now ugly gardens. They reached the stairs that led into the ground, and Sandu realized that this was it. There was no turning back now.

A ball of light sprang into Gwen's hand, and she took the lead. Mavian followed, a red orb flickering above his palm. Seanna came behind, silent save for her ragged breaths. Verdon stayed a little behind, waiting patiently as Sandu navigated the worn treads of the carved steps.

A short hallway met them, ending at an archway and yet another staircase spiraling downwards, deeper into the plateau. Sandu swallowed and rubbed his stump, horribly conscious of the pressing earth overhead. Could a whisper bring the whole palace down on them?

As they began to descend, Verdon murmured to Sandu, "I wish we had more time to speak. I would have liked to hear stories of my daughter before..."

He trailed off, and Sandu stopped himself from saying *before she began murdering for fun.* Instead, Sandu said, "She was my best friend."

Verdon stopped suddenly and gripped Sandu's arm. "You will do everything to bring her back to me, won't you?"

Sandu swallowed again. No threats laced Verdon's words, yet still Sandu found it hard to speak for a moment. He managed, "I'll try."

Farther and farther into the earth they traveled, their footsteps muffled by the compacted dirt walls. The darkness was complete, only barely touched by the mages' glowing lights.

At last, they emerged into a large cavern, its far walls

devoured by shadows. Silhouettes filled the space, vaguely human in shape and size, but misshapen, like a sculptor's first strokes into stone. Gwen stepped close to one and lifted her orb, peering at the shape. She frowned.

"This was a *fampir*," she said. "They all were. Trapped within this stone by Valder's Song."

Sandu edged away from the nearest statue. The imprint of fangs and ridges were outlined in the stone, echoes of the creature that lay beneath it. "There must be hundreds of them."

"Thousands," Verdon said. He lightly touched one, tiny flecks of stone crumbling under his fingers. "The greatest army of my kind ever created. It took years for Galiyar and Talnor to form it. They intended to take the Ossuary."

"We should keep moving," Mavian said. Sandu scrambled to keep up with him, and the rest joined them. Seanna clustered close to Gwen, her eyes wide with fear.

"What happens if they awaken?" Seanna whispered.

Sandu shivered. Gwen replied, "Their bodies are long gone. Breaking the stone should free their souls to Autorus."

"If Autorus is there to greet them," Mavian said darkly.

On the far side of the cavern, another staircase spiraled down into the gloom. Sandu's legs trembled from the last set of stairs, but he set off down them. He didn't want to be left alone with the souls trapped within stone.

✳

Down, down, down they went. Cara held her torch aloft, its glow doing little against the expansive blackness. Druam was silent, the babe sniffling in his arms. But even Landin seemed to know that he should make little noise, else risk waking the dead from their slumber.

Each cavern was much the same, its spaces full of the stone husks of ancient *fampir*, statues of monsters with open mouths and reaching talons. On the far side of the chamber, yet more stairs descended down. Cara's ears popped at some point, and she lost track of how many caverns they had traveled through.

They must be close to the bottom now. Cara's head ached with the musty scent and the overpowering feeling of smallness within that encompassing space. No matter how large each cavern was, the weight of the earth pressed in on her from all sides, and she wondered if there was enough air to breathe this deep below the surface.

Her legs ached and her calves twitched as they emerged into a cavern that teemed with husks. She had to carefully slide past them in order to make it through. Nearly every corner of the space was occupied, save for a circle in the center of the room. In that circle lay an altar and a pair of ancient skeletons, preserved only through the lack of air and moisture.

The Ossuary. Cara moved toward it reverentially. Her fingers lay upon the altar, and she trembled with the power held within it. She could hear Death itself, a chorus of misery and pain. *But Valder's knowledge? Where is it?*

Cara snapped her fingers and ordered Druam to stay at the altar. He sat down and leaned against it, his eyes half-closed in exhaustion. The baby watched her with huge eyes, its arms reaching for her. Cara turned away and began to explore the vast chamber.

It had many nooks and alcoves, but no books, no scrolls, no carved stone tablets. Nothing but dirt and rock and husks. The more Cara explored, the deeper her frustration grew. *Where's the knowledge I was promised?*

She completed an entire circuit of the room only to discover no secret library, nor another door. She cursed under her breath and made her way back to the altar.

As she drew closer, she realized her misconception. Even from a distance, a faint light glowed against Druam's back as he leaned against the altar. *Of course.* Cara hurried forward and touched the cold stone once more.

Yes, there was the power. But how to access it? How to understand?

A tendril of light reached for her hand and grazed her skin. Cara shuddered with the contact, but within it, she heard a faint question. It was not in her head, nor spoken aloud, nor even a true voice. She could *feel* the inquiry, understanding it deep inside her as an infant knows hunger or love.

Sulpari? it asked.

Yes, Cara thought.

The altar shook, and a faint seam appeared around its edge. The seam grew and grew until a lid formed. Druam scrambled up and away, his surprise showing even through his fatigue.

Cara pushed the lid. It moved aside, revealing a large hollowed space teeming with carved tablets. Each one whispered to her, promising her that it would fulfill all her dreams. Cara ran her hands over them. Most felt false somehow, like they were lying to her. But then one spoke whose voice rang true.

I WILL GRANT YOU WHAT YOU SEEK, it said to her.

I want the undead gone, Cara thought. *I want the Underworld severed from our own.*

AND I WILL HELP YOU.

Cara lifted the heavy tablet. Characters written in some ancient, dead language ran across its surface, over onto the edges and back. Her fingers touched the deep grooves, and music filled her head. It was terrible and dreadful, evoking an instinctual panic deep within her. No, not within her. Within the beast.

With a smile, Cara moved the lid back over the opening and set the tablet down.

"Don't do this," Druam croaked. He looked like a skeleton, all eyes in a gaunt face. He clutched the baby to his chest as if it were driftwood in a raging sea.

"Hush," Cara said, barely glancing at him.

"This won't just hurt my kind," Druam pleaded. "Think of all the innocent souls sent into chaos with no Underworld to guide them."

"There was once a time without Autorus," Cara said. "There can be another."

"Please..."

Cara ignored him. She focused on the tablet, and it whispered to her, *BLOOD OF THE DEAD. TEARS OF THE*

MEEK. CONVICTION OF THE MIGHTY.

She asked, *What do I do with them?*

TAKE THE FIRST TWO INTO YOUR HAND. The whisper glided over her, soothing away any doubts. *THEN ONLY A SINGLE TOUCH.*

Cara straightened. Druam backed away as she advanced on him, shaking his head and rambling at her. His words didn't matter. She struck his cheek, her talons ripping into his skin as the force of her blow sent him reeling. He stumbled away, thrusting out an arm to catch himself. The baby started to cry, its high wail echoing through the cavern.

Cara reached down and wiped her finger against the infant's wet face. Druam cursed at her, and she turned back to the altar. With blood and tears on her hand, she reached down to the tablet.

A sudden doubt bled into her heart. *Without the gem, I have no control...*

Her fingers brushed the stone.

A high wind whipped from nowhere, battering into Cara. She fell to the floor as Druam cried out. Harsh screams sounded in her ears, but she didn't know where they came from. Dust flew into her eyes, blinding her. She brushed it out and squinted at the chaos around her.

A cyclone formed above the altar, made of black light and crackling energy. It shot out in bursts of lightning, striking at the husks. Each time it hit, the husk shattered, and a faint scream came from the remains. Cara cowered against the altar, watching in horror.

What have I unleashed?

The whispers from the tablet had grown to screeching laughter. It rang out through the cavern, beating into Cara's mind: *THERE CAN BE NO CONNECTION IF THERE IS NO ONE LEFT.*

A bolt of energy struck Druam. He screamed as it ripped through him. Unlike the husks, it did not destroy him at first blow. It lifted him, drawing out his energy. Cara struggled up, but then another bolt snaked out.

It hit her chest, and spasms of electric pain buzzed through her. Cara gritted her teeth and tried to move away, but it had her in its clutches. She could not move. Her mind was a hornet's nest, her thoughts insects that hummed against her skull as every limb twitched in agony.

A third bolt blasted from the cyclone. Cara watched it in morbid fascination, unable to move, unable to stop it.

The bolt struck the crying infant, and its screams increased tenfold. Cara stared at it, the tears on her cheeks sparking with the energy in her body.

I never meant for you to be hurt.

＊

Nature was far gone from this place. Its oppressive Songs crowded into Gwen's mind, Death and Humanity at their worst. Though she could no longer understand them, their strains beat upon her head, urging her to turn back. Gwen could see the courage of the others failing, their resolute demeanors chipping away with every sordid note. Only Verdon, bright-eyed and attentive, seemed unaffected.

They passed cavern after cavern, and a rumble below their feet told Gwen that they were near. She paused at the top of the next spiral staircase. Though she could no longer feel the sweet wind or hear birdcalls in this depressing place, Gwen summoned the Songs of Nature that evoked pleasant days and peaceful streams. She Sang it, laying a hand on Sandu, Seanna, and Mavian in turn, giving them a glimpse of the world above.

"Keep your courage," she said. "We are nearly there."

Before she could take the next step down, the cavern erupted into tremors. They grasped at each other as the floor shook.

It has begun.

Cries of pain echoed from below. Then, a baby's high, heart-rending screech.

"LANDIN!" Seanna screamed. Despite the shaking floors, she pushed past Gwen and raced down the steps. Gwen recovered herself and ran after her, her light barely shining around each corner. Her breath came ragged in her lungs, her legs weary from the steady downwards climb.

They emerged into a nightmare. It was the chamber that Valder had shown to Gwen in the Underworld. But this time, it was not him against the *fampir*.

The altar pulsed with energy. Above it, a cyclone of dark energy whirled and whirled, bolts of dark lightning exploding out and striking the husks. Each one shattered, its soul crying out as the cyclone consumed it. A strange voice permeated the air:

I HAVE AWOKEN. I AM MADE.

Gwen didn't understand what was happening. She stood, rooted to the spot, gawping at the scene below her. Then Seanna dragged her forward, her cries lost amid the noise, and pointed.

Three figures were held aloft, each by a strand of energy. Two were adults, and one terrifyingly tiny. The figures writhed and shrieked, overcome by the agony of the Song that trapped them.

The strange voice laughed in glee, its bolts striking toward Seanna and Gwen. At the last moment, Gwen pulled them aside, and the energy struck at the husks behind them.

"What is that thing?" Seanna shouted in Gwen's ear.

Gwen didn't answer her. She had no answer. She huddled behind a husk and stared out at the whirling abomination. As she tentatively reached for its Song, she heard a clamorous dissonance of music and notes, a hundred Songs colliding with no thought or pattern. The Songs of Destruction and Pain, Anger and Vengeance, and many, many others which she could not differentiate from each other. Above all the rest, though, came the Song of Hunger. Greedy, depthless hunger, a creature that would devour and devour until all was absorbed into its maw.

Mavian, Sandu, and Verdon crept forward, huddling from husk to husk until they reached the women. Mavian licked his lips and pointed at the cyclone. "I hear...so much in there. All the worst Songs of Death. What is it?"

"I don't know," Gwen said.

"A soul of one of the *fampir*?" Sandu suggested.

Gwen shook her head. "No. It's not a person, it's barely sentient."

The whirlwind increased in speed, its winds tearing at the walls and sending gritty dust into their eyes. Gwen ducked her head. *We'll never get to them if we stay here.* With a great force of effort, she called up the Song of Protection. A force of energy burst out from her hands to surround their little group. The wind battered and raged at it, but the magical shield held.

In their small sanctuary, Gwen shook the dirt from her eyes. She focused again on the collection of Songs above the altar. *What are you?*

Again, the voice came into her head, and by the grimaces of those around her, she knew that they heard it, too. *I AM MADE. I WILL UNMAKE LIFE FROM THIS WORLD.*

The Songs howled through the words. Gwen's stomach dropped to her shoes as she realized what this thing was. "It's an awakened Song. A Song with...with intelligence. No, not quite intelligence. Instinct of its own. It will rampage and consume until there's nothing left."

"But how?" Mavian asked.

"The Ossuary is powerful, but it's been locked up for centuries with the souls of the undead trapped here with the Songs. I think all the Songs from those souls were absorbed into that one, and all it needed was Cara's ritual." Gwen peeked out at the morass of energy. It rippled and shifted, and a bolt of energy struck the roof above their heads. Rocks and dust showered down, and Gwen pulled Seanna out of the way of a particularly large stone. Mentally, she began to think of the whirlwind as the Song of Devouring, a bottomless pit that would take and take.

"The Song of Unmaking," Gwen said to Mavian. "We need to stop this thing before it kills the others."

Mavian nodded, his lips white as they pressed together. She turned to the others. "As we Sing, focus on Druam and Cara. Alive, whole, good. Don't think about their sins, only their goodness."

"What about Landin?" Seanna clutched at Gwen's arm. Gwen didn't respond; she doubted the child would survive for long.

The Song of Unmaking rose quickly, eager to be loosed upon the world. As Gwen struggled to hold it, humming notes over and over, she heard Mavian begin a Song of Death. She didn't know what he built around him, and could only pray that he would maintain the balance between Life and Death.

To either side of her, Sandu and Seanna's lips moved, their Songs coming out in whispers. It would have to do; there was no time to perfect their Songs' structure or boost their voices.

In the whirlwind, Gwen could feel the tethers of Earda coming undone. Cara and Druam's life forces grew fainter, and soon they would be gone. Pulling them back would not be simple; their connections to the Underworld, once strong, had been eaten by the Song of Devouring. If she wished to save their lives, she would have to sever that connection.

"Just like with Verdon," Gwen gritted out. "Sever the undead from the Underworld."

Mavian's eyes widened, his Song still coming out, though weakly. Gwen stood, drawing Devouring's attention. The shield around them sputtered and went out as Gwen put all her energy into the Song of Unmaking. It thrummed inside her, desperate to be released. It hungered with a force equal to Devouring.

Unlike on the mountaintop, Gwen did not have a reservoir of Songs to draw from. She took energy from the husks, and they burst as she drew upon their faint essences. Unmaking roiled inside her, and she could not control it. She didn't have Humanity or Death to aid her.

"The gem!" Gwen screamed. Even with those words, wisps of Unmaking slipped from her, slapping at the bolts of energy coming from Devouring. The whirlwind howled, and more lightning crackled toward her.

Mavian shouted, and Gwen felt the hard gem pressing into her hands. She raised it aloft as her vision filled with dark energy and pain enervated her flesh.

Autorus help me, she pleaded as the forces of Unmaking and

Devouring collided within her body. With all her remaining strength, Gwen tore the Songs from the gem. In a brief moment, she was inundated with vigor, and Devouring paused.

Gwen let loose the Song of Unmaking. From the cries of the others, she knew that it would not only affect her and Devouring.

In the space of a heartbeat, Gwen was no longer in the cavern under the plateau. She was once more in that space of color, that place between Making and Unmaking, a bubble of power in which she could enact the impossible.

Figures shifted behind the colors, silhouettes that she recognized. Mavian and Seanna and Sandu, all trapped within their own version of that expanse.

The colors that swirled around her were not the peaceful, wondrous shades they had been before. Blacks and blues and purples raged, Devouring fighting with Unmaking. Gwen expected to see specters as she had with Verdon. But she was utterly alone, her voice paltry in the din of Songs that battled around her.

What do I do? Gwen wanted to cry.

Just hold on, came a whisper of Songs.

Gwen didn't think she had any stamina left, but she stepped toward the battling Songs. With the last reserves of energy left in her battered body, she stuck her hands into the fray of colors and urged Unmaking onward.

Just hold on.

✳

The world was chaos and magic, bolts of lightning striking at the air around her. Seanna's lips murmured in more of a prayer than a Song, but she felt the magic move within her. Whatever she was doing, it was working. She focused on Druam, picturing him as both the proud earl and the humble gardener. He was a force for good, a man to be respected and admired.

In the next moment, the din in her ears quieted. She blinked, and the cavern was gone. Instead, a collection of color foamed around her, shifting in pastel patterns too elaborate for her eyes to follow.

She was not alone in that strange place. Druam huddled on the ground nearby, shaking from spasms of dark sparks that burst from his skin. Seanna moved toward him, then stopped. On her other side was Landin.

But he was no longer a child. He stood, tall and proud, the spitting image of his father. A crown sat on his brow, its gold setting off the blonde in his hair. His beard had grown in, and his brown eyes – eyes that matched Seanna's – stared off at something she couldn't see.

He was handsome and perfect, a king to put all others to shame. Joy and satisfaction closed Seanna's throat. *I knew I would raise the finest king Dotschar has ever known.*

Without thinking about it, she reached out for him. She paused before she could touch him.

The Song has costs, she realized.

Seanna turned back to Druam. He huddled there, his blue eyes pleading with her. Agony lined his face, and his skin twitched in spasms.

If you want to save him, whispered the Songs, *you must give up your claims to power.*

"Will I still have my son?" Seanna whispered.

He will never be king.

Seanna wavered. All her life, she had fought for her place in the world. She had endured tedious council meetings and feasts with nobles pawing at her, happily gone into an arranged marriage before losing two children in the womb, scraped and clawed her way into the respect she had finally garnered. Con Salur was back in Dotsch hands because of her. All this she had done for Landin's sake, to ensure he had a kingdom worth ruling.

The Songs whispered and laughed at her. Some urged her to save Druam, while others insisted that she be selfish again. Hadn't she given up so much already? Why should she have to sacrifice her power for the sake of one man?

Seanna didn't move, caught between the dying Druam and

the vision of King Landin.

*

Mavian took a deep breath. In this other-world of color and Songs, he could pause for a moment and consider his options.

The temptations were laid out before him, clear and simple. Two doors stood opposite each other, each with a small window showing what lay beyond. To his right, Mavian watched the life he had imagined: a study filled with books and papers, a merry fire spitting in the hearth. A beautiful woman swept in, a babe in her arms, and kissed his cheek. He could spend his final years exploring all the secrets of the Songs. Perhaps he could even be a voice for the rustics, advocating for them within the noble courts. Before everything with the Masque and Rask and the war, that was all he had wanted.

To his left, the window showed the Underworld. It was filled with souls, some weeping and wailing in Purgatory, but most content, guided by his hand to a peaceful eternity. The vision blurred, then reconstituted on Earda. Prowlers stood tall, shedding their ferocity for human visages once more. They washed and dressed, and went to find their lost kin.

Yes, Mavian had spent much of his scholarly life hoping for a better life for the rustics. But, more than that, he had longed to cure the prowlers. Ever since his father's death, he had been obsessed with them. He had lost social connections and restful nights in pursuit of that knowledge. But now that it lay so close, he didn't know if he could sacrifice everything for it.

Though he had aged somewhat, he was still young. Not even thirty. He could live another twenty years, more if he was lucky, and see what else the world had to offer. The pangs of Renna's death still burned his heart, but she was at peace now. He could move on, remarry, father his own children and teach them all that he knew.

Mavian turned back to the first door. In that vision, his other self rocked a child on his knee and read to it. It gasped and cooed and pointed at the pages. Mavian drew closer, desperate to hear its little voice. The child looked so like him at that age, full of wonder and curiosity.

Go through, the Songs urged him, their whispers dissonant all around. *Take the life you want. You never asked for Autorus's duty. You were never given the choice.*

"He forced it on me," Mavian murmured. His hands twitched at his sides. "I never wanted it."

Different Songs encouraged him to turn around. *You can do more good in the Underworld. You can cure the prowlers with this Song of Unmaking, then go forth into Death knowing that you have healed so many. Isn't that worth the sacrifice?*

Mavian's own heart murmured, *Haven't you done enough harm? Do you really deserve a happy life after all you've done?*

He couldn't answer any of the questions that assaulted him.

✳

Sandu blinked. Was he back at the Waiting Place? Surely he would have felt his own death as it happened.

No. The longer he stood there, staring at all the colors, the more he realized that this was something else entirely. He heard the choruses of music in the swirl of colors around him. *This is something magic.* The Songs within him trickled to a faint whisper, and he took stock of his situation.

He had been told to think about Cara. Not the monster she'd become, but the kind maid she once was. And he'd done that, or so he thought. He'd blocked the memory of Alex's murder from his mind, focusing instead on Cara on the road, laughing and helping herself to another portion of the stew he'd made. Cara in the tower, vulnerable and seeking help. Cara in Riverfen, her joy at seeing him and her bravery at the Masque.

Sandu turned around, and there she was. Cara, whole and hale, and utterly different than how she'd appeared in recent months. Her face was no longer contorted by fangs and ridges, her eyes a clear hazel. She swayed back and forth, trancelike and serene.

Sandu stepped closer to her, then paused. Behind her was a

monster. It was twice her height, its skin pale and scaly, its eyes burning above its gaping maw. Its arms were abnormally long, ending in talons the length of his hand. Fur grew in spiny tufts along its back.

The beast wrapped its talons around Cara, gripping her by the waist and neck. Its tongue panted next to her cheek.

From between its yellow teeth, it said in a deep, rasping voice, "If you want her, you must take her from me."

Sandu stood, paralyzed with fear. This monster was worse than prowlers. It smelled of death and decay, its breath stinking of blood. Sandu's insides constricted with terror, the edges of his vision flirting with the waking nightmares.

It's only Cara, he told himself. *She is the beast.*

Sandu took deep breaths and rubbed his leg with his hand. The nightmares fell back, and he finally looked back up at the beast.

It had Cara's eyes. Angry and red with tears, but her eyes. Sandu stepped around Cara and put a hand to the beast's nose.

"You have always been demonized," he said.

The beast huffed, its talons drawing red from Cara's throat. Sandu resisted the urge to back away.

"Even if you were separated from her, she would still hold her anger and her suffering. You are not the cause of her strife, but she has blamed you for it her whole life. If you leave her, she would still have to grapple with what she's done and who she has become. You are a representation of the darkness that dwells in her, but you are not its source." Sandu didn't know if he was speaking more to himself or to the beast. He had gone through the pains of acknowledging his own shortcomings and failures, and though he had come to accept them, they would never leave him.

The beast tilted its head, its eyes narrowed. "What if I don't want to leave her?"

Without thinking about it, Sandu ran his hand through the beast's fur. "That's not your choice. It's hers."

"And what will become of me? I will be nothing without her. I am not a soul, I have no claims to her life."

"I don't know," Sandu answered honestly. "All I know is that Cara can never come to terms with herself with you clinging onto her like that. She needs to breathe freely."

"She will still be a monster."

Sandu couldn't help but agree. "Yes, she will."

The beast nodded. "But what about the rest?"

Sandu's brow wrinkled in confusion as mirror upon mirror popped up around them. In each one, a different *fampir* was reflected, with their own beast clinging to their backs. Sandu saw Druam, then a myriad of men and women he didn't recognize.

The Song of Unmaking is heightened in the Ossuary, the Songs told Sandu. *It will not differentiate between Cara's beast and the rest.*

"So removing her beast will sever the connections between all *fampir* and the Underworld?" Sandu asked.

Yes.

"But I can't make that decision for them all!" Sandu shouted into the billowing Songs. "It's not my place!"

Mirrors of *fampir* stared at him.

"I can't free Cara without making the rest mortal," Sandu said. "And what about me? Gwen said there would be a price if I used the Song of Unmaking."

Guess you'll have to find out when all is done.

✳

Gwen held onto Unmaking, feeding it her own energy. Her arms shook, her legs threatening to give out from under her. Sweat beaded on her brow and dripped to her chest. She could feel herself slipping away.

Just hold on. You have to hold on.

A ripple of energy jolted her arms, making her bones rattle in her shoulders. Gwen gritted her teeth and dug her feet down.

Gwen Sang out an encouragement, hoping the others would hear it: "Don't give up! I can't do this alone!"

✳

Stuck between Druam and Landin, Seanna heard Gwen's voice. She startled and asked the Songs, "Can she succeed if I choose my kingdom?"

The answer came clearly. Seanna turned away from her handsome son and stooped to Druam. Her hand touched his shoulder, and the world blurred and shifted around her.

✳

Mavian paced from door to door, coming no closer to a decision. How could he choose? He had fought for redemption for so long, but it would be far easier to just choose himself. A little selfishness couldn't hurt.

Then Gwen's voice shattered his reverie, and Mavian straightened his back. His own greed would bring ruin to everyone else. There was no other answer.

I hope there's a hell in Lyael, and I hope Autorus rots there.

Mavian opened the door to the Underworld, and power even greater than what Darian had given him flowed into him. An epiphany came to Mavian's head, and he smiled. With his next blink, he departed.

✳

Sandu peered into each mirror, wondering if this *fampir* enjoyed their existence, or if that one had even wanted to be turned. He lingered at the glass showing Druam. The earl had always been kind to him, and he had worked for so long to bring about his vision. Could Sandu really take that away from him?

And, Sandu knew he would have to pay a price. What if it was his other arm? What if he'd have to leave his children behind him?

I can't lose them. Not again.

Gwen's voice whispered over the air, a plea for help. Sandu's shoulders slumped.

He knew the right thing to do. He just didn't know if he had the courage.

A cool hand took his, and Sandu jolted. Cara was smiling at him, and she nodded. Sandu wanted to ask if it was really her, or just a figment of the Songs, but he didn't have any more time. A decision had to be made.

"Release her," Sandu said to the beast.

It let go. With each thundering step back, it faded a little more. It howled, but its cry was lost in the Songs as it vanished. In all the mirrors, every beast stepped away, disappearing one by one. The *fampir* slumped to the ground, some weeping, some shrieking in agony.

Cara collapsed into Sandu's arms, and in the next moment, he left the Song-world behind him.

＊

The Song of Unmaking grew stronger with each of these acts. Devouring slithered and hissed and fought back, but it was no match for the newfound power of Unmaking. The black-and-blue of Devouring grew smaller and smaller in the eddies of color until it was no more.

But Gwen's duty was not done. Unmaking was hungry now, pulling away from her. It tried to escape her grasping hands, to leave her control and flood Earda.

Gwen screamed as she wrestled the Song. It slapped against her, searching for a way to overcome her. Its notes burned her skin, its chords ripping her hair and clothes.

From the corner of her eye, Gwen saw the three Witches, faint and distorted.

"Help me!" Gwen screamed.

Una shook her head. "You must let go."

"No!" Gwen's grip on the Song tightened. "It'll destroy everything."

The Witches vanished, and Gwen cried out again. Her body felt like it was being slowly torn apart by the Song's strength. She couldn't hold onto it for much longer.

A familiar Song came through the churning colors, its

melody full of the Woods. The force separating that place from Earda was ancient and powerful. To Unmake that force would take more power than the Song of Unmaking could provide.

Let go. Gwen released the Song of Unmaking, directing it to the Woods. It would wither and burn itself out eating away at the rift between the Woods and Earda.

Gwen swayed and fell to her knees. Her muscles were stretched and aching, her breath ragged and worn. She was weak.

She could only pray that Unmaking would not win against the Woods.

✻

Cara moaned. Her entire body hurt. Her hair was frizzed and dry, her skin cracking. She shifted a little, and groaned at the tension between bone and muscle. Everything was silent. She opened her eyes to darkness. Not a single sound penetrated the vast chamber. Reaching out, Cara's hand brushed against the cold stone altar, and she shuddered.

Somewhere in the distance, a voice gave a command. Light exploded in the black, and Cara shielded her eyes against it. After blinking out the sunspots, she focused on the glowing red orbs that slowly came toward her. Faces swam in and out of the darkness, speaking with voices that she couldn't understand.

The orbs drew close. At last, Cara could pick out the faces clearly. She thought she knew them, but couldn't recall. Two men moved toward her, while the two women went where she couldn't see.

Cara licked her dry lips. "Where am I?"

The moment she said the words, her memories flooded back. She was in the Ossuary. She had awoken a whirlwind that tried to devour her. Beyond that, she didn't know what had happened. She felt her face, but the fangs and ridges were gone. Desperately, Cara reached inside for the beast. It didn't respond. An emptiness filled the space it had once occupied.

The two men kneeled beside her. One she knew instantly.

"Sandu," Cara whispered.

"How do you feel?" he asked.

"The beast..."

Sandu nodded solemnly. "It's just as you wanted. You're cured. You're free."

Cara patted herself as if she could find the beast hiding in a pocket. "You're sure? But it was so ingrained in me..."

Sandu helped her to sit up. "It's gone."

A peacefulness settled over her. Cara grinned. Then her gaze drifted to the other man. *Druam?* No, this one had a thinner face and longer nose. Tentatively, Cara reached out for him. He stood still as her fingers brushed his face.

"F-father?" Cara asked.

The man smiled and cupped her hand against his cheek. "I'm so glad to finally meet you."

✳

Mavian was gone. Gwen could tell it as soon as they all reappeared in the Ossuary. His Song had been changed, and he was no longer the man they had once known. She wondered if he was still there, incorporeal as he transformed into a Cythra.

I can ask him when I die.

The moment they reached the altar, Seanna ran to the small bundle lying on the ground. She lifted it up, running her fingers over Landin's cheeks. The baby coughed and began to cry. Seanna sobbed as she held him.

"He's safe," she said. "He's safe."

Gwen rested a hand on Seanna's shoulder in a moment of solidarity, then moved on to the figure lying motionless on the floor. She kneeled by Druam's side and ran her fingers through his hair. A pulse beat against his neck, showing that he was still alive.

"We did it," Gwen whispered. A huge weight lifted from her shoulders, and she cried in sheer joy. "It's done."

CHAPTER FIFTY-ONE
Gwen

Weak as she was, Gwen still supported Druam on the long climb back up to the light. With no gem and no strength for Songs, they would have to make the journey on foot. Behind her, Seanna carried baby Landin, and Sandu and Verdon helped Cara, for her feet dragged and her head bent with weariness.

When they reached the final staircase, Gwen's heart lifted at the sight of sunlight. *Dawn has come.*

As she plodded toward the steps, between the husks that remained, she paused. Something traveled among the husks, a figure she recognized.

"Mavian?" Gwen called.

The figure turned toward them and moved into the sphere of light. It was Mavian, though there was something different about him. He had an ethereal grace, and the wrinkles had smoothed from his skin. It was his eyes, though, that made Gwen realize the change was complete: one eye was milky white, and the other pitch black. None of Mavian's green irises remained.

"Autorus," Gwen amended, giving him a small bow. The others followed suit, though Druam and Cara stumbled as they moved.

Autorus smiled at her. It was not Darian's mysterious smile, but Mavian's satisfied one that she saw. He spoke, and beneath the grand tones, she heard her friend's familiar voice: "I am freeing these lost souls and allowing them to join me."

"A noble task."

He turned to Verdon. "The Song of Unmaking cured the prowlers. They will be lost and afraid."

Verdon gave a deep bow. "I will help them rejoin the world of mortals."

"Good." Autorus reached out to Gwen. "The Witches wait for you above. They have a task for you."

Gwen's heart stammered, but she put on a brave face and nodded. "Of course."

She turned to the stairs as Autorus returned to his solemn work. At last, Gwen could feel the sunlight on her cheeks. She sighed and lifted her weary feet one last time to climb to the surface.

To her surprise, the dead plants of the Conservatory were gone. In their place, grey-barked trees rose to the glassy roof, the sun's rays filtering between their bare branches. Familiar shrubs and bushes lined the pathways, and brightly-hued flowers Sang in faint voices.

"The Woods are here," Gwen said. She could feel them, their Songs and their wind, their moisture and their touch. The others gaped in awe at the transformed Conservatory. *I wish Lintem were here.*

Not far away, the three Witches stood in a row. Their backs were bent and old, their hair white and no longer shining.

"You are ready to go to Lyael," Gwen said.

Una nodded. "It is our time."

Dona reached for Gwen. "You must guard these Woods for us."

Tresa smiled and rubbed her palm along the bark of a tree. "They will care for you if you care for them."

"I can't hear the Songs of Humanity and Death anymore," Gwen said. "Only Nature."

Una took Gwen's face in her weathered hands. "Death has its own caretaker. Humanity's Songs will blossom and spread from the two you have gifted with them. Worry only for Nature."

Gwen dreaded the answer, but she had to ask it, "What is

my new task?"

"The Woods," they said in unison.

Una said, "You will stay here and teach others the Songs of Nature."

"You will guard the Ossuary from those who would abuse its secrets," Dona said.

"You will never leave the Woods," Tresa finished.

I longed to return, but to never leave? Gwen's mouth was dry as she asked, "What happens if I do stray from these lands?"

Una shook her head sadly. "You will never hear the Songs again, and the Woods will forever block you from reentering."

Gwen swallowed, her throat lumped with melancholy certainty. *The Songs know the price that fits each of us. They will give me the Woods, but nothing else.*

"Your life will be long and fruitful," Dona added. "The Woods will sustain you for many lifetimes if you remain here."

Tresa took Gwen's hand and gave her a smile. "It is the price we paid. We have no regrets."

"Then go," Gwen said. "Be at peace. I will care for these Woods."

The Witches kissed her cheeks, then stepped back. As one they vanished, leaving nothing behind but faint traces of pine and sweetgrass.

Gwen turned to the rest of the group. "I can escort you to the borders of the Woods. From there, I cannot accompany you."

They walked out to the edge of the plateau and gazed upon the new forests. The Woods spread all over the city, then beyond into the River Valley, as far as the eye could see. Gwen's heart sped up; how far did they go?

She had lifetimes to discover it.

"Why not take a ship?" Seanna asked. She pointed down to the harbor. A dock jutted out from the dense woodland, and at its end lay a longboat. A gilded ship bobbed at anchor not far out.

Verdon grinned. "I'd know that ship anywhere."

CHAPTER FIFTY-TWO
Seanna

They parted with Gwen on the docks. The Forest Witch did not say goodbye to Cara, who was still in and out of consciousness, but she shook hands with Verdon and embraced Sandu. When she came to Seanna, she kissed Landin's forehead.

"He will be great no matter what path he takes," Gwen said. "Be proud of the man he will become."

"Thank you," Seanna said. She hesitated, then leaned forward and pecked Gwen's cheek. "Maybe we'll return someday and visit your Woods."

Gwen smiled. "I would like that."

Seanna thought about Druam, who had been left sleeping at the top of the plateau. "What about Druam?"

"I will watch over him," Gwen said. "There will be time enough for reunions when he has recovered."

Verdon brushed his hair from his forehead. "After everything is settled with Cara, I will return and be with him. In the meantime...can you help him scry on me? I want to speak with him, even at a distance."

"Of course," Gwen replied.

Then it was time to get into the longboat. A familiar voice greeted Seanna, "Ah, it is being the queen! Have you decided to be taking another journey with the corsairs?"

"Hello, Laaravat," Seanna said. "Is she waiting on board?"

He nodded, and Seanna settled into the bobbing boat and clutched Landin close to her bosom.

The boat skipped across the waters. Seanna watched the docks until the figures of Gwen and Druam dwindled, then turned her attention to the vessel that waited for them. It was the same as she remembered, from the writhing mermaid bowsprit to the red sails. Eager corsairs hauled up the longboat, and strong arms helped her onto the deck.

Seanna had only a moment to register the appearance of Sura Gellder before the Corsair Queen shoved her aside to get at her daughter.

"Cara!" Sura said.

Then Sura froze as she caught sight of Verdon. The two stared at each other.

Adjusting Landin in her arms, Seanna stepped forward. "We have a lot to tell you."

The whole group filed into Sura's sumptuous cabin. Sura's eyes were glued to Verdon, and not a word left her lips. She collapsed into one of her chairs and absently poured herself a goblet of wine, set the goblet on the table, and swigged straight from the decanter.

Verdon carefully laid Cara into Sura's bed before joining Seanna and Sandu. They all sat down at the table. Seanna opened her mouth to begin, then thought better of it. *This isn't about me.* Instead, she urged Landin to latch and gently rocked him as he fed.

"How..." Sura finally said, her voice weak.

Verdon reached over and laid his hand over hers. She started and glanced down at his fingers. Verdon said, "I was gone for a very long time. Gwen and Mavian brought me back through magic that, frankly, I don't understand."

"You're so...warm," Sura said. "You used to be cold."

"Well," Verdon smiled, "I didn't come back as I was. I'm mortal again."

"That's not possible."

"Neither was Cara's birth, but she's sleeping over there."

Sura finally peeled her eyes from his face. She appealed to Seanna, "This is a dream, right? I came here expecting to rescue Druam and the babe, and instead I find a forest growing where there wasn't one before and my child's father standing in front of me. None of this can be real."

Seanna patted Landin's back as she said, "It's all real. You have your family back."

"My family..." Sura's gaze returned to Verdon.

Seanna nudged Sandu and tilted her head toward the door. "I think we should give them some room."

He agreed, and they departed the cabin. The corsairs gave them a well-appointed space with two comfortable beds. Seanna kicked off her shoes and rolled onto one. She fell asleep almost as soon as her body was horizontal.

*

The ship hove into view of the port town. Seanna gripped the railing with one hand, her heart thrilling at the sight of the coastline.

Over their short journey, Sura had learned all that had transpired. Cara still had not awoken, and Verdon spent every candle at her side. Sura was there as much as possible, too, though she still needed to command her crew. A bird had come from Ropaz asking to meet at the nearest port, and so they traveled with all the speed wind could afford them.

As the ship drew closer, Sura joined Seanna at the railing. The Corsair Queen spoke quietly, "He's a good one, your son. I'm glad I could save him from that wretched elf, but I'm sorry that Cara took him. I didn't have a choice; she would have burned down my entire city, then taken him anyway."

"I have no ill will toward you," Seanna said. "You did the best you could."

Sura nodded, her gaze on the port. "Have you reconsidered what I said last time we met?"

"I have. In fact, I want you to help me draw up an official letter."

"For what?"

Seanna took a deep breath. "I'm going to abdicate the throne. I still have a dowry and jewels granted to my person, and I intend to use those to find a nice, quiet hamlet to raise Landin in. You were right; the crown isn't worth our lives together."

"Your predicant isn't going to like that."

"No," Seanna smiled, "he's not."

The ship slipped gracefully through the water and all too soon weighed anchor in the bay. Seanna climbed into the longboat and waved farewell to the rest. She took Sandu's hand and said, "I wish you the best in life. I know that Ropaz will need help finding a solution for the kingdom. He could use a perspective like yours."

Then she took the rolled scroll from Sura and gave her thanks. The boat was lowered into the water and sped to the dock. Ropaz, Portia, and Jagger all waited there, the giant forlorn without his blind companion beside him.

"Thank the gods," Ropaz said as he helped Seanna onto the shifting timbers. "I could hardly believe it when I heard what had happened."

"How did you find out?" Seanna asked.

"How do you think? Gwen visited us through scry. She told us that you were on a ship and asked us to send her nightcat to the River Valley."

As Seanna grew used to the stability of land, Jagger bowed to her and then climbed into the longboat. Ropaz said, "He's going to see Sandu, I think."

Jagger nodded and waved as the longboat headed back toward the ship. Seanna walked with Ropaz and Portia onto dry land, grateful for the feel of dirt beneath her feet.

Immediately, Ropaz set into planning. "We'll take a carriage to Con Salur. Our laborers have been working tirelessly to clear the city of elven filth. Once everything is settled, we will officially crown Landin and name you Queen Regent until he comes of age."

Seanna held out the scroll. Even if she still wanted the crown, the Songs compelled her to give it up. She knew that sitting on that throne would only result in a quick, magical death.

Ropaz frowned and unfurled the scroll. His brow drew tighter and tighter as he read, and he stared at Seanna in disbelief. "You can't just abdicate. Who will take the throne? Landin is the last of Henrik's line."

"Search farther back in the registries if you need to," Seanna said. "I'm sure a few names will surface. Besides, you're a clever man. Maybe you can convince the nobles to form a council; I'm sure they'd love not being under a king's foot."

She took Portia's hand. "I have a different idea for my life now."

"But you're the queen!" Ropaz spluttered. "After everything I've done for you and this kingdom, you're leaving? Just like that?"

"I will always treasure our friendship," Seanna said. "Besides, you'll want to visit Portia now and then."

Ropaz rubbed the bridge of his nose and sighed heavily. "Portia, you're fine with all this?"

"The castle was grand and all," Portia replied, her eyes bright, "but I think a simpler life suits me better."

At last, Ropaz nodded. He put a hand on Seanna's shoulder. "Take care of her. I'll see to the kingdom. Now come, there's a hot meal and a bed waiting for you. We can make further arrangements on the morrow."

Hand in hand, Seanna and Portia followed Ropaz to the inn. Seanna's other arm held tightly to Landin, and she squeezed Portia's fingers.

CHAPTER FIFTY-THREE
Mavian

The last husk blew into dust, its soul free at last. Mavian sighed heavily. The Songs of Death were ever-present, discordant and loud. He would have to find a way to manage them.

One thing at a time.

He emerged from the Ossuary and looked out at the horizon. A sense of contentment settled over him. He had always enjoyed having a job to do and discoveries to make. Autorus had created the Underworld, but Mavian could improve it.

After all, I have an eternity to figure this out.

CHAPTER FIFTY-FOUR
Sandu

Sandu waited for Jagger. *I'll stay just long enough for Cara to wake. Then I'll head home to Da and the twins.*

But where was home? Dunfrey was a ghost town, its denizens killed by the plague. Riverfen had transformed into the Woods, and he doubted that any people that had lingered there would stay for long. For a moment, he entertained Seanna's idea of going to Con Salur.

Me? An advisor to a king? Sandu laughed at himself for even thinking of it. He was a rustic with one arm, barely educated and with a lifetime of poor judgments. What use could the predicant have for him?

Beneath his skin, the Songs of Humanity hummed to him. He could hear the Songs of the sailors around him, and though he tuned them out as best he could, the music never quite went away. In a strange way, the knowledge that they would always be with him was comforting. No matter where he went, he would always hold that little bit of power.

Jagger climbed from the longboat and came straight for Sandu. They embraced, Jagger's strong arms lifting Sandu off the deck a little. After putting Sandu down, Jagger signed, *"He's gone"*.

Sandu pushed down the tightness in his throat. "We knew it wouldn't be long. Was it peaceful?"

Jagger nodded. *"He was sleeping."*

"Good." Sandu stared out over the water. "And now

Mavian's taken his place. I hope Darian finds peace in Lyael."

Jagger followed his gaze. *"I hope so, too."*

"What are you going to do now?"

"I think there's someone I can help. Darian showed me a lot about being gentle and good, and how to cope with my mistakes."

Sandu realized what Jagger meant, and nodded. It was a good solution. "You and Cara can work off your debts together."

"Yes."

"Well, we should go check on her. Come on." Sandu led Jagger down to Sura's cabin. The door was open, and they slipped inside. Sura and Verdon sat side-by-side on a couch they had pulled up beside the bed, Sura's hand in Verdon's lap. Sandu sank into the chair he'd been using.

"Nothing yet?" Sandu asked.

Sura shook her head. "I think we should see a healer."

"Let me try." Sandu bent over Cara and put his hand on her head, reaching for her Song. It was strange, touching someone's very soul, and he balked as he first brushed against it. Then he steadied himself and listened to her Song.

The beast was gone, its harmony replaced with a strange quietness. Cara's thoughts tumbled about, stuck in a place between dreaming and waking. As Sandu touched her music, she trembled. A thought came through, clear as speech:

Sandu?

"I'm here," Sandu murmured.

I can't feel the beast.

"Remember? It's gone. You're cured."

A single tear leaked from Cara's closed eye. *But the sand is still there.*

"Sand?"

It's all over me, closing over my heart, choking my lungs.

Guilt layered every note in her Song, making them weighted and low and sluggish.

You see it? I'm so sorry, Sandu. I've hurt you and everyone else too much; I can't face you.

"Wake up. Please."

Slowly, Cara's eyes eased open. She stared from her parents

to Jagger and Sandu, her Song vibrating with fear. Sandu heard her pain and resignation, the repercussions she knew she would face.

"Mumma," Cara whispered. "Papa."

In that moment, all Cara's sins were briefly forgotten. Sura and Verdon leaned over their daughter, murmuring to her. Sandu watched them, his thoughts full of his own children. *I need to return to them. I can't stay away much longer.*

When the reunion began to wind down, Sandu took Cara's hand. The others backed away, giving them space.

"I knew you were still in there somewhere," Sandu said. "The maid I rescued from her dull life on the estate."

"As I recall," Cara replied, "I'm the one who dragged you into the wilderness."

"Well, it was a mutual kidnapping." He drank her in, the friend he had thought lost forever. "You became a monster. You killed Alex."

"I know."

"You slaughtered innocent people and reveled in it."

"I'm sorry."

Sandu's grip grew tighter. "You betrayed me. I don't know if I can ever forgive you for all you've done."

Her head sank into the pillow. "Then why are you here?"

"Because you deserve to know the truth. Remember how we promised to always be honest with each other? Well, this is me being honest. I died three times, and only came back because I had hope of finding my children. I did this for them.

"When Gwen told me we could cure you, I wanted to give you a chance at the life you've always wanted. If there were any soldiers around, they would have shackled you and sentenced you to the block. I can't say you don't deserve that."

Sandu looked over his shoulder at Jagger. "But he got a second chance, and I think you're getting one, too. I hope you make the best of it."

Her eyes widened. "What about you? Will I see you again?"

"No." Sandu had known it since he'd come out of the Song-world and back to the Ossuary. He had done his part in stopping Cara, but that was it. He was finished with adventures and magic and monsters. "I have two children and an elderly father. I have to take care of them. You'll excuse me if I don't want you mucking that all up."

Though her lip quivered, Cara said, "I understand."

"I wish you luck." Sandu squeezed her fingers one last time, then stood and put a hand to Jagger's shoulder. "I hope you find what you seek."

"Where will you go?" Jagger signed.

After a moment, Sandu said, "The scholars will begin rebuilding in D'Clet, or maybe back in Mott. I have a bit of magic; I can help them. Maybe teach them a little. A quiet, scholarly life will suit me just fine. And maybe the university can be a haven for those like me who struggle with their heads. I can help people. I know I can."

Jagger's eyes were warm. He embraced Sandu again, then pulled back and signed, *"I know you can, too. Maybe we'll be able to share a drink again and laugh about the old days."*

Sandu stepped out onto the deck and breathed the sweet, cool air. He'd write to Frederick and invite him to live with them; one more set of hands to look after the children would be nice, and it would do them good to have the blacksmith's familiar face around. He could already see his future: studying and researching the Songs with the scholars; playing with Eaton and Elvy in the sunshine and cuddling with them when winter's breath cooled the land; losing against Da and Frederick time and again as they dealt a round of Elf's Hand; counseling those whose minds turned against them and didn't know what to do about it.

It's going to be a good life.

CHAPTER FIFTY-FIVE
Cara

The door closed behind Sandu, and the hollowness left in Cara by the beast's absence grew even deeper. She waited for it to reopen, for him to come back and rescind his words.

The door did not open. It remained resolutely closed, and her friend was gone. He would not return, no matter how many wishes Cara blew into the sea.

She rolled her head to face her mother. The tears had gone, and though Sura looked fondly on her, Cara saw a hint of fear in those hazel eyes which so resembled her own. Her father, stoic as Druam, stood quietly.

"I'm sorry," Cara whispered to them. "I...I don't know what else to say."

"Shh, my love," Sura said. She stroked Cara's arm, all her walls collapsed to reveal the woman beneath. "You need to rest. You've gone through quite the ordeal."

Cara nearly choked on the irony. "I killed too many people to count. I drank blood and enjoyed it. If it wasn't for me, none of this would have happened."

Sura brushed her hand over Cara's forehead. "Rask would still have gone to war with Druam. The elves would have invaded. The world is larger than you."

"But I destroyed Riverfen." Cara appealed to her father. "I destroyed Druam's centuries of work in mere days. I tore down his lanterns and rotted his Conservatory, I drowned his people in blood. Mumma, I burned your ships and slaughtered your sailors."

Sura's lips tightened at that, and Verdon sighed, "Yes. You did."

"So I'm still a monster. That evil is in me, beast or no. How can I atone for such things? Sandu was right, I should be executed and have done with it."

Sura shook her head and Verdon frowned, but Jagger coughed. He signed, *"Then you'd only be in Purgatory. Better atone here than there."*

"I wouldn't even know where to start."

"I'll help you. Believe it or not, I know what you're going through."

Cara couldn't argue that. "I'll leave as soon as I'm recovered."

Before her parents could respond, a sailor knocked at the door and shouted a question. Sura uttered a curse and rose. "I have to deal with this."

She departed, and Verdon said, "Jagger, could you leave us, please?"

The assassin left on silent steps, and, for the first time in her life, Cara was alone with her father.

Verdon took her hand and rubbed it between his fingers. Cara winced at all the scars that roped his skin, a tapestry of pain from living as a prowler in the wilds.

Cara opened her mouth to apologize again, but Verdon interrupted her, "It was my selfish wish for children that brought you into this world. For that, I am sorry, though I do believe I've done my time."

"Did Gwen bring you back?" Cara asked.

He nodded. "With Mavian's help. They reunited my soul and body. In the process, they Unmade my connection to Autorus. I am mortal."

Cara's mouth was dry. "Did it work? My...my spell in the Ossuary?"

He snorted. "It nearly worked to kill you. In Unmaking that spell and rescuing you from your own folly, Sandu untethered every last soul from Autorus. There are no more *fampir* now."

Cara asked, "Do you think that's a good thing?"

His unreadable expression reminded her of Druam's. He said, "I have spent much of my life as *fampir*. I'm still adjusting to being a mortal once more. The idea of Death frightens me, I'll admit. There were many of my kind who used their eternities, as Druam and I did, for improving the world around us. I wonder how history will view this change."

"But the Ossuary is still there," Cara pointed out. "Someone could recreate the experiments of the Dead's War and bring the *fampir* back."

"I doubt that. Gwen will guard it well."

Cara nodded. After a moment, she asked, "What will you do now? Sail with Sura? Rebuild with Druam?"

"I have thought much on this since my reawakening," Verdon replied. His gaze had a far-off cast to it. "I will find my fellow *fampir* and help them adjust to their new mortalities. I will spend time with Sura and Druam, enjoying their company with the knowledge that our lives have a marked ending now. I will accompany you sometimes, in those years where I find I miss my daughter."

Cara leaned her cheek against his hand and allowed herself to cry. "Do you think I deserve this second chance?"

"I think you should make use of the opportunity given to you. If I were you, though, I would not announce my identity to the world. Let Cara Gellder, Scourge of Riverfen, fade away until she is no more than a legend."

She closed her eyes, enjoying the warmth of his hand against hers. "I wish I'd known you my whole life. Maybe things would have turned out better."

He said nothing, but she felt the regret in his touch. They sat in silence as waves lapped the ship. Whatever the coming days held for her, Cara knew that he was right. She had become the very thing she had once sworn to destroy, and she had an opportunity few received to right her own wrongs.

She didn't know where she would start, only that each day would bring with it a reminder of the evil she had wrought on the world.

That is good. I should never forget it. The guilt that ate at her heart would not dissolve for a long, long time. Maybe she'd die before it truly went away, and maybe that was for the best.

Chapter Fifty-Six
Gwen

The people of Riverfen were lost in the Woods, their roofs destroyed by branches and their streets teeming with plants. Grass as red as the sunset filled the cracks between cobblestones, and between the grey-barked trees whose faces twisted in pained expressions, there were boulders shaped like trees and trees round as boulders.

Gwen Sang a message to the people who now found themselves in this strange forest: *Come to the plateau*. As she toiled up the incline, a crowd of people emerged from between the trees. They huddled together, terrified of the faces in the bark and the jeweled birds which flashed overhead. None of them spoke, their fear and confusion palpable in the foreign air.

Gwen was so tired. She hoped that Druam hadn't woken in her absence. He would be dazed, and she needed to recover her own strength before she took care of him.

People from within the palace had gathered in the courtyard as Gwen came up. They parted for her, sensing that she was not like the rest of them. Her grey-and-green streaked skin, her hair, her clothes...all communicated that she belonged in these strange Woods.

The crowd grew and grew, soldiers from Rask's army and servants from the palace and the few townsfolk that remained, all of them emaciated and worn through. Sympathy stirred in Gwen's heart. *I have to make this right*.

"People of Riverfen," Gwen said, "These are the Whispering

Woods. They have come back to Earda, bringing with them Songs and magic. If you wish to leave them, I will escort you to the borders. If you wish to stay, I will help you learn to navigate them and use their offerings for your benefit, living in harmony with the creatures and trees. For today, though, I am exhausted. You may sleep in the palace under my protection, and tomorrow, we will begin our work."

Though the people muttered, some of them spitting curses at her, Gwen walked into the palace without a backwards glance. Her steps carried up to Druam's chambers.

Druam still lay unconscious in his bed. Gwen paused at the door, reminded of the tourney when he had fallen ill from sunfever. She had sat with him and used magic to help him recover.

Gwen filled a bowl with water and brought it to his side. With calm, gentle strokes, she bathed his face and arms, cooling his fevered body. He moaned and trembled, and his eyes fluttered open.

"G-Gwen?" he stammered.

"Shh," Gwen murmured. "Rest. I'm here."

He looked around him, wide-eyed at the plants. Before he could ask any questions, Gwen said, "Cara took you to the Ossuary. You were nearly consumed by the Song of Devouring. We stopped it with the Song of Unmaking, but in the process, well..."

Gwen gestured at the vines growing through his floor. "The Woods returned to Earda."

"I feel strange," Druam said. He licked his lips and ran his tongue over his teeth. "You're not telling me everything."

"You're mortal now."

Her blunt words struck him, for he froze a moment before holding up his hands. He made a face, but nothing changed. Genuine terror shone in his eyes. "I'm not *fampir*. Gwen, what did you do to me?"

She nearly slapped him, only just resisting the urge. "I saved your life. Sandu was the one who severed Cara's connection to Autorus. But the Unmaking was too powerful; it didn't stop there. It severed you and every other *fampir*, too. You're all mortal now."

"But..." His pale face went ashen, all the color draining out of it. His blue eyes, bright in his gaunt cheeks, pierced her to the marrow. "I will die now."

"Yes." Gwen leaned forward and rested her hand on his. "You were granted an extra seven centuries beyond your normal lifespan. Be grateful for them."

"What of my city? Are these Woods..." He trailed off as he stared out the window.

"I don't know where they end," Gwen admitted. "I'll find out in the coming days. For now, you must rest. I need to scry those in D'Clet and inform them of what's happened. And then...I must sleep, too."

✳

Day by day, Druam grew stronger. Gwen tended him in the mornings and evenings, but the rest of the day she spent in the Woods, either gathering supplies or leading people to the borders. She had found the edges after many days of travel under the grey branches. The Woods covered much of the River Valley, from the coast south of Riverfen to the hills to the east and north.

Most of Riverfen's former inhabitants, as well as those who lived in villages affected by the sudden intrusion of trees, opted to move away. Gwen led them in all directions, and returned exhausted in the evenings. Some, though, wanted to try to live in the Woods. These she gathered on the plateau, planning on teaching them Songs and survival in this strange new place.

Lintem returned to her within a deshe, his powerful legs having carried him all the way from D'Clet. He reveled in the Woods' presence, and remained glued to her side. Gwen couldn't complain; she, too, found immense joy in their old routines.

One day as she explored the eastern part of the Woods, Gwen found something that made her heart leap with joy. She bounded back to Riverfen, where she found Druam in his study.

"Come with me!" Gwen exclaimed.

"What?" Druam turned to her. His cheeks had regained some of their color, his body finally fleshing out with solid meals each day. He appeared more like the man she had married.

"I have something to show you," she said, grabbing at his hand.

Druam pulled back, his gaze suspicious. "Gwen..."

She paused, finally reading his hesitation. "What's wrong?"

"There's nothing left!" he shouted. He threw the parchment he'd been laboring on out the window. "My city is gone, my people are scattered."

"I've been helping them," Gwen protested.

"You don't understand!" Druam raged, his temper flying out. "What am I supposed to do now? I have spent centuries cultivating this city, protecting it and nurturing it. I have nothing left to live for."

"Your brother is back," Gwen said.

"Yes, and we can have conversations again," Druam said, bitterness in his words. "But between his visits, what am I to do?"

"I don't know," Gwen said. "But these Woods are full of life. You were a gardener once, you made me a sanctuary in the Conservatory. You can do that again."

She grasped his hand, but he didn't move. He stared at their entwined fingers, then met her eye. "And what of us, Gwen? Last we spoke of it, you blamed me for taking advantage of you. You were right, but I still love you."

Gwen played with his fingers, feeling their whorls and ridges. "I was only a girl when we married. I barely knew myself, much less what I wanted." She took his chin in her other hand. "But I am a woman now, and I have lived in these Woods for a long, long time. We are equals, and I know myself. I know what I want."

"And what is that?" His voice came out in a whispered plea.

"I want to show you the home I built for myself in the Woods. Lintem and I found it, and I want to share it with you."

Tentatively, she stood on her tiptoes and gave him a kiss light as a butterfly's wing. "I cannot leave these Woods, but you can explore them with me. I'd like that."

His eyes bared his soul, and he swallowed heavily.

"Come with me," Gwen said, pulling at his hand.

Druam finally moved, and he followed her, their hands clasped tight.

ACKNOWLEDGEMENTS

Mom, Dad, and Brandon, who would tell me they love it no matter what – thank you for always being there for me.

Don, Matt, Michele, Dallas, Paul, Simone, Theresa, Wendy, Janet, Bruce, and Linda, who helped me polish up early chapters – thank you.

Beth, Rachelle, and Jane, who endeavored to beta read even in the midst of a pandemic - thank you.

Rodney, for creating my beautiful map and bringing it to life – thank you.

All my readers: May you have enjoyed this journey as much as I have. This chapter has ended, but I look forward to exploring the next one with you.

About the Author

Vista McDowall lives and works in the rural mountains of Colorado, where she imagines great quests over the snow-covered peaks. When she's not writing, she can be found sewing, watching period dramas, and cuddling with her two cats.

She can be found on Facebook, Twitter, and Instagram. Her website is vistamcdowall.com.

Other works:

    "The Pack," a short story in the anthology *First Encounters*

    "Faithful's Oath," a short story in the anthology *Second Law*

    "Through the Blackthorn," a short story in the anthology *We Cryptids*

    All of the above available on Amazon.com.

www.ingramcontent.com/pod-product-compliance
Lightning Source LLC
Chambersburg PA
CBHW021124260626
47169CB00005B/1432